HANNAH HOWELL

HIGHLAND GROOM

ZEBRA BOOKS
KENSINGTON PUBLISHING CORP.
http://www.kensingtonbooks.com

ZEBRA BOOKS are published by

Kensington Publishing Corp.
119 West 40th Street
New York, NY 10018

All Kensington titles, imprints, and distributed lines are available at special quantity discounts for bulk purchases for sales promotion, premiums, fund-raising, educational, or institutional use.

Special book excerpts or customized printings can also be created to fit specific needs. For details, write or phone the office of the Kensington Special Sales Manager: Attn.: Special Sales Department. Kensington Publishing Corp., 119 West 40th Street, New York, NY 10018. Phone: 1-800-221-2647.

Zebra and the Z logo Reg. U.S. Pat. & TM Off.

ISBN-13: 978-1-4201-3731-6
ISBN-10: 1-4201-3731-X

First Printing: November 2003

10   9

Printed in the United States of America

The Murray Family Lineage

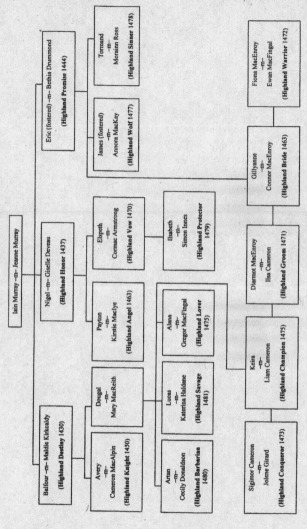

CHAPTER ONE

Scotland, Spring 1471

Ilsa groaned as eight of her fourteen brothers crowded into her small cottage. They looked around, each wearing an identical scowl of disapproval. None of them liked or tolerated her decision to move out of the keep. Unfortunately, not one of them understood that their often overbearing protectiveness had been smothering her, either. Even though one or more of them stopped by several times a day, she was enjoying her newfound freedom. That, she feared, was about to end.

"It has been nearly a year," announced Sigimor, her eldest brother, as he and his twin Somerled crouched by the cradles of their nephews. "In a fortnight the year and the day come to an end."

"I ken it."

Ilsa put two heavy jugs of ale on the huge table that occupied almost half of her main room. She had realized that she would never be able to stop her brothers from coming round as the mood struck them so had arranged her living area accordingly. The huge table, sturdy benches, and extra seats, hung upon the wall until needed, had all been made specifically for her brothers. She had arranged a small sitting area more to her liking on the other end of the great hall which made up most of her bottom floor. A low, somewhat rough addition to the back of her home held the kitchen, a tiny pantry, a bathing room, and a small bedchamber for her companion. The high loft which served as the upper part of her home was where she had done things to please herself alone. She had the sinking feeling her brothers were going to force her to leave her little cottage just as she had gotten herself comfortably settled.

"The lads need their father," Sigimor said as he let his nephew Finlay clasp his finger.

"Fourteen uncles arenae enough?" she drawled, setting eight tankards on the table.

"Nay. Their father is a laird, has land and coin. They deserve a part of that."

"It would appear that their father isnae of a like mind." It hurt to say those words, but Ilsa fought to hide her pain. "Ye want me to go crawling to a mon who has deserted me?"

Sigimor sighed and moved to join his brothers at the table as Ilsa set out bread, cheese, and oatcakes. "Nay, I want ye to confront him, to demand what is rightfully due your sons, his sons."

Ilsa also sighed as she sat down next to her twin brother Tait. She had hoped her brothers would not use her sons's rights or welfare to sway her, but suspected she had been foolish to do so. They might be rough, loud, overbearing, and far too protective, but they were not stupid. Her weak point was her sons and only an idiot would not realize it.

"Mayhap another week," she began and groaned when her brothers all shook their heads.

"That would be cutting it too close to the bone. We will leave on the morrow."

"But . . ."

"Nay. I will admit that I am fair disappointed in the lad . . ."

"He is of an age with ye," muttered Ilsa.

Sigimor ignored her and continued, "For I believed all his talk of needing to clear away some threat and prepare his keep for a wife. Tis why I settled for a handfast marriage. I felt a wee bit uncomfortable insisting upon witnessed documents, but now I am glad that I did. He cannae deny ye or the lads. We can make him honor the vows he made." He studied Ilsa closely for a moment. "I thought ye cared for the mon. Ye wanted him bad enough."

"And I thought he cared for me," she snapped. "That was obviously utter foolishness. For just a moment I forgot that I am too poor, too thin, and too red. The mon was just willing to play a more devious game than usual to tumble a maid."

"That makes no sense, Ilsa," argued Tait. "He let us ken where he lives."

"Are ye sure of that?" She nodded when her brothers looked briefly stunned. "We just have his word on that and I think we can assume that his word isnae worth verra much."

"We will still go," said Sigimor. "If we discover it was all a lie, a trick, then we will ken that we have us a mon to hunt down." He nodded when his brothers all muttered an agreement. "So, Somerled will stay here, as will Alexander whose wife is soon to bear him his first child. They can watch the young ones. I, Gilbert, Ranulph, Elyas, Tait, Tamhas, Brice, and Bronan will ride with ye. A few of our men and a couple of our cousins, too, I am thinking."

"Tis nearly an army," protested Ilsa.

"Enough to put weight behind our words, but nay enough to be too threatening."

Ilsa tried to talk them out of their plans, but failed. The moment her brothers left, Ilsa buried her face in her hands and fought the urge to weep. She had done enough of that. A soft touch upon her shoulder drew her out of her despondency and she looked at Gay, her companion and the wet nurse who helped her sate the greed of her sons. Brutally raped, cast off by her family, and then suffering the loss of her child had left young Gay terrified of men, a near-silent ghost of a girl who still feared far too many things and grieved for all her losses. Gay always hid away when Ilsa's brothers stomped in for a visit.

"Ye must go," Gay said in her whispery voice.

"I ken it," Ilsa replied. "Yet, when he didnae return for me, didnae e'en send a letter or gift, I realized I had been played for a fool and did my grieving then. I buried all of that verra deep inside of me. I dinnae want it all dug up again."

Gay picked up a fretting Finlay, handed him to Ilsa, then collected Cearnach. For a few moments, Ilsa savored the gentle peace as she and Gay fed the babies. Looking at her sons, however, at their big, beautiful blue eyes, she was sharply reminded of the man whose seed had created them. The pain was still there, deep, and, she suspected, incurable.

For a few brief, heady weeks she had felt loved, desired, even beautiful. At twenty years of age, an age when most considered her a spinster, she had finally caught the eye of a man. And such a handsome one, she mused, and sighed. That should have warned her. Handsome men did not pursue women like her. In truth, no man had ever pursued her. She had let loneliness, passion, and a craving for love steal away all of her wits. Going to the man as her brothers wished her to would only remind her too sharply of her own idiocy. Not that she ever completely forgot it, she muttered to herself.

"It must be done for the laddies," Gay said as she rested Cearnach against her thin shoulder and rubbed his back.

"I ken that, too," Ilsa said as she did the same to Finlay. "'Tis their birthright and I cannae allow it to be stolen from them. Weel, if there even is a birthright and we dinnae discover that the mon told us naught but lies. Ye will have to come with us."

Gay nodded. "I will be fine. I hide from your brothers because they are so big, nay because I fear them. They fill the room and I find that hard to bear. I will find other places to slip away to when we get where we are going." She frowned. "I just cannae abide being inside a place when so many men are about. I ken your brothers willnae hurt me, but that knowledge isnae yet enough to banish all my blind fears."

"Quite understandable."

"Do ye still love this mon?"

"I think I might, which would be a great folly. But, 'tis time to stop hiding for fear I will be hurt. I must needs seek out this bastard for the sake of the laddies, but I begin to think I need to do it for myself, too. I need to look the devil in the eye, find out just how big a fool I was, and deal with it all. Of course, if he is there, was just hoping I would fade away into the mists, tis best to confront him with his reponsibilities. And then I can do my best to make him utterly miserable."

When Gay laughed briefly and softly, Ilsa felt her spirits rise. Gay was healing. It was slow and there would always be scars, but soon Gay would recover from the hurts done to her. It made Ilsa a little ashamed of her own cowardice. If, after all she had suffered, little Gay could heal, then so could she. And, if she did meet her lover again, she would be a lot wiser and a lot stronger. She would not fall victim to any more foolish dreams.

"My children need a mother."

"Och, he is back to talking to himself again."

Sir Diarmot MacEnroy smiled at his brother Angus who sat on his right. On his left was his brother Antony, or Nanty as he was often called. They had come to attend his wedding and he was heartily glad of their company. The brother he really wished to talk to was his eldest brother Connor, however, but that man had only just arrived with his pregnant wife Gillyanne. Ignoring Gilly's protests, Connor had immediately insisted that she rest for a while and had dragged her up to the bedchamber they would share. It would be a long while before he saw either of them again. Diarmot just hoped there would be some time before his wedding in which he could speak privately with the man.

"Just uneasy about the wedding," Diarmot said.

"Thought ye wanted to marry this lass."

"I do. I just need to remind myself of why now and again."

"She is a pretty wee lass," said Nanty. "Quiet."

"Verra quiet," agreed Diarmot. "Sweet. Biddable. Chaste."

"Completely different from your first wife," murmured Angus.

"Just as I wanted her to be. Anabelle was a blight. Margaret will be a blessing." A boring one, he mused, and probably cold as well, then hastily shook aside those thoughts. "Good dowry and a fine piece of land."

"Does she ken about the children?" Angus asked.

"Aye," replied Diarmot. "I introduced her. She seems at ease with the matter. Her father wasnae too happy at first, nay until he realized the only legitimate one was wee Alice. Once assured that any son his daughter bears me will be my heir, he calmed down."

"There willnae be what Connor and Gilly have, will there?" Nanty asked, his tone of voice indicating that he already knew the answer to the question.

"Nay," Diarmot replied quietly. "I thought I had found that with Anabelle, but twas naught but a curse. Nay every mon can be blessed with what Connor has, but then no mon deserves it more." Both his brothers grunted in agreement. "I now seek peace, contentment."

He ignored the looks his brothers exchanged which carried a strong hint of pity. Since he was occasionally prone to feeling the pinch of it for himself, he did not really need theirs. It was time, however, to set his life back on course. He had drifted for too long after the debacle of his marriage to Anabelle, descending into debauchery and drunkeness which had left him with a houseful of children, only one of whom was legitimate by law even if he was not certain that little Alice was truly his child. Then, as he had finally begun to come to his senses, he had been attacked and left for dead. The months needed to heal had given him far too much time to think. That had led to the coming marriage to sweet, shy, biddable Margaret Campbell. It was the right step to take, he told himself firmly.

It was late before he got a chance to talk privately with Connor. Diarmot had almost avoided the meeting he had craved earlier, for the looks Connor and Gilly had exchanged while dining with Margaret and her family had not been encouraging. It was possible Connor might try to talk him out of the marriage and Diarmot feared he was too uncertain of himself to resist such persuasion. As they settled in chairs set before the fireplace in his bedchamber, Diarmot eyed his elder brother warily as they sipped their wine.

"Are ye certain about this, Diarmot?" Connor finally asked. "There doesnae seem to be much to the lass."

"Nay, there isnae," Diarmot agreed, "but that is what I want now."

"Are ye being prompted by your injuries, by that loss of memory?"

"My injuries are mostly healed. And, aye, my memories are still sadly rattled with a few unsettling blank spots remaining from just before and just after the attack upon me. But, those things have naught to do with this." He sighed and sipped his wine. "Not every mon has the luck ye have had in finding Gillyanne. I tried and I failed, dramatically and miserably. Now I seek peace, a woman to care for my home, my bairns, and to share my bed when I am in the mood. Nay more."

"Then why did ye wish to speak to me?"

"Weel, I havenae seen ye for months," Diarmot began, then grimaced when Connor just stared at him with wry amuement. "I think, like some foolish boy, I wanted ye to say this is right, to give your approval."

Connor nodded. "But ye arenae a small boy any longer. Ye are the only one who can say if this is right or not."

"Ye arenae going to give me your opinion, are ye."

"I am nay sure ye want to hear it," Connor drawled. "Also nay sure what ye want my opinion on. By all the rules, ye have arranged yourself a good marriage, gaining land, coin, and a sweet, virginal bride. By all the rules, ye should be congratulated by most everyone."

"But not by ye or Gilly."

"I cannae see into your heart, Diarmot. I cannae be sure what ye want, what ye seek. To be blunt, I look at that sweet, shy, biddable bride ye have chosen and wonder how long it will take ere ye have to be reminded that ye e'en have a wife."

Diarmot laughed and groaned. "About a month. I can see the same ye do, but tis what I think I need. Yet, something keeps nagging at me, weakening my resolve. One of those lost memories trying to break through the mists in my mind. The closer the time to say my vows draws near, the sharper the nagging. I have more and more dreams, strange dreams, but I cannae grasp the meaning of them."

"What is in these dreams?"

"Nonsense." Diarmot sighed. "Last night I dreamed of a scarlet elf poking at me, cursing me, and

telling me to clear the cursed mist from my puny
brain ere I do something stupid. Then there were
some angry fiery demons, near a dozen of them,
bellowing that I had best step right or they will be
cutting me off at the knees. Then, for a brief moment, all seems weel, until the first blow is struck.
Tis the beating, I think, for I wake up all asweat,
the fear of death putting a sharp taste in my mouth."

"The last I can understand," Connor said. "Ye
were helpless. No mon wants to die, but to be set
upon in the dark by men ye cannae recognize,
who beat ye near to death for reasons ye dinnae
ken, would stir a fear in any mon."

Diarmot nodded. "I can understand that part. I
just wish that, upon waking with that fear, I would
also hold the memory of the who and the why."

"Twill come. Now, elves and fiery demons? Nay,
I dinnae understand that. Gilly might. Could just
be some trickery of your mind which is struggling
to remember." He shrugged. "That would explain
all that talk of clearing the mists and the like.
Mayhap ye should postpone the wedding."

"And what reason could I give? Dreams of scarlet elves?"

"Weel, that could do it," drawled Connor, but
his obvious amusement quickly fled. "The return
of your memory. Just tell Sir Campbell ye sense a
danger behind what happened to ye and, since the
memories are struggling to return, it might be best
to wait and see if ye finally recall what that danger
is."

For several moments Diarmot sat sipping his wine,
staring into the fire, and considering Connor's advice. It was good advice. The increasingly strange
dreams he was having could indeed mean he was
beginning to remember the attack upon him. Then

he shook his head. It did not really matter when his memory returned, whether it was before or after his marriage. He might not recall what the danger was, but he was absolutely sure it was his danger alone. If it started to reach out to others, it would reach for his betrothed as swiftly as it did for his wife.

"Nay, it would just cause more trouble than it would solve," Diarmot finally said. "All my instincts tell me this danger I face is mine and mine alone."

"But if ye are wrong?" Connor asked quietly.

"Then I have already drawn Margaret into my danger by betrothing myself to her."

"True. At least, as your wife, ye would have better control o'er the protection of her. Weel, I dinnae think I have helped ye much. I sense ye are still uneasy." Connor stood up. "Years ago I would have looked at your bride's bloodline, her land, and her dowry and said 'good lad.' Once I wed Gilly, I lost that blindness."

"And if Gilly had turned your life into a near hell upon earth as Anabelle did mine? Would ye wish to risk giving any lass that sort of trust, e'en power, ever again?"

"Nay," Connor replied immediately. "Ye made your point. I just wish it wasnae so."

"So do I, but far better a wife so unexceptional I forget she is about than one who rips my heart and soul to shreds."

Connor walked to the door, but paused on his way out to look back at Diarmot. "There is a third choice and ye have until the morning to decide."

"What third choice?"

"No wife at all."

Diarmot was still considering Connor's parting words as he watched the dawn brighten the sky. He had slept very little, troubled by that strange dream again as well as his own uneasiness. Although there were any number of times in his life that he knew he should have thought twice, this constant worrying over something was unlike him.

It was possible that his memory was beginning to return, although he wished it would not do so in strange dreams. He could not understand how that should make him question his decision to get married, yet, that seemed to be what it was doing. Until the strange dreams had begun, he had been content with his choice of bride and his plans for the future. In fact, he could not figure out what scarlet elves and fiery demons had to do with anything.

Suddenly realizing he had missed the dawn because he had become so lost in his own thoughts, Diarmot cursed and rang for his bath. Enough was enough. Illness and a strange reluctance to bed any of the willing lasses around Clachthrom had kept him celibate for a year. That was what was disordering his thoughts and dreams. In a few hours he would be a married man again and he could do something about that problem.

Constant company and the final preparations for the wedding feast kept him busy and he was glad. Diarmot wanted no more time with only his own tangled thoughts for company. It was as he walked to the church with Connor at his side that Diarmot realized he was not going to be able to go blindly to the altar, marry his bride, and get it over with. Connor was tense with the need to say something.

"Weel, what is it?" Diarmot grumbled.

"I was rather hoping ye would take the third choice," Connor murmured. "So was Gilly."

"Why?"

"Weel, Gilly says Margaret is indeed sweet, shy, and biddable. She also says she is, er, empty."

"Empty? What does that mean?"

Connor shrugged. "Not much emotion in the lass."

"Good," Diarmot snapped, although Gilly's impression troubled him. "I have had my fill of emotion. Anabelle drowned me in emotions, good and bad. Calm would be a nice change."

"It could also be teeth-grindingly dull."

"I dinnae care." He looked away from Connor's expression of wry disbelief. "I may not find any fire in my wife's bed, but at least when I choose to go to her, she will be there. She may nay welcome me verra heartily, but she willnae be welcoming anyone else, either—mon nor woman."

Connor whistled softly. "Ye caught Anabelle with a woman?"

"Aye, although the woman fled ere I got a good look at her. Anabelle thought it all verra funny. Said she and the lass had been lovers for years. Tried to tell me I couldnae call that adultery. I could keep ye entertained for days on all the tales I have of Anabelle, her lovers, her rages, her wailing spells, and her wanderings. It was like trying to live in the heart of a fierce Highland storm. After that, dull sounds verra sweet to me."

Diarmot was relieved when Connor said no more. He did not like pulling forth the painful memories of his time with Anabelle. Such memories, however, did serve to remind him of why he had chosen Margaret. He craved peace, he thought, and walked toward the church with a surer step.

It was as he knelt beside his bride that his doubts trickled back. A voice in his head kept saying this was wrong, although it offered no explanation. Margaret's hand in his was cool and dry, her expression one of sweet calm. What could possibly be wrong?

Just as the priest asked if anyone knew why Diarmot and Margaret could not marry there was a disturbance at the doors of the church and a clear, angry woman's voice said, "I think I might have a reason or two."

Shocked, Diarmot looked behind him and his eyes widened. Marching toward him was a tiny woman with brilliant copper hair. Behind her strode eight large, scowling red-haired men. She held a bundle in her arms and a small, dark-haired girl walked beside her holding another.

"Weel, now, Diarmot," drawled Connor, smiling faintly, "it seems your dreams have become prophetic."

"What?" Diarmot glanced at Connor who was slowly standing up.

"Did ye nay dream about a scarlet elf and a troop of fiery demons?"

Diarmot decided that, as soon as he found out what was happening, he would pound his grinning brother into the mud.

CHAPTER TWO

Pain seemed to be coursing through Ilsa with every beat of her heart, as if it was carried in her blood. When they had been told the laird of Clachthrom was marrying, her brothers had been enraged. So had she, but she had also wished to simply turn around and go home. Her brothers had refused to allow that retreat. As they had forced her toward the small stone church, she had both hoped it would be too late and feared that it would be. Ilsa knew that the best she could hope for was that she would retain enough wit and strength to stop blood being spilled.

To see her lover, the father of her children, kneeling beside a pretty, fulsome young woman murmuring marriage vows had slashed her heart. Then rage had swept over her, a rage born of pain and betrayal. She could not believe she had spoken out before her brothers. As she marched toward Diarmot, who slowly stumbled to his feet and helped his pretty bride to stand, her fury grew. He was looking at her as if he had never seen her before.

He was still so beautiful it made her heart clench to look at him. Tall, well built, lean and strong, his form was all any woman could wish for. His hair was the color of rich clover honey, thick and a little long, hanging to several inches below his broad shoulders. His broad forehead, elegant straight nose, and well-shaped mouth with a hint of fullness to his lips formed a face that had haunted her dreams for a year despite all her efforts to banish him from her mind. Beneath slightly arced brows, and rimmed with enviable dark lashes, were eyes of a beautiful deep blue, but looking into them only added to her pain. Gone was the soft warmth she had seen before when he had held her close and sworn they would soon be together again. Now there was only a cold anger and suspicion. She fought the sharp urge to flee that look, struggled to cling to her fury.

"What right do ye have to disrupt this ceremony?" Diarmot demanded, telling himself the reason the sight of this woman made him so uneasy was that she reminded him too strongly of his strange dreams.

"The right ye gave me a year ago," she replied.

"I have nay idea what ye are babbling about."

The audacity of the mon, Ilsa thought. "Show him the papers, Sigimor."

As the rest of her brothers kept a close watch on the guests, some of whom were looking increasingly angry, her eldest brother stepped forward and handed Diarmot all the papers concerning their handfast marriage. Ilsa tried to ignore the way he paled as he looked them over. She noticed the large, fair-haired man at Diarmot's side read them as well, constantly casting her looks that held a wealth of curiosity.

"They appear quite in order, Diarmot," Connor said quietly as he took the papers out of Diarmot's limp grasp.

"What is going on?" demanded Margaret, curling her arm around Diarmot's and trying to catch a glimpse at the papers.

When Diarmot just stared at the woman, Ilsa drawled, "It appears your betrothed is already married—to me." From the uproar she could hear, Ilsa knew the bride's family was furious, but she trusted her brothers to hold them back. "Diarmot and I were handfasted a year ago."

"Handfasted? Is that all? Such marriages are set aside easily enough."

Ilsa stared at the woman, torn between an urge to gape and one to slap her pretty face. What was truly surprising was how little reaction the woman revealed to the possibility that her betrothed had deceived her, that she had almost been dragged into a false, bigamous union. Where was the anger, the righteous sense of insult? There was not even the glimmer of pain in the woman's pale blue eyes. Either Diarmot's pretty little bride had no depth of feeling for him or she was an idiot.

"It cannae be done so easily, Margaret," Diarmot said.

"It cannae be done at all," snapped Ilsa.

She unwrapped the blanket around Finlay. Out of the corner of her eye, she saw Gay quickly open the blanket wrapped around Cearnach. It shocked Ilsa a little to see that Gay looked as furious as she herself felt. For the moment, outrage had apparantly dimmed Gay's fears.

"Your sons, Finlay and Cearnach." Ilsa nodded toward each child as she introduced them. "They are three months old. These lads give me the right to claim ye as my husband. They also, by your own vow, compel ye to make me your wife before God and kinsmen, before a priest."

"Nay, they are not my get," said Diarmot.

Ilsa felt Sigimor take a step closer to Diarmot and heard him growl. There was an echo of the ferocious noise from behind her, her seven other brothers clearly sharing Sigimor's fury. Although she was feeling violently angry herself, she was pleased that the men had left their weapons outside the church as custom demanded.

"Nay, Sigimor," she said as she wrapped her son back up in his blanket.

"He insults ye," snapped Sigimor. "He insults *us.*"

"Aye, true enough, and, although there is a part of me which would like to see him stomped into a smear upon the floor, I still say nay. Ye were the one who pressed me to seek him out, to make him honor his obligations. I cannae do that if ye break him into wee, bloodied pieces, can I. It wouldnae be good for the lads to see their uncles slaughter their father, either."

"How can I be their father?" demanded Diarmot. "I dinnae e'en ken who ye are, woman."

Diarmot fought the urge to take a step away from the outrage and fury directed at him by the woman and her companions. This was impossible. Someone was trying to deceive him. He could not believe he would forget having a wife no matter how severe his injuries had been. A wife with copper-colored hair and ivy-green eyes was surely something a man would recall. He looked to Connor for help only to find his brother and the priest carefully examining the papers. When both men glanced at him, Diarmot felt panic stir in his blood. The look they gave him told him he would find little help from them.

"Is this your signature upon these papers?" the priest asked Diarmot.

"Aye, but—"

"Nay, no arguments, please. These papers say ye are bound to this woman," the priest glanced down at the papers, "this Ilsa Cameron." He cast a pointed look at the twins before returning his gaze to Diarmot. "Ye have proved verra compatible indeed, thus she is the woman I will be marrying ye to."

Before Diarmot could say another word, a unified roar of fury rose up from the Campbells. He looked for Margaret, although he was not sure of what he could say or do, only to see her standing next to the altar. She still looked sweet and calm, but there was a hint of gleeful anticipation in her eyes. Before he could wonder at that, he caught sight of a large fist headed his way, and ducked. A heartbeat later, he found himself caught up in a melee of fists and bellowed threats of retaliation.

Ilsa quickly backed up toward the far side of the church. She felt a trembling Gay keeping pace with her. When they were pressed up against the wall, Gay tucked herself up close to Ilsa's side. As she turned to speak with Gay, Ilsa saw a pretty, obviously pregnant woman with faintly mismatched eyes standing on the other side of Gay.

"I am Gillyanne MacEnroy," the woman said. "Wife to Connor, the big mon who stood at Diarmot's side."

"I am Ilsa and this is Gay." Ilsa watched as the

woman inspected the twins. "They are Diarmot's sons."

"Aye, I ken it. They have his eyes, as weel." Gillyanne lightly stroked Gay's arm. "Be at ease, child. These men will ne'er hurt ye. Big and loud though they are now, the MacEnroys and the Camerons would ne'er harm a lass."

"Most of me kens it, m'lady," said Gay, then she frowned. "Ye didnae include the Campbells, the bride's kinsmen."

"Nay, I am unsure of them." She ruffled the thick red curls on Cearnach's head. "Lovely."

"I had hoped they would have Diarmot's hair," Ilsa murmured, noticing that Gillyanne's words, perhaps her very presence, had calmed Gay.

"There is naught wrong with red and I suspect twill darken some." Gillyanne glanced toward the men and winced. "Nanty just went down. Ah, there, he is back on his feet."

Ilsa looked toward the men and noticed there were two more men who looked akin to her husband standing shoulder to shoulder with Diarmot, Connor, and a few of her brothers. "Nanty?"

"Antony, Diarmot's brother. We call him Nanty. He is to Diarmot's left. Angus, another brother, is to Connor's right. His brother Andrew and his sister Fiona remained at Deilcladach. Was that one of your brothers who just disappeared under all those Campbells?"

"Aye. Twas Elyas, but Gilbert and Tait will soon have him out. Tait is my twin."

"I am hoping this doesnae cause a bitter feud."

"Ah, that would be a curse, for certain. I will be sorry if I am the cause of such trouble. Mayhap—"

"Nay, no mayhap, no hesitation. Ye are Diarmot's wife."

A little surprised by the woman's words, Ilsa asked, "Ye believe me?"

"Och, aye." Gillyanne shrugged. "I feel things, ye ken. I can feel the truth in ye." She nodded toward Margaret. "She makes me verra uneasy, has from the start. I feel nothing in her. There are some people, like my husband, who seem to have a shield o'er their feelings I cannae get through e'en if I try, but Lady Margaret doesnae feel like that to me. She just feels, weel, empty, if that makes any sense at all."

"Some," murmured Ilsa, faintly unsettled by Lady Gillyanne's words, yet unable to question the woman's claims. "I did think it odd that she had so little reaction to my claims. She remained calm, almost serene."

"Aye, she is always calm and serene."

"That just isnae natural," muttered Gay.

Gillyanne laughed softly. "Nay, it isnae." She looked at Margaret again. "I did sense some anger now and again, but it came and went so quickly, I dare nay swear it was really there. I am verra pleased that she willnae be a part of our family."

Ilsa studied the woman Diarmot had planned to marry. Margaret stood by the priest who had given up his attempts to stop the fighting and was wise enough not to venture too close to the melee. If she had been about to marry a man only to have the marriage stopped because a wife he neglected to mention suddenly appeared, bairns in arms, she would be enraged. She would be as hurt and angry as she felt now as the instigator of this trouble. Yet, Margaret remained calm, her hands clasped lightly in front of her skirts. It did not seem to even matter to her that her kinsmen were being soundly beaten, that this incident could easily blossom into a bloody feud lasting for years. Ilsa felt uneasy just watching the woman and looked back at Gillyanne.

"At best, she appears faintly amused by all of this," murmured Ilsa. "I dinnae have your gift, but I do have some skill at sensing how a person thinks or feels. Or, I thought I did."

"Oh, ye do, Ilsa," Gay said.

"Do I?" Ilsa sighed. "If so, it utterly failed me with Diarmot. I thought him honest, trustworthy, yet he tries to claim he has no knowledge of me or our handfasting. I was obviously verra wrong in my judgment of him."

"Nay, ye were right," Guillyanne said. "He is honest and trustworthy."

"But, he said—"

"A lot of nonsense. Unfortunately, he probably believes what he says. That could be because, in many ways, it may be the truth. Shortly after he left ye, Ilsa, Diarmot was set upon and beaten nigh unto death. He made it to a crofter's small home ere he could go no farther. He retained enough wits to tell the mon there who to seek out and that mon sent word to Connor at Deilcladach. We went to fetch him and I did what I could. E'en so, we werenae sure he would survive. Once back at Deilcladach, we sent for my Aunt Maldie Murray, a reknowned healer. Despite her great skill, it was a long time before we could all feel confident he would live. Diarmot insisted upon returning here and, once we were certain he would survive the journey, we brought him back to Clachthrom. His recovery took a verra long time and, in truth, I am astonished that he healed as weel as he did. Howbeit, although he healed in body, his mind remains, weel, injured."

"What do ye mean?"

"He cannae recall anything from that time. He doesnae ken why he was where he was, when or how he was beaten, or by whom. He has little memory of the worst of his pain and illness, his time of healing. Diarmot truly doesnae remember you." Gillyanne smiled faintly when Ilsa frowned at her. "Tis hard to believe. I understand."

"I dinnae think ye lie."

"Nay, but ye think Diarmot does."

Ilsa shrugged then sighed. "I dinnae ken what I think. To forget a wife? And, his time with me came before the beating, so why would his memory of that fail him?"

"Who can say? Just try nay to let anger and injured feelings close heart and mind." Gillyanne glanced at the men. "Ye shall have to try to start anew. I ken it willnae be easy."

"Nay, it willnae." Ilsa winced as a Campbell seemed to fly over the church benches and landed near the door.

"Oh, dear," said Gay. "Sigimor has gotten verra angry. He is tossing men about."

"Aye." Ilsa briefly smiled at a giggling Gillyanne. "This foolishness will soon end. Once the Campbells see how many of them are ending in a groaning heap near the walls, they will back down."

"Your brother often ends a fight this way, does he?" asked Gillyanne.

"He says that, if they havenae got the sense to stay down when he knocks them down, they deserve to be thrown away." She shook her head as yet another Campbell went flying toward the wall, but she noticed the urge to keep fighting was slowly leaving the others still facing her brothers and the MacEnroys. "Tait says Sigimor just wearies of hitting them and wants them to go away. I think, too, that he did it once, saw how it made other men hesitate or back away, and decided it was a verra fine battle tactic."

"Aye, it is. I can see that my husband heartily approves." Gillyanne looked at Ilsa.

When the woman continued to study her, but say nothing, Ilsa began to feel uncomfortable. "What is it?"

"Just love the fool as ye do, Ilsa Cameron. Twill take time ere all is weel, but twill be time weel spent. Ah, the priest now ventures forth to try to soothe tempers."

Ilsa wanted to ask the woman what she meant by those words, but suspected she would get no answer. If Lady Gillyanne had wanted to say more, she would have. Of that, Ilsa had no doubt. She inwardly shook her head. The woman had accepted her quickly, almost without question. Yet, Ilsa could not rouse much suspicion over that, which in itself was very odd, indeed. She turned her attention to the men who were arguing with the priest and each other.

"He shamed my daughter," snapped Sir Lesley Campbell, glaring at Diarmot and the priest. "That insults me and my family."

"It wasnae an intentional slight," said Father Goudie.

"I didnae ken I had a wife, handfast or otherwise," muttered Diarmot.

"How can ye forget a wife?" demanded Sir Lesley. "Do ye truly expect me to believe that?"

"I believe I told ye of my injuries and my loss of memory when this marriage was arranged." Diarmot did not need to look at the Camerons to know they doubted his claim, too. He could almost feel their anger and suspicion.

"Ye will pay for this, MacEnroy. Ye were to take my daughter to wife, to make her the lady of this keep."

"Weel, it seems he cannae do that, can he?" said Sigimor. "He handfasted with my sister nearly a year past and those bairns give her the right to claim him as husband."

"If the bairns are really his," snapped Sir Campbell, only to take a step back when Sigimor started to move toward him.

"There will be nay more fighting in my church," shouted Father Goudie, stopping Sigimor's advance, then he gave Sir Campbell a stern look. "The papers Lady Cameron has are proof enough for me. I also ken that Sir Diarmot was grievously ill. I believe him when he says he didnae recall he had a wife already. This was nay more than an innocent error, no insult intended, and that should be the end of it."

"Ah, weel, ye would say that, wouldnae ye?" said Sir Campbell, growing bold in his anger once Sigimor had stepped back. "Ye are a Goudie, one of a clan allied to the MacEnroys."

Father Goudie stood very straight, his expression and his voice cold. "Ye grow offensive. I am a priest. My first allegiance is to God, the church, and the truth. Ye would do weel to cease your curses and allegations and thank God the truth was uncovered ere your daughter found herself the illegitimate wife in a bigamous union."

Sir Campbell glared at the priest, but said no more, simply looked toward his daughter. "Come, Margaret."

As his erstwhile wife passed by his side, Diarmot looked at her, unable to think of anything to say to make amends. She smiled faintly and he inwardly frowned. There was little expression upon her sweet face or in her blue eyes. Margaret was as calm as always which made no sense at all. Diarmot knew theirs was not to have been a love match, yet, surely, the woman should be at least annoyed. He began to wonder if what he had seen as a sweet, passive nature was actually bone-deep stupidity.

"It will all come right in the end," she murmured, then let her father drag her away.

Diarmot noticed that everyone was staring after Margaret with the same look of confusion he suspected he wore. "What did she mean by that?"

"Mayhap she is a forgiving lass," suggested Father Goudie. "She understands this was all an innocent mistake and wishes ye weel in renewing your vows with Lady Ilsa. Shall we begin the ceremony?"

It was on the tip of Diarmot's tongue to say no Goudie could possibly be that naive, but he bit back the words. Instead, he fixed his mind on the suggestion that he now marry the copper-haired woman who claimed they had been handfasted. He did not care what papers she waved about, he was certain some wretched trick was being played on him.

"I dinnae believe," began Diarmot only to have Connor drag him several feet away from the growling Camerons. "This has got to be some devious game, Connor."

"Nay, I dinnae think so," said Connor. "The papers look too real." He glanced toward the small crowd at the back of the church, many of whom had slipped inside after the Campbells had left. "I expect some of that group are witnesses." He then looked toward his wife who still stood close by Lady Ilsa's side. "Gillyanne has accepted it all."

Diarmot followed his brother's gaze, saw Gillyanne standing with Lady Ilsa, and felt chilled. "Weel, she ne'er liked Margaret."

"Why are ye being so stubborn about this? Ye were seeking a wife. Weel, it appears ye have found one."

"She isnae what I sought."

"Nay? She is a bonny lass and has given ye two fine sons, legitimate ones."

"If her claims are true." Diarmot grimaced and dragged his hands through his hair. "She isnae what I sought," he repeated a little helplessly. "She isnae calm and sweet. There is the hint of strong emotions in her and I dinnae want that."

Connor softly cursed. "She came to find the husband she thought she had, one she hasnae heard from in a year, only to find him ready to marry another. That would rouse strong emotion in any lass with some wit or heart."

That was a pointed reference to Margaret's utter calm, but Diarmot could not bring himself to defend the woman. Margaret's complete lack of emotion under such circumstances was odd. "She is too thin and too red." He cursed when Connor slapped him on the back of the head.

"Ye clearly found her enticing a year past. Aye, she may nay be sweet and calm and her curves are but gentle ones, but those bairns prove they will serve ye weel. If I judge it right, there willnae be much of a dower, either. Tis evident that that lack didnae trouble ye a year past." Connor cocked one brow. "Any other arguments ere ye do as ye ought?"

Diarmot just glared at Connor and slowly shook his head. He might be able to present more arguments, but Connor would just continue to knock them down with ease. Whatever he said now could be readily countered by the fact that it had evidently not caused him to hesitate to plight his troth to the woman a year ago, or so the Camerons would have them all believe.

"How do ye ken I signed those papers of my own free will?" he finally asked.

"And how do ye ken that ye didnae? Ye certainly cannae recall. I believe the papers real, that no game is played here. It appears that Gilly thinks the same. If there isnae any trick here, ye owe that lass vows said afore a priest. If there is some trick, then, would it nay be wise to have her close to hand? Ye say ye cannae recall her as lover or wife. Ye cannae recall who your enemy is, either. Wed her. If tis but a trick, a lie, that will be enough to end the marriage. Play the game for now."

There was a great deal of sense in what Connor said. Diarmot wondered why he hesitated, but he did. As he looked at Ilsa he felt a variety of emotions stir to life inside of him and suspected that was why. He wanted no emotions. He wanted peace. Although he could not readily identify what he felt, it was not peaceful. Taking a deep breath to steady himself, he marched toward Lady Ilsa Cameron.

Ilsa was given no chance to complain or discuss the matter before she found herself kneeling beside Diarmot. A little dazed, she said her vows before Father Goudie. Diarmot did not hesitate to say his, but there was a cold anger in his voice as he did so and it made the words she had so longed to hear just another way to wound her. His kiss to seal their vows was also cold and abrupt.

She could think of nothing to say as she accepted Finlay back into her arms, smiling faintly at Gillyanne who had been kind enough to hold him. No one else seemed inclined to speak, either. Diarmot's hand on her arm felt a little too much like a manacle. This marriage was so far removed from all of her girlish imaginings, she knew she was in shock. It was not until they entered the keep that she regained her senses enough to realize that her sons needed to be attended to before she was subjected to any more shocks or slights.

"Do ye have a nursery?" she asked Diarmot, finally resisting his pull on her arm and forcing him to stop and look at her. "Gay and I need to feed and change the bairns." She felt very uneasy when he slowly smiled.

"The nursery," he murmured and started to pull her toward the narrow stone stairs that led to the upper floors. "Allow me to escort ye there."

A murmur of protest came from Diarmot's family, but he ignored them. Ilsa was not sure why the MacEnroys did not want her taken to the nursery or why Diarmot seemed far too pleased to take her. She could not think of any reason why she should suddenly feel so eager not to go, either, but she did.

Diarmot stopped before a door, opened it, and insolently waved her and Gay into the room. Ilsa took a few steps inside and stopped, staring at the six little children who called out greetings to their papa. A part of her, the part so well trained in good manners, made her curtsy slightly to each child as Diarmot introduced them.

"Just toss yours in with the rest," Diarmot said and walked away.

As Ilsa heard the door shut behind him, she had the mad thought that it sounded like the coffin lid being nailed shut on every hope and dream she had ever had.

CHAPTER THREE

"M'lady, let me take the bairn. I think ye may be holding him a wee bit too tightly."

Ilsa blinked and looked at the plump, older woman standing before her. The woman was probably in her thirties with the hint of silver in her dark hair, and had a round, pleasant face. There was sympathy in her dark eyes and Ilsa felt that cut through some of the shock which held her so tightly in its grip. A soft whimper from Finlay convinced her to hand her son to the woman. Until she could gain some control of her rampaging emotions, Ilsa knew she could not give her babies the attention they needed. She also knew her upset could make the twins fretful.

"And ye are?" she asked, astonished at how calm and even her voice sounded. "I fear I didnae heed the introductions verra weel."

"I am nay surprised to hear it. Dinnae ken what the lad was thinking, what foolish game he played. Toss them in with the others, he says. He needs his ears twisted, he does. I am Mistress Fraser, but most call me Fraser or Nurse." The woman curtsied. "My given name is Mary, ye see, and there are a lot of Marys about. Didnae like the way they tried to put a word afore Mary to separate me from the others, so tis just Fraser or Nurse."

"Pleased to meet ye, Fraser." Ilsa touched Gay's shoulder. "This is my companion Gay. She helps me feed and care for the twins." Ilsa noticed only curiosity in the woman's eyes, but Fraser did not press for any explanations, just drew the children closer and began to introduce them one by one.

There was Alice, a pretty little girl of three with thick blond curls and big brown eyes. In a not very quiet aside, Fraser identified the girl as Diarmot's only legitimate child born of his first marriage to a woman named Anabelle. It would have been nice if Diarmot had told her that he had been married before, Ilsa mused as Fraser introduced Ivy, a girl of five with blond hair and blue eyes. Then came Odo, a sturdy little boy of five with brown hair and blue eyes. A shy little boy of four named Aulay seemed to be all shades of brown, from his thick hair to his big dark brown eyes to his slightly swarthy skin. Ewart, two, was a startlingly beautiful little boy with thick black curls and brilliant blue eyes. Finally, a thin boy named Gregor was introduced. This boy was also two, had dark blond hair, and light gray eyes.

Five bastards, she thought. Some from before his marriage, some bred during his marriage. Diarmot obviously did not honor his vows. Two children aged five and two aged two revealed that Diarmot could not even be faithful to a mistress, let alone his own wife. Her future kept looking darker and darker, she thought with a sigh.

As Fraser introduced Cearnach and Finlay to

their new siblings, Ilsa felt numbing shock slowly replaced by a searing hot rage. Telling herself that there were no children of an age to show Diarmot had been unfaithful to her did nothing to cool her anger. He had obviously scattered his seed far and wide and held no faith at all with his first wife. He had never told her that he had been married once. He had never told her that he had a small horde of illegitimate children. Diarmot could not claim he had forgotten those rather important facts, for their time together had been before his injury. In a way he had lied to her, deceived her. She could not help but wonder how deep that deception went, if everything that had passed between them had also been a lie.

And the way he had tossed her into this room, she thought and tightly clenched her fists, had been cruel and insulting. Ilsa was sure the man had meant it to be an insult. Diarmot had also insulted their sons with his parting words. That could not be allowed. If he truly had forgotten her, forgotten their marriage, he had a right to some doubts. There was no doubt, however, that the twins were his sons. She could not allow him to strike out at them no matter how angry or suspicious he felt.

Out of the corner of her eye, she caught sight of a heavy jug. Ilsa picked it up, pleased by its weight and the fact that it was empty. She turned and started out of the room. What she intended to do would solve nothing and she knew it, but she still needed to do it.

"I will return in a few moments," she told Gay.

"Oh, dear," murmured Gay as the door shut behind Ilsa.

"If she needed water, she should have asked me,"

said Fraser. "There are plenty of ready hands to fetch things."

"She hasnae gone to fetch water."

"Then why did she take the ewer?"

"She is going to throw it at her husband." Gay's eyes widened slightly with surprise when Fraser chuckled. "She is verra angry."

"So she should be. To present her with this brood without a word of explanation was badly done. Twas unkind and, I think, meant to insult her. A slap in the face, it was. The fool deserves whatever she does to him."

"She truly is his handfast wife," Gay said.

Fraser nodded. "I ken it. Dinnae need to be seeing any papers, either. There is no deception in that lass." Fraser shook her head. "Unfortunately, our laird sees deception at every turn at the moment. He has some right to be wary, but, I believe his loss of memory makes him even more so. When the lass has calmed herself, I will tell her a few things that fool lad should have told her before he had his wits rattled."

"Will that help?" Gay was not comforted when Fraser's only answer was a shrug of her shoulders.

Diarmot scowled at the Camerons. With the assistance of his family, he had told them of his injuries and loss of memory. He suspected it was only Gillyanne's presence and her word that held back their outrage and fury. The Camerons were not openly calling him a liar, but their expressions said it loudly enough. They obviously suspected him of lying to his family.

That was fine, he thought crossly, for he did not believe them, either. For one thing, he did not believe he would ever be fool enough to marry a woman with eight large brothers, ones who possessed every shade of red hair imaginable and the temper rumored to go with it. Despite Gillyanne's belief that the Camerons told the truth, for the first time since he had known her, Diarmot did not accept her word on it. He did not want to.

In what he recognized as a somewhat childish reaction, Diarmot wanted them all to go away. He wanted his meek, calm, easy-to-ignore bride back. It had only taken one glimpse of Ilsa to know that copper-haired beauty would never be meek or calm, nor would she tolerate being ignored. Nor would the Camerons shake his hand, praise the new alliance, then stay away, he thought as he studied Ilsa's brothers and half a dozen of her cousins. It appeared that, if his wife chose to, she could call up an army big enough to grind Clachthrom into the dust, and with only asking her close relations. Even more dangerous, he felt certain there was a strong bond amongst these Camerons, a true affection for each other. That explained the anger that still lingered even though he had married Ilsa as they had demanded.

"Diarmot."

Slowly, Diarmot looked toward the doors of his great hall, wondering how one sharp calling of his name could so effectively silence a whole room. He caught his breath at the sharp bite of lust he felt when he looked at Ilsa. It was obvious she was angry. In truth, he did not think he had ever seen a woman so furious. Diarmot wondered why that should arouse him, and, even more curious, why it should make him want to smile. The way Ilsa had said his name had held enough quiet but deep rage that a smart man would start running.

"Bastard," she hissed. "Lying, lecherous bastard. Ye are fouler than the slime at the bottom of a midden heap."

"Duck," said one of the Camerons.

Diarmot heard the shifting of everyone at his table, indicating that they had heeded that warning. He watched somewhat dazed as Ilsa raised the heavy jug she held. It occured to him that she intended to throw it even as she did so. Suddenly, Connor grabbed him by the arm and yanked him to the side. Diarmot heard the jug lightly scrape the top of his chair, then winced as it shattered on the floor behind him. When he sat up straight and looked toward the doors, Ilsa was gone. He thought it highly unfair when the Camerons all glared at him. After all, he was not the one cursing and hurling ewers.

"She must have become irritated upon meeting my children," Diarmot said and took a drink of his ale to hide his unease.

"What children?" demanded Sigimor.

"My daughter Alice, the only child my late wife gave me, and five others."

"Five others? Five bastards?"

"I am nay fond of that word."

"Isnae that a pity. I suggest ye gain a tolerance for it, because I suspicion ye are about to hear it a lot and nay directed at your bairns. Ye ne'er told my sister ye were wed before nor about your habit of breeding women like some cocksure stallion set loose in a field of mares in season."

Diarmot was annoyed at the way his brothers snickered, but ignored them to reply to Sigimor's insult. "Why do ye assume I ne'er told your sister? Mayhap she ne'er told ye."

"She would have told Tait."

"And what makes him so blessed?"

"He is her twin."

It just kept getting worse, Diarmot mused, and inwardly cursed. "That doesnae mean she will tell him every little secret."

"Weel, she does. He kenned about ye ere we did. And, Ilsa would have spoken up about your lechery. Aye, loud and long. Such lechery would have appalled her and ye wouldnae have gotten into her bed so cursed fast. We would have been asking ye some hard questions ere ye handfasted as weel. What did ye do, push her into the room full of your bairns with nary a word of warning?"

To his dismay, Diarmot could feel the sting of guilt's color upon his cheeks and he glared at Sigimor. "She wanted the nursery. I showed it to her."

Sigimor shook his head. "Ye werenae such an ill-tempered, unkind sod when we kenned ye. I think that beating knocked more than your senses awry." He crossed his arms over his broad chest. "I am now wishing I had let the others come along so that we could all take a turn beating some sense and charity into your thick head."

"What others? There are more of ye? Just how many cursed brothers does she have?"

"Fourteen. Three sets of twins. Ilsa is the only lass. Has two score and seven cousins, too, and only three of them are lasses, but then ye kenned all of that."

Diarmot scowled at Gillyanne who was laughing so hard she had to cling to Connor for support. All three of his brothers were doing a poor job of hiding their own amusement. He saw absolutely nothing funny about this. A doting father or brother was well known to be a problem for a husband. He was beset by a doting army of huge redheads.

"Why dinnae ye just assume I dinnae recall any of it," Diarmot said. "Play the game. Tell me exactly who Ilsa Cameron is and how I came to be handfasted to her." He gave Sigimor a cold smile. "Mayhap it will bestir my memory."

"I have heard that a sound knock upon the head can help," said Tait, slowly rising from his seat, his hands clenched into hard fists.

"Sit, Tait," Sigimor ordered, nodding when, after a moment of hesitation, Tait obeyed. He then looked at Diarmot. "Fine, we shall play your game. Ilsa met ye when she stopped our cousins Ivar and Marcus from knocking ye senseless. They considered the lass at the inn theirs, ye ken, and felt ye were trespassing. Ilsa is probably regretting the fact that she didnae see that wee incident as proof of a lecherous nature."

It was not easy, but Diarmot decided to ignore that slur. "How did I go from meeting her to wedding her?"

"By the same route many a lecherous rogue takes—seduction. Ilsa was easy prey as the fool lass thinks she isnae one to catch a mon's eye. She thinks her lack of gentlemen seeking to court her is because she hasnae got a big dowry or lush curves or a bonny face."

"When tis mostly that she has a veritable sea of strong kinsmen encircling her," murmured Gillyanne.

Sigimor nodded. "That was for the best at times. We all felt she should have her heart's choice in a mon, but didnae want her picking some rogue who would leave her poor and unhappy. Sad to say, our manner of sorting the wheat from the chaff spawned rumors that made the lads wary, the cowards. We werenae at hand when she met this rogue," Sigimor said with a nod toward Diarmot. "By the time we were, the rogue had won her heart and seduced her. Wheesht, me and five of my brothers found them trysting in the wood. Truth is, near to rode right over them. Twas clear he had taken her maidenhead and, since Ilsa wouldnae let us kill him, we demanded marriage." Sigimor frowned when Gillyanne buried her face in her hands and her shoulders trembled slightly. "It wasnae so bad, m'lady. Sir Diarmot's pride may have been a wee bit bruised, but naught else. Though, I be thinking he may have deserved more. Aye, and still might."

Gillyanne raised her head and smiled at Sigimor, revealing that she had been laughing, not crying. "I wasnae upset, Sigimor. I but suddenly realized how ye kenned Ilsa was intending to throw that jug and why it is she has such a fine aim."

"Aye, we do irritate the lass at times," he said and grinned.

"Why handfast? Why nay a priest?"

"Didnae have one. Ours died a month before Sir Diarmot arrived."

"Died in his mistress's bed," said Tamhas Cameron. "Actually, he died in his mistress and it wasnae easy to prepare him for his burial, I can tell ye. Had to get some lard and . . ." he grunted a curse when his older brother Ranulph shoved him off his seat.

"My pardon, m'lady," Sigimor said, ignoring the brief tussle which took place between his brothers before Tamhas was seated again. "The lad is but nineteen and hasnae learned his manners yet."

"Quite all right," Gillyanne said in a voice choked with laughter. "So, ye decided upon a handfasting."

"Aye. Got the lovers to tidy themselves up and took them off to the alehouse to find our cousin Liam. Set the groom in a barrel and had my brother Gilbert there," he nodded toward a very sturdily built young man with flame red hair and blue eyes, "to sit on it whilst we discussed the matter with Liam."

Diarmot slouched in his chair and drank his ale, wondering if it was possible for this tale to be any more humiliating. He forced himself to listen carefully to every word, however. It might help him to catch one of the Camerons in a lie. He stoutly ignored the small inner voice that suggested this had to be the truth, that no one would concoct such a convoluted or farcical tale if they feared being caught in a lie.

"This Liam was able to help?" asked Gillyanne.

"Aye," replied Sigimor. "He spent some time in a monastery. Being a sharp-witted lad, he learned a lot. Had to leave in the end, though, as the rules about celibacy proved a wee bit too difficult for him to follow. Liam wrote up those papers and we got Sir Diarmot to sign them. Then Liam led the handfasting ceremony. After that the bride and groom went to a wee cottage for a fortnight."

"After which Diarmot left only to be attacked. Why was your sister nay with him?"

Sigimor grimaced. "He insisted he had to go alone, that some trouble was dogging his heels and he wanted it tended to before he took Ilsa to his home. We were verra uneasy about it, but, if he was telling the truth, we didnae want Ilsa put in danger. Ilsa believed him. Poor lass tried verra hard to keep believing e'en though she neither saw nor heard from him again. When the year and the day were near done, we insisted she come to him."

"If I have figured the times correctly, he was beaten verra soon after leaving Ilsa, and right in your village."

"Nay, I cannae believe that. The whole village kenned he had married our Ilsa. Nary a one of them would do him ill."

"But, we are fair certain he was beaten in Muirladen."

"Och, that isnae on our lands. We are the Camerons of Dubheidland."

And there was irony, thought Diarmot. A vast clan of redheads living in a place called the dark headland. He wondered if he was actually caught up in one of his nightmares, was actually still asleep in his bed, then decided he had never been that lucky.

"Then who holds Muirladen?" asked Connor.

"Weel, the mon there now is a Sir Randolph Ogilvey, but I believe he holds it for someone else," replied Sigimor. "It changes hands a lot. E'en the people living on the land are nay too sure and they are a weel mixed lot, so one cannae judge by their names. Tis a dower land, always has been, and each new laird holds a different name and brings his own people who add their names to the village rolls. Twould take some searching to find the true holders of it and we have ne'er been interested as we have ne'er had any trouble from them."

"Can ye find out?"

"Och, aye, if ye think it important."

"It may help us discover who had my brother beaten near to death."

"I will send word back to Dubheidland with my brothers and set them to the task."

Diarmot tensed and frowned at Sigimor. "And why nay see to the task yourself?"

"Because Tait and I will be staying here to keep an eye on things," replied Sigimor.

"Do ye think your sister needs your protection?" Diarmot was unable to hide his outrage over the suggestion that he might hurt a woman.

"Weel, there is obviously still some trouble dogging your heels, isnae there? And, since ye have become such an ill-tempered, callous rogue, mayhap we stay to protect ye from Ilsa."

"Did ye kill him?" Gay asked when Ilsa marched back into the nursery.

"Nay. Gilbert told everyone to duck," replied Ilsa as she took a fretting Finlay into her arms, sat in a chair near the fireplace, and began to nurse him. "For a moment, Diarmot sat there, an excellent target, but Sir Connor yanked him out of the way."

Gay sat down opposite her and began to nurse Cearnach. "Tis for the best. I dinnae think the mon needs his head cracked open again."

"Nay, he doesnae," agreed Fraser as she sat on a padded stool near Ilsa's chair. "He truly was near death, m'lady. I have ne'er seen a mon so badly beaten and I didnae see him until some time after the attack. It took him months to heal."

"Weel, I had naught to do with it," said Ilsa.

"I ken it, but I fear my Anabelle taught the laird wariness, mistrust, and bitterness long before that. The beating only made it worse."

"Your Anabelle?"

"Aye. I was her companion. I kenned from the beginning that Sir Diarmot was smitten with her, but I couldnae do anything. No mon will heed ye when ye try to make him see the evil in the woman he woos. He certainly wouldnae listen to some poor kinswoman forced to bow to Anabelle's every wish. She put on a fine show, acting so verra sweet and demure."

"But she wasnae either of those things, was she?"

Fraser shook her head. "Nay. She was a spoiled, manipulative, e'en cruel, woman. She was also a whore," Fraser added with a sigh.

"She was unfaithful?" Ilsa tried to think of what sort of man could prompt a woman to be unfaithful to a man like Diarmot, but found it impossible.

"Weel, I wouldnae call all unfaithful wives whores. Some husbands deserve to be cuckolded. Or, there is no love within the marriage, but tis found elsewhere and thus the sin is committed. But, Anabelle was truly a whore. She rutted with any mon, delighted in seducing foolish men to betray liege, lover, kin, or wife. How she hid that part of her for e'en the few months she did, I dinnae ken. The truth was finally revealed but a month after the wedding when the laird caught her with two men from the village."

"Two?"

"Aye." Fraser smiled faintly. "I have often wondered about that myself, though I try verra hard nay to."

Ilsa felt herself blush when she realized the woman had guessed the path of her thoughts, then smiled. "Aye, tis one of those sinful things ye ken ye ought to ignore, but cannae stop being curious about."

She set Finlay against her shoulder to rub his

back and smiled at Alice as the child sidled up to her chair. She was a pretty child. In truth, all the children were pretty. The nursery was clean, well supplied, and Fraser was a loving attendant. Diarmot could be faulted for his profligacy, but not for accepting the responsibility for the results. The ages of the children told a tale, as well. Three from before his marriage, and, she suspected, two from after he had discovered the truth about Anabelle. None, she was pleased to note again, from the time he was pledged to her. Of course, she mused, he could simply have learned a way to prevent breeding a child.

Finlay belched and the children all giggled. Ilsa smiled at them and knew she would have no trouble caring for them. She had never believed a child should pay for the sins of its parents. It seemed most of the people at Clachthrom believed the same for, at first glance, she could see no sign of unhappiness or fear in the children. She turned to look at Alice when the little girl fleetingly touched her arm.

"Are ye to be our mother?" Alice asked.

"Aye," she replied with no hesitation, touched by the smiles the older children gave her. At only two years of age, she suspected the smiles Ewart and Gregor gave her were more imitation than heartfelt. "I will be your mother now."

"And what is she?" Alice asked, looking at Gay.

"Your aunt."

"She is your sister?"

"Nay by blood, but families can be formed from more than blood ties, lass. They can be bred in the heart." Ilsa was not really surprised when the older children all looked at Fraser. "Aye, she too could be considered kin of the heart." She smiled when the children immediately dubbed Fraser an aunt for the woman's delight was plain to see.

Young Odo moved to stand in front of her, his blue eyes very similar to Diarmot's. "So, our father has four brothers and a sister and a sister by marriage. That gives us four uncles and five aunts now. Do ye have any sisters and brothers?"

"My only sister is Gay, the sister of my heart." She waited patiently for Odo to press for more, never doubting that he would.

"Oh. No brothers?"

"A few."

"How many?"

"Fourteen." She laughed when he gaped at her, then tried to count that number upon his fingers. "And two more brothers for ye," she added, pointing to Finlay and Cearnach.

"We need more lasses," said Alice, frowning at Odo and her brothers who were cheering the fact that lads far outnumbered lasses in the family.

"I fear we are just going to have to accept being outnumbered, Alice," replied Ilsa. "Dinnae worry, lass. I will teach ye and wee Ivy how to make it more a blessing than a curse."

"How can ye do that?" asked Ivy as she moved closer.

"Weel, think on this. If someone is mean to ye, ye have six brothers and eighteen uncles, plus a father ye can call to your side."

Both little girls frowned in thought for a moment, then grinned. Diarmot obviously bred sharp-witted children, Ilsa thought, and Fraser undoubtedly nurtured it. Even more important, the children all appeared willing to accept her as their new mother. She wished their father would be as willing to accept her as his wife.

As the children gathered around her and Gay, asking questions and inspecting their new siblings, Ilsa silently made a vow. For their sake, she would work as hard as she could to make a good marriage with Diarmot. She would not allow whatever troubles there were between her and her angry, mistrustful husband to touch their young lives. These children needed her and she would try to find comfort and strength in that as she struggled to reclaim the man she had fallen in love with.

CHAPTER FOUR

"What are ye doing here?"

Diarmot closed the bedchamber door behind him, leaned against it, and crossed his arms over his chest. The woman who claimed to be his wife stood near the fire dressed in only a thin shift, her bright hair hanging in thick waves past her slender hips. It was an intensely arousing sight, despite the scowl she wore.

She looked nothing like his late wife, or any other woman he had ever lusted after. She was almost too slender, her curves subtle ones. Her breasts were plump and round, but he suspected some of that fullness would disappear once the twins were fully weaned. The shadow of her form was visible through the fine linen of her shift, revealing a small waist, slim hips and slender legs. Her body showed little sign of having borne twins only a few months ago, yet even his cynical mind could not doubt that she was their mother.

Her eyes were beautiful, the rich green visible even in the soft light from a scattering of candles and the low fire in the fireplace. They were somewhat wide eyes, set beneath delicately arced brown brows, and rimmed with impressively long, thick lashes. Her nose was small and straight, her bones delicate, and her mouth slightly wide with temptingly full lips. There was the hint of the strong jawline her brothers had, but it suited her faintly round face. For a redhead, she had few freckles marring her soft, pale skin. Her long, slender neck was perfection.

Even though she was completely different from any other woman he had ever felt drawn to, Diarmot could see why he might have bedded her. Once he studied her children more closely, he might be willing to accept that he and Ilsa had once been lovers. Accepting her as his wife would take a great deal more. He had decided, however, that if she was going to play this game, he would gain what benefit he could from it.

"I have come to join my wife in the marital bed," he replied.

Ilsa needed but one hard look at him to know he had not had a sudden revelation and now believed in her. "Ye dinnae think I am your wife."

"Nay? Mayhap I doubt your tale of what occured between us a year ago, but I dinnae doubt that ye are now my wife." He started to move toward her. "We did kneel before a priest mere hours ago and say our vows."

"And ye expect me to play the dutiful wife to a mon who thinks me a liar?"

"Since when does what a mon think or feel about his wife keep her from giving him his husbandly rights?" Diarmot gave in to the strong urge to stroke her hair, finding it soft to the touch.

That was a sad fact Ilsa could not argue with. Another sad fact she had to face was how his nearness, his touch upon her hair, was heating her blood. Although she could hide a great deal of what she felt, it was obvious she could not easily control her desire for him. Having him so close, smelling the clean, crisp scent of him, and knowing he was undoubtedly naked beneath the heavy robe he wore was rapidly stirring her desire for him to a near-feverish level.

"Ye dinnae believe I am your wife despite Father Goudie's blessing," she said. "Ye think I am trying to trick ye in some way, although I cannae understand why ye would."

"Nay? We were supposedly lovers, then handfasted, a year ago. A year ago I put my name to papers that give ye and your children claim to all that is mine. A year ago someone tried to kill me. Such great coincidence has to raise a doubt or two even in the most feeble of minds."

"I see. So, ye dinnae just think me a liar, ye think me a threat to your verra life. I am surprised ye wish to be alone with me," she snapped as she took several steps away from him and turned to glare at him. "Are ye sure ye dare to slip beneath the sheets with such a dangerous lass?"

"Nay so dangerous when ye are unarmed and naked."

"Unarmed, naked, and nay the wife ye intended to bed this night, either."

Diarmot shrugged as he walked toward her, undeterred by how she retreated before his advance, for she was backing up toward the bed. "I wanted a woman in my bed and a mother for my bairns. Aye, I also sought a sweet, biddable lass."

"Of course. Instead, ye got one ye dinnae trust as far as ye can spit."

"Probably nay e'en that far. Howbeit, until the truth is revealed, ye will do for what I seek."

"Ye have a true skill at wooing a lass, dinnae ye."

"I dinnae need to woo ye. Ye took vows afore a priest. Those vows say ye will share my bed when I wish it. Shall we leave the marriage unconsummated then?"

She frowned. "It has been consummated. A year ago."

"Nay in the church's eyes."

Ilsa felt the bed against the back of her legs and tensed. She had thought she would be given time to consider the best way to deal with Diarmot, with this marriage he so clearly resented. During the tense evening meal in the great hall, he had not revealed any inclination to be her husband in even the smallest way. Now he was demanding his husbandly rights. He might not have had a change of heart, but he had obviously had a change of mind.

If he truly had lost his memory, he had a right to be suspicious and act as if he were the one wronged, but that fact did not make his attitude any less irritating. Nor did it soften the pain she felt. Since he did not believe her, he was insensitive to her own turmoil and sense of injury. She had been deserted, had had to hunt him down, and had found him about to pledge his troth to another woman. Unfortunately, since he was in no mood to even consider the possibility that she told the truth, he had no understanding of how hurtful he was being now.

It was unfair, but Ilsa realized she was going to have to prove her trustworthiness. Since Diarmot claimed to have no memory of their time together, she was now a stranger to him. Instinct told her he would do his best to keep a wary distance between them. If she did the same, their marriage would quickly be doomed. Here, in the marital bed, there might be some chance of reaching him, of softening his bitter mistrust. Yet, to lie with a man who thought her a liar and a threat seemed wrong, would surely leave her feeling used, even shamed and humiliated.

Suddenly, she realized one reason she hesitated was because she was afraid. What if his passion for her had died along with his memory? What if he had truly loved the woman he had been about to marry? She had seen little sign of any true affection between them, but conceded that she could easily have blinded herself to such a thing. It was difficult enough to accept that he no longer cared for her, whatever the reason was for that change.

What to do? she thought, struggling to keep her mind clear as he began to toy with her hair again, his fingers brushing against her neck, shoulders, and face. Beneath all the pain and sense of insult she suffered, she still loved him. Her passion for him seemed undimmed by his rejection. Her desires and needs were oblivious to his lack of trust, his suspicions, and the fact that he intended to use her to satisfy his manly needs without love, without even much hint of liking. He was not using sweet words to get her into bed, but the dictates of the church and his rights as her husband.

"Ye simply mean to use me as ye would use some whore," she protested, placing her hands upon his chest in a vain attempt to push him back at least a step or two.

"As my lawful wife. There is a difference."

"Nay in your mind."

She suddenly realized that he had partly unlaced the front of her shift. She clutched the opening tightly shut with one hand and glared at him. It was time to decide aye or nay, to join him in bed or find some other place to sleep.

There was no denying that the vows she had just exchanged with him meant he had rights to her body. She desired him and suspected he desired her. There was a look in his fine eyes that she recognized from when he had been wooing her. So why not indulge herself, why not feed the hunger that had knotted her insides for far too long?

Hastily, she reviewed the reasons why sharing his bed would be a good idea. It would legalize the marriage in the eyes of the church. Here, in this bedchamber, there could be a chance for a truce, a chance for her to prove herself to him and ease his suspicions. If they still shared the fierce passion they had enjoyed a year ago, it could help her to inch her way back into his heart and mind. This marriage was important to the future of her sons and to the six children sleeping so soundly in the nursery. She had come here demanding that Diarmot marry her as he had promised to do. He had, and it was time for her to accept her responsibilites as his wife. She just hoped he did not use her desire and willingness to prove herself against her.

"Fine, Sir Diarmot," she snapped as she climbed onto the bed and flopped down onto her back. "I will do my duty. Have at it, then."

Diarmot was both surprised and a little annoyed when he had to bite back a smile. He did not want to be amused. That hinted at a softness within him, one she might be able to turn against him. He had placed her in his bedchamber intending to see just how far she would take this game. Since she was so obviously going to allow him into her bed, he would not turn away from what was offered, no matter how reluctantly. He would feed a need left untended for too long, no more. Diarmot shed his robe and climbed onto the bed.

Ilsa nearly groaned when he cast off his robe revealing that he was, indeed, naked beneath it. It was going to be difficult, if not impossible, to give him only duty if he was going to flaunt himself like that. Praying that she looked as calm as she was trying to be, she allowed herself to look him over. He was all lean, hard muscle. A broad chest, narrow hips, and long well-shaped legs. There was a feathering of gold hair on his chest. A narrow line of tiny curls that began just beneath his navel, thickened around his groin, and then lightly dusted those handsome legs. His feet were long and narrow. There were a few new scars upon his body, giving the touch of truth to his tale of a vicious beating. His manhood rose stout and proud from its nest of curls, indicating that he did desire her, and looking a lot bigger than she recalled it being.

Tearing her gaze from his groin, Ilsa quickly

scolded herself for that sudden flicker of unease. She was no virgin. Except for the first time they had made love, she recalled no pain, only pleasure. Since she doubted a man could become more impressively endowed in just a year, she had obviously accommodated him well in the past and could do so again.

She tensed when he crouched over her and began to remove her shift. A protest formed upon her tongue, but she bit it back. This, too, was his right. If he was planning to do more than rut on her, however, it would certainly be impossible to pretend she was giving him only reluctant duty. She blushed when he tossed her shift aside and stared at her bared body. He looked at her as if he had never seen her before. Obviously the sight of her stirred no memory, but, if she judged his expression correctly, it did stir his lust. She could make that be enough for now.

Diarmot told himself to cease dawdling and get about the business of easing his needs. He then told himself that enjoying the sight of such loveliness revealed no more than any man's natural interest in the female form. Ilsa's breasts were round and full, the nipples a dusky rose. Her waist was tiny, her stomach taut with only a few faint scars from when pregnant with her sons, and her legs were long and strong. Her skin was smooth, soft, and without blemish. Between her pale, slender thighs was a neat little triangle of copper curls that had him aching, his mind rapidly filling with thoughts of all the ways he wished to enjoy that treasure.

And why not enjoy himself?, he thought. Even the slowest of wits knew passion had nothing to do with any of the deeper emotions a man might feel for his wife. This beauty was his by the laws of the land and the church, so why not savor it? And, if he roused a little passion in Ilsa as he satisfied his own needs, so be it. She owed him some recompense for so thoroughly disrupting his plans.

He watched her eyes widen as he lowered his head to touch his mouth to hers. The soft fullness of her mouth was too great a temptation to ignore. For a brief moment, she held herself tautly, silently rejecting his kiss, but only for a moment. She then slowly curled her strong, slender arms around his neck as she responded to the gentle prod of his tongue and parted her lips. Diarmot suspected his body echoed the faint tremors that went through her as he stroked the inside of her mouth with his tongue, but he did not care. She was sweet to the taste, her body soft and welcoming as he settled himself on top of her. Passion had been missing from his life for too long and he was greedy for a taste of it.

Ilsa recognized her swift surrender, regretted that weakness, then ceased to worry about it. There was evidently no chance she could feign being no more than a dutiful wife in his bed. So be it, she decided. If this was all he had to give her, she would take it. If nothing else, lovemaking would allow her to express all the love she now had to keep hidden. And, since men rarely believed strong passion came from the heart, Diarmot would never guess how very vulnerable she was.

She tilted her head back as he moved his kisses to her throat. A soft groan of pleasure escaped her when he slid one hand up her ribcage to caress her breast, teasing her nipples to an almost painful hardness with his fingers. When his kisses finally reached her breasts, she was almost as much relieved as she was enflamed. She threaded her fingers into his thick hair as he feasted upon her breasts, laving, suckling, and even giving her the occasional gentle nip. By the time he slid his hand between her legs she was desperate for his touch. It only took a few strokes of his long fingers to make her desperate for all of him.

"Jesu, ye already weep for me," he muttered as he prepared himself to possess her.

When he thrust into her, she cried out, and he paused, afraid he had been too rough. Diarmot started to retreat only to have her wrap her strong legs around him and push him back deep inside. As he began to move, the feel of her tight heat surrounding him, the way she so perfectly matched his every thrust, and the feel of her strong lithe body wrapped around him, quickly robbed him of all control.

She cried out his name as she bowed slightly off the bed with the strength of her release. Diarmot wrapped his arm around her slim hips and held her close as he buried himself as deeply within her as possible and joined her in that blind fall. When he slumped against her, he was not sure who was trembling more, him or her.

The moment he felt he had gained enough strength to do so, Diarmot flopped onto his back at her side. He felt almost boneless. A glance at Ilsa revealed her sprawled on her back obviously suffering from the same affliction. That offered him some comfort.

There had been a sense of familiarity to it all, he realized. He not only had not been surprised by that moment of passionate oblivion, he had anticipated it from the moment he had kissed her. The feel of her, even the taste of her, had felt right. Diarmot realized he had not even been surprised by her passion, had been anticipating that as well.

That implied that buried in his memory was knowledge of this woman. It would explain his immediate desire for her despite the lack of the lush feminine curves he had always preferred before. She enflamed him, which was both intoxicating and dangerous. Diarmot knew he would not be able to turn away from the pleasure he could find in her arms, however. He would just have to make certain he did not allow it to blind him to the threat she might pose or any tricks she might play. After the hard lessons he had learned from his marriage to Anabelle, Diarmot felt confident that he could keep this madness a thing apart.

"Weel, I now believe we may have once been lovers," he said, watching her closely.

"Ah, how generous of ye," drawled Ilsa as she turned her head to look at him. "So, in addition to believing me a liar, and a possible murderess, ye also think me a whore."

"Just because ye have spread your legs for your husband, doesnae allow—mmmphf." He stared at her in shock when she clapped her delicate hand over his mouth, then he scowled at her.

Ilsa slowly lifted her hand from his mouth. "Were your monly needs adequately satisfied?"

Adequately satisfied was a paltry description of what he had felt, but he would not argue with her. "Aye."

"And, so, ye may consider demanding your husbandly rights again from time to time?"

Several times a night and probably in the morning as well, he mused, but simply replied, "Aye, I may."

"Then might I suggest ye temper your words when ye are in here with me? Despite my anger earlier—"

"When ye tried to kill me with the jug?"

She ignored that and continued, "I am able to control my temper more often than not. I ken what ye think and ye ken what I think, and I suspect we will feel inclined to voice our opinions again in the coming days. Howbeit, here wouldnae be a good place to do so. My anger might grow hot, but I suspect the rest of me would quickly grow cold."

That sounded very much like a threat, but it also made sense. If nothing else, he would put her on the defensive and that wariness would certainly dim her passion. Agreeing to a truce here meant he could not use her desire against her. There would be no trying to trick her into revealing some truth while muddled with passion. It was a loss, but not a big one. Considering what flared between them, Diarmot suspected he would have found such subtlety and deviousness very difficult.

"Ye seek a truce here, do ye?" he asked.

"Aye," she replied as she tugged the sheet up to cover herself. She tossed a corner of it over him as well, and ignored the wry look he cast her. "A truce. The battle stops at that door. I doubt we can follow that rule precisely, but, if tis set, we will at least try."

"A truce then." He was faintly amused when she

stuck out her hand, but he shook it. "Does that mean ye willnae try any tricks here? Willnae be a threat?"

Ilsa rolled her eyes and bent over the side of the bed to retrieve her shift. "That was a short truce. Nay, I willnae try any tricks or assault your poor wee body with my superior strength and skill at arms."

She certainly had a true skill with sarcasm, he mused. Worse, it carried the sting of truth as well. He watched in surprise and growing amusement when she disappeared beneath the sheet. The wriggling and soft curses that ensued told him she was attempting to don her shift under there. When she reappeared above the sheet she looked tousled and flushed.

"Such modesty is unnecessary," he said. "After all, but moments ago—"

"Weel, I dinnae feel as I did but moments ago," Ilsa quickly interrupted him. "Nay, I willnae be a threat here," she said, "not that I e'er was. And, since ye dinnae trust me as far as ye can spit, I dinnae understand why ye e'en ask for my word on that. Ye willnae believe it."

"Give it anyway and then our truce can begin."

"Do I have your word to try no tricks or attempt to harm me then?"

"Of course."

"Weel enough, then ye have mine." She shook hands with him again then got out of bed.

"Where are ye going?"

"Behind that screen set in the corner which should have told me that I had been put into your bedchamber. Ye would have no need of a privacy screen in your own room, nor I in mine." She slipped behind the screen and began to wash. "I hadnae looked about much, either, so hadnae noticed any signs that this was your bedchamber." She peeked around the screen and frowned at him. "Tis a verra plain bedchamber. Thought it was one kept ready for guests." She returned to the chore of washing. "Ye have made no mark upon the room."

Diarmot looked around his bedchamber and realized she was right. There was nothing to mark it as his unless one opened his clothes chests. Although he was not sure what he could do to change that, it was strange that he had not yet done so. Considering the many long months he had spent in the room recovering from the beating, there should have been some clear sign of his presence. Diarmot was not sure he wanted to think about the reason for that too deeply.

When Ilsa started back to the bed, Diarmot got up and strode past her to disappear behind the screen. She caught her breath so quickly at the sight of his naked form, she coughed. Inwardly cursing her weakness for the man, she climbed back into bed. If the mere sight of him affected her so, it was going to be impossible to resist him in even the smallest of ways.

Turning on her side and snuggling comfortably into the feather mattress and plump pillows, she decided to give up on all thoughts of resistance. Ilsa suspected such a tactic would only add to Diarmot's suspicions even if she could accomplish it. There was no way it would protect her from the hurts he would undoubtedly inflict in the days to come, so it was a battle lost before it had even begun.

Trying to be always sweet and biddable was also hopeless and, she suspected, would also rouse his suspicions. So she would just be herself. Honesty in word and deed would be her weapon. Although she would not speak of her love for him, she would give it. She had already given him her passion and would continue to do so. All her instincts told her it was the best plan and, after so much indecision and wrestling with plan after plan, it was a comfort of sorts to finally settle upon one. Ilsa just hoped she had the strength to hold to it until Diarmot lost his anger, mistrust, and bitterness. She also prayed that, when he did, she would find what they had shared a year ago, that she would not discover that it had all been a lie.

She tensed when she felt Diarmot climb back into bed. He moved to press against her back and, before she could act to stop him, tugged off her shift and tossed it aside again. When he pressed against her again, she could feel his arousal, and shivered as her own desire was rapidly stirred to life.

"I was planning to go to sleep," she said, not surprised to hear the huskiness of her voice, for he was caressing her breasts and nibbling her ear, sending heat through her veins.

"Weel, go right ahead," he murmured and traced the delicate curve of her ear with his tongue. "I will just carry on."

She laughed softly. "Ye cannae do that whilst I sleep." She gasped as he slid his hand between her legs and her body swiftly responded to that intimate caress. "I think I might be able to stay awake for a wee bit longer."

Hope stirred in her heart when he chuckled.

She was not foolish enough to think such compatibility would last long, but it had to start somewhere. It was a tiny crack in the wall between them and cracks could be widened enough to bring down a wall. She would have to think of ways to weaken that wall, widen that tiny opening until she could slip through. When he cocked her leg back over his and eased into her, she decided she would plot out her battle plan later.

CHAPTER FIVE

"Are all our new uncles as big as ye are?"

Ilsa smiled when Sigimor lifted up the curious Odo until they were eye to eye and said, "They are all wee, runty lads compared to me. I am the biggest, the strongest, and the wisest."

Odo giggled which prompted the other children to deem her brothers safe and venture closer. Ilsa had left the sleeping twins with Fraser so that she and Gay could take the older children outside. It had only taken one look as she reached the bailey to know that her brothers were preparing to leave. She swallowed a brief cowardly urge to ask them all to stay or take her home with them. Diarmot had been her choice. She could not hide behind her brothers simply because everything between her and her husband was not right.

Diarmot had made love to her this morning, then left. He had barely spoken to her except for the time he was uttering hot words of pleasure and delight against her skin. Ilsa supposed his silence was his way of honoring their truce, but it had quickly chilled her, stealing away all the warmth left by his lovemaking. She still believed her decision to welcome him into her bed was a good one, as was her plan to simply be herself. However, if Diarmot's plan was to make her senseless with passion every night and ignore her existence all day, building a good marriage was going to be very slow work indeed. So slow that she could easily be past caring when, and if, he ever regained some affection for her.

Ilsa started to walk around the bailey, intending to explore her new home. She had to smile when Sigimor fell into step beside her, walking along at a steady pace even though he was covered with children. Ewart in one arm, Gregor in the other, Aulay on his shoulders, Odo and Ivy each wrapped around a strong leg, and Alice clinging to his jerkin. Her brother loved children and she had to wonder, yet again, why he was so hesitant to wed. One day she would have to ask him, she mused.

"And how are ye this morning, lass?" Sigimor asked, studying her carefully.

Despite her best efforts not to, Ilsa blushed. "I am just fine. Ye dinnae see any bruises, do ye?"

"Nay, not on the outside."

"Ah, weel, the other sort are mine alone to deal with."

"Do ye believe his tale?"

"More and more. There are new scars upon his body. Lady Gillyanne and Fraser both support his tale. My doubt is bred from his claim that he doesnae remember me yet our time together came before the attack upon him. Then again, our time together was short and there is no glint of recognition in his eyes." Ilsa shrugged. "It will take me some time, I think, to decide what I believe. It didnae help Diarmot's cause when I discovered he ne'er told me he was married once, nor that he had six children. It was a lie in many ways, so one has to wonder if this is but another lie."

"Aye, I think the same." As they entered a sadly neglected garden, Sigimor divested himself of the children. "Tait and I will be staying. If naught else, a danger still lurks in the shadows. A threat to Diarmot could be a threat to ye, too."

"Do ye think ye can discover what it is?" Ilsa asked as she and Sigimor sat together on a stone bench while Gay meandered through the garden with the children. "I am sure Diarmot and his family have been trying."

"They have, but they also have lands to tend and people to care for. That means they cannae spend all their time trying to uncover this enemy. For months after the beating, their greatest concern was helping Diarmot recover. Tait and I can take up the hunt and hold fast. I may be the laird of Dubheidland, but I have a small army of kinsmen who can tend to the land and its people whilst I tend to this. Diarmot's brother Nanty intends to do the same."

"Do ye think ye can uncover his enemy?"

"It willnae be easy, but, aye, we will find the bastard." Sigimor gently brushed a stray lock of hair from her face and tucked it behind her ear. "Do ye still love the fool?"

"Aye." Ilsa grimaced. "I would rather I didnae, but it isnae an easy feeling to cast aside."

"I havenae seen much of the fool this morn, but it didnae appear as if your wedding night changed much."

"He conceded that we must have been lovers. Tis a start." She blushed faintly. "The passion is still there between us. That, too, is a start. We have also agreed to a truce within the bedchamber."

"How gracious of the mon," Sigimor grumbled.

"If he truly has lost all memory of me, then, aye, it is. And, as Diarmot said, whether he believes my tale or nay, I am his wife now and should accept that responsibility. That is exactly what I have decided to do."

"I am nay sure I understand."

"Weel, after thinking of and tossing aside several plans, I have decided to simply be his wife, to simply be what I am. I intend to try to shield my poor battered heart in whatever way I can, but, in all else, I will deal honestly with the mon. No plots, no games, no tricks. I think that is the only way to deal with a mon as suspicious and wary as Diarmot MacEnroy."

Sigimor rubbed his chin as he considered her words for a moment, then said, "Tisnae fair that ye must prove yourself."

"Nay, it isnae, but that is what I must do. Again, if he truly has no memory of me, then he doesnae ken anything about me. Since he is in danger, tis only right and wise that he suspects me, and is wary."

"Mayhap, and, aye, the best way to change his mind is to be honest in all ye do and say. He has to learn to trust in ye again. Of course, if he but plays some game with us—"

"Then ye can beat him into mash and toss him on the midden heap."

"Fair enough."

* * *

"What are ye looking at?" asked Nanty as he entered Diarmot's ledger room and moved to stand next to him by the window he stared out of.

"Sigimor Cameron covered in children," Diarmot replied, never taking his gaze from the group entering his garden.

Nanty grinned as he watched the children climb off Sigimor and skip through the garden. "Your bairns trust the mon."

"And so I should?"

"Ye should at least note that they have no fear of the mon despite his great size. One should always take notice of how a child reacts to someone. They can oftimes sense things we cannae."

That was true, but Diarmot felt no inclination to admit it. When he had first seen how his children had accepted Sigimor, he had felt a pang of jealousy for he was not close to his children. Since he had to accept the fact that that was his own fault, he then felt guilty. Uncomfortable with both emotions, he was not feeling very kindly toward Sigimor Cameron, the man who had inspired that brief, damning moment of reflection.

"The Camerons appear to be a closely bonded family," Nanty murmured.

Diarmot glanced at his brother, irritated by the false look of innocence upon Nanty's face. "Ye trust them, dinnae ye. Ye believe their tale."

"Nay need to make it sound as if I betray ye in doing so."

"Why not? They could be the ones behind all my troubles, the ones who tried to kill me."

"If her brothers had wanted ye dead, ye would-nae be here now to wonder on it. They wouldnae have left ye near death; they would have made sure ye had breathed your last ere they walked away. And, we talked to every mon, woman, and child in Muirladen, yet gained verra little useful information. I doubt that would have been the way of it if a small army of giant redheads had been in the area at the time ye were attacked."

There was another truth he could not argue with, one he dearly wished Nanty had not set in his mind. Men like Sigimor and the other Camerons were ones people noticed. It would have required only one person catching sight of them for the tale to have spread throughout the village. Since Muirladen was close to Campbell lands, the villagers would undoubtedly have recognized them, but no one had mentioned the Camerons. It was certainly something to consider as he weighed judgment on his wife and her kinsmen.

"Since the Camerons must ken how recognizable they are, they might have hired others to do the deed," Diarmot offered in argument and scowled when Nanty rolled his eyes.

"Why are ye so intent upon marking them guilty?"

"Because I dinnae have anyone else to blame." Diarmot sighed and shook his head. "Aye, I may be too hard on them, but better that than to be too trusting right now. Someone wants me dead. That beating was but one incident. There have been a few others, all of which could also have been nay more than ill luck. If the incidents before the beating were only accidents, that means the Camerons could be the ones trying to kill me. If those incidents were actually attempts to kill me, then it cannae be the Camerons. Clouded though my memory is, I am fair certain I didnae ken a single member of that family until a year ago."

"If ye ken ye didnae meet them until a year ago, then ye must be getting your memory back."

"Nay. I dinnae recall the meeting or anything else about that time. I do have a mostly clear memory of the time several months before that and they werenae kenned by me at that time."

"So, do ye feel certain Lady Ilsa isnae your wife."

"I feel certain she and I were once lovers. I was certain of that the moment I kissed her. I kenned the taste of her, the feel of her," he added softly.

"Then ye must ken that she speaks the truth when she claims ye were handfasted."

"Nay, I just ken that we were once lovers. I dinnae recall any of the times we spent together, if any promises were made, or e'en if she was a virgin."

Diarmot watched Sigimor, Ilsa, and Gay wander through the garden, the children skipping all around them. From the way they studied the garden, were obviously deep in a discussion, and occasionally stopped to study a plant or two, Diarmot suspected they were intending to resurrect the sadly ignored garden. He was not sure why or when it had fallen into disrepair. When he had inherited Clachthrom, he had brought the garden his uncle had neglected back to life. In the first days of his marriage to Anabelle, he had thought she had enjoyed its beauty, only to discover she used it to cuckold him repeatedly with any man willing to betray his laird. Diarmot suspected that was when he had ceased to care about the garden.

In fact, Diarmot had the uncomfortable feeling that was when he had ceased to care about a lot of things. What little had been done to soften the starkness of Clachthrom's keep had mostly been done before his marriage and some in anticipation of it. He now did what was necessary to keep himself out of debt and his people safe and fed, but little else. It surprised him somewhat to realize he had done next to nothing to prepare his keep for Margaret, the woman he had intended to marry. He did not like to think his wretched marriage had caused him to lose all joy and interest in life.

"She was a virgin," Nanty said after a few minutes of consideration.

It took Diarmot a moment to realize Nanty was referring to Ilsa. "Ye were there to examine the linen, were ye?"

Nanty gave him a look of disgust. "Ilsa has fourteen brothers and two score and seven cousins, mostly male. She was undoubtedly verra weel guarded. I am surprised ye managed to seduce her." He looked out the window to see Sigimor tickle a laughing Ilsa, then chase her around the garden obviously threatening to tickle her some more, much to the delight of the children. "She is the cherished only sister. Tis plain to see."

Even though he had to agree, Diarmot said, "If she is so cherished and protected, why has that girl Gay been allowed near her?"

"To help feed your greedy sons. And, I think ye ken what happened to that poor lass as weel as I do. One doesnae need to hear her tell the tale. Ye can see the truth in the way she shies away from any mon. Aye, and trembles so pitifully when she is in a room crowded with men. She nearly burrows into Ilsa. I think the lass was blessed when the Camerons took her in and, if she wasnae so terrified of men that she can barely speak to one, she would probably tell ye the same."

"Ye make them sound like cursed saints, as if I

blaspheme by e'en considering them liars or, worse, my enemies."

"Ill tempered for a mon who spent last night in the arms of a fair lass, arenae ye?"

"The woman appears at my wedding, claims things I cannae remember and none of ye ken aught about, waves some papers I dinnae recall signing under the priest's nose, and, next I ken, I am married to her. Aye, I feel certain she and I once made love. That isnae any reason to trust in her or her kinsmen. Neither is a kindness to children or a poor abused lass." He walked away from the window, tired of watching Ilsa and her brother act in a way more befitting Nanty's opinion of them than his own.

"Ye cling to your doubts and suspicions then," said Nanty as he turned to face Diarmot. "I may nay agree with them, but I can understand why ye have them. Ye go ahead and try to prove the Camerons your enemies. I will work to prove ye are wrong."

"Why?"

"Because I believe their tale. I trust in Gilly-anne's feelings about them. When ye made your suspicions about them so clear, I saw only right-eous anger in the men and hurt in the lass. And, when ye presented her with your brood, only one of whom is legitimate, I didnae see calm, sweet ac-ceptance. Nay, I saw the anger any woman with wit and a spine would feel. The lass didnae seem to then forget ye had all those bairns, either, but has taken on the care of them. She didnae refuse ye her bed, either, despite how poorly ye behaved and I would wager she warmed it most satisfacto-rily. What I think," Nanty said as he walked toward the door, "is that one year ago ye finally pulled yourself free of the misery Anabelle had drowned ye in and found yourself a fine little wife. My intention is to see that ye keep her."

"Weel, ye best work fast then as ye will only be here for a few more days."

"Oh, didnae I say?" Nanty paused in the open doorway to smile sweetly at Diarmot. "I have decided to bless ye with my fine company for a wee while."

Diarmot stared at the door that Nanty shut behind him as he left. He told himself it would be childish to throw something at that door. A heartbeat later, he picked up a heavy tankard from his writing table and hurled it at the door. That was not satisfying enough so he pulled his dagger and threw that at the door as well. He then moved to slouch in the chair facing his worktable and glared at the knife stuck in the thick door.

It was foolish to feel somewhat betrayed by his family who obviously believed Ilsa. That was their right. They also understood why he did not, could not. Unfortunately, that understanding felt a little too much like pity or sympathy for an injured man. That was difficult to tolerate.

He sighed, closed his eyes, and rested his head against the high back of the chair. It was difficult to admit it, but his family was right. A man with such large holes in his memory was injured. His abysmal marriage had left him wounded in many ways as well. He did not want to trust Ilsa because he was afraid to, an admission that made him wince. Anabelle had shown him that he could not trust in his own judgments about people, especially women he lusted after. This time a bad judgment could do more than tear at his heart; it could kill him.

There were a few faint similarities between Ilsa and Anabelle. Ilsa was emotional, as had been Anabelle, yet he had only seen temper, passion, and humor. He thought he had seen pain as well, but dared not make any assumptions upon the truth of that or the cause. When he tried to think of other similarities between his late wife and his new one, he found none, but stoutly told himself they would appear as time passed.

Despite their short acquaintance, the differences between Anabelle and Ilsa were far more distinct. He only had to look out into the garden to see one clearly and that was Ilsa's open acceptance of his children. Anabelle had not even paid attention to Alice, her own child. Ilsa's temper had been hot, but not the screaming rage Anabelle had often displayed. Even Diarmot had to admit that Ilsa had had a good reason to be angry. Anabelle had never needed a reason. Ilsa was a passionate woman, but that passion lacked the darker emotions that had tainted Anabelle's passion. Even his wary heart and mind could not foresee that happening with Ilsa, either.

Grimacing, he shifted in his chair as the mere thought of Ilsa's passion caused his body to harden with need. Ilsa's passion was hot and sweet, satisfying him in ways he could not recall ever having felt before, not even when he had thought himself in love with Anabelle. Diarmot knew that could prove a weakness, but he felt he had learned his lessons well from his late wife. He might not be able to control his desire for Ilsa, but he knew how to keep it from controlling him or blinding him to the truth.

If he was honest with himself, Diarmot had to admit he was very glad it was Ilsa in his bed instead of Margaret. He could easily understand how he and Ilsa could have become lovers. The fire they could start between them was all any man could wish for. Despite all his doubts, fears, and suspicions, he intended to take full advantage of having Ilsa in his bed, and warm himself by that fire whenever possible. It was the one good thing in the whole tangled mess he now found himself in. He would just be very careful he did not get burned.

Holding her son Cearnach while Gay held Finlay, Ilsa smiled sadly as her brothers kissed their nephews and her farewell. Sigimor and Tait were staying with her, but she knew this was just the first step in the separation of her life from her family's. Due to the unusual circumstances surrounding her handfasting with Diarmot, this painful change in her life had been delayed. Although trembling faintly, Gay stood firmly at her side enduring the farewells handed out to Finlay, and Ilsa realized Gay saw the Camerons as her family now. Ilsa took a step toward Sigimor only to pause when Elyas stepped up to Gay and held something out to her.

"Here, lass," said Elyas. "Tis a gift."

Cautiously, Gay took the sheathed knife Elyas held out and then frowned. "Tis a dagger, sir."

"Aye. Ilsa will show ye how to wear it and use it."

"Why would ye give me a dagger, sir?"

"So ye will learn how to protect yourself, e'en if only in a wee way. Ye need to feel safer, lass, to feel that ye arenae quite so helpless." He smiled faintly. "Ye can also use it to protect our Ilsa."

Gay blushed. "Thank ye most kindly, sir."

"Oh, that is so sweet," Ilsa murmured as Elyas walked away from Gay, then frowned in feigned agony when Sigimor draped his arm across her shoulders.

"Aye," agreed Sigimor, ignoring her expression. "Elyas has been troubled by how fearful the lass is."

"She is getting better."

"She is." He watched the MacEnroys say their fare-wells to his brothers. "Despite your ill-tempered husband's suspicious nature, I think we have made a fine alliance there."

"I am so verra pleased I could benefit ye and the clan." She winced in earnest when he tugged her braid in punishment for her sarcasm, then she waved at her brothers as they rode out of Clachthrom. "Twill seem so strange nay having them stomping about all the time."

"Weel, ye will still have me and Tait to stomp about ye for a wee while longer."

"How nice," drawled Diarmot as he stepped up to face Sigimor. "Odd, I dinnae recall inviting ye to stomp about Clachthrom for a wee while."

"I ken it, but Tait and I were kindly o'erlooking that lack of good manners," replied Sigimor.

"How verra charitable of ye."

"Aye, that it is."

Both men were so tense, Ilsa was surprised she was not hearing any bone or sinew snap. Diarmot was obviously angered by the implication that she needed to be protected from him or felt her two brothers were lingering at Clachthrom to make sure the devious plot he suspected them of having was successful. Sigimor was insulted by the man's suspicions. By the look upon Tait's face as he moved to stand next to Sigimor, he felt the same.

Ilsa breathed an inner sigh of relief when the rest of the MacEnroys joined them. Her relief was short-lived for Diarmot frowned somewhat accusingly at his family and strode back into the keep.

"I suspicion ye would be a wee bit irritated if I snapped his thick neck," murmured Sigimor and he glanced at the MacEnroys.

"Aye," replied Connor. "The stubborn, pouting oaf is my brother after all."

"It is going to be hard to get him to see the truth."

"Verra hard indeed. When a mon wakes up from such a deadly beating and with some verra dark spots in his memory, he feels more compelled to be wary than many another might be."

"Fair enough. And, he doesnae ken who his enemies are. Kenning there is a dirk aimed at his heart, but nay kenning the why or the who, can surely gnaw at a mon."

Connor nodded. "If that wasnae enough, he has suffered the sting of too many betrayals in the last few years."

"Weel, I can be patient." Sigimor scowled at his sibling when he snorted in derision and rolled his eyes. "I can. I havenae killed any of ye, have I?"

"Oh? It certainly has been a near thing now and again. What about that time ye tossed our cousin Maddox out the window?" asked Tait. "What was that?"

"That was exactly what he deserved and it only bruised the fool," Sigimor replied. "The lad had gathered some verra bad habits whilst flitting about the king's court with his highborn, wealthy friends. He needed some sense knocked into him."

"Ah, of course. And ye were knocking sense into

Gilbert, were ye, when ye tossed him into the river and kept pushing his head under the water?"

"I was cleaning out his earholes because the fool wasnae heeding what I had to say. That wasnae anger, it was discipline."

Knowing this game could continue for a while, Ilsa decided to return to the keep for her sons would soon be demanding a meal. Gay fell into step on her right and Lady Gillyanne quickly joined her on her left. A brief glance back at the men revealed that the three MacEnroy brothers were too entertained to leave.

"Your family reminds me verra much of my own," said Gillyanne as they entered the keep and started toward the nursery. "The Murrays are a large, boisterous lot and we, too, seem to breed more lads than lasses."

Ilsa shook her head even as she smiled. "My father had four wives and I was the only lass born. When his last wife died bearing Fergus, who is but eleven, he said he had buried enough wives and wouldnae marry again. He died less than a year later of a virulent fever that swept through Dubheidland. It took many of the elders. So, at barely eleven, I found myself being raised by my brothers and cousins, mostly male as weel." She laughed softly as, the moment she entered the nursery, Diarmot's children rushed to greet her. "Finding myself with six sons and but two daughters seems verra natural."

"And, mayhap dealing with a stubborn fool of a mon willnae seem so strange, either."

"Och, nay, not strange at all. Nay easy, but nay strange."

"Ye will prevail."

"Is that an opinion born of some foreseeing or prophetic dream?"

"Nay, just a belief in the power of love, and ye do love him, dinnae ye?"

Ilsa sighed. "I do. I but pray it can survive the tests I am sure Diarmot will put it through."

CHAPTER SIX

The speed with which her brothers and the two younger MacEnroys disappeared into the alehouse almost made Ilsa laugh. They had all muttered something about needing to quench their thirst, but she knew they sought out willing women. She had spent her whole life around men so they could not fool her about such things, even though they continued to try. Although she puzzled over why they would waste scarce coins on a brief rutting with a whore, she considered it just another one of those manly things she would probably never understand.

"They are just seeking out a rutting," grumbled Gay. "Do they think we are too dim-witted to ken it?"

"Och, nay," replied Ilsa as she moved toward the market she had come to see. "They ken that we ken exactly what they seek, but dinnae want to shock our delicate feminine sensibilities by being too truthful."

Gay snorted and rolled her eyes. "I dinnae understand men. I certainly dinnae understand how those lasses can rut with so many men they dinnae ken, mayhap dinnae e'en like."

"Ah, weel, 'tis for the coin, isnae it. Tis a hard life and some may have been pushed into it, nay chose it, but 'tis the way of the world. I suspect the lasses in that alehouse have some choice o'er which mon they bed down with. Twould be verra fine indeed if all such lasses had truly chosen that life and were pleased with their lot, but there really isnae much we can do about it. If there is a lass about here who has been forced into that life and doesnae want to stay there, that will soon be kenned and I will see what can be done to help her. Tis all one can do."

"Aye, I suppose." She gasped softly and moved to a table filled with bolts of fine cloth. "Oh, Ilsa, look here. Tis a wonder to find such richness here."

"Gillyanne said this was a verra good market for the merchants stop here on their way to the larger, richer towns." Ilsa studied an extremely fine linen dyed a deep, rich blue. "This is verra lovely."

Although she knew it was an unnecessary extravagance, Ilsa soon reached a bargain with the man selling the cloth and arranged for it and some cheaper linen to be sent to the keep. Gillyanne had shown her the fine clothes and bolts of cloth left by Anabelle and Ilsa was willing to alter them for herself, but she also wished something new, something a little special and all her own.

She moved through the many displays of goods selecting ribbons for herself, Gay, and her new daughters. At one table she purchased a gentle scent for Fraser, at another something for each of Diarmot's children. Ilsa suspected it would not be appreciated that much, but she bought a wedding gift for Diarmot. It was a beautifully wrought silver buckle, decorated with the swirling patterns favored by the ancients and a griffin with garnet chips for its eyes. They had been married only three days so she knew she could still disguise her urge to buy a gift for the man she loved as little more than custom or a courtesy. She might even hold fast to it until matters grew less uncertain between them.

Drawn by the scents of lavender and roses, Ilsa paused to survey the wares of the local herb seller and healing woman. The supply of medicinal herbs at the keep had been sadly depleted and, until she could restore the garden, she would have to buy what she needed. She was impressed by the variety offered and praised the white-haired woman for the quality of her goods.

"Ye are the new lady of the keep, are ye?" asked the woman.

"Aye," Ilsa replied and introduced herself and Gay.

"Heard that the laird married another lass than the one he walked to the kirk, one he had forgotten about. Saw the Campbells ride away that day." She stuck out one surprisingly clean, smooth hand. "I be Glenda, the midwife."

Ilsa shook the woman's hand and, realizing the tale of her marriage had already spread through the village, decided to be perfectly honest. "The laird's memory was damaged by a severe beating."

Glenda nodded. "So tis said. I didnae have much to do with his care as the Murray women are skilled healers and his kin. Tis right and proper they came to his aid. I tend most other ails and hurts."

"Aye, and e'en sold the laird the potion he used to kill his wife, ye old witch," snapped a dark-haired man as he moved to stand beside Ilsa.

"Ye ken weel that I deal only in the healing arts, Wallace," said Glenda.

Wallace ignored the woman's protest and looked at Ilsa. "Ye best watch what ye eat or drink, m'lady. Lady Anabelle didnae and she is dead. He couldnae abide the truth, that his lady preferred another mon to him, so he killed her."

"I find it verra hard to believe that Sir Diarmot would kill a woman," Ilsa said, her voice hard and steady even though she felt chilled by his angry accusation.

"Then I pity ye, m'lady, for we will soon be burying ye as weel."

Ilsa watched the man stride away and told herself not to heed his words. He was a handsome man, young and strong, and she suspected he had been one of Anabelle's lovers. That would taint his opinion about the woman's death, his probable jealousy of Diarmot making him see guilt in Diarmot's every word and deed. Despite the logic of that argument, Ilsa felt uneasy and knew it showed in her face when she turned to look at Glenda. The look upon that woman's faintly lined face was one of gentle sympathy.

"Wallace speaks from anger and jealousy, m'lady," said Glenda.

"Is what he says what the people of Clachthrom think and believe?" Ilsa asked.

"Nay all of them. I hate to speak ill of the dead, but Lady Anabelle wasnae weel loved." Glenda sighed and shook her head. "She was a strange lass. She had a handsome husband who cared for her, a fine keep to rule, and, though the laird isnae as rich as some, coin to spend. Yet, she was e'er unhappy, unsatisfied. Twas as if she wanted to have every mon alive beguiled by her. I think she bedded near every mon about Clachthrom, those who werenae too ugly or too old, leastwise."

It was almost beyond Ilsa's understanding. For a woman to be so repeatedly and flagrantly unfaithful to a laird seemed mad. Punishment for such behavior was usually severe. The woman had been fortunate that all Diarmot had done was turn from her. Unless Wallace's accusation was true, she mused, then struggled to banish that thought.

"Were ye called to the keep to tend her when she was dying?" Ilsa asked Glenda.

"Nay. Lady Anabelle refused my help. She had tried to force me to sell her a potion to rid her womb of a bairn." Glenda nodded when both Ilsa and Gay gasped in shock. "I held firm against her for I dinnae deal in such things, but she was angry with me. Verra angry."

"Do ye think she found someone who would give her such a thing or tried to make one herself?"

"M'lady, I think a great many things about how and why Lady Anabelle died, but few of them point the finger of guilt at the laird." Glenda shrugged. "And, if he did have a hand in it, I cannae fully blame him. She shamed him time and time again and she told me herself that the bairn wasnae his."

"Diarmot wouldnae kill a bairn," Ilsa said, hating the tickle of doubt in her mind. "Whether twas his or nay, I cannae believe he would hurt a bairn, in or out of the womb."

"That is my belief as weel, m'lady, but, if the tale troubles ye, speak to Lady Anabelle's woman."

"Fraser?"

"Aye. She tended Lady Anabelle whilst she was dying."

"Are these suspicions often spoken of?"

"As often as most gossip."

Ilsa cast a nervous glance toward the alehouse her brothers had gone into. "I think I best gather a few facts as quickly as possible." She chose what she needed from the selection of herbs, and asked Glenda to send it to the keep before hurrying in that direction herself.

"Do ye think the laird killed his wife?" asked Gay.

"Nay. And, yet?" Ilsa shrugged. "All that has happened has weakened my trust in the mon, I fear. There is a verra small part of me that wonders if it is possible. Diarmot is a proud mon and Anabelle repeatedly shamed him, made him look a fool. That woman is the reason he is so bitter, so mistrustful of women. For the brief time we were together, I did catch glimpses of such wounds to the heart, but I thought I had soothed them. There was arrogance."

"Weel, it might have been true ere he got his wits rattled."

"Possibly. What is important now is to get to the truth about Anabelle's death."

"To soothe that tiny doubt?"

"Aye, for I dinnae wish to become as wary and lacking in trust as Diarmot. There would be no hope for our marriage if that happened."

"And for that ye need to do this so quickly we near run back to the keep?"

Ilsa shook her head. "Nay, I need to do this quickly so that I have the truth ere my brothers hear the gossip."

"Oh dear."

When Gay began to run, Ilsa nearly laughed, then she also began to run. She had not been in the village very long before hearing the gossip so there was no doubt in her mind that her brothers would hear it as well. If they had not all lingered within the walls surrounding the keep, Ilsa suspected they would have heard it a lot earlier. Ilsa hoped that the lack of such tales within the keep meant those who lived there did not believe Diarmot guilty. This new problem could take a long time to solve if there were ones within Clachthrom eager to keep her brothers suspicious of the laird. That would prove a slow, dripping poison to any hope of peace in her new home.

Ignoring the startled glances of the ones she and Gay ran past, Ilsa led her companion straight to the nursery. She was pleased to find Gillyanne there with Fraser and requested a few moments of privacy with the two women. After assuring Gay she would let her know exactly what she learned, and assuring the children she would soon return, Ilsa left Gay to watch over the nursery. She then led an openly curious Gillyanne and Fraser to the small solar she had claimed for her own.

"What do ye need to tell us?" asked Gillyanne as she sat down beside Fraser on a well-padded bench.

"I heard some rumors in the market today," Ilsa said.

"Oh, dear," murmured Fraser.

"What rumors?" Gillyanne asked at the same time.

"I was warned about my husband's inclination to poison his wives." She nodded at Gillyanne's gasp of shock. "Tis clear ye havenae been to the village much since Lady Anabelle died, Gilly, but Fraser kens what I speak of."

Fraser grimaced. "Aye. I had hoped that foolishness had waned, good sense killing all suspicion. Tis clear nay everyone there has any regard for a laird who has worked hard to keep them safe and their bellies full. Who told ye this wretched tale?"

"A young mon named Wallace."

"Ah, one of Anabelle's many lovers. A foolish lad who thought her a poor troubled soul and believed the laird the one to blame for it. Anabelle was troubled, but she was also mean-spirited, selfish and vain. Of course, he ne'er saw that. The laird had naught to do with Anabelle's death."

"*I* am nay the one who needs to be convinced. My brothers are gathered in the alehouse and will undoubtedly hear this rumor." Ilsa nodded when the other two women winced. "Exactly. I need to ken everything that happened ere they return to Clachthrom."

"Which could be soon and with fire in their eyes," said Gillyanne.

"I fear so," agreed Ilsa. "I cannae be sure Angus and Nanty will be able to stop them, either, or will e'en ken what is happening. Diarmot has made no attempt to ken the men my brothers are, nor allow them to learn who he is. Diarmot still thinks they are liars, mayhap e'en the ones behind the attempt to kill him, and that insult sits poorly in my brothers' bellies, plus makes them suspicious of Diarmot. Sigimor and Tait will be strongly inclined to beat Diarmot, drag me home, and listen to explanations later. Mayhap. After a sennight or two."

"Weel, we cannae have that," said Fraser. "Anabelle found herself with child. It wasnae the laird's for he had cast her from his bed many months before, near to a year, I believe. Most here at the keep kenned that, thus they would ken that she was carrying some other mon's child."

"Considering all else she had done, I am surprised that would concern her."

"True. She made no secret of her whorish ways, seemed to flaunt them, in truth. By then, however, I think she wasnae quite right in her mind. She also didnae want the bairn. She ne'er wanted Alice, either, and seemed to forget the wee lass existed from the moment she bore the child. Since Anabelle had an easy birth, I cannae believe she feared the bearing of a child."

"So, she got herself a potion to cleanse her womb of the bairn."

"Aye. The healer Glenda in the village refused to give her one. Anabelle ranted about that for a few days, then seemed to calm herself. I had thought she had accepted it all, but, nay, she had her potion. She took it one night after having a fierce argument with the laird. Nay o'er the child, though. I dinnae believe the laird kenned Anabelle was carrying. Within hours we all kenned it, kenned what she had done, and kenned that she might soon pay for her sins with her verra life."

"Ah, dear." Gillyanne sighed and patted Fraser on the shoulder. "Ye couldnae stop the bleeding."

"Nay," replied Fraser. "We tried everything, worked all through the night. We would think it had stopped only to have it begin all over again. Twas a surprise in some ways for she was but two months along, mayhap e'en less, and she didnae suffer much when she miscarried the bairn. Ah, weel, sad to say, Anabelle died unrepentant, blaming everyone save herself as had e'er been her way. She e'en lost the chance for absolution and last rites for, when Father Goudie was summoned, she cursed him and wouldnae let him do it. Some of the things she screamed at the mon were appalling. I was shamed for her, although Father Goudie didnae look as shocked as I would have expected him to be."

"He is a Goudie. They are a rough lot. I doubt much would shock him e'en though he oftimes displays a surprising naiveté for a Goudie." Gilly looked at Fraser. "She didnae happen to say where she got the potion, did she?"

"Nay, but it wasnae from the laird. Truth is, she cursed him tenfold for nay helping her in her time of need."

"A statement which would imply that he did ken about the bairn," said Ilsa.

"'Tis what I thought and remarked upon it, but she said he didnae," Fraser replied. "When I thought o'er her ravings later, trying to make sense of it all, I decided the laird had failed her because he wouldnae let her seduce him back into her bed."

"And thus give her the chance to claim the bairn was his." Ilsa cursed softly and sat on a stool facing the other women. "That was probably what they argued about. Yet, considering how openly Anabelle shamed herself, it makes no sense at all that she would care that she would soon bear a child most kenned couldnae be her husband's get. Unless, of course, she thought she might have a son." Ilsa's eyes widened slightly when Gillyanne cursed.

"That was probably her game," Gillyanne said. "She had lost her hold upon Diarmot, might e'en have begun to fear he would find a way to set her aside. But, if she gave him a son, she wouldnae need Diarmot any longer, and could be rid of him.

She may have thought she could then rule Clach-throm through the child."

Ilsa thought about that for a moment, then shook her head. "Some mon would have been given the charge of the land and the child."

"As Fraser said, Anabelle was vain. She probably thought she could control that mon as she could nay longer control Diarmot."

It was a sad story, Ilsa mused, and it explained why Diarmot clung so fiercely to his wariness and the bitterness he could not always hide. The shadows in his memory hid the healing she was certain had begun when they had been together a year ago. Added to the scars left by his wife were new ones caused by an unknown enemy. It was not going to be easy to bring back the Diarmot she had known and fallen in love with, not unless his memory returned. Ilsa fought back the urge to just give up and go home.

Worse, when her brothers returned eager to tear Diarmot into tiny pieces, as she knew they would, she was going to have to tell them this whole sordid tale. Diarmot would be painfully reminded of why he had no faith in women for Ilsa knew she would probably not be lucky enough to keep him out of the way. He would undoubtedly be right there to hear all the details of the humiliation he had suffered at the hands of his late wife. It was enough to make Ilsa want to weep and scream.

In fact, the more Ilsa thought on all she had learned of Lady Anabelle, it was somewhat of a miracle Diarmot had been such a caring lover, had even married her. There must have been something in the air, she thought wryly. She did wonder if she had really known Diarmot at all. It was increasingly obvious that he had told her very little about himself.

"Did ye fear the rumor might hold some truth?" Gillyanne asked. "Ye must ken that Diarmot—"

Ilsa held up her hand to halt Gillyanne's defense of Diarmot. "For one brief moment I wondered. Twas a verra small doubt. And that doubt concerned the death of his wife, for I had already learned enough to ken she was a curse. I couldnae believe he would cause the death of a child, however. Nay, not e'en one barely begun in the womb. Tis just that he isnae the same mon I kenned a year ago, although I now begin to fear I didnae ken him much at all. Tis now clear that he hid a great deal from me."

"Men dinnae like to stir up painful memories. When I was first married to Connor, most of what I learned about him came from others. He was a verra controled mon who saw near every emotion as a dangerous weakness. He is still verra controled, but it doesnae trouble me now for I ken that he loves me."

"Aye, that knowledge can give one the strength to deal with many things. Unfortunately, I dinnae ken if Diarmot loves me. E'en before the beating, he didnae actually say the words to me. In fact, if my brothers hadnae found us that day, I am nay longer sure that Diarmot would have married me. He didnae fight the handfasting nor did he show any anger or resentment o'er it, but he may ne'er have actually chosen me if it had been left to him alone."

"Weel, ye are married firm now," said Fraser.

"That I am," agreed Ilsa, smiling faintly. "And tis what I want when I dinnae feel like throttling the fool." Her smile widened briefly when both women chuckled. "I but need to hold firm until his memory clears and he finds out who his enemy is. However, right now, I just need to make sure my brothers dinnae kill him."

"Then we had best get down to the bailey to meet them as they come charging in," said Gillyanne as she stood up.

Ilsa stood and brushed down her skirts. "There is a part of me that would like to let my brothers knock my husband down at least once. Tis that part which is angry o'er the secrets he kept. Howbeit, once the fighting begins, twill be verra hard to stop it. I doubt Diarmot's brothers would stand quietly by and allow my brothers to pound him into the mud, either. So, I shall hie to my husband's rescue."

Once out in the hallway, Fraser left them to check on Gay and the children, promising to join them soon. Recalling how Sir Connor never let his pregnant wife go up or down stairs alone, Ilsa kept a gentle hold on the woman's arm as they descended the narrow stone steps. She had not asked Gilly or Fraser to help her, but was glad of the support they so readily offered. The confrontation she was sure was coming would not be pleasant.

Once outside, she and Gilly sat on a bench near the steps that led into the keep and which faced the gates. It was a sun-warmed spring day and Ilsa wished she could enjoy it. Her brothers could be exceptionally stubborn when they felt they were protecting her and Diarmot was not in a mood to be conciliatory. It really was not a confrontation she wished to put herself in the middle of, but she had no choice. When Fraser arrived and sat with them, Ilsa was pleased with the added company and the diversion it promised. Waiting for a confrontation was almost as bad as being caught up in one.

"All is weel in the nursery?" she asked.

"Aye," Fraser replied. "Gay is a wonder with the bairns. She is trying to feed your lads some gruel and tis a fine mess they are making, much to the delight of the others."

"Tis a wee bit early to try gruel and mash with the lads, I suspect, yet they seem to need something more than the breast."

"They are going to be big lads," said Gillyanne. "My firstborn Beathan was ready for more verra early as weel. I could easily have weaned him completely at, mayhap, a sixmonth, but his wee sister still nursed. So, I would nurse her whilst feeding him his gruel, then nurse him a wee bit."

"That is comforting to hear. There are so many rules and opinions about it all. What rule do ye follow?"

"I have one hard and fast rule. I am nay sticking any part of my body in the wee devils' mouths once they get teeth."

Ilsa laughed along with the other women. There had been few women around Dubheidland, especially after her father's fourth wife had died, and none of those were of the same rank as she. Although she had cared little about that, the women had. Most of them had also been far more interested in the vast array of handsome Cameron males than in a too-thin, small girl child. Her brother Alexander's wife had arrived shortly after Ilsa had married Diarmot and moved to the cottage, so she had not really gotten the chance to know the woman well. Now, having enjoyed the companionship of Gay, then Gillyanne and Fraser,

Ilsa realized she had missed a lot, that a need she had not fully recognized was now fulfilled.

For a brief moment she felt guilty, as if she betrayed her brothers in some way, then told herself not to be foolish. She loved her brothers, had been happy in their company, and would always seek them out, even miss them when they were not close at hand. They had each other, however, and had often seemed beyond her understanding, just as she had often been beyond theirs. Even they would have to agree, there were simply some things a woman could not adequately discuss with her brothers.

"Ilsa, I believe your brothers are approaching," Gillyanne said. "'Tis but two men so they must have eluded Angus and Nanty."

It took but one look at her rapidly approaching brothers for Ilsa to know they had heard the rumors. "Oh, dear."

"Weel, they arenae charging the keep so, if they have heard the gossip, mayhap they intend to be reasonable."

"I doubt it. Sigimor is wearing his enraged bull look."

"How can ye see his face so clearly from here?"

"Dinnae have to see his face. His head is lowered a wee bit, his shoulders are hunched up, and he is stomping along with his hands clenched into fists. Aye, he has heard the gossip and he is in nay mood to be reasonable."

"Ah, weel, at least ye have a chance to soothe his temper before he sees Diarmot."

Catching sight of Diarmot and Connor coming out of the stables and walking toward them, Ilsa sighed. "Luck isnae on my side this day, I fear."

Seeing Diarmot and Connor, Gillyanne looked back toward the Camerons. "It appears they will all reach the same area of the bailey at the same time."

Ilsa stood up and squared her shoulders. "That cannae be allowed."

"What do ye intend to do?"

"I intend to grab the bull by the horns, as they say."

"Oh, dear," murmured Fraser.

CHAPTER SEVEN

"Move out of the way, Ilsa."

Ilsa met Sigimor's glare with one of her own. She had quickly placed herself squarely between Sigimor and Tait, and Diarmot and Connor. Even though the MacEnroys had no idea yet what had upset her brothers, they had already tensed in reaction to the fury her brothers revealed. The way her brothers had fixed their glares upon Diarmot as they had entered the bailey and immediately started toward him made Ilsa doubt they would have taken the time to offer any explanations before attacking her husband.

"Aye, move out of the way, Ilsa," said Diarmot as he stepped up closer behind her.

One glance over her shoulder was enough to tell Ilsa that Diarmot was as eager for a fight as her brothers were. "Oh, do hush, Diarmot," she snapped, too annoyed to enjoy his look of utter astonishment. "Ye dinnae e'en ken why they want to pummel ye."

"I dinnae need a reason and, mayhap, I will pummel them," Diarmot said.

"Fine. As soon as I have this all explained and settled, have at it. At least then it will just be one of those strange monly things, and not something done out of a complete misunderstanding."

"Strange monly things?" Diarmot muttered.

Ilsa ignored him and glared at her brothers again. "Now, ye are going to listen to what I have to say."

"Of course," said Sigimor.

"Good. I am glad ye have decided to be reasonable," Ilsa said carefully, not really believing his swift capitulation.

"I intend to be verra reasonable. Whilst Tait and I beat your worthless husband into the mud, ye can go and collect Gay, the bairns, and all your belongings. Then ye can talk all ye wish to as we take ye back to Dubheidland."

"Oh, leaving me so soon, my love?" said Diarmot. "I am devastated."

Ilsa rammed her elbow into Diarmot's stomach. A part of her was pleased to hear his breath leave in a gasp and another part of her was a little appalled by her actions. A brief peek at her husband revealed him bent over clutching his belly as he fought to regain his breath. She winced, but quickly turned her attention to her brothers again.

"Curse it, Ilsa," snapped Sigimor. "Now we have to wait until he can breathe again. Wouldnae be fair otherwise."

"Listen to me while he recovers then. I ken what ye heard in the village," she began.

"Then ye ken why ye cannae stay here. The mon poisoned his last wife."

"Nay, he didnae. She poisoned herself."

Sigimor snorted in disbelief. "From what little I have heard of the woman, she wasnae the type to kill herself."

Ilsa was pleased to hear that Sigimor had learned some of the ugly truths about Lady Anabelle. It would make it easier for him to believe what she had to tell him. It also meant she did not have to say too much about the woman's behavior while Diarmot was listening. She desperately wanted to avoid reminding him too much of all the betrayals he had suffered in the past. Lady Anabelle's malevolent shadow caused her enough trouble already.

"She didnae try to kill herself," Ilsa said. "She was trying to rid her body of a bairn."

"Is that what he told ye?"

"Nay, Fraser told me all about it when I asked her why such rumors were being whispered about."

"She would defend him. He is her laird."

"Actually, although he is my laird now," Fraser said, "I came here as Lady Anabelle's companion."

Ilsa realized Fraser and Gillyanne had moved closer, obviously hoping their presence would cause the men to hesitate before coming to blows. "There, ye see, Sigimor? She would ken the truth better than most. Lady Anabelle didnae want the bairn and asked Glenda the village healer to give her a potion. Glenda refused for she doesnae deal in such things. So, Lady Anabelle got one from someone else or e'en tried to mix one up herself. It rid her womb of the bairn, but it also drained away all of her life's blood."

"That makes no sense. Why rid herself of a bairn? She had already had one and she was married."

"It wasnae Diarmot's bairn. It couldnae be and most all here would ken that."

"Aha!" Sigimor raised his fists a little. "That is why he gave her the potion that killed her. He couldnae abide the fact that she carried another mon's child. Tis said he already had to bear that shame once."

"Wee Alice isnae a shame," Ilsa snapped, "and I best nay hear ye say so again. Try thinking, Sigimor, if it willnae cause ye too much pain to do so." She ignored his scowl and Tait's snicker. "The mon has a nursery full of children most men would ignore or disdain. I doubt the five women who gave him those bairns were all virgins when he bedded them, so he would have questioned their claims that he was the father of their children. Yet he took them in, he accepted the responsibility for them. Does that sound like a mon who would give a woman a potion to kill the bairn in her womb?"

"Weel, mayhap he didnae ken there was a bairn. He was just trying to be rid of his wife."

Her brother had stumbled upon one truth, but Ilsa was not about to let him know that. Sigimor and Tait were looking calmer. Agreeing that Diarmot had not known his wife carried some other man's child would start them on yet another round of arguments and explanations.

"And exactly who told ye the rumors that would cause ye to make such an accusation?" she demanded.

"A young mon named Wallace," began Sigimor.

"Och, aye, Wallace. He is the same one who whispered poison in my ear in the market. The same Wallace who accused poor Glenda the healing woman of giving Lady Anabelle the potion, e'en calling her a witch. He was one of Lady Anabelle's lovers, ye ken. It doesnae make him a verra unbiased talebearer, does it. Howbeit, if ye must accept the word of a mon who would betray his own laird in such a way, so be it."

"Ilsa," Sigimor began.

"A mon who dearly loved the woman he sinned with." Ilsa sighed and clasped her hands against her breasts. "A mon who thought her naught but a sad, troubled woman, driven to despair and sinful ways by her cruel wretch of a husband. A young mon who felt certain he could save her from herself with his love only to lose her to a cold, unforgiving grave. A mon who—"

"Enough," growled Sigimor as Tait rolled his eyes in disgust.

"Ah, so ye have decided ye erred in heeding the words of an angry, embittered adulterer?"

"Aye, and I have also decided that I cannae abide listening to any more of that mawkish nonsense ye were just spouting. God's toes, another moment or two of that, and I would have been emptying my belly into the dirt."

"Too true," murmured Tait.

"Then there is nay a need to be pounding my husband into the mud," said Ilsa.

"Nay, I suppose there isnae," agreed Sigimor, his disappointment clear to hear in his voice. "Of course, I suspect I could think of a few other verra good reasons to pummel the fool."

"Dinnae let me stop ye from trying," said Diarmot.

Ilsa rolled her eyes. "Have at it then. Pummel away. Indulge yourselves in your odd monly rituals until ye are broken and bleeding." She started toward the keep, Gillyanne and Fraser at her side.

"Where are ye going?" demanded Sigimor.

"I have important things to do."

"That was verra weel done," said Gillyanne as they entered the keep.

"Thank ye," Ilsa replied. "When one grows up so heavily outnumbered by men, most of whom are much bigger and stronger than ye are, ye have to be particularly clever."

"And devious."

"Aye, that is verra helpful as weel." Ilsa laughed with the women, then said, "Weel, let us go and rescue poor Gay."

Sigimor watched Diarmot idly rub his belly as he watched Ilsa walk away. The moment the door of the keep closed behind the women, Diarmot looked at him, and Sigimor asked, "Hurts, does-nae it?"

"She is stronger than she looks," admitted Diar-mot.

"Aye, she is, and that pointy, wee elbow of hers is a dangerous weapon. Be glad she used it on your gut. She caught our cousin Dennis in the groin once and I swear the poor lad walked funny for a sennight."

"Pointy wee elbow?" Diarmot murmured and briefly frowned at Connor when he laughed.

"Wheesht, ye didnae raise the lass weel, Sigimor," said Tait.

Sigimor punched him. Tait cursed as he stag-gered backward, then fell hard, flat on his back. He propped himself up on one elbow, rubbed his sore jaw with his other hand, and glared at his brother.

"What did ye do that for?" Tait demanded.

"Ye were impertinent." Sigimor idly cracked the knuckles on each hand. "I also spent the whole walk from the village readying myself for an enjoy-able fight, only to have our sister talk me out of it.

Left me feeling a wee bit tense. I feel better now," he said and strode off toward the keep.

A still-chuckling Connor helped Tait to his feet. "All right, lad?"

"Aye," replied Tait as he brushed himself off. "He didnae hit me hard."

"Sigimor raised Ilsa?" Diarmot asked, unable to quell his sudden curiosity about his wife.

"Aye. Raised all of us. My father's fourth wife died birthing Fergus, who is eleven and some months now. Father died a few months later. A fever swept o'er Dubheidland. Took the verra old and the weak bairns, as such things always do, but it also struck hard amongst those about thirty and older. Took Da, two of my uncles, and one of my aunts. Left a lot of orphans and a fair number of widows. Left Sigimor laird of a lot of needy people and he barely twenty. He had his twin Somerled to help, but also had a dozen younger siblings to care for and a lot of younger cousins either orphaned or without a father."

"There wasnae any kinswoman to take her in?"

"Several of them offered, but, either they were widows with a large brood of their own or didnae live on Dubheidland lands. Sigimor thanked them all kindly, but said Ilsa's place was with us. A lot of orphaned cousins came to live with us and they were all males, too." Tait shrugged. "She may be a wee bit rough, but she willnae be troubled by a nursery full of wee lads to tend to, either."

"Nay, that has been clear to see." A little surprised at how kindly he felt toward his wife at the moment, Diarmot turned his attention to the rumors that had brought Ilsa's brothers to the keep eager to break his bones. "So, the people of Clachthrom and the village think I killed my wife?" He had thought those suspicions had died, but admitted to himself that he had mostly closed his ears to them.

"Only the mon Wallace spoke of it. No one here at the keep has e'er implied it." Tait grimaced. "Ilsa was right. We should have paused to consider the mon making the accusation, mayhap asked him a few hard questions. If Ilsa wasnae concerned, Sigimor would have hesitated to listen to a mon who openly confessed to cuckolding his laird. Probably would have just knocked the fool senseless and carried on with his drinking and wenching."

"And with leaving Ilsa wandering about with only Gay for protection." He may not want Ilsa for his wife or trust her, but it was his duty to protect her. "Didnae ye heed me when I told ye some danger stalked me?"

"Ye, nay Ilsa," Tait said, but frowned slightly. "Ye truly think she may now be in danger, as weel?"

"If ye truly arenae the ones who tried to kill me, then, aye, tis possible." Diarmot was a little disappointed when Tait did little more than glare in response to that subtle insult, and then frowned in thought.

"I cannae see what anyone would gain by hurting Ilsa."

"Neither can I, but I dinnae ken who seeks to harm me or why. The why may include harm to my wife and bairns." Diarmot dragged his hand through his hair. "I should ne'er have thought to marry. I should have cleared this trouble away first, as ye say I had planned to. After the beating naught much else has happened and it has been verra quiet, verra safe o'er the last few months. Mayhap the beating was nay more than ill luck for

I was robbed, yet, unclear though my memory is, I feel certain that it was much more than that."

"Weel, my brothers and cousins will search out the truth."

"Dinnae ye think we have tried?"

"Aye, but ye arenae weel kenned by the people of Muirladen. The Camerons are. Some of my kin have wed lasses from those lands. Ye were but a stranger hurt whilst traveling o'er their lands. I suspicion my brothers will make full use of the kinship we have with some of the Muirladen folk." Tait frowned. "Might set Liam to searching out nay only who holds those lands, but who might rule o'er that mon."

"Cannae ye just speak with the mon holding the keep now?" asked Connor. "I tried, but he wasnae there and we needed to get Diarmot away so I couldnae linger. He hasnae answered any of the queries I have sent him, either."

"And he probably willnae," said Tait. "He hides in that keep like some troll. His wife is long dead and there were no children. I think he isnae supposed to be laird there now and tries to remain quietly out of sight and mind. If I am right, he certainly willnae help anyone seeking his laird, the true owner of the land. Liam will ken where to look. It has to be recorded somewhere. One of the elders in Muirladen might have a name to give us, too."

"I hope so. My instincts say the answers lie there." Connor looked at the two young men strolling through the gates. "Didnae ye notice the Camerons had left ye behind?" he asked Nanty and Angus.

Angus frowned. "Aye. Did wonder on their leaving for Sigimor and Tait hadnae done any wenching yet." He grinned at Tait. "Maggie was fair disappointed to find ye gone when I was done with her."

"Is she any good?" asked Tait.

"Would be better if she would just stop talking and expecting ye to talk to her."

"Hilda didnae talk much," said Nanty, "though she does smell strongly of onions." He frowned at Connor. "Were we supposed to keep a watch on the Camerons? We did hear someone say they thought they had come here to pummel the laird, but ye look fine to me, Diarmot."

"They changed their minds." Connor succinctly explained what had brought Tait and Sigimor back from the village and how the ensuing confrontation had been resolved.

"Do ye want us to go and have a wee word with this Wallace?" offered Angus. "He may be the enemy ye seek, Diarmot."

"I doubt it." Diarmot declined to point out that the Camerons ought to be watched for the same reason because he knew his family did not share his suspicions. "Once I was recovered enough to do so, I began to investigate my late wife's lovers."

"Ye kenned who they were?" Tait asked in surprise.

Diarmot sighed. "My wife kept meticulous records of everything she did, from when and how she cleaned her teeth to each mon she rutted with." He decided they did not need to know that Anabelle had not only listed who, but how, where, and how often. Only a few times had the name been missing. "Almost to a mon it was nay more than succumbing to a need and a beautiful woman. A few thought that cuckolding their laird was a daring coup. Only Wallace showed any sign of anger or jealousy, but he didnae have the coin needed to hire someone to beat me, nor will he."

"My wife's family has almost completed an investigation of the more weelborn lovers the woman had," said Connor. "Tis much the same. A few raised some doubt, but that begins to look as if it is simply a reluctance to confess to cuckolding a mon."

"Jesu." Tait shook his head. "I am astonished that ye didnae kill her, Diarmot."

"She wasnae worth hanging for," Diarmot said, then turned and headed back into the keep.

As soon as the door shut behind Diarmot, Connor looked at the three younger men. "Diarmot is probably right about Wallace, but I think it wouldnae hurt to give the mon a second, hard look."

"Agreed," said all three.

"And try nay to do it from the alehouse," he drawled as he strode away from the three blushing young men.

Diarmot paused at the door to his bedchamber. He could hear the sound of softly splashing water. The thought of catching Ilsa naked and relaxing in her bath had him reaching for the door latch. He slipped into the room and quietly shut the door behind him.

It took but one look at Ilsa to stir his desire. Her lithe body was only lightly shadowed by the soapy water of her bath. She was resting her head against a drying cloth folded over the rim of the tub, her glorious hair hanging down the outside to pool slightly on the floor. Her strong, slender arms rested on the sides of the tub, her eyes were closed, and her face was slightly flushed. Diarmot wondered how any mon could not think she was beautiful.

He hesitated to move, fighting the urge to shed his clothes and join her in that bath. It was not a good time for him to lose himself in the passion they shared for he was feeling a dangerous softness toward her. She had defended him to her brothers and he could not deny that he had been touched by that. Instinct told him a seed of doubt had been planted in her mind when Wallace had spat out his accusations, but it did not matter. She had not rushed to him with accusations, but gone to Fraser and Gillyanne to seek out the truth. It was more than many another had done. Her own words had also told him that, whatever else she may have briefly thought, she had not been able to believe that he would harm a child, in or out of the womb. It was impossible to harden himself against that.

When, despite what good sense was telling him to do, Diarmot took a step toward the bath, Ilsa's flush darkened and she slowly opened her eyes. He kept his gaze upon her as he shed his clothes. The way she pulled her legs up close against her body and wrapped her arms round them did nothing to cool his blood. She had beautiful legs.

"What are ye doing?" she asked. "Ye cannae mean to get into the bath with me?"

"Tis exactly what I mean to do," replied Diarmot even as he shed the last of his clothes.

"Ye willnae fit."

"Aye, I will."

Ilsa cursed softly in surprise as he stepped into the tub, bringing the level of the water dangerously close to the edge. Try though she did, she could not stop herself from looking at him. She liked the look of him far too much. The sight of his lean, strong body, and his obvious arousal stirred her blood. The way he studied her as he bathed should have made her uncomfortable, but only aroused her more. The heated looks he gave her made her feel almost beautiful.

"Such modesty isnae necessary between a wife and her husband," Diarmot said, smiling faintly at the way Ilsa continued to huddle at the far end of the tub.

He certainly was not troubled with it, Ilsa thought a little crossly, but said, "A bath is a private, intimate thing."

"So is what I intend to do verra soon."

"Now? But, we must soon go down to the great hall for our meal."

"Aye, I dinnae intend to miss that, either."

Her eyes widened as he stood up and stepped out of the tub. The bath had obviously not dimmed his lust at all. She squeaked when he suddenly grabbed her by the arms and lifted her out of the tub, setting her down facing him on the cloth she had spread out on the floor. She murmured a protest when he tugged one of her arms away from her breasts and began to dry it. Slowly, with a sensuous care that sent her passions soaring, he dried her body.

Ilsa was so caught up in how he was making her feel that by the time he knelt before her to begin to dry her feet, she was only briefly concerned about how exposed she was. The way he dried her stomach then heated it with kisses quickly killed that soft flicker of modesty. He did the same to each leg, lingering over her thighs until she was trembling. She groaned softly as he nudged her legs wider apart to dry betwen them.

When Diarmot dropped the cloth, Ilsa was

more than ready to go to the bed. Then she felt his mouth upon that part of her he had just gently patted dry. She tensed in shock and tried to pull away, but he grasped her by her hips and held her steady. Ilsa was not sure if what he was doing was right, but it took only a few strokes of his tongue for her to decide she did not care. She clung to his shoulders as she lost herself in the pleasure he gave her. Only his hold on her kept her from collapsing as her release tore through her with dizzying force.

Although still dazed as Diarmot slowly rose, kissing his way back up her body, Ilsa felt a twitch of renewed desire. Then she noticed that Diarmot was still damp. Eluding his grasp, she picked up the drying cloth. *Turnabout is fair play,* she decided, and enjoyed the way his eyes widened as she started to dry his arms.

By the time Ilsa reached his taut stomach, she could feel the faint tremors in his body beneath her lips. His passion was running hot and wild. Afraid he might end her play before she was ready, she stepped behind him, almost smiling at his soft grunt of disappointment. As she dried his back, then kissed, licked, and occasionally nipped his warm, smooth skin from his broad shoulders down to his strong calves, she felt her own passion rise. When she moved in front of him again to start at his ankles and moved upward, she was more than ready to be as bold and intimate in her attentions as he had been. She was eager.

Diarmot was not sure how much more he could endure as Ilsa dried and kissed her way up each of his legs. When she meticulously dried the damp from his groin, he tensed, wondering if she would be bold enough to bless that area with her kisses. He shuddered with delight when she dropped the drying cloth, ran her fingernails lightly over his thighs, and touched her warm, soft lips to his aching shaft. Although he was not sure he was very coherent, he muttered his approval and encouragement. He threaded his fingers in her thick hair to hold her close as she drove him to near madness with her lips and tongue.

The feel of her mouth lightly enclosing the head of his staff told Diarmot he had to stop this play. It was both too late and too soon to enjoy such pleasure. Too late for him to grasp enough control to savor it and, despite her apparent willingness, probably too soon to request her to gift him with the intimate pleasure he now craved. He grasped her by the arms and pulled her away, then gently pushed her back onto the drying cloths scattered over the floor.

"Oh. I thought ye liked that," Ilsa said, afraid she had shocked or offended him with her boldness.

"I did. Too much." He knelt between her legs. "Another time, when I am nay so needful of being within ye."

He looked her over, noting the flush of passion upon her skin, her taut nipples, and the rapid pace of her breathing. Placing his hand over her womanhood, he felt the hot damp of welcome and saw the way she shivered at his touch. Diarmot realized her passion had been stirred by making love to him and the last thin restraints he had clung to snapped. He fell on her, thrusting himself inside her heat, blind need driving him onward. Even as his release shook him, he heard her cry out and felt her body tighten around him. The only clear thought he had as he collapsed on top of her, was that at least he had not hurt her.

Ilsa blinked when, after several minutes of lying together, sated and a little dazed, Diarmot got up. She clumsily wrapped a drying cloth around herself and sat up. It irritated her when she saw that Diarmot was silently dressing. Surely he could at least manage some inconsequential talk without threatening the truce they had agreed to. Her eyes widened in surprise when he paused on his way to the door to press a kiss to the top of her head.

"Dinnae tarry too long," he said. "The food will be set out soon," he added even as he shut the door behind him.

Staring at the closed door, Ilsa quickly suppressed the urge to throw something at it. She would fix her mind on that brief, affectionate kiss. It could mean that she was slowly winning her battle to conquer his heart and mind. As she rose to get dressed, she told herself not to let her hopes rise too high. It was early days yet and a man as scarred in spirit as Diarmot was would not cast aside his bitterness and wariness easily. They were his defenses against pain. Ilsa just wished she did not have to suffer as she struggled to prove to him that she would never hurt him.

CHAPTER EIGHT

Gillyanne handed Finlay to Ilsa after kissing and cuddling the boy, then did the same to Cearnach before returning him to Gay's arms. Ilsa was a little surprised at how painful she was finding this farewell. She had only known Gillyanne for a fortnight, yet felt a strong bond with the woman. It was not simply because they were married to brothers or the mothers of twins, either.

Ilsa looked around the bailey. Everything was readied for Gillyanne, Connor, and Angus to leave. It pleased her in a strange way to see that Diarmot was as irritated by Nanty's insistence upon staying at Clachthrom as he had been by Sigimor's and Tait's. Her husband plainly resented the implication that either he needed protection or she did.

"Twill be a tough battle ahead for ye," said Gillyanne as she stood next to Ilsa. "I wish I could stay longer."

"I wish ye could, too," said Ilsa, "but nay for that. I am the only one who can fight the battle for Diarmot's trust, the only one who can make him believe in me."

"Ye dinnae fight for his heart, for his love?"

"The trust must come first, especially with Diarmot. Until he feels he can trust me, he will protect his heart as if it was the Holy Grail." She smiled faintly when Gillyanne laughed. "Lady Anabelle left behind a lot of scars."

"Aye, she did. She was vicious, e'en hateful. In truth, despite her whorish ways, I oftimes felt she hated men."

"That makes some sense. After all, e'en the biggest, meanest, strongest men can be made weak by passion, lust, or e'en love. She did make fools of a great many men. She had power of a sort and that can be a heady and corrupting thing."

"Weel, ye have chosen a wise strategy. Just cling to it."

"I intend to, although it isnae easy to just hold fast and nay try to argue my innocence. Dinnae mistake me, I dinnae meekly bow before any slur or accusation he tosses my way. There are times, howbeit, that I fair ache to tie him in a chair and give him a severe talking to, mayhap slapping him upside the head now and again to make my point."

Ilsa smiled when Gillyanne laughed. She suspected the woman knew she was only partly jesting. Dealing with Diarmot's constant wariness was far more tiring and hurtful than she had thought it would be. Now that she was with him again, was his wife by all the laws of church and court, she wanted the man she had fallen in love with back. She wanted that joy she had too briefly enjoyed a year ago to return now. For all her plans and determination, Ilsa found she lacked patience. She had to continually give herself stern lectures on how good things came to those who waited. They did not help much.

"Twill come," said Gillyanne. "A mon wouldnae work so hard to protect his heart unless he kenned it was in danger." Gillyanne laughed when Diarmot's children gathered around her to say farewell.

Although she tried hard to fight it, hope was stirred by Gillyanne's words. Ilsa could not deny the truth of them. If Diarmot felt nothing for her beside a man's natural desire for a woman, he would have no need for all his defenses. He would bed her as he pleased and continue on as he had before her arrival at Clachthrom. Instead, he avoided her as much as possible and was obviously on guard whenever she was around.

The children left, rushing off to encircle Fraser. Gillyanne took Cearnach from Gay so that young woman could go and assist Fraser. Ilsa tensed when Diarmot walked up to them for he rarely approached her when the twins were with her. She found his apparent lack of interest in his sons the hardest thing to endure. Even as she decided to take Cearnach from Gillyanne and leave Diarmot and Gilly alone to say farewell, little Gregor fell down and started to cry. The boy was not accepting the comfort of Gay, Fraser, or his siblings, but crying for his mama. At least Diarmot's children accepted her, Ilsa thought as she shoved Finlay into a startled Diarmot's arms and hurried over to Gregor.

Diarmot stared at the small child in his arms. The boy stared right back. The child had a surprisingly thick crop of bright red curls. He also had deep blue eyes. The same color as his own, Diarmot thought, then told himself blue eyes were not so rare. When the child gave him a toothless grin, Diarmot could not stop himself from smiling back and gently tousling the boy's wild curls.

"That is Finlay," said Gillyanne. "He possesses a more cheerful nature than Cearnach here and has a wee scar on his arm to mark him as the first born. Sigimor has a similar one and says tis a tradition to mark the bairns in such a way. In a family beset by twins twas quickly seen as necessary."

"Ye believe they are mine," Diarmot said even as he found the scar she spoke of on Finlay's small forearm.

"Aye. Ye would ken it, too, if ye but looked at them once in a while."

"Tis a busy time of the year. I cannae lurk about the nursery."

He ignored Gillyanne's look of mild disgust, then winced as Finlay grabbed a handful of his hair and yanked it forward to shove it in his mouth. Diarmot was a little surprised at the strength of the child's grip and the look of stubborness that settled upon Finlay's sweet face even as he worked to free his hair. Grimacing at the wetness of his hair when he finally freed it and tossed it back over his shoulder, Diarmot's eyes widened at the speed with which Finlay grabbed one of the laces of his doublet and shoved that into his mouth.

"Do ye think he is hungry?" Diarmot asked a grinning Gillyanne.

"Nay," she replied, kissing Cearnach's forehead when the child rested his head against her shoulder. "He just likes to chew on things. He has to be watched verra carefully. Your other bairns are verra good about that."

"My other bairns? I admit, I now believe Ilsa was

once my lover, but that doesnae mean the twins are mine."

"They have your eyes."

Diarmot thought so, too, but was feeling too obstinate, too cornered, to admit it. "Blue isnae such an uncommon color." He shrugged. "I cannae be any more sure my seed bred these bairns than I am with the others."

"Ilsa is right. Ye need a slap upside your thick head," snapped Gillyanne. "If ye keep treating Ilsa as if, at any moment, she is going to stick a dagger in ye and twist it, ye will ruin all chance of a good marriage."

"Oh? And what makes ye think I can have one?"

"Tis just like a mon to trust a lass who didnae deserve to be trusted, and nay trust the lass who does. Ilsa had been here a fortnight and hasnae done one thing to deserve the unkindnesses ye heap upon her. I ken she warms your bed verra weel indeed. She tends your home and tis looking better each day. She defended your sorry hide when her brothers thought to flay it from your bones because of those foolish rumors ye do naught about. She cares for the people of this keep and on your lands, winning the affection and trust of them all. Ilsa also cares for your bairns as if they were her own, something few other women would do. Fine, cling to your doubts and suspicions, e'en though ye risk waking up one day to discover that is all ye have to cling to, but ye could at least treat her with more courtesy."

He was still stinging from Gillyanne's words and struggling to find some reply, when Ilsa rejoined him. "Here, take your brat," he snapped, setting Finlay in her arms and tugging his doublet lace free of the boy's mouth. "I am too busy to play nursemaid."

Ilsa calmly turned to Gillyanne. "Would ye mind holding Finlay for a moment?"

"Of course not," replied Gillyanne, accepting the little boy into her hold, easily balancing him and his brother on her hips.

Diarmot watched in stunned fascination as Ilsa balled up one hand into a tight fist and swung at him. The force of the blow on his jaw was such a surprise, he staggered back a few steps. He cursed as he stumbled over a patch of uneven ground and sat down hard.

"Thank ye, Gillyanne," Ilsa said, retrieving the twins and setting them on her hips as Gilly had done. "Have a safe journey, and, please, let me ken when the bairn comes." She kissed Gillyanne on the cheek and strode back into the keep.

As he rubbed his jaw, Diarmot became aware that a small crowd was gathering around him. He looked up to find his brothers, Ilsa's brothers, his children, Gay, Fraser, and Gillyanne all staring down at him. He did not bother looking beyond them, certain he would find everyone else in the bailey craning their necks to have a look as well. The women all looked disgusted with him, his children looked curious, and his and Ilsa's brothers all looked far too amused for his comfort. Diarmot stood up and brushed himself off.

"Said something insulting or just plain ignorant, did ye?" asked Connor.

"I thought ye were leaving," grumbled Diarmot.

Connor grunted, draped his arm around Gillyanne's shoulders, and started to escort her to the cart readied for her. "I think ye had more than your memory knocked out of ye. Seem to have lost what few manners ye had, as weel."

Diarmot ignored that since the rebuke was earned. He busied himself with the final farewells. The moment his family left, Gay and Fraser took the children back inside. Sigimor and Tait headed toward the stables after assuring Nanty they would bring his mount out to him. Diarmot frowned at his brother when Nanty stood in front of him with his arms crossed over his broad chest. All amusement had faded from Nanty's face and he looked nearly as disgusted as the women had.

"Where are the three of ye going?" Diarmot asked, hoping to divert the lecture he knew Nanty wanted to give him.

"Hunting," Nanty replied.

"We have enough meat."

"Nay that sort of hunting. We are seeking the who and the why behind your beating as I told ye we would. Ye think someone wants ye dead, and we are trying to find out if ye are right. Of course, if ye continue to act like such a fool, the number of your enemies could swiftly grow." He grinned suddenly. "Ye could be courting a wee pointy elbow in the groin."

Since Nanty appeared to be completely on the side of the Camerons, Diarmot did not bother to point out, yet again, that they should also be considered suspects. "The woman has a bad temper."

"I suspect most of it comes from your skill at stirring it to life with a barrage of insults." Nanty shook his head. "Your idiocy could soon cost ye a verra fine wife. I just pray the Camerons and I can find the true enemy ere ye succeed in making Ilsa one, too."

Diarmot watched Nanty stride off to join the Camerons and ride out of Clachthrom. It stung to see how well his brother got on with Ilsa's brothers. He felt both jealous and a little betrayed. Even if Nanty did not agree with his doubts about the Camerons, he could at least attempt to keep a cautious eye on the brothers. Reluctantly, Diarmot admitted to himself that he sorely missed the comraderie Nanty was now enjoying. Except for a rare time or two with his brothers, Diarmot realized he had become very much alone since his ill-fated marriage.

Anabelle had started to isolate him, although he suspected that had not been her intention. Her attempts to seduce his brothers had caused them such discomfort their visits had grown less frequent and shorter. He had taken fewer journeys for Anabelle would shame him wherever he went, and, if he tried to leave her behind, she had followed only to behave even more outrageously. Diarmot knew he had also become an angry, bitter man, and poor company. And considering how many men Anabelle had bedded, there were many who found it uncomfortable to be near him, unable to look in the eye a man they had cuckolded.

Somehow he was going to have to shake free of all that, he decided as he turned to go back into the keep only to come face-to-face with his son Odo. The little boy stood with his hands on his hips, scowling up at him. One thing had certainly changed since Ilsa's arrival, he mused as he clasped his hands behind his back and calmly met the child's belligerent look. His children were no longer unseen and unheard.

"I dinnae think ye should be out here all on your own, lad," he said.

"Aunt Fraser said I could come talk to ye," replied Odo. "Mama and Aunt Gay are busy in Mama's solar and Aunt Fraser is watching us rest. The others are resting, but I needed to talk to ye."

"Ah, and what would ye like to say?"

"What did ye do to make Mama hit ye? Were ye mean to her?"

Noting how the boy now held his two small fists up before him, Diarmot realized that he was in danger of changing from the father who had little to do with his children, to the enemy. For a moment he blamed Ilsa for that, but his own strong sense of justice would not allow him to cling to that unfair judgment. If his children found it easy to see him as the enemy, it was his own fault. He was too much the stranger to them, had left them to the care of others. Ilsa, on the other hand, had become their mother, and even he could not deny the honesty of her care for them.

"Have ye come to defend her?" he asked.

"Aye, she is my mama. We have ne'er had one before and, if ye are too mean to her, she might go away."

"Weel, I deserved the punch, but adults oftimes make each other angry. It doesnae mean Ilsa will leave. Ye want her to stay, do ye?" Odo's belligerent stance eased slightly and Diarmot decided the boy had accepted that explanation.

"Aye," replied Odo. "She is a true mama. She talks to us, and plays with us, and tells us stories, and," he grimaced, "she kisses us a lot. I dinnae want her to go away. I want her to stay," he stood up very straight and his expression bore the hint of martyrdom, "e'en if she keeps kissing me."

It took a moment for Diarmot to control his urge to laugh, then he said, "She is my wife. She will stay." He put a hand on Odo's shoulder and turned the boy toward the keep. "Now, I shall take ye back to Fraser." He frowned slightly as, taking the child by the hand, he started back toward the keep. "Did ye ne'er consider Mistress Fraser as a mother?"

"Nay. She said she was only the nursemaid. Now she is our aunt."

Diarmot nodded, understanding that the woman had felt it best to keep her position clear, for she could not be sure if he would take a new wife. Allowing the children to see her as their mother could easily have caused strife within the household when and if there was a new lady of the keep. He knew Margaret would not have cared what position Fraser took with the children, probably would not have even cared if Fraser had taken his brood far away and never returned. The fact that he knew, without any doubt, that Margaret would have been as uncaring a mother as Anabelle had been, proved it. Since one of the reasons he had stated for marrying again was to get a mother for his children, he had to wonder what he had been thinking of to choose Margaret.

Ilsa had been thrust upon him, claiming a past and promises he could not remember, yet she was proving to be a very good mother to his children. He doubted he could have chosen a better one. Ilsa did not berate him to his children, as far as he could tell, and she did not take her anger at him out on his children, either. She might scorn him for his licentious behavior which had led to their birth, but she treated the children themselves exactly as she treated her own sons. Despite all of the other problems besetting him and Ilsa, it appeared he had inadvertently gotten one thing he had been seeking—a mother for his children.

He quietly entered the nursery, looking around as he released Odo's hand. This room, too, had been changed a little. Fraser had made it clean and comfortable, more so than many another room in the keep, but it had still been a little stark. Ilsa was making her mark here as well. He could not name each change precisely, save for noting cushions on benches and a few wall hangings, but the room was definitely softer, more cheerful and welcoming.

Even though he told himself to leave, that he had a lot of work to do, Diarmot moved toward the twins. The babies were sprawled on their backs on a soft pallet near Fraser's chair, awake but looking sleepy. One just stared at him and the other smiled. Finlay was the smiling one, he decided. He recalled Gillyanne's description of the differences in the boys' nature and was a little surprised at how clearly he could see it now. It was almost as if Cearnach waited and watched before giving his approval whereas Finlay simply accepted most everyone. Although it seemed foolish to credit such small children with those attributes, Diarmot could not easily scoff aside his impression.

Nor could he ignore how greatly those big eyes resembled his. Diarmot knelt by the twins, reached out to touch Finlay's curls and sighed with resignation when the baby grabbed one of his fingers and shoved it in his mouth. He glanced up at Fraser who was grinning as widely as Odo who now sat on her lap.

"Go lie down now, Odo," Fraser said. She gave the child a kiss, set him on his feet, and gently nudged him toward his bed at the far end of the room. "I hope Odo didnae trouble ye too much, m'laird."

"Nay," replied Diarmot. "One cannae fault the wee lad for the reasons he came to speak to me." He watched how the twins followed the conversation with their eyes. "They appear to be bright lads despite Finlay's compulsion to see near everything at hand as food."

Fraser chuckled softly. "Aye, they are. Bright and strong. Do ye still wonder if they are yours?"

"I sometimes wonder if any of them are truly mine," he murmured, then grimaced, wondering if he sounded as petulant as he thought he did. "Ah, weel, they are certainly all mine now, aye?"

"Aye, m'laird. Tis my feeling that they are all yours. Most women, e'en those of easy virtue, ken who fathered their bairns. Most arenae as Anabelle was, left with too many choices to be certain. These two laddies are most certainly yours, though I ken twill take more than my word on it to convince ye."

Since Finlay had fallen asleep, Diarmot gently extracted his finger and stood up. "Aye, it will. And, as for the rest of them, I fear their mothers might have had the same reason to doubt as Anabelle did."

"Mayhap. Most of that sort dinnae bother kenning names or faces and dinnae trouble themselves with the fates of their wee ones, however." Fraser returned her attention to the small shirt she was mending. "Lady Ilsa isnae like that and I think ye ken it. She wouldnae have to puzzle o'er who fathered these dear bairns for a moment. Lady Ilsa isnae like those other women and ne'er could be."

"How can ye be so certain of that?"

"Because I lived with one of that ilk, m'laird."

"So did I."

"Aye, ye did, but I wonder if ye truly learned the right lessons from that misery."

Diarmot snorted. "I learned ne'er to trust any lass, especially nay one who stirs my blood."

Fraser sighed but did not look at him. "Tis as I feared. Ye brand all for the sins of one."

There really was no response to make to that so Diarmot left the nursery. It was a cowardly retreat, but he did not falter in making it. Fraser was not so many years older than he, but she displayed a true skill at making him feel like a foolish child. She could also quickly and precisely ferret out the truth of a person's heart, which was another good reason for him to get away from her. His heart was filled with far too many tangled, conflicting emotions at the moment to allow anyone to stare into it.

Once inside his ledger room, he poured himself a tankard of wine, and sat in a high-backed chair before the fireplace. It was a moment of glaring into the low fire and sipping his wine before he noiticed the heavily carved oak chair he sat on was a lot more comfortable than it had ever been before. He looked to see what he sat on, then studied its match on the other side of the chest he used as a table. There were cushions on the seats and a thick, soft sheepskin draped over the back of each chair. Ilsa was obviously not satisfied altering the rest of the keep to her tastes; she had entered his sanctuary. Diarmot wondered if she had spent her youth plucking bald every goose in Scotland and was now turning to skinning the sheep.

Diarmot slouched in his chair and drank his wine. He was sulking and he knew it. He also knew he was being unreasonable. The chair was comfortable and the needlework upon the cushions was exquisite. The design was of a large griffin encircled by thistles, not some far too feminine display of flowers. It was foolish to feel as if she had unforgivably intruded. Complaining about it would only make him look petulant. It was his wife's job, after all, to make her husband's home more comfortable, more elegant and welcoming. Considering how often he retreated into this room, he did wonder when she had managed to change it without him discovering it until now.

He had a brief vision of Ilsa lurking outside the room, waiting until he left, then dashing in to toss cushions about and he smiled. And hang tapestries, he thought, as he finally noticed the one over the fireplace. Diarmot frowned slightly as he looked around seeing two others, one behind his ledger table and one on a wall near the door. Where was the woman finding all of these things? He did not recall her bringing that many chests of goods with her.

A rap at his door drew his attention and he called out, "Enter."

His man Geordie walked in, smiling faintly as he looked around. "Tis looking verra fine in here, m'laird," he said as he shut the door behind him. "S'truth, the entire keep begins to look verra fine."

"Aye, my wife has been verra busy indeed," he murmured. "I was just wondering where the devil it was all coming from."

"Ah, weel, from a storage room down in the dungeons. Tis a perilous warren of passages and rooms down below. Her ladyship insisted upon wandering through it all and found a veritable treasure trove."

"No one has e'er made mention of it."

"We all thought ye kenned it, but wouldnae

touch it because it had been gathered by your uncle. The mon gathered up many fine things, yet ne'er used them, or used verra few. Tis as if he liked bonny things but didnae ken what to do with them. He must have been a wealthy mon."

Or would have been if he had not tossed it all away on things he couldnae use, thought Diarmot. He felt the return of an old anger as he recalled how little his uncle had helped Connor in caring for his family and his clan, in rebuilding Deilcladach after the devastation wrought by years of war. That his uncle had hoarded wealth while he and his family had fought starvation was simply more proof of how badly his uncle had wanted them to fail to survive. It also explained why the man had never brought any of them to Clachthrom, even in an attempt to hide his guilt and hate behind simple familial charity. One of them could have discovered his wealth, rousing their suspicions about him.

Diarmot pushed aside those dark thoughts and asked, "Do ye think he was a thief?"

"Nay," replied Geordie. "Those who were here in his time all mutter about his waste of coin on things he ne'er used. Her ladyship was told of the things when she began to ask if there was anything set aside that she might use to add some warmth and color. She had already raided Lady Anabelle's rooms. Your late wife also hoarded many lovely items."

After finishing his wine, Diarmot had Geordie take him to his uncle's treasure. Shock held him silent as the man showed him two large rooms in the bowels of the keep that were filled with more riches than Diarmot could easily comprehend. His uncle had indeed been a wealthy man and now he was. Once he put his fury at his murderous uncle back into the past where it belonged, Diarmot suspected he would be pleased.

"With all of this, Clachthrom could become as fine as a king's palace," he murmured, idly looking over a collection of fine tapestries.

"Aye, m'laird," replied Geordie. "I believe Lady Ilsa thinks the same."

Diarmot suspected Geordie was right and wondered why that did not bother him as much as it should. Ilsa was inching beneath his shields, plucking away at his barriers with passion, as well as the care of his children and his home. If he was not careful he would wake one morning to find himself dangerously besotted. What truly terrified him was how easily she was doing it.

CHAPTER NINE

Ilsa glanced behind her and had to bite back a grin. Odo, Ivy, and Aulay were following her in a tidy line, marching along like proper little soldiers. She still felt a little pang of guilt over leaving Alice behind, even though the little girl had accepted the reasoning that such treks through the woods and hills were not for the wee ones. Ilsa had told her that she had to be five, or as near to it as Aulay was. She suspected that the very day Alice turned five, the child would be demanding her turn.

And she will get it, if I am still here, Ilsa thought and sighed. In the fortnight since Gillyanne and the other MacEnroys had left, little had changed. Her brothers and Nanty doggedly continued the search for Diarmot's enemy while Diarmot doggedly searched for more ways to keep a distance betwen them. He was a passionate lover every night and a cold stranger every day. Ilsa was not sure how much more she could endure. Her attempts to win her husband's respect and affection were beginning to feel less like determination and more like self-flagellation. At what point did she cross that fine line between patience and humiliation?

Deciding it was too nice a day to fret over such things, Ilsa stopped to study the rocky hill she ached to climb. It was not high and there was a path of sorts. Her final destination was only part of the way up and she suspected the children could make the journey to the little cave without any real difficulty.

She turned to face the children. Their guard Tom, not much more than a boy himself at seventeen and somewhat thin, had brought the pony up close behind them. Since she had never seen his skill with a sword, Ilsa was not exactly sure how good a protector he would be, but he was good with the children. There had been no sign of danger or trouble of any sort in the month she had been at Clachthrom so Tom was probably guard enough, Ilsa told herself. She shook off her sudden unease and smiled at everyone.

"We are going to climb the hill now," she began.

"Why?" asked Ivy, frowning as she studied the obstacle before them.

"Weel, there is a wee cave up there," she replied and saw the two little boys immediately become intrigued. "All about it and inside are just the sort of stones I am looking for."

"Dinnae ken why we have to tote stones about," muttered Tom. "There is a lot of them at Clachthrom."

"And I am using them," Ilsa said, "but there are nay too many of the sort I want for the paths in the garden. Tis difficult to explain, Tom. Ye would have had to see the gardens I saw. Our priest had the most beautiful gardens. E'en those which held the vegetables and herbs were made to look beautiful."

"Is that the priest who died in—"

"Aye," she hastily interrupted, not wishing him to speak of the priest's undignified and very unpriestly demise in front of the children. "One of the things about his gardens was how orderly they were. Each section clearly set apart from another and beautiful stone pathways winding through the whole place."

"Weel, if ye wish it, then I suspicion tis fine enough." Tom took the small sacks from the back of the pony after tethering the animal to a bush. "Here ye are," he said as he handed each child a sack before giving Ilsa hers. "Dinnae fill them too full or they will be too heavy for ye to carry."

"Up the hill then, my brave ones." Ilsa began to climb the path. "Watch how ye step."

"What if we fall?" asked Ivy.

"Tom is right behind us to catch anyone who stumbles."

"Will there be dragons in the cave?"

"Wheesht, there isnae any such things as dragons," muttered Aulay.

"Are, too," said Ivy. "Odo told me. He says that a dragon makes those noises in the night and that the stink is from its foul breath. And, Odo should know because the dragon always gets verra close to his bed."

Having grown up surrounded by boys of all ages and sizes, Ilsa knew all too well what the noise and the stink was. After quelling the urge to laugh, she glanced back at Odo. There was the hint of a blush upon his cheeks, but he was grinning like the little imp he was. Aulay and Tom were doing a poor job of smothering their laughter. Odo, Ilsa decided, was one of those most dangerous of creatures—a clever little boy. It was a good thing there was not a drop of meanness in him.

"Weel, we shall have to discover why that dragon slips into the nursery so verra often," said Ilsa as she turned her attention back to the path. "Then we can be rid of it."

Once they reached the little cave, Ilsa carefully instructed her troop on what type of stones she sought. The ground on the ledge in front of the cave was littered with them. She went into the cave, the children and Tom following. Tom made quick work of examining the small cave, and, after making a small fire to give Ilsa more light, went back outside. Odo soon followed, leaving Ilsa with Aulay and Ivy to help her collect the stones littering the bottom of the cave.

As Ilsa and Ivy studied a particularly interesting rock which, although too large for a path stone, was also too pretty to leave behind, Ilsa heard an odd sound. It was as if something had just shifted over their heads, but she saw nothing when she studied the roof of the cave. Ilsa suddenly feared the cave was unsafe, that it was littered with stones because it was slowly collapsing. She opened her mouth to tell the children they would be leaving when a louder, more ominous sound echoed through the cave.

Tom's warning shout sounded even as the first rocks began to fall. Ilsa gathered Aulay and Ivy into her arms, tugged them away from the mouth of the cave, and huddled over them, desperately trying to shield them with her body. She prayed Odo and Tom had gotten safely out of the way as rocks, large and small, cascaded down the hillside.

It was quiet for a full minute before Ilsa dared move. She felt a dampness on her face, reached up and wiped it away. Even in the dim light of the fire, she recognized the blood upon her fingers. She soon realized she had other small wounds on her back and arms. In her blind need to protect the children, she had been oblivious to the pelting of stones she had suffered. When she looked to find the mouth of the cave completely blocked by stones, she decided her many little wounds were the least of her problems.

"Those are verra big rocks," said Ivy in an unsteady voice.

"Aye, lass, that they are." Too big for her to move all by herself, thought Ilsa.

"Mama! Mama!"

"Odo, is that ye? Are ye all right?"

"Aye, Mama, but Tom, Tom is all covered in rocks. I think he is dead."

"Stay here," Ilsa told the two frightened children with her before moving toward the blocked mouth of the cave.

There had been a high, tremulous note in Odo's voice. The child was obviously terrified. Although she knew it was risky, Ilsa carefully picked away what stones she could until she had opened up a small crack at the top. Odo peered in at her and she breathed a hearty sigh of relief. He was filthy, but he looked unharmed. She wondered what he was standing on, however, and prayed it was stable.

"Were ye hurt, Odo?" she asked, unable to see much more than his face.

"Nay, Tom was on top of me," he replied. "When the rocks stopped falling I wriggled out from under him, but he isnae moving, Mama."

"That doesnae mean he is dead, my sweet."

"Should I take the rocks off him?"

"Nay, love. Ye wouldnae be able to help e'en if ye did. Now, I ken ye are a verra clever and brave lad."

"Aye, I am." He rubbed a hand over his face, smearing his tears into the dust and dirt upon his face.

"That is what we all need now. Ye have to go get help, Odo, help for your brother and sister and help for Tom."

"And ye, Mama. I have to get help for ye, too. But, Tom—"

"Odo, ye have to be a hard wee mon and ignore poor Tom. Ye need to get some strong men from Clachthrom and bring them here. That is the only way to help us all. Do ye ken how to get back to Clachthrom?"

"Aye, I do. Plodding kens the way, too."

"Good. Now, ye must go down the path verra carefully, then get on Plodding, and ride to Clachthrom. Tell them what has happened and that Tom has been hurt. Can ye do that, my wee brave knight?"

"Aye, I can."

"Go carefully, Odo. We need ye to get to Clachthrom safely."

"I will, Mama."

Ilsa listened intently when Odo left, but heard nothing to indicate any trouble as he went down the hill. When, despite all her efforts, she could hear no more, she moved back to sit with Aulay and Ivy. She held them close, her gaze fixed upon the small opening she had made. Their rescue depended upon a frightened little boy of five. She prayed she had not put the child in danger by asking too much of him, yet she had had little choice.

"Odo will save us, Mama," said Ivy. "Odo is verra clever and verra brave."

When Aulay nodded in agreement, Ilsa realized why the children had become so calm. Their faith in their brother was absolute. She tried to ignore the fact that they, too, were only five, and find reassurance in their confidence in Odo.

Diarmot frowned when Fraser suddenly paled, her gaze fixed upon something over his shoulder. He had stopped the woman as she had returned from the stables where she had been showing Gregor, Ewart, and Alice the kittens. In the last fortnight he had been trying to come to know his children better. It was hard work, but he had been enjoying a rather lively discussion about the kittens when Fraser had suddenly begun to act as if she had seen a ghost.

"Are ye ill, Fraser?" he asked.

"Odo," she whispered and started to move toward the gates of the keep.

Keeping pace at her side, Diarmot saw the little boy ride in on his pony. "He shouldnae be out riding all alone."

"He wasnae. He left with Tom, Ilsa, Aulay, and Ivy."

A chill siezed Diarmot as he strode to the pony's side and took a trembling Odo into his arms. He told himself it was born of a fear for the children, but it was Ilsa he had first thought of. There were many reasons for that, but few of them were good as far as he was concerned. It hinted at a weakness and, as soon as this problem was solved, he would have to recognize it and fight it. The Camerons had not been cleared of all suspicion yet.

"What has happened, Odo?" he asked the boy, touched by the way the child clung to him without hesitation.

"The rocks fell down," Odo replied. "Mama, Aulay, and Ivy are stuck in a cave and Tom has a lot of rocks on top of him."

"Do ye ken if Ilsa or the children have been hurt?"

"Nay, they are just stuck in the cave. The rocks are too big for them to move."

"How did ye get away, Odo?" asked Fraser as Diarmot set the boy down and snapped out orders to his men.

"I was outside with Tom when the rocks fell," replied the boy. "Tom covered me and the rocks fell on him instead. Then I crawled out and called for Mama. She made a little hole so she could see me when I stood on a rock and told me she, Ivy, and Aulay werenae hurt. She told me to come here and get help."

"Ye did weel, lad," Diarmot said, lightly ruffling the boy's thick curls. "Ye did verra weel." He frowned when Nanty, Sigimor, and Tait rode in, returning from one of their many attempts to track down his enemy.

"What has happened?" asked Sigimor, looking from Odo and Fraser to Diarmot.

"It appears there has been a rock slide which has trapped your sister and two of my children within a cave," replied Diarmot even as he mounted the horse his man Peter had brought to him. "My men and I are going to get them."

"Tis a good thing we returned when we did then, aye?"

"Take me," said Odo, holding his arms up to Diarmot. "I have to show ye where it is."

Diarmot opened his mouth to tell the boy he knew where it was, that the child should stay with Fraser, but quickly swallowed the words. Odo had earned the right to join in the rescue. Reaching down, he picked the boy up and set him before him in the saddle. He was irritated by how much Fraser's smile of approval pleased him.

Leading the others out of Clachthrom, Diarmot allowed Odo to point the way. Considering his tender years, Odo revealed a remarkable sense of direction and a keen eye for the sort of markers one noted to find one's way. Diarmot felt a distinct glow of pride and realized that, despite his occasional doubts about the children being bred from his seed, he had accepted them as his. Recalling the woman who had borne this child, named him as Odo's father, and handed him the boy, Diarmot was suddenly glad the child had been given into his care. Despite carrying the mark of bastardy, Odo apparently had all that was needed to better himself. There would have been no chance for that at all if Odo had stayed with his mother and that would have been a sad waste.

As they neared the hill where the accident had occurred, Diarmot could see the clear signs of a serious rock slide. He felt uneasy, unable to fully excuse it as natural. He himself had been climbing over that hill but a sennight ago and had noticed no weakness, seen no hint of unsteady ground. Nor had there been any heavy rain which might have weakened the area, loosening the earth beneath some of the stones. Yet, he could not think of how or why anyone would cause such an accident. There were too many easier and more certain ways to be rid of someone.

And now was not the time to puzzle over the

how or the why, he told himself as he dismounted and helped Odo down. His wife, children, and poor Tom needed help. It was all well and good to be wary, but if he began to see plots and threats behind simple acts of unforgiving nature he would have edged far beyond wary. The last thing he wished to become was one of those sad creatures who saw an assassin behind every tree leaf.

"Lead on, Odo, my lad," he said. "I suspicion Ilsa and the others will be eager to get home."

"Mama! Mama! Tis Odo! I have brought help."

Ilsa sent up a brief prayer of thanks and moved to the mouth of the cave when she heard Odo's voice. Enough time had passed for Aulay and Ivy to begin to waver slightly in their confidence in Odo. Since her own had never been very firm, she was heartily glad she had not been pressed to raise their hopes. When she peered out the opening in the rocks barring her escape, it was not Odo's eyes she looked into, but her brother Sigimor's.

"Might I ask what ye were about?" asked Sigimor.

"I was collecting rocks," Ilsa replied. "I wanted some rocks to make pathways in the gardens."

"Of course." He glanced over the pile of rocks separating them. "I think these might be a little difficult to walk on."

When she heard Aulay and Ivy giggle, she knew they would recover from their fright. Although that pleased her, she managed to scowl at her brother. "Such a clever wit, ye are." She quickly grew serious. "Tom?"

"Was waking e'en as we reached him," Sigimor answered. "Since he is also cursing and moving about as the rocks are lifted off him, I assume he is only battered and bruised."

"Thank God. And Odo? He looked weel enough, but I couldnae see him all that clearly."

"Dirty, nay more. Ah, your charming husband approaches."

Before Ilsa could prepare herself, she was staring into Diarmot's eyes. She did not need to see him very clearly to know he was angry. His gaze was hot enough to melt the rock. She inwardly sighed. Even if he could not find a way to blame her for this, she suspected what little freedom she had enjoyed was about to be seriously curtailed.

"What the devil are ye doing in there?" Diarmot demanded, not sure what annoyed him more, the danger she had been in or the fact that he had been afraid for her.

"Waiting for some burly lads to come and let us out," she replied.

"She was collecting rocks," said Sigimor, and, even though Ilsa could not see her brother, she was sure he was smirking.

When Diarmot looked at the pile of rocks he would have to move to free her, Ilsa snapped, "Nay those. Wee ones. I have been collecting rocks to make pretty pathways in the gardens."

Diarmot looked at her as if she was completely witless and Ilsa growled softly. She was getting very tired of that look. Her plan for the gardens was obviously one of those things that was beyond a man's understanding and, so, as with too many men, her husband assumed it was idiocy. Unfortunately, after this, it would be a long time before she gathered all the stones she needed, finished her pathways, and could show him the value of her plan.

"Best ye stand back whilst we move these

stones," Diarmot said. "They could tumble inside
and I wouldnae want ye to suffer yet another blow
to the head."

Even as she obeyed, pulling the children back
with her, Ilsa realized he was implying she had already had her wits rattled and she silently cursed.
The only ones in danger of suffering a blow to the
head at the moment were her husband and her
chuckling brother. Perhaps she could draw Diarmot
a picture to make her idea clearer to him. And, if
that did not work, she could shove the picture down
his throat. It was an enjoyable plan to contemplate
as she waited to be freed.

The moment an opening was made that was big
enough to climb through, Ilsa handed the children out. Ignoring the muttering of the men, she
put out the fire, picked up the sacks of rocks they
had collected and handed them out. As she started
to climb out, Diarmot caught hold of her and
nearly yanked her through the opening. Ilsa suspected what little patience Diarmot had had been
sorely tested. Since Sigimor draped an arm around
her, she leaned into him, suddenly in need of the
support.

"Ye are looking sorely battered, lass," Sigimor
said, gently grasping her by the chin and frowning
as he studied her face.

"Some of the smaller stones were flung into the
cave," she said, becoming achingly aware of each
and every place she had been struck. "Where is
Tom?"

"He is already on a litter and being taken back
to Clachthrom," replied Diarmot, wondering why
he felt so annoyed by the fact that Sigimor was the
one offering comfort and support to Ilsa. "I think
he is just badly bruised. It was clear naught was

broken on the outside. Twill be a day or two ere we can be sure naught was injured inside the lad. Ye will need some tending as weel." He frowned at the sacks she had handed out of the cave. "Do ye expect us to tote these back to Clachthrom?" His frown deepened when Odo set two more down with the others.

Since she considered that a foolish question, Ilsa ignored it, and smiled at Odo. "Ye did weel, my wee brave knight."

"Thank ye, Mama." Odo frowned at her. "Ye got hurt." He looked at Diarmot. "We have to take her home so that Fraser can care for her. She has blood on her."

"A fine idea, lad," said Sigimor and started down the path keeping a firm grip on Ilsa.

After staring at his wife's unsteady progress for a minute, Diarmot looked down at the sacks of stones. "I suppose I am expected to bring these along with us."

"We worked hard to collect them, Papa," said Ivy. "We want to help make the garden pretty."

Diarmot tossed a sack each to a grinning Tait and Peter, then started down the path carrying the other three. Peter and Tait followed, keeping a close eye on the children. When they reached the horses and Diarmot saw Ilsa already seated before Sigimor on the man's horse, he tossed Nanty the sacks and ignored his brother's look of surprise. Tait took Ivy up with him and Peter took Aulay. So, instead of riding back to Clachthrom holding a grateful Ilsa, Diarmot found himself sharing a saddle with Odo again. Diarmot supposed that was only fair. Odo was the true hero of the day.

Once back at the keep, Ilsa and the children were

quickly taken away by Gay and Fraser. Diarmot made
certain Tom was comfortable and cared for, then
joined Ilsa's brothers and Nanty in the great hall.
He helped himself to some of the ale, bread, and
cheese that had been set out, but he had barely
begun to slake his thirst and hunger when he realized his companions were unusually quiet. He
looked at them and found them staring at him as if
they expected him to say something.

"Ye have something ye need to say?" he asked.
"Everyone was saved, the injuries are nay severe,
and that is the end of it, aye?"

"One would think so," said Tait, "yet I cannae
shake away the feeling that it wasnae as simple as it
appeared. I looked around, but couldnae see any
reason why those rocks came tumbling down. Couldnae see any signs that twas done by a mon, either.
But that is what troubles me, that lack of any sign
of why it happened."

"Rocks fall. It could be as simple as that."

Diarmot was pleased, however, to discover that
someone else shared his unease. He just wished it
was not a Cameron. This incident stole a lot of
strength from his suspicion that they were his enemies. He knew, without even a flicker of doubt,
that they would never put their sister in danger
nor would they put children at risk. They might be
guilty of other things, but not this. And, after a
month of their company during which not one
suspicious thing had occurred, he was finding it
increasingly difficult to believe they were responsi-
ble for his beating. Even the possibility that they
played some game to get their sister a laird for a
husband was losing its importance.

"And how could someone have accomplished

it?" asked Nanty, drawing Diarmot's attention. "It would require planning."

"It wasnae any great secret that Ilsa was going there today," said Tait. "Some planning was needed ere she set out. It wouldnae have been difficult for someone to prepare this accident, ready it for her arrival at the cave. Ilsa has been there before and spoken of the place. Only a few stones needed loosening and then a push. Once rolling they would bring anything loose on that hillside right along with them."

"Why would someone try to hurt my wife and children?" asked Diarmot. "If I am right in believing I have an enemy, that the things which have happened to me were more than accident and ill luck, then I am the target, nay Ilsa."

Tait shrugged. "Tis nay so strange for an enemy to strike at those who are close to a mon. Until we uncover the truth, who your enemy is if ye have one, and why he is your enemy, I cannae see this accident as simple fate."

"Reasonable. The children and Ilsa must be closely guarded then, until we have those answers." He looked at each man and carefully asked, "I assume ye dinnae have any yet."

"Nay," Nanty replied. "We have eliminated a growing number of people as ones who might be guilty. It doesnae appear as it is anyone from Clachthrom. Wallace talks a lot, but doesnae act." Nanty smiled faintly. "We had a wee chat with the fool about the slander he is spreading about. Sigimor was especially convincing in making the fool understand that he is lucky he can still breathe after the way he betrayed his laird. Howbeit, I begin to wonder if we look in the wrong direction." He shrugged. "We will continue, however, until we see something to lead us elsewhere. That may happen when we finally discover who holds the lands upon which ye were nearly murdered."

"I, too, begin to wonder if we chase a chimera." Diarmot considered the possibility for a moment, then shook his head. "Nay, I am certain someone wanted me dead, that the beating at Muirladen wasnae simply a robbery."

"Have ye remembered something?"

"Only a little, a glimpse. I can now hear a rough voice saying someone best make sure I was dead, that they wouldnae get their reward if I was still breathing. That rather implies that someone hired the men."

"Aye," agreed Sigimor, "and it tells me the answers lie at Muirladen. I will give my family another fortnight to find the answers we seek, or show that they make progress. If there is none of either, then Tait and I will go there to have a look for ourselves. Until we find some answers, however, ye are right to say Ilsa and the bairns must be guarded. If what happened today wasnae an accident, then ye do have an enemy and he now strikes at your family. I just wish ye could remember why ye had been traveling upon our lands."

"Nay more than I," Diarmot said, "for I also grow more certain every day that the answer to so much lies there."

CHAPTER TEN

It was sad, that was what it was, thought Ilsa as she propped herself up against the pillow to watch Diarmot wash and dress. She held the sheet over her breasts and fought the urge to sigh. It was a pleasure to watch him like this, to see how gracefully he moved, to study the ripple of muscle below his fine skin. She was glad that he never bothered to make use of the privacy screen except to relieve himself. What was so sad was this hard proof that she was utterly enthralled despite all of her efforts to protect her heart. Diarmot, however, seemed to have protected his heart with the finest Spanish steel.

There was one very thin ray of hope. She hated to cling to it, but could not seem to stop herself. Yet, since the accident at the cave a fortnight ago, Diarmot had ceased to treat her as a threat. Outside of the bedchamber, he was not warm, but he was also not as cold and distant as he had been. The occasional muttered remark told her that he still doubted her tale that they had been handfasted, but, more and more, he behaved as if he accepted her as his wife. Even more important, he behaved as if he accepted the twins as his sons.

She tried not to act surprised when he paused by the bed. He did not simply give her a brief kiss and leave, but stood frowning at her, his hands on his hips. It was obvious he was actually going to speak to her. Ilsa prayed he was not about to break their truce. She was not at her sharpest in the morning, certainly not sharp enough to effectively defend herself if he began to utter some of those suspicions he still clutched so close to his armored heart.

"I plan to take Odo and Aulay with me today," he said.

"Where?" she asked, tensing slightly as she fought the urge to demand he explain himself. Odo and Aulay were his children, his sons, and he had every right to do as he pleased with them.

"To ride with me o'er my lands." He shrugged. "To tally the livestock, inspect the fields, speak to the people. Odo and Aulay cannae be my heirs, but they are my sons and part of this clan."

"Oh, aye, but is it safe for them to go?"

Diarmot realized he had expected her to be concerned. That was why he had consulted her about his intentions, something he had not needed to do. No matter what else he thought about her, it was clear that he had fully accepted her place as the mother of his children. He supposed he ought to take some time to consider how her complete acceptance of his children, her unquestionable affection for them, contradicted all of his suspicions about her.

"It willnae be just the three of us," he replied.

"There will be half a dozen men with us. I havenae gone many places on my own for a long while." He gave her a brief kiss and started to leave. "They will be weel guarded."

Ilsa slumped against the pillows and frowned at the door as he shut it behind him. She was not quite sure what to make of it. Diarmot had consulted her about the children, something he had never done before. Did that mean he had accepted her as their mother or would he have done the same with Fraser if he had no wife? It was one of those puzzles she would probably drive herself mad trying to solve.

She got out of bed and moved to wash up, then dress. There were still a few discolorations on her skin from the battering she had received at the cave, but that was all. Tom had recovered quickly as well. For a fortnight all had been peaceful so she told herself not to worry about Diarmot, Odo, and Aulay. In fact, everything had been so very quiet she was tempted to leave the confines of Clachthrom herself, but fought the temptation.

"Good morning," called Gay from the doorway. "I have brought ye something to break your fast."

"Ah, good. Come in, come in," Ilsa muttered as she finished lacing up her gown and stepped out from behind the privacy screen.

"Oh, that gown looks lovely, Ilsa." Gay shut the door, then set the tray she carried on the chest near the fireplace. "That dark green is a good color for ye."

"One of Lady Anabelle's." Ilsa ran her hand down the side of the skirt, astonished at the softness of the wool. "Fraser fitted this one for me. I am nay sure I wish to think too much on how much of Diarmot's money was tossed away on such finery. The woman must have had a gown for every day of the month."

"Mayhap two months. All in rich colors. All of the finest cloth. Ye would think she had been handmaiden to the queen." Gay set a stool by the chest where she had placed the food. "Come, sit on this and I shall tidy your hair."

"Her wardrobe reveals her vanity, I think," said Ilsa as she sat down and helped herself to a honey-sweetened oatcake. "And a part of me can easily understand the craving for so many pretty things. However, Nanty said she nearly beggared Diarmot, making it difficult for him to care for his lands and his people. That is unforgivable."

Gay gently combed out Ilsa's long hair. "Weel, now his lordship can repair his lands and his purse. That woman left so many gowns and so many bolts of cloth, ye willnae have to buy anything for years."

"Oh, dear. That makes me feel guilty for buying that lovely blue linen."

"Nonsense. Ye deserve a wee pleasure. A bolt of cloth now and again willnae beggar the mon. Ye deserve it for being so careful with your mon's coin, as weel."

"How can buying a bolt of cloth keep Diarmot from poverty?"

"Ye have made good use, or will, of the gowns Lady Anabelle had. Many another wife would have refused to do so. Wouldnae want to touch the belongings of the first wife."

"Superstitious, I suppose."

"Could be. Could also be that the second wife would be afraid she wouldnae look as good in the clothes as the first wife did. And, ye can cease looking like that."

Quelling the sudden urge to remove the gown, Ilsa said, "Ye cannae see my face. How do ye ken what I look like?"

"I ken ye weel, Ilsa. Ye have oft called yourself too red, too small, too thin. Weel, ye are none of that. Ye look verra fine in that gown and ye best nay be thinking of taking it off."

"Impertinent wench." Ilsa sighed. "From all I have heard, Anabelle was a verra beautiful woman. Considering where, and how much, we had to adjust this gown so that it would fit me, Anabelle had the sort of form that makes men's tongues hang out and their eyes roll back in their heads."

"There is a lovely picture," murmured Gay, then she laughed softly. "Sounds like a fit."

"A fit of lust. Anabelle apparently drove men mad with it. She could make men betray their laird, risk death to have her. I cannae do that, ne'er have, ne'er will."

"And would ne'er wish to. Your husband comes to your bed every night, aye? I suspicion he doesnae just pat ye on your wee head and go to sleep. He is the only mon who matters, the only one ye want to make his tongue hang out and his eyes roll back in his head, although it sounds most unpleasant."

Ilsa laughed. "Aye, it does."

"There, ye look tidy now." Gay sat down in the chair on the other side of the chest and helped herself to an oatcake. "I suspicion every lass would like to be so beautiful men would risk life and fortune to have them. I am nay sure Lady Anabelle was, precisely. Oh, she was bonny, but I think there was a wild lustiness about her that drew men. Mayhap she drew men by her beauty, too, but I think they also hoped they would be the one who tamed her." Gay shook her head. "Or, mayhap, she was just a vain whore and men are fools who think with their rods."

"That is a strong possibility," Ilsa drawled and laughed again. "Weel, there is nay kenning what drew men to Lady Anabelle and twas probably something different with near every one of them. I may fret on occasion that I am nay the beauty she was, but naught else. The only ghost she left behind is a vile one, her legacy one of anger, pain, and mistrust. I am certain Diarmot doesnae love the woman any longer. I just fear that she has left him unable to love again."

"Nay, I dinnae believe that. Wheesht, if all feeling had been killed, the fool wouldnae have to work so hard to guard his heart, would he?"

"That is what Gillyanne says."

"And tis true, I am certain of it. Aye, his late wife left him filled with bitterness and mistrust, but I think he clings to it now like a shield. He softened to ye once; he will again."

"I hope so, Gay." She smiled faintly. "Ye seem to be giving all of this a great deal of thought."

"Weel, I want ye to be happy, dinnae I? I also feel a need now to look closely at the many ways men and women act with each other, the many ways they treat each other. It helps me to start to believe that what happened to me had naught to do with all that, that it was naught but a particularly vicious way to beat me." She blushed. "I suspicion those bastards felt some odd sort of tainted lust, but nay for me. They would have done the same to any poor lass they got ahold of. They just wanted to stick their rods in some woman, thought it would make them look all big, strong, powerful, and monly. I just happened to be the first poor lass to come within their reach. Slowly, as I watch others, it helps me understand that."

"I am so glad, Gay. And ye will continue to heal, I am certain of it. Ye are too strong a lass to let those men rob ye of all spirit and future." She held up her hand to stop Gay's response. "Ye will have a future. Whilst ye are noticing so much else, I suggest ye notice that no one shuns ye, and they have all guessed what happened to ye. A good mon, the sort ye could make a future with, will ne'er condemn ye for what happened."

Gay nodded. "Each day I begin to believe that more and more. Twill settle firm in my heart soon, I think, for I can see the truth of it in your brothers, your cousins, and the men here at Clachthrom." She smiled faintly. "And, it helps to be learning how to use the knife Elyas gave me."

"As soon as I have finished eating and visit with the bairns, ye shall have another lesson. Best to take advantage of the fact that Odo and Aulay arenae here to pester us to teach them." She frowned. "I hope they are all right."

"Of course they are. They are with their father. I think it verra good that Sir Diarmot is starting to take an interest in them."

It was, and by the time they returned, Ilsa told herself she would be over the pinch of jealousy she felt.

"Who lives in this cottage, Papa?" asked Odo as he peeked into the empty pot hung over the fire.

"No one now," replied Diarmot. "The old couple who used to live here died a few years ago."

Yet the little house looked remarkably clean, thought Diarmot as he looked around. It had been the sense of occupancy that had caused him to stop and look inside. It was not unusual for someone to take possession of an empty house, but he saw no sign that someone was actually living here. There were no clothes, no food, and no scent of a recent meal or a fire in the hearth. A clean straw mattress was upon the bed, however, a blanket folded neatly at the foot of the bed.

A trysting place, he thought, and smiled faintly. That made sense, explaining the cleanliness yet no sign of actual residency. Some lovers had stumbled upon the abandoned house and decided it was the perfect place to meet. Diarmot began to look for some clue as to who might be using his cottage. Just as he began to think it a waste of time, he caught sight of something wedged between the rough wooden leg of the bed and the wall. Diarmot got down on his stomach, smiling when Odo and Aulay did the same, flanking him.

Diarmot was just tugging what appeared to be a message free when a gruff voice said, "Weel, will ye look at the laird with his bonny face in the dirt."

A bone-chilling cold flooded Diarmot. He was back in Muirladen, sprawled in the mud, too broken and bloody to move. He flinched, his body remembering the booted foot that had struck him in the side, cracking a rib. For a moment, Diarmot felt caught tightly in his nightmare, could feel the bitter taste of fear in the back of his throat. Sweat broke out all over his body as he waited for another blow.

"Papa! Are ye stuck?"

Odo's childish voice and the feel of four small hands tugging at his clothes pulled Diarmot free of those dark memories. He scrambled out from beneath the bed, covertly shoved the note in a pocket within his doublet, and struggled to smile at his sons. They looked concerned, which touched him, and he wondered how long he had been held in the grip of his memories.

"I am fine, lads," he said as he stood up. "Aye, I was a wee bit stuck."

Diarmot looked around the cottage for the owner of that voice which had so deeply affected him, but saw only Geordie. The man stood in the doorway of the cottage, his thickly muscled arms crossed over his broad chest. Had the voice come from inside his head or had a harmless remark by Geordie stirred that memory? Diarmot suspected one of the attackers had said something very similar and that was why Geordie's words had had such an unsettling effect upon him.

"What were ye doing under there?" Geordie asked as he moved to let Diarmot and the twins walk outside.

"I thought I saw something, but twas naught," replied Diarmot, not wanting to reveal his discovery until he was certain no one would suffer for whatever might be written there. "I shall have to find new tenants for this cottage. Tis a waste for it to sit empty, the land about it left fallow, and the fields ungrazed. Ye ken the people hereabout weel, Geordie, so mayhap ye ken someone who would be interested in becoming a crofter here."

"Aye, m'laird, I will look about."

There was an odd note to Geordie's voice that caused Diarmot to frown after his man as Geordie walked away. Was he the one trysting at the cottage? Diarmot resisted the urge to immediately study the message he had found. Instead, he turned his attention upon his sons and getting them mounted. Aulay sat before Tom and Odo sat before Diarmot, both untiring in their questions and observations as Diarmot led his men back to the keep.

A chill still infected his blood and Diarmot struggled to fight it off. He realized he had not suffered from a nightmare since his marriage to Ilsa. Having her lithe, warm body tucked up close to his every night had obviously kept the nightmares away. That seemed odd as she would not be much protection if he was attacked. Diarmot decided that it was simply because he was not alone. He had been starkly aware of being all alone the night he had been attacked and that feeling had clearly lingered.

It was possible his memory was struggling to return. That would explain suffering his nightmare in the daylight and while he was awake. It would probably explain why Geordie's words had affected him so deeply. Diarmot hoped that was true, for he was sure some of the answers he needed were locked up with those memories. Even one small clue would be welcome for it would help them direct the search for his enemy more exactly.

The moment they rode through the gates of Clachthrom, Diarmot looked for Ilsa. He wanted her and doubted he could wait until they retired for the night. It galled him to admit it, but her passion would be the surest cure for the chill that had settled inside of him.

After leaving the boys with Fraser, Diarmot washed up in a room off the kitchen, and then searched for Ilsa. He was pleased to find her in the first place he looked. Since that was their bedchamber, it was also convenient.

Ilsa smiled at Diarmot as he entered the room, then frowned a little warily when he shut and latched the door behind him. "Is something wrong?"

She set aside the cushion she had been sewing and rose from her seat by the fire as he walked toward her.

"Another cushion?" he asked, smiling faintly.

"There are a lot of hard seats in this keep. Are Odo and Aulay all right?"

"Tired and dirty, nay more." He ran his hand down her arm, pleased to see her shiver a little in response at his touch. "This gown looks verra fine. The color suits ye."

A compliment, Ilsa thought in surprise, then eyed him with suspicion. In the six weeks she had been his wife, Diarmot had rarely complimented her, except when he was feeling passionate. She could not believe he was thinking of doing that when it was only late in the afternoon, but it would explain the locked door. It would also explain why he was not wearing his doublet.

"Thank ye," she murmured, then realized his hair was damp. "Ye have had a bath."

"Aye, I smelled too strongly of sweat and horses." He slowly tugged her into his arms, smiling at the faint scowl she wore. "I didnae wish to offend your wee nose."

Diarmot kissed the tip of her nose, then kissed the hollow by her ear. She gasped faintly and clutched his shirt. He traced the delicate shape of her ear with his tongue and felt her tremble. Here was the warmth he needed. Although it troubled him that he did need it, he found consolation in the fact that she did not recognize his weakness.

"Tis only the middle of the afternoon," she protested, but could not find the will to pull away.

Since her protest was so weak, Diarmot ignored it. He kissed her, fighting to keep enough of his wits about him to undo her gown. The moment it slid to the floor, he picked her up in his arms and carried her to the bed. After setting her in the middle of the bed, he removed her shoes, then hastily undressed. Ilsa looked beautifully flushed and a little dazed, but Diarmot did not want to give her enough time to shake free of desire's grip. Despite six weeks of sharing a bed, Ilsa retained her sense of modesty. He did not want her to become aware of the fact that she was half naked in bed with the sun shining brightly through the window.

Ilsa watched Diarmot shed his clothes with a speed that revealed a flattering eagerness. She did love to see the man naked and he looked especially glorious in the sunlight. She frowned, pulling free of the stupor his kisses always put her into, and started to look toward the window. Just as she was becoming painfully aware of how much light there was in the room, Diarmot settled himself on top of her, diverting her.

His kiss banished all concern about the time of the day from her mind. By the time he started to tug her shift down, she was so lost in her desire, she readily pulled her arms free of it. Ilsa clung to him as he followed the descent of her shift with hot kisses and strokes of his tongue. It was not until he tugged it completely off and tossed it aside that she again became aware of how much light shone into the room. When he crouched over her and she saw where he was staring, Ilsa felt as if she were blushing all the way down to her toes.

"Oh, nay," she whispered and placed her hands over her groin.

"Oh, aye," he said, clasping her hands in his and holding them captive against the bed.

She tensed with embarrassment when he kissed

the inside of each of her thighs then touched his lips to the place that so ached for him. A heartbeat later embarrassment was burnt away by searing need. Ilsa freed her hands and threaded her fingers into his thick hair as she opened herself to his intimate kiss. She tried every trick she could think of to control her passion, even counting backward, so that she could savor the pleasure he gave her, but it was a losing battle. Knowing her release drew near, she tugged on his hair, eager to have him join with her. By the time he had kissed his way back up her body, she was shaking from the force of her need. He kissed her, thrusting his tongue in her mouth at the same time he joined his body to hers.

Ilsa felt herself shatter. She kissed him as if she were starved for the taste of him. She used her arms and legs to hold him close, to push him deep inside. His movements became fierce, the hard, swift thrusts of his body renewing her passion. When he groaned out her name and filled her womb with the heat of his seed, Ilsa felt herself shatter a second time. Blindly, she clung to him as he collapsed on top of her.

Unsure of how long she lay there, sated and oblivious, Ilsa slowly became aware of her surroundings. She winced at the bright rays of sunlight spilling in through the window. The sight of Diarmot sprawled on top of her was rather pleasing, but, when she recalled all they had just done, she nearly groaned. Then she caught sight of her legs splayed out on either side of him.

"Jesu, I am still wearing my hose," she muttered.

Diarmot turned onto his side and looked her over, smiling at her blushes. "Ye look verra tempting."

Ilsa growled and turned onto her side, her back to Diarmot. She saw her shift on the floor, grabbed it, and hastily put it on. By the time she had laced it up and turned back to look at Diarmot, he had redonned his hose and shirt. Ilsa prepared herself for his abrupt leave-taking now that he had gotten what he wanted, but he stood there scowling down at what appeared to be a tattered letter. She moved across the bed to kneel at his side.

"What is that?" she asked.

For a minute, Diarmot hesitated, then sighed. She had already seen the message he had found at the cottage so there was no sense in trying to hide it again. A clever lie was beyond him at this point. In truth, he no longer believed she would try to kill him. It did not mean she was innocent of all trickery, he sternly reminded hismelf, but if she wanted him dead, she had had numerous occasions to accomplish the deed since coming to Clachthrom. So had her brothers, he thought, then quickly shook that thought away. *Someone wants ye dead, Diarmot,* he reminded himself for what had to be the hundredth time, *and the Camerons are still the ones with the most to gain.* Telling Ilsa about the ruined message he had found would make no difference, either in proving her guilt or innocence, or in prompting her to change her plans in any way.

"I found this in a cottage at the western border of my lands," he replied. "The cottage should have been empty, dirty, and showing all the other signs of several years of disuse. It did not. Decided it might be a trysting place for some pair of lovers, then found this. It was wedged between the leg of the bed and the wall." He handed the note to her.

"The wall evidently isnae completely free of leaks. Damp has made it nearly illegible."

"Aye, it has." She studied the message. "It was written by a woman."

"How can ye tell that from this mess?"

"Some words are clear enough. Tis the script a woman would use, I am certain of it. And, tis nay verra old. Though soiled and smudged, the paper shows no sign of age and the ink is still dark." She frowned at it for a moment. "Tis a love letter, I think. The greeting looks to be an endearment, as does the ending. No names, just an endearment. I can see a few words such as 'meet me,' 'must talk,' and 'taking too long.' A tryst, although the words 'growing impatient' imply all is nay weel, I should think."

Diarmot nodded and tucked the letter into a small carved box on the table by the bed. "I had hoped to find out who was using the cottage. If naught else, the place needs new tenants." He rose, selected a clean doublet and slipped it on. "It isnae good to have an empty place upon one's lands and tis a waste to have the land sit unused."

"Mayhap ye should look for a couple who are soon to be wed, but will have to live with her family or his. Or some young couple already in such a position. Such ones may be eager to become crofters, would be grateful for the chance."

"And their gratitude would be to their laird thus inspiring loyalty."

"Without a doubt."

Diarmot kissed her and moved to the door. "A verra good idea, wife."

Ilsa stared blindly at the door after it shut behind him. That was definitely a compliment and

Diarmot had not been feeling the slightest bit lustful when he had given it. Even though he had hesitated for a telling moment, he had shared his discovery with her. Ilsa felt a stirring of hope concerning their future and she knew it would take a great deal more than lecturing herself to kill it this time.

CHAPTER ELEVEN

"Where is he?"

Ilsa was almost able to smile at the expression upon Tom's face, and the way he looked around a little desperately in search of a way to escape her question. She would not allow it. Diarmot was nowhere to be found within the walls of the keep and she had to wonder why. From what she had seen as she had hunted him down, if he had gone outside the walls of Clachthrom, he had done so alone. In the three weeks since the incident at the cave, none of them had been allowed to leave Clachthrom alone.

Tom sighed. "He is out riding. Tis a fine day and he had an itch for it."

"I dinnae suppose he had an itch to take anyone with him."

"Geordie went with him."

"I just saw Geordie. He was sitting in the great hall drinking ale and talking to Peter."

"Ah, weel, he came back a wee while ago. He

said the laird would be soon to follow." Tom scowled at the gates.

Ilsa wondered if Tom thought that stern expression would cause Diarmot to come running home like a good boy. She could fully understand Diarmot's need to break free of all constraints for a while. That same urge had been what had driven her to hunt him down. She had thought they could escape those constraints together. It was why she was standing there holding the reins of her mare Rose demanding Tom tell her where Diarmot was. If she had gotten another vague reply, she had intended to ride out on her own. It appeared that was exactly what she was going to do.

"What are ye doing, m'lady?" asked Tom.

"I do believe I am mounting my horse, Tom," Ilsa replied sweetly as she settled herself in the saddle, amused at how hard a blushing Tom tried not to look at her stockings before she could arrange her skirts a little more modestly. "I am going to look for my husband. Do ye have any idea where he might be riding?"

"Mayhap ye should wait, m'lady. The laird could return soon. Mayhap your brothers and Sir Nanty will return and they could ride with ye."

"My brothers and Nanty have traveled far afield this day, Tom. They may nay be back until the morrow. I dinnae think I should leave the laird wandering around by himself until then, do ye? Now, do ye ken where he might be?"

"Geordie said the laird was riding along the ridge. Some lambs have gone missing and he wanted to see if they had gotten themselves trapped or had fallen. Ye can sometimes save the pelt," Tom began, then gasped as Ilsa started to ride past him. "Ye cannae ride about on your own!"

"Verra soon I willnae be on my own," she called back to him. "I will be with my husband."

She heard Tom cursing as she rode away. She felt a brief twitch of guilt over her actions, but swiftly pushed it aside. If anyone ought to feel guilty, it was whoever put Tom in charge of manning the gates. Not only was Tom a little young and untested for such an important post, but he simply could not be threatening or authoritative. She would just have to be very careful not to be injured in any way or Tom would feel at fault.

She took a deep breath and sighed with enjoyment. She knew the air outside the gates was the same as the air inside the gates, but it seemed sweeter. Over the last few weeks she had done her best to behave, to go nowhere alone. Raised mostly by her brothers, she had always had great freedom. The fact that there seemed to be a cousin around every corner had allowed her to come and go as she pleased, safe and secure in the knowledge that no one at Dubheidland would hurt her or let harm come to her. She had also been taught when to heed orders given for the sake of her own safety, however, and she knew her brothers would not be pleased with her disobedience, no matter how much they might understand and sympathize. Ilsa hoped she could return to Clachthrom safely, with her husband at her side, preferably without her brothers discovering what she had done. Although she was a married woman, and a mother, Sigimor would not hesitate to lecture her and she hated those lectures. Sigimor had truly mastered the art over the years.

Reaching a thick stand of trees, Ilsa slowed her pace to a cautious one. There were a lot of very wild places on the Clachthrom lands, she realized.

Harshness and wild beauty marched side by side. The children were going to have to be carefully taught to respect the land around them and the dangers it might hold. She idly wondered if she could keep them tethered to the keep until they were twenty and laughed softly. Although she liked to move freely, she obviously did not like the thought of her children doing the same.

The unmistakable sound of clashing steel abruptly cut through the peace of the wood. Ilsa tightened her grip on the reins as she fought back the instinctive urge to gallop forward to see what was happening. One of Sigimor's most repeated lessons went through her mind and she took several deep breaths to calm herself. Caution was a person's strongest shield, her brother was fond of saying. Ilsa held tightly to that thought as she tried to decide what to do. Since she was certain Diarmot was just ahead, that the sounds of fighting meant he was in danger, calm and caution were difficult to cling to.

She could not go racing to his resuce. Although she considered herself strong and able, she was no warrior and, at the moment, the only weapon she had was a dagger. A horse could also be a weapon, but Rose had never been trained in such skills.

Ilsa dismounted, tethered Rose to a tree branch, and began to move toward the sounds of battle. She needed to see exactly what was happening, what the enemy's strength was, before she could do anything. It would take too long to race back to Clachthrom and get help. There was always the chance that no help would be needed.

At the very edge of the wood, she caught her first sight of all she had feared. Diarmot was in a

fight for his life against four men. She quickly
sprawled on her stomach on the ground and peered
around a knot of brambles growing at the base of a
tree. Unless the men ran into the wood, she felt
sure they would not see her.

Every part of her tensed with the need to race to
Diarmot's aid, but, despite the icy fear that she was
about to witness her husband's murder, Ilsa held
fast. Her sudden appearance might well serve to
distract the men attacking Diarmot, but it could
also dangerously distract her husband as well.
Worse, she could easily fall into the hands of Diarmot's foes and become just another weapon to use
against him. Yet, to do nothing seemed wrong.

Ilsa decided charging the group on Rose was
her only choice. She was good with her dagger,
very good, and felt sure she could take down at
least one man with it. Even Sigimor liked to brag
about her keen eye in throwing her dagger. She
would just have to hope Diarmot would be quick
to take advantage of the distraction she caused.

Just as she started to move, all hope of saving
Diarmot was lost. Ilsa pressed her fists against her
mouth to stop herself from screaming as Diarmot
disappeared off the edge. Her whole body shook
with the need to move, to run to the place where
Diarmot had fallen, but she stayed hidden, watching her husband's murderers through tear-filled
eyes.

Forcing herself to concentrate, Ilsa studied each
man as he stood there peering over the edge of
the ridge. As the men argued the wisdom of lingering long enough to make sure Diarmot was
dead, she fixed their images in her mind. She also
studied their horses, fighting to recall all the little

ways Tait had told her how to distinguish one horse from another beside their color and size. Ilsa was determined that these men would be hunted down and brought to justice.

After a futile attempt to catch Diarmot's horse Challenger, the men rode away, but Ilsa still did not move. She needed to be sure the men would not return, would not suddenly decide they did need to make sure they had killed Diarmot. Ilsa realized she was also terrified to see that Diarmot was truly dead, broken upon the rocks, and that this was not just some horrible nightmare.

When she finally moved, her whole body ached and she realized how tensely she had held herself as she had fought her need to run to her husband. She finally began to move, each step easier than the last, and went to get her horse. As she led Rose toward the ridge, she discovered she had lost all urge to run. She did not want to view her husband's body; she wanted to race back to Clachthrom and send someone else to do it. Ilsa took several deep breaths and beat down her fear and grief. This was her duty as Diarmot's wife.

The moment she reached the spot where she had last seen Diarmot, Challenger trotted up to her. "Och, laddie," she murmured as she stroked his neck and saw several wounds marring his gray-speckled hide, "ye gave it your best try, didnae ye?" She took a moment to make sure the wounds were shallow, then lightly tethered the gelding and her mare to the same stunted tree struggling to grow in the rocky soil. "Just be patient, laddie. We will soon get ye home and have your wounds tended to."

Her first glance over the edge made her heart

clench with grief and fear. Diarmot was sprawled facedown on a narrow ledge, but had not fallen all the way down the rocky slope to break upon the large stones at the bottom. Ilsa pulled the back of her skirts through her legs and secured them at her waist so they would not get in her way as she climbed down to Diarmot.

It proved a relatively easy climb, despite the steepness of the slope. Ilsa was surprised at least one of the men who had attacked Diarmot had not tried it, but also relieved. If there was even the smallest chance that Diarmot had survived the fall, those men would have cut his throat.

Ilsa knelt at Diarmot's head and clenched her hands into tight fists, afraid to touch him and feel the undeniable chill of death. He certainly looked dead, pale and covered with blood as he was. The blood from whatever head wound he had suffered showed clearly upon his fair hair and was smeared over the side of his wan face. It was no wonder the men thought him dead.

Ignoring how her hand shook, she reached out to touch him. Beneath her fingers his skin was warm. Her heart lodged in her throat. As she tried to edge her hand beneath him to search for a heartbeat, he groaned. Ilsa collapsed slightly, bending forward until her cheek rested against his hair, and she wept. It took her a few moments to compose herself.

"Diarmot?" she called softly as she wiped some of the blood from his face with her handkerchief. "Diarmot? Can ye hear me?"

"Ilsa," he whispered.

She waited, but he said no more and did not open his eyes. As carefully as she was able—terrified he would move and she would not be able to stop his fall from his precarious resting place—she checked him for broken bones. Ilsa finally decided he had miraculously escaped that fate and sat back on her heels to plan what to do next.

"I could ride back to Clachthrom and get help," she said and then looked around. "Nay, that will-nae serve. Ye move at all and ye could fetch up at the bottom of this rise. The rocks down there are monkillers for certain."

One glance up the rise revealed that the climb was not as easy a one as she had thought. Desperation and some skill at climbing had caused her to underestimate the challenge. Although she could get back up and down again, she had no idea of how she could get Diarmot up that steep rocky ridge. There was nothing to secure him to while she went to get help, either.

"Dinnae ye move, dinnae e'en twitch," she ordered her unconcious husband and then started to climb back up to the horses.

When she reached the top, she studied what tools she had at hand. They were few, but very useful. Diarmot clearly planned for every need when he rode out to tend to his lands.

Securing one end of a coil of rope to her horse, Ilsa gently lowered the rest over the ledge. She wrapped a blanket and her cloak around her neck, and climbed back down the hill. As soon as she reached Diarmot, she hurriedly tied the other end of the rope around him beneath his arms so that she no longer needed to worry that, at any moment, he could move and fall the rest of the way down the slope. She tied the blanket so that it covered his back and used her cloak to wrap his head for she knew that his journey back up the hill would be rough.

Although she ached to somehow direct his body up the rise, to try to prevent every bump he would suffer, she knew that was impossible. Not only did she need both hands to climb, but Rose would need to be coaxed to pull Diarmot up. Ilsa climbed down a few more feet to retrieve Diarmot's sword from where it had caught between two rocks and returned it to his scabbard. As best as she could, she pushed and pulled his limp body until he was seated, his blanket-covered back against the rocks.

Once back up with the horses, Ilsa took a moment to catch her breath, then grasped hold of Rose's reins. "Now, lass, step gently and let us pull Diarmot back to safety with as much care as we can."

When Ilsa judged Diarmot reaching the top, she moved to the edge to look over, then went back to Rose to lead her mare along another few steps. Ilsa had to go back and forth twice more before she was able to get a grip on Diarmot. Urging Rose to move and cursing Diarmot for being so big, Ilsa finally got her husband onto the ground several feet away from the edge. She untied the rope around him and Rose, tethered Rose and, after taking her cloak off Diarmot's head, sat down beside him.

"I cannae just leave ye here," she said, staring at Diarmot's chest and taking comfort in the way it rose and fell with each breath he took. "Ye are helpless and tisnae only the ones who wanted ye dead one needs to worry about. I could just set here and wait for someone to come looking for me." A quick glance up at the dark clouds on the horizon made her shake her head. "Nay, no time for that. I am going to have to think of some way to drag ye back to Clachthrom myself. Or," she frowned at the horses, looked back at Diarmot, and cursed. "Nay, I cannae get ye on the back of one of the horses." She patted his chest, holding her hand over his heart for a moment to savor its steady beat, then untied the blanket she had used to protect his back, spreading it out beneath him.

The slowly increasing wind and the chill it carried told Ilsa she could not rest long. She stumbled to her feet, spread her own blanket over Diarmot, and fetched the small axe from where it hung on his saddle. Ignoring the increasing damage to her hands, she cut what wood she needed to make a rough litter. She used the lacings from his boots to lash it together. After she had used the rope to attach the litter to her horse, she stood and looked down at Diarmot.

"I will confess, love, that, at this precise moment, I truly dinnae appreciate that fine strong body of yours," she muttered. "I have spent my whole life surrounded by braw oafs," she grumbled as she grasped the blanket he was on top of and pulled him toward the litter, inch by arm-wrenching inch, "but where are they now, I ask ye? Are they here to help me get your carcass on the litter? Och, nay. They are trotting o'er hill and dale looking for your enemies when your enemies are right here knocking ye off cliffs."

When the blanket suddenly came out from beneath Diarmot, Ilsa fell back and sat down on the ground, hard. Cursing softly, she rose to her knees, tossed that blanket over the litter, grabbed one of Diarmot's arms and pulled him toward the litter. Then she did the same by grasping one of his legs. She continued the arduous process until she had his body propped up on the edge of the litter.

"I think my arms are going to be several inches longer after this," she said, reaching across the litter to grab him by his doublet and pull. "If ye wake up after I get ye on this litter, I will be verra angry." She pulled again. "Twould be just like a mon, though. Let the woman do all the hard work whilst he rests his heavy bones, then wake and smile and ask what there is to eat."

"Ilsa."

By the time Ilsa recognized the voice which had called her name, she had already turned toward it, pulled out her dagger, and prepared to throw it. Sigimor was quicker, however. He caught her by the wrist and took her knife from her hand.

"Curse it, Sigimor, I could have stabbed ye," she said, accepting her knife back and sheathing it. "Ye shouldnae creep up on a person that way." She smiled weakly at Tait and Nanty as they moved closer.

"If ye dinnae wish to be surprised, ye should be quiet," said Sigimor, bending to lift Diarmot and set him down on the litter. "Ye didnae hear me because ye were too busy complaining about men. What happened?"

Irritated by how easily Sigimor had gotten Diarmot on the litter, Ilsa answered his questions somewhat succinctly. She was becoming far too aware of all her aches and pains. She did not wish to think of what Diarmot suffered. It was undoubtedly a blessing that he was unconcious.

"The men's horses stood over there," Ilsa pointed toward the spot where Diarmot's attackers had left their horses, "and rode north when they left." As soon as Tait went to study the ground for any clear markings, Ilsa looked at Sigimor and asked, "Why are ye here?"

"Returned to Clachthrom earlier than we thought we would and Tom told us the two of ye were out here alone, had been for quite some time. Decided we best see if all was weel. Now, let us get the laird home." He looked toward his brother. "Tait, ye follow that trail as far as ye can ere this storm starts. We may be lucky and they willnae go verra far, which will allow us to catch them up on the morrow."

"We will need Glenda from the village to help tend Diarmot's wounds," said Ilsa even as Sigimor picked her up and set her in her saddle.

"I will go after her," said Nanty.

Ilsa watched him and Tait mount their horses and ride off in different directions before looking back at Sigimor who was checking Challenger's wounds. "I think he will be fine, dinnae ye?"

"Aye. None of the wounds are deep." Sigimor patted the gelding's strong neck, then went to mount his own horse. He rode back and picked up Challenger's reins before looking Ilsa over carefully. "Can ye hold on til we get ye back to the keep?"

She obviously looked as weary as she felt, Ilsa mused, and nodded. "I will be fine. I will be eased by a hot bath and a rest. Tis Diarmot who suffers. He hasnae roused since he fell."

"The way Nanty was riding, that healing woman will be at the keep waiting for us. Your laird will be weel, Ilsa." He winked at her and then nudged his horse forward. "Ye did weel, lass. Verra weel indeed."

Even as she urged Rose to follow him, Ilsa felt herself blush with pleasure. Wife and mother she might be, but there was clearly enough of the child left within her heart to be thrilled by Sigimor's praise. She just hoped she had done well enough to keep Diarmot alive.

"Ye look much better, lass."

Ilsa smiled at Glenda and very cautiously approached Diarmot's bed. It had been difficult to put his care into the woman's hands and leave, but she had been given little choice. Gay and Fraser, aided by Sigimor's threatened assistance, had pulled her from Diarmot's side. After having a bath, enduring the tending of her many small wounds, and assuring the children she would be fine, Ilsa had been unable to fight the urge to rest. It took only three hours, however, for the sharp edge of her exhaustion to be dulled and then her fear for Diarmot had wakened her. She studied him, then looked across the bed at Glenda.

"Will he be all right?" she asked.

"Aye, m'lady," Glenda replied. "No bones broken and no sign that he is hurt inside. Bruised and battered, but little else."

"The blood upon his head," Ilsa began, lightly stroking his newly cleaned hair.

"A wee cut. Such wounds bleed freely and always look gruesome. I could feel no injury in the bone beneath it. Ye can set with him now, if ye wish."

"Are ye certain?" Ilsa asked, but did not hesitate to sit in the chair that had been set close by the bed. "I am no healer."

"Dinnae need to be. Just watch him for fever, for too much pain, for anything ye think worthy of concern. I have been given a fine wee room in the keep where I will stay for a few days until he wakes and looks certain to heal. If ye have need of me, I can be fetched right quick."

The door had barely finished shutting behind Glenda when it was opened again and Sigimor walked in. He sat at the end of the bed and frowned at Ilsa until she felt like squirming in her seat. If he ever planned to get married, he was going to have to do something about that stare, she thought crossly, for no woman would be able to endure it for a lifetime.

"Ye should have stayed abed longer, lass," he said. "This fool isnae going anywhere for a while."

"Sigimor," she said in a scolding tone, "Diarmot could be sorely injured."

"Nay, I dinnae think so. Glenda doesnae, either. Still, if ye must fret o'er him, may as weel do it here."

"So kind of ye. Has Tait returned?"

"Aye. Followed the men to a wee village. I have come to see if ye got a good look at the fools."

"I did. I made certain I looked hard and long at them and their horses." Ilsa proceeded to tell Sigimor everything she could remember about the men and their horses. "Do ye think catching them will be any help to us?"

"Mayhap, mayhap not. We have found so little in our searches that we were beginning to think there was no enemy, that tis nay but a plague of accidents, and the beating was only a robbery. This was an attempt at murder, nay question about it. The one doing this is clever, though, or we wouldnae be running in circles as we have or doubting if there is any enemy at all."

"Ah, and so these men may ken nay more than who pays them for their work."

"Exactly, but that someone could lead us to another someone and on it goes." He got up, kissed Ilsa on the top of her head, and started toward the door. "In truth, the who doesnae bother me near as much as the other thing."

"What other thing?"

"How this cursed enemy so often kens where ye or your laird will be."

Ilsa stared at the door he had shut behind him for a moment before slumping in her seat and cursing. Sigimor was right to worry about that. The concern had crossed her mind a time or two but, she was ashamed to admit, had not lingered very long. It was alarming to consider the matter even now, but she forced herself to do so. There was a traitor at Clachthrom. In fact, Diarmot's enemy could actually be one of the people right here in the keep. She shivered for it meant no place was completely safe.

"Ilsa! Jesu, the men! 'Ware the men!"

"Hush, loving," Ilsa said as she moved to sit on the edge of the bed and stroke his forehead. "Hush, ye are safe now." She started slightly when he opened his eyes to stare at her, but saw that they were not clear and alert, that he was not awake. "Ye are safe."

"Nay, the men," he said, then sighed and closed his eyes. "'Ware the men. Four of the bastards."

"Aye, there were, but they are gone now. Ye are safe abed at Clachthrom."

Diarmot continued to mutter about those four men for several minutes, but Ilsa finally calmed him. She knew he had not been completely con-

scious, but it was somewhat reassuring that he
called her name and still held the memory of this
latest attack. It would be nice if a few of those
memories he had lost now returned, she mused as
she retook her seat, but she would not hold out
any hope for that.

Gay slipped into the room carrying Finlay and
Cearnach. Right behind her came Fraser with a
tray of food and drink. Ilsa joined the two women
by the fireplace, feeding Finlay as Gay fed Cearnach,
and sharing a quiet meal with the women. It was
not long before Ilsa found herself unable to stop
yawning.

"Ye didnae rest enough, lass," said Fraser as she
took Finlay into her arms.

"Enough for now," replied Ilsa. "I just need to
see him through the night, or until he wakes and is
sensible."

"Cursing o'er his aches and pains and the need
to stay abed."

"Aye." Ilsa smiled, then kissed each of her sons
on their cheeks. "Howbeit, one good thing has
come of this. We now ken for certain that someone
wants Diarmot dead and we ken the four men who
tried to accomplish the deed this time. Tis a start."

Fraser nodded. "A path to follow instead of just
trying to find the cursed path."

"Quite so. I ken I can trust ye two to keep this
quiet and I feel ye should be told. Someone at
Clachthrom works for the enemy. As Sigimor said
earlier, what troubles him is how this enemy so
often kens where I or the laird will be. There is but
one way, isnae there."

"A spy," said Gay. "A cursed traitor. And we will
keep it quiet, ne'er fear, for we ken it could warn

the bastard. Howbeit, we will also keep ears and eyes open."

"Thank ye." Ilsa moved back to the bed, stared down at Diarmot, and gently brushed a lock of hair from his face.

"Dinnae fret, lass," Fraser said as she and Gay paused on the other side of the bed. "He will heal."

"Aye, I think he will." Ilsa smiled a little. "I just hope that, when he wakes, he hasnae forgotten me again."

CHAPTER TWELVE

Diarmot slowly opened his eyes. He felt as if he
had been trampled by a warhorse. In fact, he felt
very much as he had when he had finally regained
his senses after the near-fatal beating of a year ago.
There was one immediately evident difference this
time, however. He remembered everything.

Cautiously, he turned his head to look at the
woman sleeping at his side. She was fully dressed
and sprawled on top of the blankets. A few scratches
and a bruise marred her fair skin and the shadows
of exhaustion tinged the skin beneath her eyes. He
looked down at the delicate hand resting upon his
arm and saw a few more scratches and cuts, remnants of her valiant struggle to help save him. The
sight of her upon the ledge with him had not been
a dream, he thought. She must have found him and
run for help. All too aware of how he had treated
her since her abrupt arrival at Clachthrom, he had
to wonder why she had bothered.

His wife, he thought as he looked at her face
again, admiring the thick curl of her dark lashes.

Passionate little Ilsa Cameron, now MacEnroy. Diarmot could now recall most all that had passed between them before hard fists had pounded those memories into some dark hole in his mind. He had tried to resist her allure because of her passionate nature, only to revel in that same nature once he had lost the battle to hold her at a distance. Their farewell was clear in his mind, their lovemaking as well as his promises to be with her again.

How it must have hurt her when he did not return, did not even send word. He winced to think of all the ways he had hurt her since she had appeared in the church. Diarmot thought it was just his luck that, when he would like to suffer a loss of memory, he could not. It was no wonder she had spoken no words of love since their marriage. He would not be surprised to find he had succeeded in killing all the love in her heart.

Tentatively, he moved his other arm so that he could place his hand over hers. Despite the aches and pains he felt, he could still move and that was a relief. He was battered but not broken. That meant he would not be helpless for long. Soon he could renew his search for this shadowy enemy who had tried so hard to kill him and Ilsa.

But, what to do about Ilsa, he wondered as he watched her begin to awaken. Diarmot now understood why she stirred his blood, why he had often needed to remind himself not to trust her, and why, despite all his efforts to keep her tucked away in some remote corner of his life, he had become more and more entangled with her. His mind may have forgotten her, but not his heart. It was no wonder he had spent so much time confused and fustrated. When she finally opened her eyes, he smiled at her and tried not to be hurt by the wariness that darkened her expression.

"How do ye feel?" Ilsa asked, not sure what she should read into his almost tender expression.

"As if someone staked me to the ground and a score of heavy lads danced a reel on top of me," he replied.

Ilsa smiled briefly. "We didnae think anything was broken."

"Nay, I am fair sure I am still in one piece. Tis just a verra battered piece. How do ye feel?"

Before Ilsa could reply, there was a rap at the door. She quickly went to open it, both relieved and slightly disappointed when Geordie entered. Diarmot would no doubt welcome the man's assistance. Although a part of her wanted to stay and explore this apparent change in Diarmot's demeanor, another part wanted to flee from the chance that she would see more than there was and make a fool of herself. She decided to listen to her cowardly side and, murmuring a few vague remarks about needing a bath and a meal, she fled the room. The soft look in Diarmot's eyes had given her hope, but she had felt hope before only to have Diarmot crush it. It was far past time that she gained some sense of caution.

"Astonishing what a clean body, clean clothes, and a full belly can do for a mon," said Diarmot, leaning back against his plumped-up pillows while Geordie tidied the room.

Geordie nodded, paused to look at Diarmot, and scratched at the black-and-gray beard stubble upon his somewhat prominent chin. "What is a wonder is how a knock upon the head can bring back the memories stolen by a knock on the head."

"Aye." Diarmot grimaced. "Some, but nay all, nay yet. Still, I have some apologies to make, especially to my wife."

"Aye," Geordie agreed as he picked up the tray that had held Diarmot's meal and started out the door. "Tis a shame ye were near killed so soon after signing them papers and so lost a year with the lass."

Diarmot stared at the door as it shut behind Geordie. Although he had not been making any accusations, the man's words had abruptly stolen away the peace Diarmot had been feeling. He slumped against his pillows, suddenly all too aware of every one of his aches and pains. All of his doubts and fears had returned as well. He did not want to be suspicious of Ilsa, but that made him even more determined to be wary. Diarmot had trusted blindly before and it had cost him dearly. He would not do so again.

Ilsa groaned softly as she woke up and she became all too aware of how much her body ached. She was not as battered as Diarmot, but she had pushed herself hard, too hard, in her efforts to save him. Opening one eye and looking toward the window, she saw that it was morning. Once assured that Diarmot was awake, sensible, and not severely injured, she had bathed, eaten, and collapsed into bed. Exhaustion had demanded such a long sleep, nearly a full day's worth, but she still felt a pinch of guilt. If nothing else, the children would wonder where she was and, after seeing their father so badly injured, they needed all the comfort and reassurance she could offer.

As carefully as she could, she sat up. If the aching stiffness she suffered was any indication, she would be walking like a very old woman for the next few days. If she had known that one of her duties as his wife would be dragging her husband up a cliff, she would have married a much smaller man. Just as she managed to inch herself around until she was sitting on the side of the bed, Gay arrived, and Ilsa breathed a sigh of relief. Although she hated to admit it, she was going to need some help in getting dressed.

"Weel, ye look like ye were dragged through the brambles backwards, ye do," said Gay as she set a tray of bread, cheese, and cider down on the chest next to the bed. "Sore?"

"Aye." Ilsa winced as Gay helped her stand up. "Stiff, too."

"I am nay surprised. Did ye think ye were Sigimor that ye could haul that large husband of yours about and nay suffer for it?"

"I couldnae let him die."

"Nay, ye couldnae, though considering how he has treated ye, I doubt many women would have blamed ye."

Ilsa smiled faintly as Gay helped her walk to the bowl of water set near the fire so that she could wash herself. "There is at least one reason to keep the ill-tempered fool around." She caught Gay watching her intently as she rubbed her teeth clean with a dampened rag. "What troubles ye?"

"Ye like him in your bed, dinnae ye?"

"Och, aye. He makes me burn. The passion that brought us together to begin with is still there, still strong. I have told ye before, Gay, what was done to ye had naught to do with passion. Twas an attack, an assault. From what ye said the other day, I thought ye understood that now."

"Aye, I think I do begin to understand, most times. Soon it will be all the time. Diarmot's anger made me fear for you, yet ye went to his bed night after night and came to no harm. Even if he is bellowing, he ne'er strikes ye. Every time he touches ye, I can see no sign of him using his strength to hurt ye. Tis so different from all I kenned, I am slow to believe in what I see."

"Those men—"

"I dinnae mean just the men who hurt me. My father was cruel to my mother. My sisters' husbands are cruel to them. My father never hesitated to raise his fist to any of his children. I have spent my whole life seeing men being cruel, harsh, and brutal to their women. Then I came to stay with you and saw little of men and women together. Now I begin to see that what I had accepted as the way of things isnae completely true."

"Nay, it isnae," Ilsa replied as, with Gay's help, she shed her chemise and began to wash herself. "Far too common, but nay the only way. Ye must ken by now that my brothers would ne'er raise a hand against a lass. Neither would the MacEnroys. I believe we can trust Lady Gillyanne's word upon that."

"Aye. Watching her with her verra large husband was good for me, too. That laird is a hard mon, so strong he could snap her wee neck in a heartbeat, but she has nay fear of him. It didnae take me too long to see that he would rather cut out his own heart than hurt his wife." Gay smiled. "Oh, the mon is rough in manner and speech, so the care he has for his wife may nay be that clear to see, but tis there. And, once, I neared them as they were climbing the stairs to their bedchamber. He was fondling her rump like some rough mon at arms, but Lady Gilly was giggling. And then," Gay clasped her hands together, held them close against her breasts, and sighed.

"And then, what?" Ilsa pressed when Gay did not continue.

"And then he called her 'my joy,'" Gay replied in a soft voice. "Such little words, but the feeling behind them ran deep. Ye could hear it in his voice." She shook her head and began to help Ilsa dress again. "I realize I am indeed mending in heart and mind for I found myself wishing that, some day, a mon would speak so to me."

Ilsa was pleased beyond words that Gay was recovering so well from the brutality she had suffered, but she also felt a deep stab of envy. "That ye would wish for such a thing shows clearly that ye are healing." She sighed as Gay finished lacing her gown and gently urged her to sit down upon a stool. "And, ye are right, it would be a wondrous thing for any lass to hear."

"Ere he lost his memory, Sir Diarmot must have spoken to ye that way," Gay said as she brushed Ilsa's hair.

"He did. Such love words are naught but a dim memory now."

"Does he ne'er soften, ne'er speak sweet words?"

"Weel, I dinnae ken if ye could call what he says sweet. When passion grips him, he forgets he doesnae trust me, that he thinks me a liar and a possible threat. Aye, when his blood is running hot, he doesnae speak love words, but he does utter some verra earthy compliments. And, when sated, he rarely returns to his accusations, insults, or angry words. There is a truce between us for a wee while."

"That is a good thing, isnae it?" Gay asked as she finished braiding Ilsa's hair.

Ilsa cast a wry look at Gay as she slowly stood up. "Aye, but it could also be simply that he wants to feed his monly needs and suspects I might cry him nay if he spouts too much of his cynical, e'en insulting, nonsense. I threatened as much in the beginning."

"Possibly. Then, again, I think there are a few lasses about Clachthrom who would be willing to feed those needs if ye kicked him out of your bed."

"Not if they wish to celebrate their next saint's day," drawled Isla as she started out of her bedchamber.

Gay laughed briefly as she fell into step beside Ilsa who was headed toward the great hall. "Weel, I wouldnae scorn his passion. I ken some say the way to a mon's heart is through his stomach, but I suspect the path lies a wee bit lower."

Ilsa grinned, then shook her head. "With Diarmot the path lies buried in his memory. When he first awoke from his sleep this time there was a look in his eyes that made me think he remembered me, that his new injuries had knocked his memory back into its proper place this time. Then Geordie arrived."

"Ye shall have to see if the laird has recovered his memory when ye return to his bedside, then," said Gay as they entered the great hall and walked to their seats.

One of the serving women hurried over to set out bread, cheese, apples, and two tankards of goat's milk, so Ilsa said nothing in reply. Ilsa savored a thick slice of the bread covered with thick honey, and almost smiled at the growing look of impatience upon Gay's face. The girl was definitely recovering from her ordeal and the grief it had brought her.

"Ilsa, ye are going to return to your husband's bedside, arenae ye?" asked Gay.

"Oh, aye," replied Ilsa. "Tis a wife's duty to tend to her husband when he is ill or injured. I will return to sitting by the bed watching him sleep. Later."

"Later?"

"Aye, after I eat and after I see the children. Mayhap after I tend the herb garden, as weel."

"That could take all day."

"Indeed it could." She smiled when Gay laughed, but then grew serious. "I ken I havenae been all sweet smiles and acceptance, but I have done my best. I understand what troubles him and have been most forgiving despite his unkindness and insults. Weel, I have just saved the fool's miserable life, and if he cannae bring himself to trust me, to believe in me, after that, there isnae much else I can do. Tis clear I cannae turn cold on him, but I willnae struggle to prove myself any longer. As of today, I intend to walk my own path. No more fretting o'er how to get him to remember me, trust me, or care for me. When, and if, my husband sees the truth, then he and I can resume our marriage as it should be. I will still be his wife, share his bed, love his bairns, and tend his household, but I willnae keep trying to make him see the truth. I believe tis now his turn to prove himself to me."

"Ye remember everything?" asked Nanty as he sprawled in the chair next to Diarmot's bed.

"Aye." Diarmot sipped his ale trying to ignore the twinges of pain even that small movement caused him. "Weel, almost everything. Some parts are still lightly shrouded, but I am certain that, too, will pass."

"So, ye now ken that Ilsa is your wife."

"Weel, aye, I recall the handfasting now."

Diarmot also recalled the sweet promises they had made to each other. She had taken the bitterness away, soothed the pain, and given him joy. Then, after signing those papers giving her all rights as his wife, he had nearly been murdered. His besotted mind did not want to believe Ilsa had anything to do with the attack upon him, but he resolutely buried those doubts about her possible guilt. Someone wanted him dead and, at the moment, Ilsa really was the only one who would gain from that. Diarmot knew he could not allow himself to ignore that simply because she made his blood burn.

"What has ye scowling?" he asked Nanty when he became aware of his brother's dark stare.

"Ye still dinnae accept her," replied Nanty.

"Someone is trying to kill me, as this last attack proves, and she is the only reasonable suspect right now."

"If she wanted ye dead, then why did she risk her own life to save your worthless carcass?"

"What are ye talking about?"

"I thought ye said ye got your memory back."

"So, I did, or some it, but when I tumbled down that cliff I was knocked unconcious and didnae regain my senses until yesterday. When I first woke and saw her scratches and bruises, I thought she had helped to save me, but now I wonder why she would have been there at all. I cannae ken exactly what happened whilst I was senseless."

After studying Diarmot closely for a moment, Nanty related all Ilsa had done. It was astonishing to think the small, slender Ilsa had achieved so much. Nanty was right to argue that someone who wanted him dead would not work so hard to keep him alive. Diarmot fought the urge to immediately exonerate Ilsa of all guilt. She could be a pawn in some devious plan her family had devised. Without one of them there to prod her, Ilsa had been unable to leave him to die. As an explanation for her brave act, it was rather thin, but he struggled to cling to it.

The return of his memory was certainly a relief, despite the remaining gaps, but it was obviously going to cause him some difficulty in holding fast to a necessary wariness. He wanted to believe in Ilsa as he had a year ago, wanted to return to that time of joy and peace, but his life was at stake. The only people he could allow himself to trust completely were his family.

"Ilsa didnae look badly injured," Diarmot said when Nanty completed his tale.

"Weel, she didnae fall off a cliff, did she?" replied Nanty. "As ye saw for yourself, she is bruised, scratched, and suffers a few aches and pains, but naught else. She slept from the time ye woke right through til this morning. There is a stiffness to her movements, but she is up and working again."

"She hasnae come here and tis late in the afternoon."

"Mayhap she needs a wee rest from being insulted and accused by her own husband."

"Curse it, Nanty, someone is trying to kill me," snapped Diarmot. He tried to place his empty tankard upon the table by his bed, but the movement needed proved too painful. "Thank ye," he muttered when Nanty moved to take the tankard and set it aside. "Ye refuse to admit that Ilsa and her kin have the most to gain from my death, yet ye offer me no other suspects," he said as Nanty retook his seat.

Nanty sighed, stretched out his legs, and rested his feet on Diarmot's bed. "Ere Angus had to return to Alddabhach, we tried to find someone who might think his claim to Clachthrom was stronger than yours, but there is no one. This has been MacEnroy land for too long and we are the last of this branch of the MacEnroy tree, wee thing that it is. Sigimor, Tait, and I then wondered if it was one of your late wife's lovers, someone who blames ye for her death, believes the rumors."

"She died because she took a potion to rid herself of a bairn. She succeeded in that sin, but the bleeding couldnae be stopped. Ilsa told her brothers that when they heard the rumor that I had killed her. Gillyanne and Connor heard the tale, too. Twas nay my bairn," Diarmot reassured his shocked brother. "I hadnae touched her for near to a year."

"Ye hid that truth from us, didnae ye."

"Aye. Nay sure why. The whole world and its mother kenned she was a whore." He grimaced. "Mayhap twas because she was dead and there was no reason to blacken her name any further."

"Nay, but that kindness has kept the rumors alive and may have led someone to believe ye killed her, poisoned her. Mayhap the one whose child she was carrying. Mayhap he kenned there was a bairn and blames ye for that death as weel. I dinnae believe tis anyone here at Clachthrom. We certainly havenae found any suspects. Tait and Sigimor are hunting the men who attacked ye this time. They might tell us something useful."

Diarmot sighed and slumped against the pillows piled up behind his back. "Anabelle couldnae e'en guess who fathered the bairn. It could have been any one of a dozen men from a dozen places."

"The truth doesnae have to matter. Tis only what some fool believes that must be considered. If some mon was enthralled with her, thought her his love and he hers, he could seek to avenge the deaths of his love and their bairn."

"I cannae believe any mon could be so witless. Anabelle shed the sweet guise she wore to catch me in her net within a month after we were wed. The first time I caught her with another, she ceased to play that game. Tis why I cannae be certain wee Alice is my bairn. Anabelle was faithful to no mon and ne'er pretended to be."

"Weel, it makes more sense to me that some fool mon was bewitched by Anabelle and seeks to make ye pay for her death, than that tis Ilsa and her kin trying to kill ye for greed."

"Until I discover who is my enemy everyone save my own family is suspect. At this moment, all that makes Ilsa a perfect suspect cannae be ignored. Neither can I ignore the fact that, after putting my mark to papers giving her such generous rights, within hours after leaving her I was nearly murdered. Give me something that looks more suspicious than that and I will readily consider it, if only for the sake of my sons."

"As ye wish," said Nanty. "I still hold to my right to believe ye wrong about Ilsa, but I will continue to keep a close eye upon everyone. Shall I spy upon Odo as weel? He is only five, but he is a clever lad. Can be devious, too."

"How verra amusing ye are. If I wasnae near crippled, I would show ye how verra amusing I think ye until ye are naught but a puddle in the mud." Diarmot heard his stomach rumble and frowned at the door. "Isnae it time for a meal?"

"Do ye expect your wee wife to tend to ye?"

"Why shouldnae she? She is my wife. Tis her duty to see to her husband's needs."

"Tis glad I am Gillyanne isnae here to hear ye say that." Nanty gave an exaggerated shudder, but then grew serious. "Ye expect a lot of a woman ye treat so poorly."

"She is the one who came here demanding a proper marriage." Nanty was making him feel guilty and unkind and it was very annoying. "I may nay trust her, but she still has her uses."

"I am surprised ye let her into your bed. Arenae ye afraid she will work her evil on ye?"

"She cannae do much harm to me when she is naked and spread out beneath me."

Even as he uttered the words, Diarmot regretted them. He regretted them even more when he heard the door to his bedchamber open. Instinct told him it was Ilsa. When he looked toward the door, he inwardly winced. She was holding a tray filled with food and drink. The look upon her face told him she would thoroughly enjoy emptying the whole lot over his head. Diarmot tensed as she strode toward the bed, then inwardly breathed a sigh of relief when all she did was set the tray down on the table by his bed with enough force to rattle the plates. He hoped he did not look as uncomfortable as he felt as he met her glare.

"I could always try to rip your throat out with my teeth," she drawled and decided the look of shock on his face was almost enough to ease the sting of his crude words. "Eat. Ye need your strength."

"Where are ye going?" he demanded when she turned to leave.

"To eat in the great hall, after which I shall bid the bairns good sleep, and then I shall seek my bed."

"Your bed is here."

"Nay. Tis in the room across the hall."

"A wife's place is in her husband's bed. Ye will move your things back in here."

Ilsa struggled with the urge to pummel the man, sternly telling herself he was bruised enough already. She briefly considered refusing to share his bed, then accepted the sad fact that it would gain her nothing. He would probably just see it as another trick or proof of the basic perfidy of women. The bed remained their only neutral ground, their mutual passion the only source of any lessening of his anger and mistrust. She could not give it up, for then there would be no chance of changing his mind and heart. In truth, she doubted she could turn aside from the desire that flared between them for very long anyway.

"I will return here when ye have healed," she said. His response was a soft grunt and the faintly smug look that crossed his face made her clench her fists. "After all, since I have a husband," she said too sweetly as she headed out of the room, "twould be foolish not to avail myself of the one thing he is good at."

Diarmot gaped at the door as it shut behind her, then looked at Nanty. "Did ye hear the impertinent wench?"

"Aye. At least she said ye were good at it," Nanty said in a choked voice; then he began to laugh.

It was evident he had no true ally in Nanty, Diarmot thought crossly. At least not in his suspicions about Ilsa. He gave the chuckling Nanty a hard glare and turned his attention to his meal. The first thing he would do when he felt better was make love to his impertinent wife until her eyes rolled back in her head. The second thing he would do was pound his cackling brother into the mud.

CHAPTER THIRTEEN

"Weel, that was an unpleasant way to spend the morning," Diarmot muttered as he slouched in his chair at the head table in the great hall, then took a deep drink of ale.

"Hangings always are," said Sigimor as he slathered honey on a thick chunk of bread.

Diarmot could not see any sign of upset or distaste in Sigimor. Nanty and Tait at least looked a little pale. It had taken all of Diarmot's strength not to empty his belly right in front of the gallows. Sigimor was as hard as Connor, Diarmot decided. Recalling that the man had been left laird at but twenty with a horde of younger siblings and cousins to raise, he supposed it was understandable.

Sigimor, Tait, and Nanty, along with a few Clachthrom men, had found his assailants two days after the attack. Two men had survived the ensuing battle and had been brought back to Clachthrom where they had sat in the dungeons for another two days until Diarmot had been recovered enough to judge them. Although the men had had little to say that was useful, they had confessed to being the men who had attacked him in Muirladen as well. The man they had dealt with, the one Diarmot now recalled having spoken derisively about the laird having his face in the mud then kicking him, was always masked.

And then he had sentenced them to hang. He sighed and took another hearty drink of ale. Diarmot knew he had had no choice. The men had tried to kill him twice. They had not cared who he was or why someone wanted him dead, only that the money was good. Such men undoubtedly had blood on their hands. Such men would also not be reformed simply because they had been caught and had briefly faced the consequences of their actions. Diarmot knew he had done the right thing, that a laird had to be strong enough to enact the law, but he much preferred dispatching his enemies in battle with a sword.

"Ye had no choice," said Sigimor. "They were willing to kill ye just to gain a few coins for ale and whores."

The fact that Sigimor had guessed at his unease did not please Diarmot at all. "I ken it. It certainly would have made me look a weak fool if I hadnae. Tis a gruesome way to send a mon to his death, however. I dinnae think we e'er had one at Deilcladach."

"Tis that peaceful there, is it?"

"Nay, of course not. We had enemies, but they died by sword or dagger. And, few of those once there was a truce between us, the Goudies, and the Dalglish clan. I suppose that, after years of feuding, people were too busy simply trying to survive to break laws. We didnae have anything worth stealing for many years, either."

"Weel, ye are blooded now. I was blooded when I was two and twenty. Had to hang one of my own cousins."

"Jesu, what had he done?"

"Enough to get him hanged a dozen times. The lad was ne'er right. Had a cold viciousness in him that we ignored for too long. He had a liking for rape. Tried banishing him, but he slipped back onto the lands, though we didnae ken it for a long while. He had decided rape wasnae enough. He still did it, but then murdered the poor lass when he was done with her. He had killed four lasses and was about to kill his fifth when we caught him. Those deaths weigh heavy on my heart for I made the decision to banish the lad the first time for all the wrong reasons. Couldnae abide the thought of hanging a kinsmon. That weakness allowed him to put four lasses in their graves, and they didnae die easy. I didnae hesitate when we finally caught him."

Despite the quiet horror of the tale, Diarmot almost smiled. He had just been lessoned by Sigimor. Diarmot had the strongest feeling the man probably had dozens of such tales, all true, and all with a message or a moral. Considering the fact that he was nearly of an age with him, Diarmot supposed he ought to be irritated, but he was not. It was quite possible he was coming to like Ilsa's brothers. A little voice in his head warned him to be cautious, but it was beginning to lose its ability to sway him. The more he came to know these men and all he could recall of them from a year ago, told him they would not be a part of any devious scheme. The problem was that no other suspect was coming to light. Nor could he yet recall everything that had happened between him and Ilsa.

"Ye dinnae need fear that madness is in the blood," Sigimor continued. "We kept a close watch on the rest of the lad's family and there wasnae a glimmer of it. He had a different mother than the rest and we decided it might have come from her. She did try to kill the blacksmith once."

"And Aunt Elizabeth," said Tait. "Chased her through the village trying to take her head off with an axe."

"Aye, true enough. She drowned when she attacked poor cousin David."

"She drowned?" asked Diarmot, unable to envision the way that might have occurred.

"Aye," replied Sigimor. "She was running after him, knife in hand, and he jumped into the loch to get away. She jumped in after him. He could swim. She couldnae."

Diarmot wondered how the man could speak of such chilling events with what could only be called a touch of humor. "Aye, I would say the madness came from his mother." He sighed, all amusement fleeing. "About all we have learned from this wretched business, however, is that I really do have an enemy. A mon who hides his face and pays others to try and kill me. He doesnae always come round to watch or make sure tis done right, either."

"Ye still cannae recall why ye were in Dubheidland?"

"Nay, that part remains mostly shadowed. Howbeit, since some of it has returned, I must assume the rest will soon follow. I obviously found some clue or had some suspicion which drew me there.

Tis a pity I didnae think to confide in anyone. I fear I got some notion into my head and simply acted on it."

"And took none of your men with ye. Where could ye have gotten the idea?"

"I dinnae ken. That, too, will undoubtedly come to me in time. I have only had my memory back for four days now, or what there is of it. I cannae think those memories still trapped just beyond my reach willnae break free soon, too. The healing has begun, so it must surely continue."

Sigimor nodded. "That makes sense. Tait, Nanty, and I were going to go to Dubheidland and find out if anything has been discovered, nay matter how small. We will wait here another week now. If ye do remember more, it may save us from riding about blindly whilst there. I grow weary of that game."

Diarmot suddenly tensed. "I think I had been reading my wife's journals. The memory isnae clear to me as to when I was doing it, but since one of those still-shadowed memories comes right after this clearer one, it may be that I found some clue there. Jesu, but I dinnae wish to look at them again." He held up his hand to halt the words Sigimor was ready to utter. "I must. I ken it."

"Are they that bad?" asked Nanty.

"There arenae pleasant reading," replied Diarmot. "Tis probably for the best that I didnae discover them until after I had suffered through several accidents that, e'en then, I thought might be attempts upon my life. Despite kenning they might hold important clues, the urge to hurl them into the fire was almost too strong to resist." He finished his ale and stood up. "I believe I will begin now. Viewing a hanging has probably put me in the proper mood." He strode out of the great hall and hurried toward his ledger room where he kept the journals.

"Tait?" Sigimor said as soon as Diarmot was gone.

"Aye?" Tait glanced at his brother, then returned his attention to spreading a thick layer of dark honey on a a piece of bread.

"If I e'er cast my eye upon a woman who seems to be e'en faintly akin to Lady Anabelle, I give ye leave to beat some sense into me."

"Twill be my pleasure."

Diarmot groaned, slumped in his seat, and rubbed his hands over his face. He had been studying Anabelle's writings for most of the day, taking a respite only when something else required his attention. Although reluctant to do so, he had returned to the chore soon after the evening meal. Now he felt only sickened by it all, sickened by Anabelle, and sickened by the fact that he could have been so blinded by her beauty when he married her. Worse, it was beginning to look as if he had suffered for naught for he had found nothing.

He had realized a few things about his late wife that he had not seen in the first readings he had done, when his mind and his heart had been clouded by anger and hurt. Anabelle had loathed men. She had seen them as sad, pathetic brutes who could be led around by their privates. The way she wrote about the far-too-numerous sexual romps she had indulged in made them all sound like some battle with her as the victor. In some ways, she sounded akin to the worst of callous seducers, men who used women and found satisfaction in the number of women they could lure into their beds, more than in the women themselves.

The reason he had gone to Dubhleidland, to that area, was in these writings. Diarmot could not shake the feeling despite the fact that all he had gained so far was a painful headache. That was not quite true, he mused, as he stared at the journals. He had discovered one thing, something that mattered only to him. It did not hurt anymore.

Anabelle was gone from his heart, her grip on his mind and pride broken. When he read her words, it was as if he read about a stranger. In most ways, she had been a stranger to him. The Anabelle he had married had been only a chimera created by a mind besotted by her beauty and drunk with lust. The scorn she had heaped upon him in her writings no longer stung for he realized it was no more than the scorn she felt for all men. She had not known him any better than he had known her.

A soft rap at the door distracted him and he bade the person to enter. His eyes widened slightly when Ilsa slipped into the room. In the four days since she had overheard his crude words to Nanty he had seen little of her. Diarmot knew he should apologize for that remark, yet he hesitated. He recalled a great deal about their time together a year ago, but still fought against giving her the trust he had given her then. The attack in Muirladen had beaten it out of him and rereading Anabelle's journals had sharply reminded him that his judgment was not always sound.

As she approached him, he knew he was willing to accept one thing about their relationship without hesitation or question, and that was the passion they shared. Now that they had both apparently healed from their ordeal at the ridge, he wanted her back in his arms. Since Ilsa had sought him out, perhaps she was ready to return to his bed. He had missed her at his side and, after reading Anabelle's dark, sordid writings, Diarmot realized he hungered for the clean honesty of Ilsa's passion.

"What has kept ye hiding in here all the day and into the night?" she asked as she reached his side.

"My late wife's writings," he replied. "I cannae shake the feeling that something I read here sent me hieing off to Dubheidland or someplace near there."

"Ye cannae recall the reason yet?"

"Nay, that memory hasnae returned yet. Tis there, but tis just out of my reach." He watched her pale slightly as she read from the journal open on the table. "Ye dinnae wish to see that filth," he said and closed the book.

Ilsa looked at Diarmot as she pushed aside her shock over what she had just read. "Ye didnae find anything?"

He shook his head, curled his arm around her waist, and tugged her down onto his lap. "Naught."

"Should I read them for ye?"

"They arenae easy reading, Ilsa, and are filled with the same sort of sordid rantings ye just read."

"Nay doubt, but I believe I can endure it. I didnae ken Anabelle, have only heard about her. I was ne'er wronged by her so I can read what she wrote without hurt, anger, or any other emotion. Aye, I suspect I will be shocked, but that will fade. I am also a woman and may see something ye, as a mon, cannae see."

"Words are read the same way by men and women."

"Aye, but the meaning of them can differ, each one who reads the words understanding something different from them. Believe me when I tell ye that a woman can write or say something that will mean one thing to a mon and something verra different to a woman. Howbeit, if ye would rather I didnae—"

"Nay, read them. Ye are right. E'en if there arenae any odd messages that I didnae catch, I am still missing whate'er I saw there before. Ye might find that answer."

"Are these all of them?"

"Nay, there are more, but they are from years past. The woman spent a small fortune on these books to record her rantings." He kissed her ear, felt her shiver, and nearly grinned.

"Did ye read those, too?" She leaned back against him and murmured her pleasure as he nibbled her ear.

"Aye, when I first found them, but I felt those from later years, from our marriage, held the answers I seek."

"Mayhap, but it may weel be that there was something in those earlier ones that at least made ye curious."

Diarmot softly cursed, set her on her feet, and moved to fetch those early journals from the shelf where he had stored them. He briefly thought he should read them, that he might find the answer he sought and save Ilsa from having to read Anabelle's rantings, then shook his head. Ilsa was right in saying a woman, one who had never met or been wronged by Anabelle, could read the journals with the cold eye of a stranger. He set the older journals on top of the newer ones, picked up the whole pile, and looked at Ilsa.

"Is this why ye sought me out?" he asked, hoping it was not.

"Nay, I came to tell ye that I have moved back into your bedchamber."

She sounded almost martyred, he mused, and nearly grinned. "Our bedchamber. Good, tis where ye belong," he said as he turned and headed out of the room. "Snuff the candles and bank the fire ere ye leave."

Ilsa wished he had not taken the journals because she would like to toss a few at his head. She sighed and began to do as he had ordered. After she had sulked for a day or two, she had sternly lectured herself. Diarmot had begun to remember their time together. Wariness still lingered for there had been two attempts to kill him since their handfasting, and her mind could accept that as reasonable even as her heart ached. That wariness would never be banished if she avoided him, however. He remembered that they had handfasted, remembered they had been lovers, and it was up to her to try to make him remember why. She could not be certain he had loved her, but she knew she had made him happy, that he had felt at peace with her. It would be impossible to remind him of all that from across the hall.

The man was a basketful of contradictions, she decided as she headed toward their bedchamber. He held her at some distance, yet obviously wanted her in his bed. He wondered if she might be a threat to him, yet held her close at night and accepted her as mother to his children. He was suspicious of her brothers, yet let them run tame over Clachthrom and appeared to accept their hunt for his enemy as genuine. As she opened the door to their bedchamber, Ilsa wondered if the man was aware of just how confused he was, then she stepped into the bedchamber and lost all track of her thoughts.

Diarmot was sprawled upon their bed wearing nothing more than a smile. She could see the lingering bruises and small, mostly healed, wounds he had suffered. She could also see the stout proof that he was healed enough to feel very randy indeed. Ilsa closed the bedchamber door and walked over to the bed.

"Impressive," she murmured.

"Thank ye, m'dear." He scowled when she turned and walked away. "Where are ye going?"

"Did ye expect me to start tearing my clothes off in a fit of unbridled lust?" she asked as she stepped behind the privacy screen and finally gave in to the urge to grin.

"That would have been satisfactory."

"For ye, nay doubt, but I am rather fond of this gown. And I have seen it all before, after all."

She struggled to muffle her giggle when he grunted in response to that idle disregard of his charms. In the smile he had given her as she had entered their bedchamber Ilsa had seen the ghost of the playful Diarmot she had once known. That made her feel even more certain of her decision. This time there might be only a glimpse of the man she had loved, only a brief return to the joy she had once known, but she was sure there would be other times, that little by little the Diarmot who had so beguiled her a year ago would return.

Ilsa hurried to shed her clothes and wash. She brushed out her hair then donned the lace-trimmed night shift she had made from the fine blue linen she had bought. The way Diarmot watched her as she walked back toward the bed told her she had not been foolishly vain to think it flattered her.

"Verra fetching," Diarmot murmured. "In truth, there is only one thing I might suggest to make it look even more fetching."

"Oh? And what would that be?"

"Drop it on the floor."

She could tell by the challenge in his gaze that he did not think she would do it. A pinch of the modesty she could not fully shake free of caused her to hesitate, but she pushed it aside. This would be their first night together since his memory had begun to return. It was the perfect time to be bold. Ilsa gave him a faint smile and slowly removed her night shift. Still smiling, she held it out at arm's length and dropped it.

"There. Ye think it looks more fetching now?" She noticed he was not looking at her night shift.

"Oh, aye." Diarmot reached for her and cursed softly when she eluded his grasp. "Now where are ye going?"

"Nay to the great hall to pour wine, that is for certain. I thought I had best bank the fire."

"Tis fine. Come back here and tend to this fire instead."

Ilsa moved to the foot of the bed, climbed up on it, and began to crawl toward him on her hands and knees. "There is a fire here that needs banking, is there?" She reached his legs and moved up them slowly, kissing and stroking every strong inch of them with her hands, her lips, and her tongue.

"Och, aye, and tis getting hotter every minute."

Diarmot wondered if she had any idea of how sensuous she was. The way she had crawled up the bed, every move of her strong, slender body holding invitation and promise had been a pleasure to watch. The look upon her face, the tempting curve of her smile, and the heat in her gaze had made his passion soar. The way her long, bright hair had swirled around her had simply been the coup de grace. She enthralled him and he knew that should worry him, but it did not. Instead he sprawled there, savoring the feel of her small hands, the heat of her mouth and tongue, and the silken caress of her hair as she inched her way up his legs.

His whole body shook with pleasure when she began to use that clever tongue on his manhood. When the moist heat of her mouth enclosed him, he propped himself up on one elbow, and brushed her hair aside with his other hand, needing to see as well as feel her gift him with this delight. Despite all his efforts to cling to some control, to make it last, it was not long before he knew he needed to be inside her. He sat up, grasped her under her arms, and set her astride him. Although he had done nothing to prepare her, he felt only the hot damp of welcome as he entered her, and he groaned at this proof that she could be so stirred by pleasuring him. She moved upon him with a natural skill and a sweet greed that made him tremble, and he gave himself over completely to their passion.

Ilsa roused herself from a sated doze and felt

the first tickle of embarrassment. Returning from the delicious oblivion Diarmot could send her to and finding herself sprawled in his arms was not so strange. It was recalling how she had behaved that made her uneasy. Such wanton behavior might not be the best way to win a wary man's trust, especially when that man had been wed to a woman like Anabelle. She eased herself off him, glanced at his face, and caught him frowning at her.

"Ye do that verra weel," he muttered.

Sometimes, Ilsa mused, there was no joy in being right. "What? Moving?"

"Ye ken what I mean."

"Aye, I am afraid I do." She leaned over him, picked up her night shift from the floor, and yanked it on over her head. "Ye want to ken how many men I have done that to. I couldnae possibly have simply thought to do to ye what ye have done to me. Och, nay. That would be too simple. There must be more to it. Nay, it couldnae be that there isnae any great trick to it that I can see, either." She got out of bed and went behind the privacy screen. "Just stroke, kiss, lick, and stick it in your mouth. As long as ye dinnae scream in pain or start bleeding, tis being done right."

Diarmot had to choke back a laugh. Ilsa was so angry he doubted she realized half of what she was saying, would probably shock herself if she did. Now she was just muttering. He suspected it was a good thing he could not understand what she was saying now for it would either insult him or make him laugh. She had a right to be angry for his remarks had been both unkind and unwarranted, but she was a delight to listen to when she was ranting. All his amusement faded when she came out from behind the privacy screen and walked toward the door.

"Where are ye going?" he demanded, thinking he was getting sick of asking that.

"To the room across the hall," she replied. "I willnae stay here—"

She screeched softly when Diarmot was suddenly there by her side. He picked her up and carried her back to the bed. Before she could protest, he had them back in bed with her tucked up against him and was pulling the covers over them.

"This is where ye belong," he said, adjusting her a little in his arms so that her firm little backside was nestled comfortably against his groin.

"Ye are a verra confusing mon," she said. "All welcome one moment, then a strong right to the jaw."

"If it confuses ye, try to imagine how it all seems to me at times."

Ilsa winced slightly, recognizing the truth of his words. Diarmot was clever enough to know he was behaving in a very odd way at times, being contradictory in his feelings, words, and actions. To have such large gaps in one's memory had to leave him feeling lost, uncertain. She suspected having some of the memories return, but not being able to grab hold of all of them was not much better. It did not excuse his unkind words, but she also suspected that Diarmot openly admitting to his own turmoil was as close to an apology as he would get.

"Are ye trying to tug at my sympathy?" she asked.

"Will that get ye to take your shift off?"

"Nay. If I cannae go away and sulk, then I am keeping my shift on."

"Fair enough." Diarmot kissed the top of her

head and decided not to argue. Ilsa slept soundly.
He would just wait until she fell asleep and take
her shift off later.

"Poison?"

Margaret glared at the man. "Aye, poison."

"What am I to do with this?"

She bit back the urge to tell him to drink it and
paced the small cottage in an attempt to calm herself. Her gaze passed over the tiny bed where she
had just serviced the oaf, the remembered feel of
the straw mattress and rough woolen blanket still
making her itch. She wanted to leave, to return to
her cousin's home and wash the stink of the man
from her body. After taking a few breaths to quiet
the rage that was becoming harder to control, she
faced the man again.

"Put it in her drink or her food."

"I dinnae serve her."

"Wait until she has been busy at some chore for
several hours, then bring her some wine and, mayhap, something to eat. Tell her her husband sent
it."

"That may work. Why her? I thought ye wished
the laird dead."

"I do, but that isnae being accomplished, is it?
Mayhap, if another of his wives dies, he will be
seen as the murderer he is and will be hanged. It
willnae be as satisfying, but twill serve. If not, he
will be a widower again, and I can marry him.
Then I will be able to deal with this myself as I had
planned to ere that red-haired slut interfered."

"I am nay sure ye will be able to. They say his
memory begins to return."

"Then ye had best succeed at this so that I can get close to the laird again. We dinnae want him wandering back to Muirladen, do we. If he does regain all of his memory, ye and I could find ourselves in a great deal of trouble."

CHAPTER FOURTEEN

Ilsa grimaced and rubbed at the ache in her back. She had been studying Anabelle's journals since right after breaking her fast and it was now late in the afternoon. A brief time spent with the children as she nursed Cearnach had been her only respite. She was tired and somewhat disheartened. She also felt battered by all she had read.

Fraser had said Anabelle was a troubled woman. That was far too gentle a word for the woman she had found in these journals. If there had been a time in Anabelle's life when she had not been filled with anger and hatred, it had been before she had begun her journals. Anabelle had scorned and ridiculed everyone.

Not quite everyone, Ilsa thought, as she glanced over the entry she had just read. Whoever her Precious Love was had been spared for most of the time. Every now and then Precious Love had obviously misbehaved and Anabelle had been scathing in her denunciation, ranting about betrayals and a need for vengeance. Then Precious Love would be forgiven, even though, in Ilsa's opinion, that had not been a very good thing for Precious Love. Anabelle's love appeared to have been a dominating, all-consuming thing. It had demanded complete subjugation, blind adoration, and unwavering obedience. Ilsa had to wonder about the sanity of any person who would endure that for so many years.

She gasped and sat up straight, feeling the thrill of discovery. Precious Love was the only person mentioned with any consistency through the years. Others, such as Diarmot and Fraser, were mentioned more often than others, but none had the constancy of Precious Love. That annoying name had been sprinkled throughout every journal. Whoever it was had obviously been an integral part of Anabelle's life.

Just as she started to glance through the journals to confirm her observation, Ilsa was distracted by Geordie's entrance into her solar. It annoyed her a little that he had not asked permission to come in, but she scolded herself for that unwarranted irritation. She had left the door open partway so that she could hear if any of the children cried or called to her. Geordie had obviously thought that meant anyone was free to come and go. She smiled at him as he set a tray of wine and sweetened oatcakes down on her table.

"This was kind of ye," she said.

"Oh, it wasnae my idea, m'lady," Geordie said. "The laird thought ye may want some." He glanced at the journals. "Ye have been working all day on these books. Have ye found anything important?"

"Nay," she replied and wondered why she felt the need to lie to the man. "I begin to think my husband is right, that something else had compelled him to come to Dubheidland."

"So, ye will be putting them aside soon, aye?"

"Aye." She sipped at her wine, finding it a little bitter, but decided it would probably go well with the sweetened oatcakes. "I believe I might suggest the burning of them as it wouldnae be good for Alice to stumble upon them someday."

She exchanged a few idle pleasantries with Geordie before he finally left, then frowned. She had lied to him and had no idea why she had felt it necessary to do so. Diarmot apparently trusted the man and it was no secret that she was digging her way through Lady Anabelle's journals for some clues about Diarmot's enemy. Yet, the moment he had asked if she had found anything, she had grown wary and secretive. Mayhap Diarmot's suspicious nature was infecting her, she mused as she returned to her reading.

A glass of wine and several oatcakes later, Ilsa had her suspicions confirmed. Precious Love had been a part of Anabelle's life from the beginning. The meeting had occured while Anabelle was fostered with the woman she referred to only as L.O. Ilsa judged Anabelle's age to have been about fourteen at that time, yet the girl had obviously already had several lovers by then. The first man had not been welcome, of that Ilsa had no doubt. It was possible that had been when Anabelle had begun to hate men.

Except for Precious Love, Ilsa corrected herself as she poured herself another glass of wine. Yet, if Anabelle loved this person why had she not married him? Why had she been so consistently unfaithful? It also appeared that Anabelle and Precious Love had talked about those other men, scorned and ridiculed them together. Ilsa found that beyond strange.

Not sure why she did so, Ilsa sought out entries concerning private moments with Precious Love and lined up all the journals, each opened to such an entry. Sipping at her wine, she read each, from the first to the last. The way Anabelle wrote of her lovemaking with Precious Love differed in many ways from her writings about all her other lovers. The tone lacked the usual scorn, although there was the hint of triumph, so he may have been a reluctant lover at times. Precious Love had soft hands, soft skin, and smelled sweet. Not once did Anabelle describe Precious Love's genitals, something the woman had delighted in doing when writing about every other lover. Precious Love was smaller than Anabelle and had beautiful hair.

Ilsa cursed, finished her wine, and carefully reread every entry. She was so certain she had just discovered something very important her heart was pounding. Soft hands, soft skin, smelled sweet, small, beautiful hair, a lovely voice, and dainty feet. Ilsa made careful note of each description, wrote them down, and read her list twice. Then she very carefully added one line of praise contained in a tale about a brief tryst: Precious Love kens how to touch a woman, kens a woman's needs and desires as no mon e'er could.

"Curse it, how did I miss that?" she muttered, and stood up, eager to find Diarmot.

Sweat broke out all over her body and Ilsa clutched the edge of the table. She did not feel well and was rapidly feeling worse. Certain she was about to be ill and not wanting to ruin the journals, she moved away from the table. The pain that gripped her insides was so intense she screamed and collapsed to her knees. She emptied her belly on the floor and—for a moment—felt better, then the pain struck again. Clutching her belly, she tried to stand, but when it proved impossible, began to crawl toward the door. She could hear someone rapidly approaching and tried to call out only to be sick again. Ilsa managed to move away from that foul mess and then curled up, huddled in a ball in a vain attempt to ease the pain tearing away at her insides.

"Ilsa!"

"Something is wrong," she said when Fraser and Gay knelt by her, Fraser cradling her in her strong arms.

"Tis obvious ye are verra ill," said Fraser. "We must get ye to bed." She cursed when Ilsa began to writhe.

"Jesu, tis an agony," Ilsa cried out. "Get it out!"

Diarmot entered the room only a step behind Sigimor, Tait and Nanty right behind him. He watched Ilsa tear free of Fraser's hold just as Sigimor reached for her. She was violently ill and Diarmot felt his belly clench in sympathy. Sigimor picked her up and started toward the door.

"The wine," she moaned.

"What about the wine?" asked Diarmot.

"Tis bitter. Too bitter." She started to writhe again and Sigimor tightened his hold on her. "The wine is burning me!"

"Fraser, put that wine somewhere safe so that we can look at it later," ordered Diarmot and then he hurried after Sigimor, pausing only to tell Peter to have someone fetch Glenda.

It took him, Sigimor, Fraser, and Gay to get Ilsa out of her clothes, into a clean shift, and hold her in the bed. Tait and Nanty waited helplessly by the door. She was violently ill only twice more, but the pain obviously continued. The things she said proved she was not completely in possession of her senses. Diarmot tried to talk to her, as did Sigimor, but he knew she was not understanding them. He was beginning to think they would have to tie her to the bed, when she suddenly swooned. Fraser was the first to ascertain that it was only a swoon, reassuring him and Sigimor who had both been afraid to move.

"Help me clean up this mess, Gay," Fraser said.

"Nay, dinnae touch that yet," cried Glenda as she hurried into the room.

Diarmot took the dampened scrap of linen Fraser handed him and gently bathed Ilsa's face as Glenda inspected what had come out of Ilsa. He tried to be patient when the woman moved to the side of the bed and thoroughly examined Ilsa. Then Ilsa opened her eyes and looked at him. He frowned for she briefly looked afraid of him.

"The wine," she said, her voice little more than a hoarse whisper. "The wine is bitter."

"What wine?" demanded Glenda and was taken to the tray of wine and oatcakes by Fraser who had brought it into the room with her.

"Where did ye get that wine, Ilsa?" Diarmot asked.

"From ye," she replied and moaned, clutching at her stomach. "He said ye thought I would want some. But the wine was so bitter. Tis burning me!"

"Tis poison," announced Glenda as she hurried back to the bed. "Twas in the wine."

"Nay," Diarmot whispered and hurriedly stepped back as Sigimor advanced on him.

Diarmot drew his sword a heartbeat after Sigimor drew his. Tait moved to stand by his brother even as Nanty moved to stand next to Diarmot. Both young men drew their swords, too. Fraser cried out, but no one paid her any heed.

"Ye tried to kill her," said Sigimor. "Got weary of trying to drive her away with all your unkind-nesses, did ye?"

"Nay," protested Diarmot. "I would ne'er—"

"She said it herself. The wine was poisoned and ye sent it to her."

Sigimor tensed to attack and Diarmot heard Nanty curse. A chill coursed through Diarmot's blood. His wife could be dying in agony and her brothers were eager to make him do the same. He had no defense to make the Camerons pause, Ilsa's words carrying far more weight than anything he could say. Diarmot tensed to meet the attack, not sure how this could end without one or more of them dead, when he heard a distinct thud. For a moment, Sigimor stood, his eyes wide and his ex-pression one of shock. Then, slowly, he collapsed onto the floor, obviously seriously stunned. As he fell, Diarmot could see Gay standing behind the man holding the heavy walking stick Diarmot had used while recovering from the beating he had en-dured in Muirladen.

"Sometimes ye just have to knock some sense into a mon," Gay said, staring down at Sigimor who was already shaking free of the effects of her blow.

After staring at his small assailant for a moment, Sigimor slowly sat up and rubbed his head. "Ye could have killed me with that log ye are wielding," he said.

Gay snorted. "Nay likely. I needed to get your at-tention and there was nay hope of doing it politely once ye started to wave your swords about, was there? Nay, your blood was up and ye were past being reasoned with."

"Curse it," Sigimor snapped. "Ilsa said he gave her the wine and the wine is poisoned. Do ye expect me to shake his hand?" He carefully stood up, then rubbed his head again where she had struck him.

"Aye, she thinks he gave her the wine. Twas what she was told." She sighed when all four men just stared at her. "After she said Diarmot had given her the wine, she said, 'he said ye thought I would want some.' Someone else brought her the wine and told her Diarmot sent it."

"Sounds like an accusation to me," said Sigimor, but he sheathed his sword.

"Could be, but could also be no more than what she said. Someone brought her wine and said Diarmot sent it. Was he told that by someone else? Sir Diarmot says he didnae send her any wine. Dinnae think ye have enough proof of a crime there to start hacking each other to bits and leaving we women with more mess to clean up."

Sigimor scowled at her. "Ye had to choose this moment to get bold and impudent, did ye?"

"It seemed a good time," Gay replied calmly. "Now, ye will cease this fighting until we can find out exactly what has happened. If ye cannae do it whilst ye are in the same room, best ye separate."

"Diarmot!" screamed Ilsa as she began to writhe upon the bed. "The journals, see the journals."

Sheathing his sword, Diarmot hurried back to Ilsa's bedside and grabbed hold of one of her hands. "Hush, Ilsa."

"The journals. Ye need to read them, Diarmot. Ye need to."

"I have, Ilsa. Several times."

"Precious Love. Read about Precious Love. My notes are there. Ye must read my notes."

Before he could say anything, she screamed and, yanking her hand free of his, began to claw at her stomach. The brief moment of clarity she had just had was gone again. Diarmot found himself pushed from her side by Tait. When he took a step toward the man, intending to take his rightful place by Ilsa's bedside, Fraser and Nanty each grabbed him by an arm, and started pulling him toward the door.

"I should stay with her," he protested, watching as Gay and Glenda wrapped thick cloths around Ilsa's hands so that she would not hurt herself.

"Those two men may have stopped trying to gut ye," said Fraser, "because Gay talked some sense to them, but that doesnae mean they trust ye near Ilsa. The last thing that poor sick lass needs is four big fools fighting o'er her."

Diarmot realized Fraser and Nanty had pulled him out into the hall and he watched as Fraser shut the door, barring him from Ilsa's side. "I didnae poison her."

"Och, I ken it, laddie." Fraser patted his arm. "She is sick, probably didnae ken what she was saying or didnae say it right. She kens ye wouldnae hurt her."

"Does she? When she saw me at her bedside, she looked afraid of me."

"Weel, mayhap, for a wee moment, she wondered. Someone told her ye sent the wine. But then she was trying to tell ye something about those journals. Now, she isnae going to try so hard to tell ye something that important if she thinks ye are the one trying to kill her, is she?"

"Nay, mayhap not. Her brothers think I poisoned her, however."

"Aye and nay. Ye cannae expect them to think clearly when their only sister is in such pain. And, ye havenae exactly endeared yourself to them, either. Now, why dinnae ye go and—" Fraser looked down the hall and cursed.

Diarmot followed her gaze and echoed her curse. Only a few feet away stood Odo, Aulay, Ewart, Gregor, and Alice. Ivy was probably with the twins waiting for news. Alice was crying silently and the boys all looked as if they wanted to do the same. Little Ewart and Gregor would be easy enough to soothe, their tender years making them less apt to question what they were told. Diarmot fixed his gaze upon the one he knew would require the most careful handling. He moved toward Odo, Fraser and Nanty going toward the others. Diarmot suspected it would be some time before he got to those journals.

"I am bleeding," Ilsa whispered. "I am bleeding."

"Nay," said Sigimor, "ye are just sick, loving. Tis poison ye suffer from, nay a wound."

She moaned softly and shook her head. "Nay, I am bleeding. I shouldnae be bleeding. Oh, tis so sad."

Glenda yanked back the covers and cursed when she saw the blood. "Is it time for your menses, child?"

"Has the poison done this?" asked Sigimor when Ilsa did not reply to Glenda's question.

"Nay." Glenda almost smiled when she looked at Sigimor for both he and Tait were alarmingly pale and had their gazes fixed steadily upon the walls. "I fear she is losing a bairn." Glenda examined Ilsa more closely, noting how much she had bled. "Nay, I believe she has already lost it. That would explain why the pain was so severe. Stiffen your backbones, laddies. Gay and I are going to need help to clean the lass up."

Many harrowing moments later, Sigimor held his now clean, blanket-wrapped sister and watched Gay and Glenda strip the bed. He was all too aware of how small Ilsa was. How could such a delicate woman survive all this?

"Are ye certain she lost a bairn?" he asked.

"Aye," replied Glenda. "I wasnae at first, but, aye, she lost a bairn. Twas but newly begun, nay much more than a promise. She suspected. Tis why she said she shouldnae be bleeding and that it was sad. Tis for the best. Twas surely damaged or killed by the poison. Best to clean the womb and start agin. It would have been nay more than a lingering poison in her body."

"Do ye think she has been damaged?" asked Tait as he gently brushed a stray curl from Ilsa's forehead.

"Nay, twas a clean loss," replied Glenda as she helped Gay put clean linen on the bed. "The bleeding is nay more than it should be. Your sister's body is its own healer, best I have e'er seen. The way it was throwing out that poison was a wonder."

"Weel, Ilsa has always been quick to, er, throw out what her body didnae like. E'en as a wee lass. She would eat something which didnae agree with her and, I swear to ye, it couldnae have been in her belly many minutes before it was flung out."

"Aye," agreed Sigimor. "Ye kenned it was coming, too, for she would get the oddest look upon her face."

Glenda crossed her arms over her chest and gave Sigimor a knowing look. "And, of course, her brothers ne'er gave her something just to watch what happened." She chuckled when he and Tait blushed faintly. "Aye, tis just what lads would do. Set her in the bed." The moment Sigimor did so and tucked the blankets around Ilsa, Glenda felt Ilsa's face. "Sleeping weel. She will be weel, lads. Ye hardly needed my help. Her body was doing my work for me, throwing out all the bad as fast as it could. I didnae e'en have to purge her. She was purging herself better than I e'er could."

"So, the poison is out of her?"

"She willnae be dying of it. Suspicion some lingers and she will be sickly for a few days. I will try to force some healing potions down her and all. She willnae be able to eat anything too hearty, either. Oh, and she cannae nurse the bairns." She sighed. "Ere I would feel that would be safe, I suspicion her milk will have dried up. That willnae please her. That and losing the bairn, weel, her spirits will be fair low for a wee while."

"Diarmot," began Gay.

"I am nay letting that bastard near her," snapped Sigimor. "He tried to poison her. She said so herself." His eyes widened slightly at the way Gay growled at him. "Wheesht, lass, ye sound like a Cameron."

"I am nay surprised. I have been with ye lot long enough I have probably caught the disease. Diarmot didnae give her that poison. Someone told her he had sent the wine. Nay more. The mon may act like an idiot, but he isnae a murderer."

"Aye," agreed Glenda. "Heed the lass. The laird

is a troubled mon, but he would ne'er do this."
She held up her hand when Tait and Sigimor both
started to protest. "Fine, be wary if it pleases ye,
but nay more than that. Keep him away from her if
it makes ye happy, but, if ye take a sword to the
fool, ye will be guilty of killing an innocent mon.
Aye, and the mon your sister loves, the father of
her sons. Are ye willing to bear that weight just because ye cannae hold your tempers for a wee
while?" She nodded when both men grimaced.
"Good. She will soon wake and set ye right, anyway."

"I will sit with her for now," said Gay. "The
bairns will be needing to be fed in a few hours and
one of ye will have to come here then. Best if I take
my turn now." The moment Sigimor and Tait left,
Gay looked at Glenda. "Ye were telling them the
truth?"

"About Lady Ilsa getting better?" Glenda kissed
Gay on the cheek. "Aye, lass. Twill be a few days ere
she heals, but she will heal. The hardest thing will
be convincing those two lads that the laird wasnae
guilty of this."

"Not if Ilsa doesnae believe her husband is
guilty. The Cameron brothers may act witless at
times, but they arenae. They will just need some
time to think it all over. I ken they are nay sure
e'en now for they let me stop them from killing
the laird. If they really believed he had tried to kill
Ilsa, we would still be mopping up his blood."

Glenda grinned and nodded. "Aye, we would.
Nay doubt about it. Weel, I will go to that wee fine
room they gave me last time and have a rest. Ye
ken where to find me if ye need me," she added as
she left.

Gay settled herself in a chair by Ilsa's bedside.

She was exhausted, but knew she would not sleep until she had seen Ilsa wake up and speak sensibly at least once.

"Ye will have a bit of a mess to clean up when ye wake, Ilsa," she said. "Ye are going to have to convince your stubborn brothers nay to skin your husband and hang his carcass on the stable wall. Weel, mayhap it will do the mon some good to get a taste of the meal he has been serving ye since ye got here." She crossed her arms over her chest and nodded. "Aye, let the laird see how it feels to be thought a threat to ye. It might just knock some sense into his fool head."

"Curse it, I just want to see how she fares, ye fool," Diarmot complained even as he allowed Nanty to pull him away from Ilsa's bedchamber door. "Ye would think I was planning to slip in and cut her throat." He exchanged a final glare with Sigimor who guarded the door.

"Ye talked to Glenda," said Nanty, "and she said Ilsa will recover. Until Ilsa recovers and clears up this confusion, her brothers willnae let ye near her. Accept it. She has had to put up with it from ye for weeks." When Diarmot started toward Ilsa's solar, Nanty released his grip upon his arm. "Suspicion has become a cursed plague in this keep. E'en Odo was putting us through an inquisition."

"I kenned Odo wouldnae accept some vague soothing words," said Diarmot, pleased to talk about something beside the fact that he was getting a hearty dose of his own medicine and disliking it intensely. "Ilsa told me to ne'er underestimate the lad. She said he is what she considers the most dangerous of creatures." He smiled faintly at the memory.

"Oh? And what would that be?"

"A clever little boy." He nodded when Nanty grinned. "And he is. If I hadnae kenned the way to the cave that day, he would have led me to it without any hesitation. He was terrified that day, but got to Clachthrom to seek help and told me exactly what I needed to ken. He rules that nursery, but kindly, and by the will of the others. And, the way his wee mind works is a wonder. I dinnae think Ivy witless, yet Odo has her convinced that tis nay him letting wind in the night, but a dragon making the noises and the stink is the dragon's breath." He chuckled along with Nanty as they entered Ilsa's solar. "Aye, Odo holds great promise."

"Are ye sorry he isnae your heir?"

"Aye and nay. To be my heir, I would have had to marry his mother and that would have been a misery. If he doesnae choose to go elsewhere, he will serve the twins verra weel indeed, however. Odo has a keen sense of the order of things, has e'en asked me which of the twins will be the laird. I believe Ilsa and Fraser have made it clear to them all how the rules work and without hurting feelings or stirring resentment. I doubt I could have done it so weel."

"It doesnae hurt that your wife treats them all as if they are her own, either. What is wrong?" Nanty asked when Diarmot scowled at Ilsa's table where the journals were. "The journals are still here."

"Aye, but closed," said Diarmot, looking around the room once before returning his gaze to the table. "They were open when we first ran in here after hearing Ilsa scream. I noticed that when she spoke of the wine and I looked for it. They were spread out and all opened."

"Weel, someone has cleaned up all signs of her illness. Mayhap they cleaned other things."

"Nay. The yarns for the tapestry she works on are still scattered about on the seat near the window. Her sewing is still scattered about near the fireplace. Her quill and ink were not put away. Aye, someone cleaned up the vomit, but naught else was touched except for these." He touched the journals. "They have all been closed. The notes Ilsa told me to look at arenae here either, yet tis clear that she had done some writing."

Nanty cursed and dragged his hand through his hair. "She found something, didnae she?"

"Aye, which could prove a danger to her, but that isnae what worries me the most."

"Nay? If she made notes and someone has them, that means your enemy now kens what she has learned."

"True, but what troubles me the most is, who took them? It would appear that my enemy has an ally at Clachthrom." He nodded when Nanty cursed again. "Exactly. The enemy I cannae find, cannae recognize, has set an adder in my nest."

CHAPTER FIFTEEN

If there was a part of Ilsa which did not ache, she suspected it would be a while before she found it. Then the memories began to crowd her waking mind and she nearly cried out. Someone had tried to poison her. It had been in the wine, wine sent to her by Diarmot. Before fear and suspicion could grasp hold of her heart, her mind banished it. Someone wanted Diarmot to be blamed. There were a lot of things concerning her husband she was confused and uncertain about, but not her belief in his innocence. The question that needed answering was not whether or not Diarmot had tried to kill her, but who would want everyone to think he had.

A dull ache low in her belly sharply recalled her to what else she had suffered. She had lost the child she had only just begun to suspect she was carrying. She knew that, because of the poison, it was probably for the best, but that eased her grief only a little. Ilsa felt the warmth of tears upon her cheeks and heard someone move near the bed.

"Diarmot?" she whispered and struggled to open her eyes.

"Nay, love. Tis Tait." He gently bathed the tears from her face with a damp square of fine linen. "Do ye want a drink?"

"Aye, please." She finally managed to get her eyes open as he held her up slightly and helped her drink some water. "Where is Diarmot?" she asked, a little disappointed not to find him nursing her.

"Why would ye be wanting to see him?" Tait held her against him as he arranged the pillows behind her back. "He gave ye the poisoned wine," he said as he settled her against the pillows.

"Where did ye come by such a strange idea?"

"Ye said it. When we asked where ye got the wine, ye said Diarmot sent it to ye."

"Weel, what did ye listen to me for? Tis clear I was verra ill."

"Aye, for nearly two days. Actually, ye were verra ill for a few hours, then ye slept, and have done little else for two days. Glenda has been pouring healing potions down ye." He sighed when Ilsa briefly touched her breasts. "Ye cannae feed the twins any more. Glenda says she cannae tell how long some poison might linger in your body or if it would e'en taint your milk, but felt certain ye wouldnae want to take any chances."

"Nay, I wouldnae. I am surprised it all disappeared so quickly, though," she murmured.

"Glenda had a potion to help that, too. Ye havenae eaten for two days, either." He smiled faintly. "She says your body is a better healer than she is. She didnae e'en have to purge ye, that your body did it without aid. She said ye cleansed yourself, rid yourself of near all the poison."

"And my bairn," she said and saw Tait pale, confirming it. "Dinnae look so worried. Tis a grief, but a wee one. I had only begun to suspect I was carrying so hadnae become, weel, attached. And, I am certain the poison killed the poor wee thing ere it e'en got a chance to settle in."

"Glenda called it little more than a promise. Also said ye were nay damaged in any way. Said it was for the best."

"It was." She took a deep breath and pushed aside her grief. "Does Diarmot ken it?"

"Ilsa, the mon may have tried to kill ye."

"Nay," she began to argue.

"I ken ye have feelings for the fool, but—"

She placed her fingers against his lips to stop his words. "Diarmot would ne'er try to harm me. I cannae say what he feels, he may e'en wish I would just go away, but he would ne'er hurt me. And, my feelings dinnae have much to do with that judgment. Ye ken I was reading Lady Anabelle's journals." When he nodded, she removed her fingers from his lips, and continued, "She wrote of the day, about a month after Diarmot married her, that he found her romping with two men."

"Jesu." He frowned slightly. "Two men?"

"Aye, but dinnae expect me to tell ye how that worked e'en though Anabelle was quite explicit. She wrote of the confrontation and made it verra clear that she thought Diarmot a pathetic weakling. And do ye ken why? Because for all he cursed her, he didnae raise a hand to her. He ne'er did and I cannae tell ye how hard she tried to push him to it."

"Are ye certain? Mayhap she pushed so hard he gave her the potion that killed her."

"Nay, he didnae. Anabelle wrote in her journal

right up to the day she drank the potion that killed her. I wouldnae be surprised if she wrote in her journal just before she drank it. She ranted on about her failure to lure Diarmot into her bed so that she could blame him for the child she carried. Wrote about how she was going to be rid of it. She also heaped praise and gratitude upon the one who gave her the means to do so—Precious Love."

Tait frowned. "Ye mentioned something about a Precious Love when ye were so ill."

"Has Diarmot told ye about it, then? About what he thinks?"

"Ah, nay. We havenae been speaking to each other."

"Idiots. Weel, I need to speak to him." She sighed when Tait just frowned again. "Ye ken I speak the truth. If a mon cannae e'en bring himself to strike his new bride when he finds her romping with two men, do ye really think he could hurt any lass?"

"Nay, probably not. Do ye want me to send one of the women in first?" he asked even as he started out the door.

"Aye, please," she replied.

After getting Fraser to go to Ilsa, Tait hunted down Sigimor. He found his brother in the great hall sitting before the massive fireplace cleaning his sword. Tait poured them each a tankard of ale, handed one to Sigimor, then took the seat facing him.

"Ilsa finally woke up and she wants to speak to Diarmot," said Tait.

"I hope ye made her see sense," replied Sigimor.

"Actually, she made me see sense." He told Sigimor everything Ilsa had told him. "She is right. He wouldnae do it. Once I kenned she wouldnae die, I thought it all over and found it difficult to believe. Ilsa simply confirmed my doubts."

Sigimor took a long drink of ale, then sighed. "I had doubts as weel. Nay once since we came here have I seen any cruelty in him. Och, he may nay be verra kind to Ilsa in some ways since his wits are sadly rattled, but he isnae cruel. She knocked him on his arse in front of everyone and he did naught in retaliation. And, I also got to thinking on how he looked when he saw she was in so much pain and emptying her belly all over the keep."

"Nay the look of a mon who was but waiting to see if his plot would be successful."

"Nay, and the fear on his face wasnae that of a mon thinking he might be caught, either. Yet, Ilsa is in danger because of him. And, who the devil gave her the wine saying it was from Diarmot?"

"Curse it, I forgot to ask. Do ye think the one who brought her the wine is the enemy or can lead us to him?"

"Mayhap. I shallnae hold out any hope, though. We havenae had much luck with all of this so far." He looked toward the door when Diarmot and Nanty entered. "Here be the fool now."

Diarmot poured himself some ale, glanced at the Camerons, and cursed softly when he caught them both staring at him. He was trying to be patient and understanding, but being treated like a mad dog ready to attack anyone at any moment was difficult to accept. He was sure he had not been treating Ilsa this poorly. It was even harder to calmly accept being kept from Ilsa's side, having to talk to Glenda just to find out how his own wife was faring.

"Ilsa is asking to see ye," announced Sigimor. Barely stopping himself from spitting out the ale he had just put into his mouth, Diarmot's mood quickly went from surprised to suspicious. "What did ye just say?"

"Wheesht, are ye deaf as weel as stupid? I said Ilsa is asking to see ye," Sigimor repeated in a loud voice.

"And ye are just going to sit there and allow me to go to her? Are ye sure ye dinnae wish to search me for weapons? Mayhap march me up there with a sword at my back?"

"Now, why would we do that? Tis your bed-chamber. Rather thought ye kenned the way there."

For a moment Diarmot was torn between the urge to hurry to Ilsa's side and the very strong inclination to punch her brother so hard the smirk he wore ended up on the floor. He finished his ale and started to leave the great hall, expecting to be stopped every step of the way, or acquire a large red-headed shadow. When neither occurred by the time he stepped out of the hall, he started to move faster, nearly running to Ilsa. There was always the chance Sigimor could change his mind.

Ilsa was startled by Diarmot's abrupt entrance. If she did not know better, she would think he had run to her room. When he peered back out the door as if looking for someone, she frowned. They were undoubtedly well protected now. Then he shut and latched the door. Before she could ask why he was acting so oddly, he was seated on her bedside, kissing her. Ilsa gave silent thanks to Fraser for the woman's efficiency in freshening her up, then gave herself over to the pleasure of his kiss.

"Have my brothers been troublesome?" she asked when he ended the kiss, sat back, and took her hand in his.

"What do ye think?" He smiled faintly when she grimaced. "Ye certainly look better than ye did when last I saw ye. The children will be pleased to ken ye are recovering so weel."

"Fraser said she would bring them round for a kiss good night ere she puts to bed. I was willing to see them now, but she said I should rest another day or two ere I deal with eight children."

"Wise advice." He took a deep breath to calm himself, a little disturbed by the wealth of emotions afflicting him. "Ilsa, I didnae send ye that wine."

"I ken it. Geordie brought it and told me ye thought I might be wanting some. That was probably what I was trying to explain, but it didnae come out right. If I thought otherwise, twas but for a moment."

"I shall have to speak to Geordie, then, and find out where he got the wine. How do ye feel, Ilsa? Glenda was kind enough to tell me everything. How ye fared, the loss of the bairn, the fact that ye cannae help to feed the twins now. So many hard blows. I am sorry."

"Tisnae your fault. Aye, losing the bairn is a sorrow, but tis for the best. And, weel, the twins are already needing more than the breast. Gay can continue to feed them milk whilst I do the rest. So, let us put those sorrows aside, and speak on what I found in the journals."

"I dinnae ken what ye found."

"Oh? Was my script so poor then?"

"Nay, I ne'er saw the notes ye made. When I reached your solar the journals were all closed and there were no notes." He nodded when she started to look alarmed. "Someone didnae want me to see what ye had found. Whoever shut those journals and took your notes probably thought ye were soon to die and whatever ye had discovered would die with ye. I have spent the last two days trying to find out who went into your solar after ye took ill. Young Jenny cleaned the mess upon the floor, but swears she touched naught else, and I believe her."

"Aye, so do I." Ilsa shook her head. "A traitor in our midst then. After those men tried to kill ye at the ridge, Sigimor wondered about that. It seems he was right to do so."

"That is rather galling."

Ilsa laughed softly. "Ah, weel, fetch the journals then and some writing supplies."

"Nay, ye need to rest."

"And ye need to see what I saw, to judge its importance as quickly as possible. We have already lost two days. Someone tried to kill ye on your own lands, Diarmot. If the incident at the cave wasnae an accident, they also tried to kill me right upon your own lands. They have poisoned me right here inside this keep. That brings the enemy too close to our bairns for my liking. I can rest after I show ye what I found."

Diarmot nodded and went to get the journals. Ilsa was right. They needed to find this person, needed to find the traitor within Clachthrom. Although it infuriated him to admit it, he knew the only men he could trust were Nanty, young Tom, and the Camerons. He knew it was probably unfair, but he would not include Geordie on that list until he was absolutely certain about where the man got that wine. He could also trust Gay, Fraser, and Glenda. There were one or two others, such as little Jenny, but none of them would be much use in protecting his wife or his children.

He was collecting up what he needed when

Nanty walked in and said, "I thought ye were visiting with Ilsa."

After he explained, Diarmot recognized the curiosity Nanty could not hide. "Bring the writing supplies. Your hand is better than mine," he said as he started out of the room. "I am surprised the Camerons arenae lurking about."

"Once they kenned ye and I were staying here, they went hunting rabbit. Sigimor likes rabbit stew."

"So it isnae just me they dinnae trust."

"Oh, they trust ye now. Seems they only trust each other, ye, me, and young Tom. Then the women, of course. Gay, Fraser, Glenda, and little Jenny. Tait thinks Peter is probably trustworthy, but wasnae ready to add him to the list. Or Geordie."

"Their list matches mine. Comforting, if irritating." He smiled faintly when Nanty laughed.

Diarmot hesitated a little when he entered the bedchamber and saw that Ilsa's eyes were closed. Before he could turn and leave, however, she opened her eyes and smiled at him. He cautiously approached the bed.

"Are ye sure ye dinnae wish to rest some more first?" he asked as he set the journals down on the bed.

"Nay. This would prey upon my mind so vigorously I wouldnae be able to rest." She started to look through the journals, finding the pages she had left them open to. "This Precious Love is mentioned here and there from the first journal to the last. I believe Anabelle met Precious Love when she was fostered with a certain L.O. She was probably fourteen then."

"A longtime love? That sounds unlike Anabelle. And, she wasnae faithful, was she?"

"Never. So, one wonders why she didnae marry

Precious Love. Why so consistently unfaithful? At times, she and Precious Love talked about Anabelle's lovers. There." She looked at the journals she had before her, then at Nanty who sat next to the bed. "I am going to read ye a word or two from each of these and I want ye to list them."

When Nanty nodded, she began. As the list grew, so did the looks of confusion on Diarmot and Nanty's faces. Ilsa carefully set to the side the journal with the sentence she considered the coup de grace. She held it when she finished with the others and watched Diarmot read the list Nanty had made. When both men looked at her, she just smiled. There was the glint of understanding in their eyes, but also hesitation.

"Precious Love sounds a verra odd sort of mon," murmured Nanty.

"Verra odd," agreed Ilsa. "Now, write this down as I read it. 'Precious Love kens how to touch a woman, kens a woman's needs and desires as no mon e'er could.' " She watched both men read it again, then curse.

"I did catch her one time with a woman," said Diarmot. "I didnae see the woman though. It was dark, I was drunk, and the lass burrowed into a cloak and fled ere I could get a good look at her. Yet, sin though the church is wont to call it, it doesnae mean this woman is the one we seek."

"Mayhap not," agreed Ilsa. "It wasnae actually the discovery that Precious Love was a woman that made me think this is what sent ye hurrying out to Dubheidland or thereabout. Yet, Precious Love was verra important, was a part of Anabelle's life since they were both verra young girls. From all I read, Anabelle ruled that woman with an iron fist, controlled her, enslaved her, if ye will. It gives me the shivers, but Anabelle wrote of times when she demanded a penance and got it, even to making the woman crawl to her on her belly, naked. Think of what that woman must be like, how she must have felt about Anabelle to allow herself to be used that way. One has to wonder. From the time she was a young lass, Anabelle was her love."

"A sick sort of love," muttered Nanty, "and nay because it was between women. No one speaks of it, but we all ken that such love can exist between men. Why not women? Nay, tis the rest of it. Penances? Crawling to her? That is what sets one's stomach to twitching." He frowned. "And Anabelle wasnae only her love, was she? She was her master. She was probably her whole life."

Ilsa nodded. "She couldnae marry her love, either, had to watch her marry elsewhere, had to watch her belong to someone else and give that hated mon a child."

"And she believes that mon killed her," said Diarmot.

"Ah, nay, though the woman may have made herself believe that," said Ilsa, slumping back against the pillows as weariness began to overtake her. "Precious Love gave Anabelle the potion which killed her."

Diarmot cursed again, then began to pick up the journals. "So how does one find this woman?"

"I think ye guessed. L.O. is all Anabelle called the woman she and Precious Love fostered with."

"Rest, Ilsa." Diarmot kissed her. "Ye have given me a great deal to think on. Whether this Precious Love is the one who tried to kill me or nay, she will have at least some of the answers I need. I just need to find her."

The moment Diarmot and Nanty left, Ilsa made

herself comfortable in the bed and closed her eyes. She had used up what little strength she had had, but decided it had been worth it. In her heart, she felt this woman was their enemy. If Precious Love had been a man, she was sure Diarmot and Nanty would have immediately agreed. It was often difficult for men to think a woman could be dangerous in any important way, but Ilsa suspected a few certain men were about to learn an important lesson. If a woman wanted to, she could be as ruthless and deadly as any man.

"Precious Love?" Sigimor muttered between bites of rabbit stew. "What a ridiculous name. Almost puts one off one's food."

"Tis a good thing ye have a strong stomach then," said Diarmot. "Anabelle called her lover that."

"And her lover was a woman? Does this woman hate men, too?"

"Aye. As Anabelle, I think that loathing was bred at a verra young age and probably through rape. I believed Anabelle's tale of rape, the one she told me to explain her lack of a maidenhead. Now, after reading the early journals more closely, I see why. She was actually telling me a true story. From what Anabelle wrote, this other woman was also raped, and at a verra young age."

"And so she decided to love women?"

"Nay, I doubt rape or loathing men did that. What few women I have kenned who suffered from a mon's brutality didnae want any lover, mon or woman. If they recovered, as Gay seems to be recovering, they wanted a mon. This lass probably always preferred women. Anabelle rarely mentions

Precious Love having another lover, a mon. My wife apparently liked anything." Diarmot shrugged. "We ne'er question those men who prefer men, just accept it as so. It must be the same with women. It just is."

"Aye, I suppose." Sigimor took a large chunk of bread and dipped it into his stew. "If one thought of this lover as a mon and gave him all those same reasons for going, weel, mad with grief and wanting revenge, I suspicion we wouldnae be having this discussion. We would be out hunting the bastard. Tis just a wee bit galling to think some lass has been leading us about in circles and nearly succeeding in killing ye and Ilsa right under our noses."

"Weel, we cannae be certain this woman is the one who tried to kill us," said Diarmot.

"Tis her. She obviously has someone helping her, but tis this Precious Love behind all this trouble." He rolled his eyes. "Best pray we find her ere she succeeds. Ye dinnae want 'Murdered by Precious Love' on your crypt stone." Sigimor winked and shoved the stew-soaked chunk of bread into his mouth.

Diarmot gave both Tait and Nanty a look of disgust when they laughed. Sigimor had a very odd sense of humor, he decided. He understood the need for a moment or two of foolishness. The last few days had been very long and weighted with anger and uncertainty. Until the one who had tried to kill him and Ilsa was gone, however, Diarmot could not share in it.

"Ye cannae remember why ye were riding about our lands yet, can ye?" asked Sigimor.

"Nay," replied Diarmot. "I searched through all of Anabelle's writings, as did Nanty, but we could not find anything that pointed me toward Dubheidland or Muirladen. I ken whatever did is still there, it just doesnae want to reveal itself. Nothing in Anabelle's writings brings it forth. Fraser couldnae help us, either. Anabelle rarely spoke of her past. And, as Fraser says, Anabelle didnae see her as a confidante, merely a servant. Cannae think of who L.O. might be, either."

"If tis someone near Dubheidland, it could be one of several people. It all depends upon whether the L stands for a title or a Christian name."

"I believe it is the name of the woman Anabelle and her lover were fostered with, the one who was training them."

"How many years ago would that have been?"

"About ten. Ilsa feels Anabelle would have been about four and ten when she began the journals. This Precious Love was a wee bit younger." He shook his head. "That means that both women were ill-used whilst little more than children. It gave them yet another bond. I went to Dubheidland or Muirladen looking for answers. I may nay recall why, but it still seems the best place to start looking for L.O."

Sigimor nodded. "I have been eager to go there anyway, to find out why I havenae heard from any of my kinsmen. Nanty, Tait, and I will leave in two days' time. I want to have a look at the journals written whilst your wife was being fostered first. I ken the land and people all round Dubheidland better than ye do and might see something that tells me where to start my search."

"Fair enough. I want to go with ye."

"Nay, that would leave no one to watch o'er Ilsa and the bairns."

Diarmot winced. "There would be young Tom, Peter, Father Goudie, and the women. And Geordie."

"Geordie is the one who brought Ilsa the poisoned wine."

"He explained that. One of the maids gave him the tray and told him it was by my order. His story is given the weight of truth by the fact that the maid is gone. She disappeared soon after Ilsa took ill. Fraser and Glenda say they will prepare all the food for Ilsa and the bairns. They all ken nay to go anywhere alone." He grimaced and dragged a hand through his hair. "I just feel as if there is a strong chance I will restir those elusive memories if I return to Muirladen."

"That does make sense, Sigimor," said Tait. "Tis certainly worth a try."

"Then I shall stay here," said Nanty. "Ye go, Diarmot. Tis the wisest choice. I dinnae ken the land or the people there and I have no memory that needs prodding. I can keep watch here as weel as ye can."

"Thank ye, Nanty."

"And ye can reacquaint yourself with all of Ilsa's kinsmen," Nanty drawled, then laughed along with the Camerons.

Diarmot smiled and helped himself to some rabbit stew. Now that plans had been made his appetite had been revived. He felt the thrill of the hunt course through his veins, but he also felt the first real stirring of hope since his ordeal had begun. There was finally a real chance of getting some answers, of ending the constant expectation of another attack. He could finally put a name and a face to his enemy. That would put an end to the need to watch every shadow, to wonder which of the many people at Clachthrom could be trusted.

He would have some semblance of peace again. Time in which he could take a long, hard look at what did or did not exist between him and Ilsa. Time in which he could repair his marriage and make a proper family of them all. He could only hope that, by clinging so fiercely to his doubts and fears for so long, he had not lost the chance to do so.

CHAPTER SIXTEEN

It felt good to be clean from head to toe, Ilsa decided as she brushed her hair dry before the fire. The gentle washings given her when she had been ill and while her bleeding had lingered had not been enough to really make her feel clean. The moment Diarmot had left the room this morning, she had called for a bath and had luxuriated in it, shamelessly. Now the outside of her felt as good as the inside.

Glenda was too modest, she thought. The woman insisted Ilsa's own body had done most of the work. Ilsa knew she was a quick healer, but also knew Glenda's herbal remedies had helped her keep up her strength and cleanse the poison from her body. The medicines had also helped to dry up her milk with little discomfort, soothe her battered insides, and ease the loss of her child. Ilsa just wished the woman had a potion to ease the sorrow that still lingered over that loss.

She gasped softly when Diarmot suddenly strode into the room. He was supposed to be busy prepar-

ing to leave for Dubheidland. That was one reason
she had insisted upon a bath. She had wanted to
look her best when she bid him a good journey.
Her eyes widened when he grinned and latched
the door.

"Ye have had your bath," he said as he approached her.

"Aye." Ilsa suddenly felt very naked despite the
heavy robe she wore.

"So your bleeding has ended then."

Ilsa blushed. "Aye."

"Ah, good."

Ilsa felt her eyes widen again as he began to
shed his clothes. "I thought ye were leaving soon."

"I am. After," he said.

"After? Oh! I see how it is. Ye think to have a wee
frolic ere ye ride off into the mists."

"'Tis a fine, sun-filled day. Nary a mist in sight."
He ignored her irritation and continued to un-
dress.

"When are ye leaving?" she asked, suddenly suspicious and trying hard to ignore the fact that he
wore only his braies now.

"In an hour." He picked her up in his arms and
carried her to the bed. "That should be time
enough for a proper, hearty fareweel."

"Weel, that was certainly hearty," Ilsa murmured
when she was finally able to catch her breath and
felt Diarmot chuckle against her skin.

Proper it was not, however, she mused, as she
looked over the man sprawled in her arms. Fast,
furious, and a little rough, but not proper. She
supposed she ought to be outraged that he would
ravish her then tug on his boots and ride away but,

with her body still warm and alive from his love-making, it was impossible. She had not been able to satisfy his needs until now and this was a journey that could no longer be delayed.

It was probably foolish, but she actually felt a little flattered. Diarmot had obviously understood the implications of her having a bath and, despite how important this journey was to him, had rushed to her side. Since it had only been six days since they had last made love, Ilsa knew it was not the urgency of long deprivation that had brought him there. The fact that he would be leaving Clachthrom with the memory of the passion they could share still fresh in his mind was certainly a good thing. No, she thought, Diarmot might be dashing from her bed to saddle his horse and leave, but she could see no cause for complaint about what had just happened.

"I would like naught more than to stay here," Diarmot said, kissed her, and got out of bed, "but I cannae."

Ilsa sat up, clutching the sheet to her breasts, and watched Diarmot dress. "Did Sigimor find any clues in Anabelle's journals?"

"He hasnae said. I asked, but he just shrugged. Said he wants to talk to Liam first. Liam is the clever cousin, aye?"

"Och, aye. I like to think all we Camerons are clever," she exchanged a brief grin with Diarmot, "but Liam is our shining light."

"Every family has one. The twins are too young to ken their strengths, but, right now, Odo is ours, I think."

It was not easy, but Ilsa hid the emotion which swelled up within her over the way he had called Odo "ours." "Nay question about that."

"I must be on my way." He gave her a quick, fierce kiss before starting toward the door.

"Dinnae ye dare to ride away until I get down to the bailey."

"Be quick about it then. I am nay the only one eager to get to Dubheidland."

He laughed softly when she started muttering as he left. It surprised him that she had not objected more to his rushing her into bed, vigorously tumbling her, and then hurrying away again. The moment he had realized what her calling for a bath meant, however, he had been unable to resist going to her. It certainly made for a nicer farewell than a mere wave, he thought, and grinned as he stepped out into the bailey.

"I am nay sure, Tait," drawled Sigimor, "but, as Ilsa's brothers, I think it might be our duty to slap that look off that rogue's face."

Diarmot just smiled sweetly at Ilsa's brothers and moved to check the saddle on his horse.

"I think we ought to slap that look off his face simply because he is wearing it and we arenae," said Tait.

"Aye, that would be justice," said Nanty.

Before that nonsense could continue, Fraser and Gay brought the children out to say farewell. Diarmot looked over the eight children he claimed as his. He could be certain of only the twins, and that was a judgment he had made only recently. It no longer mattered, however. Until Ilsa's arrival, the children had been a rarely seen responsibility, but she had brought them out of the nursery, made him come to know them, and he was glad of it. They were yet another reason for him to make this journey, to reclaim lost memories, good and bad, and to find the truth.

A slightly disheveled Ilsa hurried out of the keep and Diarmot suddenly knew exactly what he wanted, what he needed. Here was the family he had thought to build when he had married Anabelle. His children and his wife were all gathered to wish him God's speed and they would be waiting to welcome him upon his return. He had been laird of Clachthrom for nearly six years and had never had that. Now it was within his reach. All he had to do was clear away the lingering confusion and doubt so that he could grasp that promise without hesitation.

Once away from Clachthrom, after exchanging several waves with his children, Diarmot looked at Sigimor. "Will ye tell me what ye think ye discovered in Anabelle's journals now?" he asked

"I am nay sure I discovered anything save that your wife was, weel, how can one say it?" he replied.

"A whore?" Diarmot discovered that the only feeling he had concerning Anabelle now was a twinge of embarrassment over the fact that he had been fooled enough to marry the woman.

"Aye." Sigimor grimaced. "I read near all of them, deciding to see if there were any hints about her past further along which might prove helpful. Aye, she was a whore, but, since it wasnae for money or because she had a hunger that couldnae be satisfied, I found myself wondering why."

"Did ye find an answer?"

"Mayhap. I think she wanted the power."

"How would that give her power?" asked Tait. "How could she think she was powerful just because she had some fool thrusting into her? Seems to me a woman is fair vulnerable in that position."

"I would think the mon is fair vulnerable as weel," said Diarmot.

"In many ways, aye," agreed Sigimor. "She was shown her own weakness with the first rape." He glanced at Diarmot. "I think there were other abuses, mayhaps other rapes."

Diarmot nodded. "I got that feeling, too."

"So, Lady Anabelle came to the decision to turn that weapon, as she saw it, against men. Her trysts were written of as if they were battles waged and won. She had a strong fascination with a mon's private parts."

"I noticed those things finally. Anabelle turned that mon's weapon into a mon's weakness."

"She certainly tried her best. Some men think getting a lass into their bed means they are handsome, or monly, or great lovers. Some women think getting a mon into their beds means they are beautiful, desirable, may e'en think it means they are loved. Lady Anabelle thought it proved her strong and the mon weak, fools whose will and wit rest in their rods. As I read her writings, I got the distinct impression that Anabelle saw every mon who succumbed to her allure as a weakling. She especially enjoyed turning so many of your people into traitors, Diarmot. Pushing them to betray their laird in her arms. She considered it a galling defeat when she couldnae get any of your brothers to succumb. She loathed Lady Gillyanne."

"I suspicion that is because Gillyanne saw what Anabelle was all too clearly."

"Aye, I believe so. At times your late wife sounded as if she was on some vengeful crusade. Since we now ken many of the men simply wanted to bed a woman, tis clear Lady Anabelle was deluded in thinking she had accomplished any more than giving a mon what he wanted. A verra troubled woman."

"And the young lass she made her lover wasnae, or isnae, much saner, I suspect."

"Nay, and reading your wife's writings has only made me e'en more certain that that woman is the one we seek."

"But, ye willnae tell me if ye found some hint as to where or who, will ye?"

Sigimor shook his head. "Nay, for I cannae be sure. I need to talk to Liam. Talking on what few suspicions I have now will serve nay purpose, may e'en falsely raise your hopes."

Diarmot did not think his hopes could get any higher, but he made no further argument. He had tried very hard not to let his expectations grow and had failed miserably. Every instinct he had told him he would soon find the answers he had sought for so long. He was not sure he could endure another disappointment.

Anger, bitterness, and fear had ruled his life for too long. The anger and bitterness had faded, time working its magic on the wounds Anabelle had inflicted. Ilsa had aided that healing as well, and it was past time he recognized that gift. The fear lingered, fed by his still-incomplete memories and his unknown enemy. It had been bad enough when the enemy had been his alone, but now his foe sought to kill his wife and had shown that he, or she, cared nothing about the lives of his children, either. He wanted that enemy gone, the fear scoured from his life, and the threat removed from his family. It was past time this game ended. He briefly glanced back in the direction of Clachthrom. When he rode back through those gates, he wanted to do so as a man who remembered the past, but was free of it.

* * *

"Do ye think he will find the truth?" asked Fraser as she sat beside Ilsa at the head table in the great hall.

Ilsa looked at Fraser, Gay, and Glenda who were obviously making the most of enjoying a midday meal but could not completely hide their intense curiosity. She had called the women together for a council of war, as she liked to think of it. Since Nanty was with the four older children and Jenny was watching the four youngest, it seemed a perfect time.

"Aye, I think he will, or most of it," Ilsa replied. "E'en before that fall brought so many of his memories back, Diarmot's memory was stirring. A few words or some incident would yank free an odd memory now and again. He is now riding to the place where it all began. The truth, however, may nay give him all the answers he seeks."

"Oh, ye mean he may nay find his enemy?"

"There is that chance, but I think tis a small one. I just worry because this enemy has remained nay more than a chimera for so long. Diarmot's lack of memory helped, tis certain. I e'en think that beating happened because Diarmot had drawn too close to the truth. What puzzles me is, why did naught else happen for so verra long?"

"Because, if he couldnae remember anything, what was the need to kill him?" asked Gay, then frowned. "Nay, that makes no sense, for someone seems to have been trying to kill him before that."

"Aye, e'er since Anabelle died, Diarmot appears to have become an extremely unlucky mon," said Ilsa.

"Ye are certain that is when it all started?"

"Aye. I decided to ask about, to see if there was a

clearly marked time when all of Diarmot's troubles began. There was. But, puzzling o'er all that isnae why I wished to have this wee talk."

"Nay? Ye dinnae want to ken the answers to all of this?"

"I do, desperately. I feel those answers will only help me. Howbeit, tis truly only Diarmot who can hunt down all those answers for they are all tangled up in the memory he still cannae grasp."

"So, why did ye want this meeting? And that is what this is, aye?"

"Aye." Ilsa folded her hands upon the table and looked at each woman in turn. "Since the men seek out the who and the why, I think tis our duty to seek out the traitor. I think that can be done e'en if we dinnae ken the who and the why."

Fraser nodded. "It can. Ye dinnae always need to ken why a mon becomes a traitor to discover his betrayal."

"Couldnae it be dangerous?" asked Gay.

"I was poisoned in my own solar, right within these walls," said Ilsa. "I think the danger is here already."

"Ah, of course. Still, I think Nanty is searching for the traitor."

"It willnae hurt if we do the same. In truth, since Nanty is the laird's brother, he may have some trouble getting many people to talk freely to him. His murderous uncle didnae win many people's hearts. Then, shortly after he became laird here, Diarmot wed Anabelle and she only added to the unease and mistrust that still clings to this place and its laird. I fear Diarmot's unhappiness and then his wariness, his suspicious nature, didnae win many allies, either."

Glenda shook her head. "Nay. He cares for

these lands and the people better than his uncle
did, but he was e'er distant, an anger clinging to
him that kept people wary. The lad ne'er had a
chance to bring this wee clan together ere he was
mired in his own troubles. And, after that beating,
weel, he didnae have to accuse anyone to his face
for most to ken he was eyeing them all as if they
held a dirk at his throat."

It was all so sad, Ilsa thought as she chewed on a
thick slice of bread layered with soft cheese.
Diarmot's uncle had spent most of his life drunk,
jealous of his own brother, and sunk in plots that
kept three clans tearing at each other's throats
until they had nearly obliterated each other. The
man had done nothing to strengthen his own
lands or people. She suspected that when Diarmot
had arrived to take his place as laird, there had
been a brief flicker of hope only to have it crushed.
The new laird had quickly become all caught up in
his own troubled, unhappy life. Some things had
improved, but no sense of unity or loyalty had been
established. To the people of Clachthrom, their
laird was a morose stranger. To Diarmot, the people of Clachthrom were all possible threats.

Once all this trouble was behind them, Diarmot
would have a lot of work to do. He was going to
have to bring this small branch of the MacEnroy
clan a sense of unity, that sense of family that made
a clan so strong. Clachthrom had promise and he
was going to have to win the trust and respect of
his people to fulfill it. Ilsa did not think it would be
too difficult. In many ways, he had already improved the lot of his people. Diarmot just had to
let them come to know him as a man.

"That constant air of suspicion around Diarmot
can be wearying," Ilsa said. "One may understand

why tis there and sympathize, but it can still set one's teeth to grinding. Twill be better soon, once Diarmot kens exactly who his enemy is."

"But, can he forget and forgive?" asked Glenda. "I dinnae care to think on how many of the men on these lands cuckolded him."

"He didnae banish the men or hang anyone, did he? No beatings? No cut throats?"

"Nay, nary a one. I think he put most of the blame upon his wife, then simply stopped caring."

"Weel, I dinnae see the men as quite so blameless. After all, Diarmot's brothers resisted the woman. She wasnae raping the men. Mayhap some of the trouble round here is caused by guilt. But it matters not. Diarmot willnae be punishing anyone. He didnae then, and he willnae now. I think he just wants Anabelle set firmly in the past, all wrongs and sins forgotten. That will soon be clear to all those cuckolders. We must concern ourselves with only one mon now."

"The traitor," said Gay. "Do ye think it a mon?"

"Aye, I do," replied Ilsa, "and I cannae tell ye why I do. That doesnae mean we should ignore the women, however. I could be wrong. It could be one of them. All I ken is that someone is helping our enemy, that a traitor walks the halls of this keep and that brings the danger too close to the bairns for my liking."

All three women heartily agreed and Fraser asked, "Who do ye suspect?"

"Everyone save ourselves, Jenny, Nanty, and Tom."

"Geordie, too?" asked Gay. "Your husband believed what the mon said about the poisoned wine and that maid is still missing."

"It may be the truth," replied Ilsa, "and Nanty intends to hunt down that maid. Yet, I just cannae fully trust the mon. Dinnae ask me to explain why, as I cannae. Tis mostly a feeling. Could be instinct giving me a warning I should heed. Could be I just dinnae like dour men and Geordie is a verra dour mon. I will watch him."

"And I will find out what I can about the women working at the keep," said Glenda. "Gay can help some." She smiled faintly at Fraser, a hint of apology in her look. "I am nay sure ye can be much help there. Ye are tied too closely to the old lady of the keep and now the new one."

"I ken it." Fraser took a sip of wine, then frowned. "Isnae Gay tied rather closely to the new lady also?"

"Some, but she is the wet nurse, common born, and verra young. E'en though many people can see she is treated verra weel, nay like a servant, she is more one of them than ye are. And Jenny can help. Ye and her ladyship can watch the men."

"If the women would have trouble confiding in Ilsa or me, why should the men be any easier to get information out of?"

"Because ye are a woman." Glenda laughed softly at Fraser's look of confusion. "As long as ye dinnae set the fool in a chair and openly question him, a mon willnae guard his words as carefully around a woman as he will a mon. Most men simply cannae see a woman as a threat. Since they dinnae feel threatened, they speak freely. Tom and Nanty will also be watching each and every mon, too, but as some poor, weak, foolish woman, I suspect ye have a better chance of uncovering some clue." Glenda winked and the other women laughed.

They talked over their plans as they finished their meal and Ilsa felt hopeful. The number of people she and Diarmot could trust might be small, but they were clever and loyal. Since the traitor had to watch closely, gather information, and get that information to his master, he had to leave a trail. Things had moved swiftly since her poisoning and the men's attention had quickly become fixed upon finding the enemy who would, in turn, lead them to the traitor. Ilsa would dearly like to present them with that traitor when they returned.

Gay and Fraser excused themselves but when Glenda also began to leave, Ilsa briefly grasped her by the hand, halting her. "Dinnae mistake me, Glenda, I am verra pleased ye have decided to come live at the keep. That said, I feel the need to ask if ye are certain this is what ye really want."

"Och, aye." Glenda patted Ilsa's hand. "I had a nice wee house, but twas all it was. A nice wee house. A nice wee empty house. Aye, I have some friends in the village, but we can still visit each other. Here, weel, it certainly willnae be lonely. I can also do my healing work for all who need it, but dinnae have to worry about keeping warm, or dry, or my belly full. And here I can be safe."

"Was there some danger for ye in the village? I ken Wallace said—"

"Wheesht, that was just an angry young fool saying hard words without thought. Yet there have been times when fear or grief made people turn angry eyes upon me. Tis the lot of a healer. The same gift of healing and herb lore they all seek when they are hurt or ill becomes dark and threatening when there comes an illness that cannae be cured. Or a blight or drought which can bring hunger. Ye cannae always depend upon good sense prevailing in time to save ye from harm. Weel, here I nay only have companionship when I want it, and all my wordly needs met, but I have

verra thick walls guarded by some fine, burly men
to hide behind if tis necessary. Nay, I want to stay
here, lass."

"Weel, then, weelcome to Clachthrom."

Ilsa rested her forearms on the walls and stared
out over the moonlit lands of Clachthrom. She
had tried sleeping, but was too restless. She thought
on what Diarmot was doing, whether he would
succeed in his quest, and whether it would change
anything between them. A sigh escaped her when
she finally admitted to herself that she hated sleeping in that bed all alone.

"What are ye looking at, Mama?"

Odo stepped up beside her and Ilsa gave him
what she hoped was a very stern frown. "Ye shouldnae be up on these walls, my fine lad. I cannae believe Fraser let ye come up here alone. Nor would
anyone else."

"I had to talk to ye, Mama. I have come up here
before, too."

"Alone? At night?"

"Weel, nay."

"Odo, my love, ye are a verra clever boy, but I
think ye need to try harder to remember that ye
are still just a wee laddie. Climbing up to the top of
the keep's walls, at night, isnae something a lad of
but five should be doing."

"I am sorry, Mama."

Ilsa put her arm around the boy. "Just try to remember that ye are a little boy. Ye will grow to be a
mon soon enough. Now, what was so important
that ye had to follow me here and risk a scold?"

"Why is Papa unhappy?" asked Odo.

"Ah, I hadnae realized ye had noticed. There are many reasons. None of them have anything to do with ye. Ye do ken that, dinnae ye?"

"I think so, but he didnae like us before ye came."

"He didnae spend time with ye. That is verra different. There was trouble with his wife, the Lady Anabelle, then there was a lot of work that needed to be done here because his uncle wasnae a verra good laird, and then he was verra, verra ill. Now, that doesnae excuse him for ignoring ye children, but he didnae ignore ye because he didnae want ye or like ye. And he doesnae like ye now just because I got him to pay attention to ye. In truth, he did it all on his own. I didnae do much more than bring ye out of the nursery now and again and talk about ye."

Odo frowned for a moment, then nodded. "He got busy and didnae understand that we needed attention."

"Exactly. Is that all ye wanted to talk about?"

"Will he and my uncles find the bad person and kill him so that Papa and ye will be safe?"

"Aye, Odo, that is their plan. I wish there was some way to make your Papa safe without killing anyone, but I fear it will all end that way. Ye dinnae need to worry. Your father is strong and clever and surrounded by Camerons."

"Which undoubtedly makes Diarmot half mad," said Nanty as he walked up and scowled at them. "'Tis verra hard to guard people who willnae stay where they are put."

Ilsa allowed herself and Odo to be ushered back into the keep. She did think Nanty overdid the scolding, but bit her tongue to keep from complaining. Telling Nanty he sounded like a fussing old woman would probably not set a good example for Odo. As soon as she could, she kissed Odo good night and fled to her bedchamber. It might be lonely, but Nanty would not follow her in there.

CHAPTER SEVENTEEN

The keep at Dubheidland was impressive. Its walls were thick and high, its gates intimidating, and its great hall well furnished. It was also so filled with redheads, Diarmot was astonished that his eyes did not hurt. As he was led to the big head table, Sigimor abruptly introducing every man or youth they passed, Diarmot suspected it would take him many years to be able to remember all the Camerons by name. He could almost be grateful for Somerled, Sigimor's twin. That at least was one man he would clearly recall.

As he sat down and a faintly smiling Somerled served him wine, Diarmot became uncomfortably aware that very few of the looks he was receiving were friendly. Whatever tale the other brothers had told upon returning from Clachthrom had not won him any friends. He was not sure that whatever Sigimor chose to tell the gathered throng would help change that.

"Did Alexander's wife have the baby?" asked

Sigimor as he sat down between Somerled and Diarmot and helped himself to some wine.

"Aye, wee Mairi gave Alexander a son," replied Somerled. "They named the lad James and have gone to show her family the boy. Tis the first male born to that family for quite a while. He may weel be named heir, for there havenae been any other bairns born, either, and it doesnae look as if there will be."

"That will suit our Alexander fine, I suspect, although he didnae marry the lass for gain." Sigimor looked around and scowled at his brothers and cousins. "Why are ye all looking so fierce?"

"Why have ye brought Ilsa's mon and nay Ilsa?" asked a tall, thin youth with hair very similar to Ilsa's. "S'truth, from what Gilbert told us, I cannae understand why ye havenae gutted him."

"I cannae go about gutting your sister's husbands, Patone," Sigimor said. "Now, either Gilbert didnae tell the tale weel or ye didnae listen clear. So, clean out your earholes ere I do it for ye, and listen. I am only going to tell the tale once."

It only took a few moments for Diarmot to decide once was more than enough. Sigimor told no lies, but he softened no truths as he saw them, either. Diarmot did think the man did not need to repeat the fact that he considered his sister's husband's wits sadly rattled as often as he did. By the time Sigimor had finished, however, most of the looks cast his way were a little friendlier. Some, unfortunately, looked as if they expected him to start drooling.

"We were wondering why we havenae heard from ye," Sigimor said to Somerled. "I would have thought someone would have discovered something by now."

"Actually, Liam was preparing to go to Clachthrom in a day or two if we didnae hear from ye soon," said Somerled.

"What has he discovered then?"

"I sent Gilbert for him the moment ye were seen. He ought to be here soon, and he can tell ye himself."

"'Tis time for a meal. I am surprised he isnae here already. The lad hates to miss a meal."

"He hates to miss something else, too, and he was off getting a wee bit of the other when ye rode in."

"Nay wonder the lad ne'er gets fat from all the food he shoves down his gullet. He is tupping himself bone-thin every day and night. Do I ken the lass?"

"Nay. She isnae married and I doubt she will try pressing for marriage, either. I think Liam finally listened to some of what ye told him. I would ne'er have thought near drowning him in a horse trough would make him heed your words of wisdom, but it seems to have done so. Either that or he fears for his life," Somerled murmured and ignored Sigimor's scowl.

"I thought ye said Liam would settle down after a wee while, that he was only acting like a randy goat because he had been with the monks and they wouldnae let him have any," said a young boy with reddish-blond hair.

"Aye, I said that, Thormand," replied Sigimor. "And, I was right."

Thormand scowled at Sigimor. "He has been tupping near every lass for miles about for near to two years now."

"Weel, he was with the monks for five."

Diarmot took a quick drink of wine to smother his urge to laugh. He could tell by the look upon the youth's face that he desperately wanted to argue that ridiculous reasoning, but was not sure it was a good time to do so. Many another in the hall were doing exactly what Diarmot was doing. Sigimor wore that smirk that so irritated Diarmot when it was directed at him, and he could sympathize with the youth's blatant annoyance.

The man who strode into the hall at that moment quickly grabbed firm hold of Diarmot's attention. He knew this was the famous Liam because of all the somewhat lewd remarks directed at him as he strode past his kinsmen. With him was Gilbert, but Diarmot's reply to that man's greeting was only half-hearted.

Liam Cameron was a beautiful man. Diarmot hated to think of him so, yet could think of no other way to describe him. He was much like Gillyanne's cousin Payton, but bigger. Long dark copper hair threaded with gold, perfect features, a perfectly proportioned lean, strong body, and grace in his every step. When he neared them and smiled, Diarmot met the man's friendly blue-green gaze and suddenly sympathized with Connor's many grumbled complaints about Payton Murray. Such manly perfection was irritating.

"He is a good lad," Sigimor said, smiling faintly at Diarmot. "Still, someone that bonny can feel like a splinter under the skin at times."

"Aye," agreed Diarmot, for once not troubled that Sigimor had guessed his thoughts. "Lady Gillyanne has just such a cousin and I was suddenly able to understand why Connor keeps saying the lad needs seasoning, in the form of a broken nose and a few scars."

Sigimor chuckled, then looked at Liam who had

seated himself beside Diarmot and was filling a plate with food. "Worked up an appetite, did ye?"

"It was a long walk here," Liam drawled, then he looked at Diarmot. "How is my sweet cousin Ilsa? Did ye bring the bonny wee lass with you?"

"Nay," Diarmot replied, knowing he was being taunted. "I left her home with my eight children." He smiled faintly at the look of shock on Liam's face.

"Dinnae prod the mon, Liam. He is smarter than he looks," said Sigimor. "Now, tell us what ye ken."

"Ye need to go speak to Lord Ogilvey," Liam said.

"That is all ye have to say?"

"That is all I am going to say. Ye have to go and talk to Lord Ogilvey. Ask him about his wife, Lorraine."

Diarmot looked at Sigimor and suspected he was wearing the same look of shocked recognition that man was. "L.O. Lorraine Ogilvey." He looked at Liam. "Why will ye say no more?"

"Because a lot of what I have been told is gossip, nay more. Tis also sordid—sinful, if one heeds the monks—and I willnae blacken any woman or mon's name on gossip alone. Talk to Lord Ogilvey and I will confirm or nay what he says."

"Ye will be able to do that quickly, too, for ye will be going with us," said Sigimor.

Diarmot looked around the small clearing amongst the thick oak trees and fought to regain his composure. He knew the four Camerons riding with him sat on their horses a few feet away watching him, and suspected they knew why he had suddenly veered from the trail and come here. For several moments he had been so caught up in the return of a memory lost for too long that he doubted he would have noticed if they had ridden right over him.

As they had almost done once before, he thought. He had made love to Ilsa here several times. It had been a favorite trysting spot of theirs. Here was where her brothers had found them that day. Here was where he had taken her maidenhead.

Everything she had told him had been the truth. He had begun to believe it, but it was a relief to have his own memory now confirm it. Finlay and Cearnach were his sons, could be no other man's. That, too, he had decided upon his own, but could not help but heartily welcome the memory that proved it, the memory that took away all chance of insidious doubt.

Without saying a word, he remounted and rejoined the others. They, too, said nothing, simply continued on their way to Ogilvey's keep at Muirladen. He was grateful for their silence as he needed time to accept this new flooding of memory, time to calm himself and prepare himself for the confrontation to come. Despite some rather bloodcurdling threats from Sigimor, Liam had refused to say any more, and Diarmot found that ominous enough to feel that his wits had to be very sharp before he met Lord Ogilvey.

It was tempting, however, to leave them and the trouble ahead and return to the copse where he had first made love to Ilsa. He wanted to savor that sense of joy he had found that day, the passion followed by a peace and happiness he had not known in far too long. It had swept over him along with the return of that memory. The words she had whispered while held fast in his arms had seemed to echo in the copse, sweet words that he had not heard since. Her voice alive with passion and joy, Ilsa had told him that she loved him. He knew now as he had known then that she spoke the truth.

He wanted that back. In some ways, it was his own fault it had slipped through his fingers. Diarmot knew he could not completely blame his memory loss for the way he had treated Ilsa. He also knew it would not help his cause to return with his restored memory and try to pull from her all he had pushed aside during these last weeks. It had been a mistake not to let her know when he had begun to change his opinion of her, when his feelings for her had begun to eat away at his mistrust. Doing so now was going to have Ilsa think it was only the return of his memory that drove him, that washed away the mistrust.

There was no time to fret about that now, he thought with an inner sigh, as they rode through the gates of Muirladen. As he and the Camerons dismounted, Diarmot looked around and suddenly knew he had been here before. At that time the laird had refused to see him and he had ridden away angry and swearing to return, only to be beaten that night and forget the man altogether. This time he would not be turned away.

Even as he came to that decision, Sigimor and Somerled began to remove the opposition. When the fact that Sigimor was a neighboring laird did not get him in the door, he simply picked up the guard and tossed him aside. Somerled did the same with the one standing in front of him. The other men standing around began to edge away. With Somerled and the rest of them watching his back, Sigimor strode into the great hall of Muirladen.

"Ye have to admit my cousin has a memorable way of introducing himself to the neighbors," murmured Liam as he stood next to Diarmot.

Diarmot shook his head. He was beginning to think that all the Camerons were just slightly mad. The way Lord Ogilvey was staring at the Cameron twins told Diarmot he was thinking the same. When Sigimor and Somerled sat down flanking the laird and helped themselves to some of the man's wine, Diarmot looked at Liam. That man just shrugged and moved to sit next to Somerled. With Tait at his heels, Diarmot moved to sit next to Sigimor; Tait sat down next to him.

"What are ye doing here?" demanded Lord Ogilvey.

"We came to ask ye a few questions about your wife," began Sigimor.

"Lorraine has been dead for eleven years."

"And the two girls who fostered with her at about that time."

Lord Ogilvey paled slightly. "I dinnae wish to talk about those spawn of the devil."

"I really dinnae care what ye want, m'laird," Sigimor drawled, his voice icy and hard. "Ye will tell me what I want to ken. Ye see, it may help me keep my wee sister alive. Since I am rather fond of my sister, she being the only one I have, I willnae be verra happy with anyone who doesnae help me protect her."

"I havenae e'en met your sister. I am nay doing anything to hurt her."

"I didnae accuse ye. What ye ken from years ago is what I seek, for I believe it will lead me to my sister's enemy. Do ye recognize this mon?" he asked Lord Ogilvey and nodded toward Diarmot.

"Nay," replied Lord Ogilvey. "Why should I?"

"Because I tried to speak to ye a year past," said Diarmot, and nodded in reply to the question in Sigimor's quick glance. "I remember coming here after leaving Dubheidland to go home, but this mon refused to speak to me."

"And that night he was beaten near to death in the village here," added Sigimor. "Are ye nay curious as to why he wanted to speak to ye or why someone would feel compelled to try and silence him?"

"Ye are nay going to go away, are ye?" Lord Ogilvey asked in a weary, defeated voice.

"Nay, m'laird, we arenae," replied Sigimor.

"I believe my late wife was one of the lasses who fostered with your wife, ten years ago or more," said Diarmot. "Anabelle." His eyes widened at the foulness of the curse Lord Ogilvey spit out.

"My poor Lorraine had no bairns," the laird said. "She thought it would be wondrous to have two girls here to teach and help raise. The woman had such plans, expected sweet lasses who would learn from her and bring her joy. Instead she got two demons from hell. Your Anabelle was fair on the outside, but black as night on the inside."

"If the ones sent to her were so bad, why did she allow them to stay?"

"Stubborn. My Lorraine could be stubborn. She wasnae going to let two lasses beat her." He frowned. "I think she also began to believe it was her duty to try and save them." He snorted. "I could have told her there was no saving those two, that they were damned ere they arrived here. If I had kenned what they would cost me, I would have thrown them out myself."

"What did they cost ye, m'laird?" asked Liam quietly.

"My wife. Och, I cannae prove it. If I had had proof I would have had the little bitches hanged from the walls. Weel, that Anabelle for certain. Nay sure I could have survived hanging the other one e'en though I am sure she was the one who did the killing."

"Why would hanging her have been so dangerous?"

"Powerful family."

Diarmot became aware that this was not the first tankard of wine the man had drunk. Lord Ogilvey was teetering on the edge of drunkedness. The ragged look of the man told Diarmot that Lord Ogilvey spent a great deal of his time in that state.

"What happened to your wife, m'laird?" he asked, anxious to get his answers before the man was too drunk to provide them.

"That Anabelle was a whore," Lord Ogilvey replied and shook his head. "She was a viper-tongued slut. My wife tried everything she could think of to change the girl. At first she just lectured Anabelle, tried to talk sense into her. Naught worked. When she caught Anabelle with the shepherd's lad, she had the girl locked in her room for three days, no food, only a wee drink of water. My wife was nearly killed falling down the stairs that night. She couldnae say for certain whether she was pushed or not, wouldnae believe the girls would do it. I believed they would. Lorraine wouldnae heed me. She was so certain that discipline was all that was needed."

"But discipline didnae work?"

"Nay. Each time she disciplined Anabelle something happened to her. Then she caught Anabelle doing something that shocked her to the bone. She wouldnae tell me what. Lorraine was a godly woman and whate'er she had seen was too sinful for her to put into words. I tried to convince her that the church calls a lot of things sinful that are-nae so verra bad, but Lorraine believed all the priest told her about sin. There was nay any may-hap or compromise about that. She had Anabelle beaten. Nay as badly as I thought the lass deserved, for past sins if nay the one that had Lorraine so upset. My Lorraine was dead two days later."

"Dead? How?"

"I dinnae ken, but she died screaming. I think she was poisoned in some way, but no one could find out how. I sent those bitches away and buried my wife." He rubbed a hand over his eyes. "All Lorraine wanted was a child. She wanted one so badly she was willing to borrow someone else's for a wee while and she got two demons who mur-dered her."

"Who was the other lass?"

"I think she was the worse. Anabelle was brazen, didnae hide what she was. She was the enemy ye could see, if ye catch my meaning. That other one was so sweet, so calm. It took ye a while to see the evil in her, for when ye suspected it, ye had to doubt. How could such a bonny, quiet lass be evil? Ah, but she was. Behind that sweet face was a cold, evil woman, a killer. She was the enemy lurking in the shadows. She hadnae been here verra long when I began to see that she wasnae right, but Lorraine wouldnae heed me. The way that lass would sit there, so sweet, but with a coldness in her pale blue eyes that would chill ye to the bone, made me so uneasy I oftimes couldnae bear to be in the same room with her."

Diarmot felt a chill invade his bones at the man's words. Sweet, calm, pale blue eyes. There was only one woman he knew who fit that description, but he scolded himself for jumping to conclusions. There could be other women like that, and Lord Ogilvey's description did not have to be that accurate. Even so, he could not shake the suspicion growing inside of him.

"Who was the other lass, m'laird?" he asked again.

"Why, the daughter of my laird."

When the man said no more, Diarmot had to fight the urge to get up and shake him. "And who is your laird, Lord Ogilvey?" he pressed, trying to be polite, but feeling as tense and aggravated as the Camerons looked.

"Sir Lesley Campbell. He was so pleased that Lorraine was willing to train his lass Margaret." He frowned, vaguely cognizant of the shock in the men seated at his table. "There was some trouble with the lass recently, I think. Some marriage she was supposed to make, but didnae. I suspicion that is why she is gone to her cousin's."

It was taking all of Diarmot's strength not to race out of Muirladen and ride straight to Clachthrom. "Her cousin's?"

"Aye." Lord Ogilvey frowned. "Let me think. The woman lives in a wee cottage nay far from some oddly named place. Crackdrum? Clackhum?" He shrugged. "The woman's name is Elspeth Hamilton, if that is any help."

Diarmot was not sure what he said to the man, but the next clear thought he had was that he was going to beat the Camerons senseless as soon as they let go of him. He struggled in Sigimor's tight hold, but the man was far stronger than he was. They were outside in the bailey of Muirladen, but the Camerons obviously had no intention of letting him get on his horse.

"Calm yourself, lad," Sigimor said.

"I have to get back to Clachthrom," he said, even as he struggled to do as Sigimor commanded. "The woman Lord Ogilvey called a demon is living but an hour's ride from my lands. She can get to Ilsa at any time she pleases."

"Aye, and she has been there for a while, hasnae she? A few more hours willnae make any difference. Your brother Nanty and Tom are watching o'er Ilsa, as are the women. She is protected for now. Twill be dark soon and, if ye go hieing yourself off now, ye will just end up with your fool neck broken. That willnae help her, either."

Diarmot took several deep, slow breaths and felt Sigimor's grip loosen. The man was right. It was too late to ride out now. Waiting for dawn would be wiser, safer, and give him time to plan what he would do when he got there. The danger had been there all the time. It was not any more acute now than it had been just because he knew about it.

"Cease calling me lad," he muttered as he mounted Challenger. "I am of an age with you."

"As ye wish," said Sigimor as he, Somerled, Liam, and Tait mounted and followed Diarmot out of the keep. "What would ye wish me to call ye? Rogue? Fool? Lecherous swine? Debaucher of my only sister?"

"How is it that your kinsmen have allowed ye to survive for so long?"

"It wasnae easy," muttered Liam from the safety of riding on the side of Diarmot away from Sigimor.

That started an argument and, by the time they

returned to the great hall of Dubheidland, Diarmot was in control of himself. Since he knew the Camerons were not very good at restraint, he suspected they had used the argument to gain control of themselves, as well. He was a little surprised that it was Sigimor who had retained the sense to halt a mad dash to Clachthrom. Since it was a temptation still almost too strong to resist, Diarmot sat next to Sigimor at the head table and poured himself a large tankard of ale.

"I cannae believe I almost married the woman," he muttered, then grimaced when he realized he had spoken that thought out loud. Worse, Sigimor had heard it.

"Ye mean the calm, sweet, face-like-an-angel Margaret?" asked Sigimor, sipping at his ale as he watched Diarmot closely. "The one who was going to give ye peace in your life? The one who wasnae beset by troublesome emotion? Weel, aside from that urge to kill people."

Diarmot decided he was getting accustomed to this brother of Ilsa's for he just quirked a brow at the man and said, "I believe ye saw the lass. Did she look like a murderess to ye?"

"Nay, I will give ye that."

"So kind."

"Weel, tis certain ye havenae got much sense in choosing wives. Tis a verra good thing we convinced ye to choose our Ilsa."

It was, but Diarmot was not about to admit that to this man. "Ye mean Ilsa who throws ewers at my head? Ilsa who knocks me on my arse in the bailey in front of most of my men and some of my family? Sweet wee Ilsa who says I am fouler than the slime at the bottom of a midden heap? That Ilsa?"

"Aye," Sigimor agreed, laughter shining in his

eyes. "At least ye need nay worry she will sneak up behind ye and cut your throat."

"True. Although, she did threaten to rip it out with her teeth once." He winked at Somerled who was laughing along with Tait and Liam, but then he grew serious. "Margaret is the one trying to kill me and Ilsa. I am certain of it. Margaret is Precious Love."

"Aye," Sigimor agreed with equal seriousness. "She was wedding herself to ye so that she could kill ye with ease. I wouldnae be surprised to hear, if ye think on it a wee while, that your meeting the lass and the march toward the altar were all her doing. Sweetly and calmly, of course. That would explain why there was that time of peace and safety. Her attempts to kill ye in other ways having failed, she had planned to get as close to ye as a woman can and deal with the problem herself. Ilsa ruined that grand plan."

"Thus the return to random attacks and the attempts to kill Ilsa. Now we have our enemy. I just need to discover who her ally is within Clachthrom. It could be mon or woman." He frowned. "She left behind two maids, one of whom went missing after Ilsa was poisoned."

"Why did she leave them behind?"

"The lasses claimed they had no one to go back to and were needed at Clachthrom, could be more use, and, I suspected, gain a higher standing. I e'en thought they might have found lovers at Clachthrom." He frowned and took a deep drink of ale. "I concede I didnae pay much heed to the lasses, yet they did their work. The woman who rules o'er the lot of them said they were good workers. Ye would think someone would have noticed if one or both of them were slipping off somewhere too often or asking too many questions."

"Weel, we can find the answers to those questions when we get back to Clachthrom. May find your brother already has a few. He was thinking about trying to find that maid."

"That might help. What I am finding difficult to understand is why Margaret would try to kill Ilsa. Tis evident the marriage was but a means to seek revenge upon me, and that she has found men to help her try again to kill me. I am nay sure I can think of a reason for her to kill Ilsa. What could that possibly gain her? Ilsa has ne'er wronged her, either."

"Except to arrive at the church and ruin a verra good plan," said Liam, then shrugged when everyone looked at him. "Ye are dealing with someone who isnae quite right in the head, and ye expect to find logic in her actions? Ilsa ruined her plan to marry ye and wed ye. She tried to kill ye with hired fools again, and again failed. So, kill Ilsa and go back to the other plan of marrying ye and then killing ye. Actually, there may weel be a strange logic there."

"Do ye think she may have given up her plan of killing me for the moment and fixed her attention upon Ilsa?" asked Diarmot.

"There is a verra good chance of that. The poison was meant for Ilsa, there was no error there, nay a sad mischance. Ilsa was supposed to die. That would seem to prove that she has returned to her plan of marrying ye and becoming a widow as soon as possible."

"We dinnae leave until dawn," Diarmot said when he caught Sigimor watching him intently. "I ken it. I just pray I will find everything as I left it when I get back to Clachthrom."

"Everything will be fine," said Sigimor. "Ye have good men and women watching o'er Ilsa."

"That I do, but kenning that isnae really enough to still all my worry."

"I am nay sure anything could do that."

"Nay, especially since I doubt ye can assure me that my wife willnae do anything foolish." He sighed and nodded when none of the Camerons present offered him that assurance.

CHAPTER EIGHTEEN

There was such a dark look upon Nanty's face as he strode into the garden that Ilsa felt her heart skip with alarm. Diarmot had been gone a sennight. There had been time enough for him to have reached Dubheidland, get into some trouble, and have someone return to Clachthrom with the bad news. She slowly rose from the herb bed she had been weeding, telling herself to be calm, that she could easily be fretting over nothing. It did little to ease her sudden trepidation.

"Is something wrong?" she asked Nanty as he came to a stop in front of her.

"I am nay sure," he replied. "A lad has just come to Clachthrom to say he and his father have found the body of a young woman in a ditch."

"Oh, dear, do ye think it the maid who went missing?"

"I cannae be sure, yet who else could it be? No one else has reported that any other lass has gone missing."

"Nay, they havenae. So, ye must ride away and find out what this is all about."

"I am supposed to be guarding ye, Ilsa." He held up his hand to silence her protests. "I ken I havenae been at your side every hour of every day, have e'en left the keep for wee forays outside these walls. Yet it sorely troubles me to do so now. If this is the missing maid, and if she has been murdered, that alters a great many of the assumptions we have made since ye were poisoned."

"Ah, of course." She wiped her hands upon her apron. "Her murder could mean she wasnae the one who poisoned me. It could mean that the poor lass was led away and murdered just to make us all believe she was guilty. How sad."

Nanty dragged his hand through his hair. "'Tis far more than sad, Ilsa. That would mean the one who did poison ye is still within these walls. E'en worse, that person is one who thinks naught of murdering some poor, innocent lass just to hide his own trail."

Ilsa grasped him by the arm and started to lead him out of the garden. "Then ye had best find out if that is what has happened, hadnae ye?"

"I told Diarmot and your brothers I would watch o'er ye."

"And ye have. This is also watching o'er me. We need to ken if this is the maid, if she died by accident whilst fleeing from her crime, or if she was naught but a pawn in someone else's deadly game. Twill tell us if the killer still lurks within these walls and that is verra important."

Nanty laughed softly when they reached the part of the bailey near the stables. "And, I cannae disagree with ye because ye have just spoken aloud all I have been thinking. Yet, curse it, Ilsa, if it does mean the killer is still here—"

"He or she has been here all along. And managed to poison me when Diarmot and my brothers were here to help ye, er, watch o'er me. I dinnae think it will make much difference if ye ride off, for a few hours e'en. The danger is still within the keep. Dinnae forget, I have the women to watch my back."

"I could leave young Tom—"

"Nay, take him. Ye need someone to watch your back. If that trouble at the cave wasnae an accident, our enemy has already revealed an utter lack of concern for anyone who gets in his way. Or, mayhap, a lack of patience. Who kens when he might decide that ye are in the way. Take Tom."

"I will return as quickly as possible," he vowed, then strode away calling for Tom.

Ilsa smiled faintly as she headed into the keep to clean away the dirt from the garden. Nanty was trying very hard to make sure nothing happened to her or the children while Diarmot was gone. The man's sense of responsibility ran very deep. It was comforting even though it could cause him to be annoying at times.

She sighed as she entered her bedchamber. Her instincts told her the maid was no more than a pawn. Considering how long she had been missing, there might not be any way to tell how she had died. That would make this possible murder a successful one, giving the killer the time he sought. That would be beyond irritating, Ilsa decided as she scrubbed her hands and face clean.

As she patted her face dry with a soft linen cloth, Ilsa moved to look out the window at her ever improving garden. From here she could see the progress she was making. She could also see Geordie. The man looked around several times as he made his way toward the high walls that bordered the garden on two sides. Since no one could get up onto the walls from the garden, Ilsa was immediately suspicious. She gasped as Geordie walked to the far corner, then seemed to just disappear.

Lacing up her gown as she ran, Ilsa made her way down the stairs and out into the garden as quickly as she could. It was not until she was in the same place she had last seen Geordie that she saw how he had managed to slip from view so completely. Hidden by a gnarled apple tree was a thick door set in the wall. It was a lovely old door with intricate carvings upon it, but it was also a deadly weakness in Diarmot's wall. She had to wonder how Diarmot had missed it or, if he did know about it, why he had allowed it to remain.

Ilsa took a deep breath, eased open the door, and found herself facing a stone wall. It took her a moment to see that she had to move sideways, that an attempt had been made to hide the door with an irregularity in the wall. Once at the edge of the wall, she peered around it and looked for Geordie. The man was just disappearing down the far side of the rise upon which Clachthrom was set.

A dozen thoughts raced through her mind. She should find someone to go with her as she followed Geordie. Geordie could be the traitor. The man could be dangerous. If he was meeting the one who was trying to kill Diarmot, both men could be dangerous. If she did not hurry, he would be impossible to follow, and whatever answer to their mystery he might provide would be lost.

Lifting up her skirts slightly, Ilsa hurried after

him. Once he was on the far side of the rise, he made no attempt to watch out for anyone following him. Nonetheless, Ilsa did her best to stay out of sight, but she had to wonder if his behavior was a sign of arrogance or of innocence. When he stopped at a small, roughly built shelter and brought out a sturdy pony, she cursed. Although the pony would not be able to go very fast with such a large man upon its back, it would still require her to move a lot faster to keep up with him.

Geordie looked around once, mounted the pony, and trotted away. She waited only a moment before hurrying after him. She was just beginning to think she would have to give up the chase when he reined in before a small cottage. A beautiful black mare waited there and, as Ilsa slumped against a tree to catch her breath, she knew whoever Geordie was about to meet had to have a comfortably full purse. Such a horse was not a poor man's mount.

A woman shrouded in a cloak answered Geordie's rap at the door. When Geordie pulled the woman into his arms, kissing her even as he pushed her back inside the cottage and shut the door behind them, Ilsa cursed. She had exhausted herself to discover a tryst. Just to be certain that really was all it was, Ilsa sat down and leaned against the trunk of the tree to watch the cottage. No one else came or went and, at what Ilsa decided was about an hour, Geordie came back outside.

The woman was heavily cloaked yet again, which Ilsa found a little odd. Geordie's leave-taking was not affectionate, either. No kisses, no lingering glances, no touching. Either the lovers had had an argument or the love affair was growing cold. Geordie rode back toward Clachthrom and, after watching him for a while, the woman walked back inside the cottage and slammed the door. As Ilsa started on the long journey home she did not rush, and tried to convince herself that it had not been an utter waste of her time. She had discovered a door that, although cleverly disguised, was a serious breach in Diarmot's protective walls. Ilsa hoped Nanty had a great deal more luck than she had had.

Nanty held a cloth over his nose and tried desperately not to disgrace himself by becoming ill. The maid had obviously died shortly after she had disappeared. A shallow grave had not been quite enough to protect her from all the carrion, small and large. It was impossible to tell at a glance how she might have died. A closer inspection might tell him more, but Nanty was not sure he could stomach it.

"Tis the lass ye have been looking for?" asked the father of the boy who had fetched Nanty.

"Aye," replied Nanty. "The hair and the gown match what the women all told me to look for. She is also missing the third finger on her right hand, the result of a rather nasty childhood accident."

"We can wrap the poor lass in a blanket, put her in the cart, and take her to be buried. Unless she has people who will be wanting her body."

"Nay, no people, Duncan. We shall do as ye suggest in a few moments. I must see if there is any sign of how she died." He grimaced and started to kneel down only to have the older man grab him by the arm and pull him back up onto his feet.

"I will do it, lad," said Duncan.

"Tis my duty," began Nanty.

"By the look upon your face, ye willnae do much

looking ere ye empty your belly all o'er the lass's body. I have a strong stomach and nay much sense of smell. What are ye looking for?" he asked even as he knelt by the maid's body.

"Some sign that she didnae die of natural causes, of a fall or the like."

"Och, aye, there is a sign, right enough. Throat was cut."

"Are ye certain?"

"Verra certain. A big, deep cut from ear to ear, poor lass. Whoever wielded the knife had a strong hand. Didnae need such a vicious cut to kill such a wee lass with her having such a wee throat." Duncan stood up and brushed himself off. "Was that what ye were looking for?"

"Aye." Nanty sighed. "I wish we hadnae found it, but, aye, tis what I was looking for."

"Do ye ken who would have killed the poor lass?"

"I fear I dinnae, but I do mean to find out. My brother, the laird, will, too."

Nanty managed to gain control of his uneasy stomach long enough to help Duncan and Tom get the maid's body into the cart. He and Tom then followed Duncan and his son to the church. It eased Nanty's embarrassment over his own weak stomach when Father Goudie had the same trouble. After burying the maid, Nanty joined Father Goudie in his rooms at the rear of the small stone church.

"I would have thought ye weel accustomed to death," Nanty said after watching Father Goudie take a very hearty drink of wine.

"Death from illness," Father Goudie said. "Death from old age, from an accident, and a rare hanging or two. I have been blessed by peace for near all my life. Few battle deaths. This, this slaughter of a young lass? Nay, this isnae something I have dealt with before." He shivered. "And most of the bodies I see are, weel, fresh."

"Ah, aye, that was most unpleasant."

"This has to do with your brother's troubles, aye?"

"I believe so. This was the young maid who went missing on the day Ilsa was poisoned. Either she was taken away and murdered simply to make us turn our attention on her or she had some part in the poisoning and was killed so that she wouldnae chance to reveal anything. This is all so devious, with twists and turns and unknowns. I am nay good at this. Give me an enemy who spits right in my eye and faces me sword in hand and I ken what to do. This? In this, I stumble at every turn." He shook his head. "If I e'er find the one behind all of this, I swear I will gut him simply for being so cursed troublesome."

"Or her."

"Ah, of course. Although, a woman didnae do this. Of that much, at least, I am certain. As Duncan said, the hand that made that cut was a strong one." He finished his wine and stood up. "Tis best I return to the keep now,"

"Aye, ye shouldnae leave her ladyship alone, unguarded, for too long, and the sun is setting. Twill be dark ere long," said Father Goudie as he walked Nanty to the front of the church.

"Weel, I wouldnae say she was unguarded, nay with Gay, Glenda, Jenny, and Fraser all watching out for her."

"But they are women."

Nanty grinned. "Aye, they are. Weel, two of them are nay much more than girls. But they watch her verra weel. Tisnae their ability to guard Ilsa that worries me for I ken they will do as weel as any mon."

"Then what does worry ye?"

"My brother's wife isnae verra good at staying where she is put."

Ilsa slipped back into the garden and breathed a sigh of relief. Getting back inside Clachthrom unseen was not as easy as getting out. The men upon the walls were watching all approaches very carefully, as they should. Since she did not wish to be caught outside alone, she had had to be very careful. The dread of enduring another lecture from Nanty had been very inspiring.

As she walked through the gardens, something drew her attention. She frowned slightly as she picked up a small wooden horse from beneath a rose bush. It was Alice's favorite toy, one carved for her by young Tom. The girl never went anywhere without it. Ilsa tucked it into the small leather bag she wore at her waist and hurried toward the keep. It could be that Alice had dropped the toy and had simply not yet noticed it was missing, but it made Ilsa uneasy.

She stepped into the nursery, smiled absently at Fraser and Glenda and looked around. Odo, Aulay, Ivy, Gregor, and Ewart were all present, quietly playing with their toys. The twins, Alice, and Gay were the only ones missing. Ilsa sternly told herself that that was not unusual as she sat down on a padded stool near Glenda and Fraser. As she touched the little bag holding Alice's horse, she felt an odd increasing chill, however.

"And where have ye been?" asked Fraser, frowning with a hint of severity. "Gay was looking for ye."

"Why? Was something troubling the twins?" Ilsa asked, reluctant to tell Fraser what she had been doing. Fraser was as fond of lecturing her as Nanty and she did it far better than he did.

"Nay. She wanted to take the bairns into the garden. She got that maid Lucy to help her take them outside. Alice went along as weel. Gay was hoping that ye might join them there later."

"Fraser, I was just in the garden and didnae see any of them."

"Ye would have had to see them or meet them as they returned here."

"I did neither," Ilsa said as she stood up and headed toward the door.

Fraser rose to follow. "Odo, Ivy, watch the young ones," she ordered when Glenda moved to join her.

Ilsa did not wait for the two older women, but raced down to the gardens. It did not surprise her, however, when they were only a few steps behind her as she entered the garden. In silent agreement, they began to search the garden, although Ilsa suspected they were as uncertain about what they looked for as she was.

"O'er here," called Glenda.

Fraser fell into step beside her as Ilsa hurried toward Glenda. The woman was crouched down on the far side of the raised herb garden, bending over something on the ground. Ilsa gasped when she saw that it was a bound and gagged Gay. She fell to her knees beside Gay even as Glenda removed the gag on Gay's mouth and Fraser untied the ropes binding her thin wrists together behind her back, then her ankles.

"Gay, the twins? Alice?" Ilsa asked, fighting to calm herself even as fear twisted her insides into tight knots.

"Gone," Gay replied. "They took them."

"They? Who are they?"

"The maid I was with and Geordie."

Ilsa nearly cried out in dismay. She had been so close to Geordie, might have been able to stop him. Instead, she had just been disgruntled over wasting so much time following him to a tryst. Or so she had thought. Ilsa now suspected that what she had seen had been a final meeting before the enacting of this heinous plot to steal her children. She had to take several deep breaths before she was calm enough to speak again.

"Gay, I need ye to tell me exactly what happened," Ilsa said, taking her friend's hand in hers while Fraser placed an arm around Gay's slender shoulders.

"I thought it would be nice to bring the bairns out into the sun for a wee while. I looked for ye, but couldnae find ye anywhere. Where did ye go?" asked Gay.

"I will tell ye in a wee while. Your tale is far more important."

"Twas odd now that I think upon it, but suddenly Lucy was there. She started talking about taking the bairns into the garden, how her old mother always thought a wee bit of sun was good for the wee ones. Weel, since I was planning to do that anyway, I thought her appearing was most convenient."

"Aye, too convenient," muttered Glenda.

Ilsa nodded. "I fear so. A plot and our Gay didnae e'en have to be tricked into playing along.

Lucy probably couldnae believe her good fortune. Go on, Gay."

"We fetched the bairns," said Gay. "Alice wanted to come, too, and of course I said she could. For a brief moment I got the feeling Lucy wasnae pleased about that, but she was already smiling and chattering again so my uneasiness faded. We couldnae have been in the gardens verra long when I was grabbed from behind."

Knowing what fears must have risen up inside of Gay, Ilsa was not surprised when her friend shuddered. She tightened her clasp upon Gay's hand a little, silently offering her the courage to continue. Fraser tightened her arm around Gay's shoulders slightly as well, giving the girl a small hug.

Gay took several deep breaths before she could continue. "Lucy had been standing verra close to Alice and she had the poor wee lass gagged and bound verra quickly. The mon who gagged and bound me then set me down here and looked at me. He was masked, but I kenned who it was. I recognized his voice, his size, the wee scar by his mouth, and his hands. Geordie has big, strong hands with large knuckles and thick tufts of hair on the backs of his fingers. Aye, twas Geordie."

Either Gay had a naturally keen eye or she had been carefully studying everyone at Clachthrom. "Did they, did they hurt the children, Gay?"

"Nay. Geordie said ye must come to a wee cottage," she pulled a piece of paper from inside her bodice, "and he has left ye a map. He wants ye there within an hour after the sun starts to set. If ye dinnae appear ere the sun finishes setting, the bairns and wee Alice will be killed. He says they will be killed if anyone follows ye, too."

After looking at the map, Ilsa cursed. "I ken where this cottage is. I was there today." She nodded at the shock on the faces of the three women. "I saw Geordie in the garden, saw him from my bedchamber window. He walked toward the wall then, weel, disappeared."

"Tis just what he did this time. I kept twisting about to watch him and Lucy. They went to the old apple tree then they were gone. I couldnae see how or to where."

"There is a wee door set in the wall. I followed Geordie. He has a sturdy wee pony stabled nay far from here. He rode to this cottage to meet with a woman. Since he kissed her and then disappeared into the cottage for about an hour, I decided it was naught but a tryst. Now I ken different. I was so close. I could have done something to prevent all of this."

"What? Charged the cottage bellowing fierce war cries and slashed the mon with your eating knife?" said Glenda.

Ilsa blinked in surprise over the sharp tone of Glenda's voice then sighed as she recognized the truth behind her words. Even if she had guessed that the man and his lover were plotting against her, she could not have done anything at that time. She had been alone and unarmed. By the time she had returned to Clachthrom, her children had been taken from her. She could have returned faster, but, since she had had no idea that a threat to her children loomed, there had been no reason to exhaust herself by trying to beat Geordie back to Clachthrom.

"Who was this woman he was meeting?" asked Fraser.

"I ne'er saw her," replied Ilsa. "She greeted him at the door, but she was weel concealed by a cloak, the hood pulled up o'er her head and shadowing her features. Twas the same when Geordie left."

"Which would seem to imply that she doesnae wish to risk being seen by anyone, that she kens she will be easily recognized by everyone at Clach-throm."

"I will ken who the bitch is verra soon," said Ilsa as she stood and helped Gay to her feet.

"Ye are nay thinking of going there alone, are ye?" asked Fraser as she and Glenda also stood.

"That is what has been demanded," replied Ilsa. "If I do anything else, I will risk the lives of my children. I cannae do that."

"Ilsa, they want ye dead."

"I ken it, but what choice do I have? The twins are so wee they cannae do anything more than cry until they make a person's head ache, and Alice is but a tiny lass of three. They cannae help themselves. They would be as easy to slaughter as a day-old lamb. I have to go."

"I am sure the men would ken how to follow ye so that no one would see them."

"Probably, but I have seen the cottage, Fraser. Tis set in a verra open area. Aye, they could get close, but those last yards hold nary a rock for them to hide behind. They would be seen as they made the last rush to the place. Mayhap they could stop the killing of one or two of the bairns, but I am sure our enemies would have time to cut the wee throat of at least one, if nay all of them." She nodded when the women cursed.

"This will give them a verra large victory," said Glenda.

"Nay as big as they think," said Ilsa. "Despite his attempt to hide his face, Geordie was recognized. The traitor has been found. E'en better, he doesnae ken that he has been uncovered. Through him, Diarmot can find his enemy."

"Before or after he buries ye?" snapped Fraser.

"I am nay a day-old lamb, Fraser," Ilsa said as she started toward the keep, needing to gather a few things before she went to the cottage. "I willnae be so verra easy to kill. The woman isnae a great threat, I am thinking," she continued as the three women hurried to follow her. "She has done none of this herself. She hires men. Tis Geordie I must worry about."

"I ken what ye are thinking, that ye have no choice, but shouldnae ye at least take a wee moment or two to try and think of one?" asked Glenda.

"I havenae got a moment or two," replied Ilsa.

The women all followed Ilsa into her bedchamber. She could hear them whispering amongst themselves as she collected up three daggers and hid them as carefully as she could on her person. She also slipped a packet of strong herbs into the little pouch at her waist. If the opportunity arose, they would serve well to temporarily blind her opponent.

"Ilsa, I cannae like this," said Fraser.

"I have nay choice," she repeated. "Ye ken that. Ye must. Now, if Nanty returns, I cannae stop ye from telling him, but I would ask that ye use careful judgment. If he returns ere I have e'en gone o'er the rise, that would be too soon. He would hie out after me and then the game would be lost. Instead of the chance of burying me, we will all be standing o'er the graves of my children."

"Do ye really think ye can fight these people?"

"I grew up surrounded by brothers and male cousins. I am nay some sweet, gentle maid. I may be small and slender, but I can be verra vicious, e'en dangerous. If luck is with me, aye, I have a chance of defeating these pigs. It will all depend upon how the children are held. If there is an actual knife held to the throat of one of them, that will cause me to hesitate to act."

"Mayhap just one mon," began Gay as she joined Fraser and Glenda in following Ilsa back to the garden.

"Once I am there, once I appear to have obeyed their commands, I think there is a chance someone could get near the cottage unseen. I can keep all eyes upon me. Dinnae tell me what ye are planning now that I have said that," she added quickly when Fraser opened her mouth to speak. "I dinnae want to ken. All the way to the cottage all I will be able to think of is that plan and how terribly wrong it could go. Once I am at the cottage, I will make sure the ones there have all their attention upon me. Tis all I can do." She paused at the little door which led out of the garden and kissed each of her three friends. "Remember to tell Nanty about the door here, and about Geordie."

"And Lucy," said Gay. "She is the other traitor."

"I dinnae think we will need to worry about Lucy."

Fraser frowned after Ilsa slipped out through the hidden door then started back to the keep with the other two women. "I dinnae like this. I understand there isnae much choice, but I still cannae like this."

"Nay," agreed Glenda. "There must be some trick the men have that would help Ilsa and the bairns. Yet, if we say anything about this, they will-nae be heeding us about the dangers or risks. Once we tell anyone, the matter will be completely out of our control. I wouldnae be able to stop worrying that, instead of helping Ilsa and the bairns, we have helped to kill them."

Gay suddenly cursed. "I dinnae think it matters. Ilsa didnae return the map to the cottage."

"She did that apurpose," said Fraser, and sighed heavily as they entered the nursery. "We can tell anyone we please what has happened, but it will-nae do any good if we cannae tell them where it is happening." She frowned as she studied the too quiet group of children near the fireplace. "Where is Odo?"

"He went to the garderobe," Ivy replied.

The way the girl could not look straight at Fraser told the woman she was lying. "Ivy, I ask ye again, where is Odo?"

"He went to see what was happening in the garden," she replied.

"I didnae see him."

"He was there. Then ye left, but he didnae. He was looking all about the garden. When ye came back, he hid. We didnae see him again until Ilsa left and then ye started to come back here. We saw him walk into the wall just like Ilsa did."

"That boy has followed her," said Glenda, shaking her head.

"I will get Jenny and we will go after him," said Gay.

"Nay, ye cannae. That wee boy can probably follow a flea from bed to bed in a monastery. He will be able to find his way back here. And if he is seen, I dinnae think Geordie or his allies will think much of it." Fraser shook her head. "He willnae be seen. Howbeit, several adults running about trying to find the lad will be seen, and heard. Geordie could think it a trick, a threat. Nay, let the boy go."

"Are ye sure, Fraser? He is but five."

"Near six. Letting him run about the land alone isnae safe; I ken it. Yet, he has a natural skill. Tis probably only a wee danger for him, but he could help us pull Ilsa and the bairns out of a far greater one. He saved her before, didnae he."

"Aye, he did. I but pray he is as good as ye believe he is, that he can help us save Ilsa and the bairns. Then all we shall have to worry about is how to explain to Ilsa that we allowed one of her precious bairns to run about alone."

Fraser grimaced. "And explain it in a way that eases her first inclination."

"Which would be?" asked Glenda.

"Rather bloodthirsty, I fear."

"Oh, dear."

CHAPTER NINETEEN

A faint rustling in the brush behind her made Ilsa jump. She searched the area behind her and to either side, but could see nothing. Sternly telling herself she was allowing her fears to disorder her mind, she strode into the clearing surrounding the cottage. She used the walk to calm herself, to push all her fears down, deep inside of herself. If she was to have any chance at all of saving the children or herself, she was going to have to be cold-blooded and clear-headed.

There was a part of her that was already coldly determined, the part that wanted these people dead. It was a ruthless, vengeful part. These people had threatened her children, callously endangered the lives of innocent bairns. There was no mercy in her heart for them. If she got a chance to kill them, she would not hesitate. It might appall her later, but she suspected she would find all the comfort she needed every time she saw her bairns smile.

Just as she reached the door, it was flung open, and Ilsa came face-to-face with Geordie's lover. The woman wore no concealing cloak now. Ilsa was shocked, but did her best to hide it as she met Margaret Campbell's ice-cold gaze. Those pale blue eyes were not empty now. They glittered with fury, a touch of triumph, and what Ilsa suspected was madness. She had the fleeting thought that she would have to tell Gillyanne she had been right about that anger.

It all made sense now. Margaret was Anabelle's Precious Love. Diarmot would certainly have found peace with this woman, the peace of the grave.

The fact that no one was guarding the approach to the cottage suddenly occured to Ilsa. Margaret had obviously been watching for her, but Geordie was not at the window watching for anyone else. They had believed she would do exactly as they had commanded and had apparently not planned for any other contingency. Ilsa dearly wished she had known that. She would have brought an army with her.

"Greetings, Ilsa Cameron," said Margaret, speaking loudly so that she could be heard over Finlay's wailing.

"I believe I am Ilsa MacEnroy now or have ye chosen to ignore that as thoroughly as ye have ignored all good sense and reason?" asked Ilsa, fighting the urge to run to her child.

"I dinnae need to acknowledge something that will prove to be so verra short-lived." She stepped to the side. "Do come in."

Although it was tempting to stick one of her daggers in Margaret as she stood there so exposed and vulnerable, Ilsa resisted the urge. She walked into the cottage and briefly looked around, taking note of where everything and everyone was, just as Sigimor had taught her. Alice sat on the small bed, Cearnach lying on her right. She rubbed his back as she watched Lucy try to calm a screaming Finlay. Geordie sat at a small table drinking ale and eating oatcakes, occasionally glaring toward Lucy and Finlay.

Margaret slammed the door and also glared at Lucy. "Cannae ye shut that brat up?"

"Mayhap he is hungry," Lucy said.

"Mayhap he just doesnae like ye touching him," murmured Ilsa as she walked toward Lucy and took Finlay into her arms.

The baby's crying shuddered to a halt. Ilsa ignored the surprise Lucy, Geordie, and Margaret could not hide and rubbed Finlay's little back until he was breathing more evenly. She almost smiled as, once Lucy moved away, she set Finlay down next to Alice, for she was now between the children and the ones who wished to hurt them. It was obvious that they did not consider her any more of a threat than the children. Sigimor would find that very amusing.

"Weel, tis plain to see that ye arenae much use," Margaret said, frowning at Lucy.

Ilsa realized what was happening barely in time to cover Alice's eyes. Lucy had sat down next to Geordie. The moment Margaret spoke, the maid began to look uneasy. Margaret gave Geordie one long, hard look. He shrugged, wrapped his big hands around Lucy's neck and, before the girl could even gasp, he snapped her neck. Lucy's body slipped to the floor and he calmly went back to eating and drinking.

When Margaret idly poured herself a goblet of wine, Ilsa shivered. The complete lack of emotion the pair revealed as they had executed the maid was chilling. Lucy had served her purpose and they had tossed her aside with the ease of a diner casting a bone to the hounds.

These were not people who could be reasoned with, Ilsa decided as she took her hand from Alice's eyes, and rubbed the trembling child's back. Alice may not have seen the killing, but, young as she was, she had the wit to know what had just happened. It was an ugliness Ilsa could not shield her from now. There were far more important matters to deal with than Alice's tears. Ilsa could only pray she would have the chance to dry them later.

"Would ye like some wine?" Margaret asked Ilsa and she smiled faintly.

"Nay, thank ye," Ilsa replied. "I have tasted your wines before and found them too bitter." She noticed that Geordie paused in drinking his ale.

"Margaret?" he growled.

Margaret looked at him and sighed. "Geordie, ye wound me. I could ne'er have succeeded as weel as I have without your help and devotion. Do ye truly think I would reward that with a cup of poison?"

Geordie studied her for a moment, then returned to drinking his ale. Ilsa had to wonder if the man was so certain of his own charm he could not believe his lover would harm him, or if he was just lacking in wit. The fact that those who helped Margaret tended to end up dead should at least make him wary.

"Alice looks a great deal like her mother," Margaret said as she studied the child. She took a step toward Alice, but hastily stepped back again when

Finlay began to whimper. "What is wrong with that bairn?"

Finlay quieted the moment Margaret stepped back and Ilsa shrugged. "I would guess that he doesnae like ye."

"Dinnae be ridiculous. He didnae cry when he was taken from the garden."

"Aye, he did," said Alice and she briefly glared at Geordie, "but Geordie gagged him. Near choked my brother to death in the doing of it, the swine."

"Hush your mouth, lass, ere I silence ye myself," growled Geordie. "I dinnae need to tolerate impudence from some whore's wee bastard."

Ilsa saw Margaret pale slightly and realized it was fury which caused that look. " 'Ware, Geordie. Ye shouldnae speak of Lady Anabelle that way."

"What do ye care? The laird's first wife is naught to ye," he said.

"Aye, she was naught to me, less than naught. She meant something to Margaret, though." Ilsa fixed her gaze upon Margaret. "Didnae she, Precious Love?"

"Ye think ye are so verra clever, dinnae ye?" Margaret shook her head. "Ye have nay proof."

"Diarmot soon will. He and my brothers will soon find out all they need to ken. The truth is there, at Muirladen, isnae it? Tis why he went there a year ago. Tis why ye set those men on him."

"He willnae find out any more now than he did then."

"Oh, I think he will. Ye havenae been able to kill all who kenned the truth. Diarmot willnae be marrying ye when he returns to find himself widowed. Ye will be verra lucky if he doesnae hunt ye down like the rabid animal ye are." She tensed when

Margaret hissed and started toward her, but then Finlay started to cry, and Margaret quickly retreated again.

"How are ye making the bairn do that?" Margaret snapped.

Although Ilsa was rather astonished by Finlay's behavior, she calmly brushed a thick curl from his forehead. "I am doing naught. He just doesnae like ye."

"Weel, he will be a verra quiet laddie soon," she murmured, then took another sip of wine. "I will only have to speak to Diarmot to make him believe he has heard naught but lies about me, evil lies. The mon was eager to wed with me ere ye ruined everything. He saw in me all he wanted in a wife, all he loved in a woman."

"Aye, placid stupidity."

There was such a flare of rage upon Margaet's face, Ilsa decided it was probably fortunate for her that Geordie distracted the woman by snorting with laughter. Ilsa was a little surprised that Geordie did not wilt beneath the look of furious loathing Margaret fixed upon him. It was possible Geordie thought himself the more important partner, thought himself safe because of what he knew or could do to help Margaret. Ilsa doubted Margaret saw it that way.

"Ye think ye suit him so much better, do ye?" Magaret snapped as she returned her attention to Ilsa. "Ye with your disgusting red hair and a form that is more bone than flesh? Aye, and with all those cursed red-haired brothers whose wits are as thick as cold mud?"

"Aye, and ye best nay forget about my brothers in all of your planning, Precious Love. They and my two score and more cousins will ne'er rest until they find the ones who killed me and my sons. Ye willnae ken one moment of rest until they set ye in your grave. They will be unrelenting in their hunt."

"Margaret?"

For a moment Ilsa thought Geordie was going to discuss the problem of all those enraged Camerons, but then she saw his face. He was dripping sweat, his face as white as bleached linen. His eyes slowly widened as he began to realize that he had been betrayed.

"I would suggest ye hurry and start emptying your belly," said Ilsa. "Repeatedly."

"Ye filthy bitch, Margaret," he said, his voice hoarse with pain, as he tried to stand up.

"I am nay the one who is filthy," sneered Margaret. "Ye must pay for befouling me."

"Befouling ye?" Geordie finally stood up only to stagger to the right, bump into the wall, and slide down it to sit upon the floor. "We were lovers. Ye were the one who pulled me into your bed. I let ye seduce me, fool that I am."

"Jesu, dinnae remind me. Ye were hesitant to help me." Margaret shrugged. "Letting ye rut on me served to rid ye of that hesitancy. It was nay more than that. I had to take such drastic measures in order to make that bastard Diarmot MacEnroy pay for my Anabelle's death. Think of this as a kindness I now do ye."

"A kindness?"

"Aye, ye will suffer less from this than from the hanging ye would face once they kenned ye had killed lady Ilsa and the bairns."

"Ye are utterly mad," he said, panting out each word.

"Did ye only just notice that?" Ilsa asked the mon. "Didnae ye e'er wonder o'er her need to kill Diarmot because she blamed him for his first wife's death? She was nay blood kin to the woman."

"She said she loved Anabelle like a sister," Geordie said.

"I think not. They were lovers, Geordie. Margaret was Anabelle's Precious Love, was her lover for many years. She blames Diarmot for Anabelle's death, but twas dear Precious Love who gave Lady Anabelle the potion that killed her. Ye have sent your soul to hell for naught."

"Och, weel, it was bound for there ere I met this bitch. 'Ware," he whispered, "she reaches for my sword."

Ilsa tensed as she watched Geordie try to grab Margaret when she drew his sword from its scabbard only to fail. Margaret quickly danced out of his reach when he tried to grab her by the ankle, and, with a groan, Geordie fell onto his side. He curled up, much like a small child, and Ilsa knew he would soon be dead. The way Margaret held the sword and eyed her told Ilsa she might soon join him if she did not come up with a plan.

Nanty was just leaving the stable with Tom, wondering how he was going to explain what he had discovered to Ilsa, when there was a brief disturbance at the gates. The men had been shutting them since the sun was setting, but were now scrambling to open them again. Even as he hurried over to see what the trouble was, Diarmot rode in, followed by Tait, Sigimor, a man who looked far too much like Sigimor, and a fourth redheaded young man.

"Ye have returned sooner than was planned," said Nanty as Diarmot dismounted. "Ye discovered something?"

"Aye," Diarmot replied and introduced Somerled and Liam to Nanty and Tom, then frowned at the small group of women who inched their way in through the gates. "Do ye recall Gillyanne's cousin Payton, Nanty?"

"Och, aye." Nanty studied Liam for a moment, then looked at the women who were all staring at the man. "Oh."

"I think this one might be even worse. May we help ye?" he asked the women.

The six women all muttered varying excuses about needing to visit Glenda or some kinswoman and fled into the keep. Nanty laughed. "And there they will stay for a while, I am thinking. Oh, I found the maid." He paused when a young maid approached with a tray of tankards brimming with ale. She served all the men, but kept her gaze fixed upon Liam. "There might be some advantage to having a Liam about," Nanty said, taking a drink and watching Sigimor scowl the young maid into retreating.

After enjoying a deep drink of the ale, Diarmot looked at Nanty. "Ye said ye had found the maid? Dead?"

"Aye, her throat was cut," Nanty replied. "I have just returned from where the body was found. Weel, actually, from the church where we took her to be buried. She was either murdered because she knew too much or taken away and murdered to turn our eyes in the wrong direction."

"It could easily be either one. Margaret Campbell is Precious Love."

"Jesu, and the maid came with her. So did another. I believe her name is Lucy. Margaret is truly the enemy?"

"Difficult to believe, aye?" Diarmot told Nanty everything he had discovered about the woman he had almost married.

"She fooled us all. E'en Gillyanne in some ways."

"Weel, Gillyanne tried to warn me, but couldnae be verra clear about why Margaret troubled her. I wouldnae have survived that marriage for long."

"Papa! Papa!"

Diarmot turned to see Odo running toward him from the far side of the keep, the side where the gardens were. Even as the little boy flung himself at Diarmot's legs, Gay, Fraser, Glenda, and Jenny hurried out of the keep toward him. He noticed that Gay and the two older women greeted Liam cordially, but no more. Jenny seemed stunned. Then a chill entered Diarmot's blood as he realized this was no welcome home. Something was wrong.

"Ilsa?" he asked.

"She isnae here," Gay said and quickly told Diarmot all that had happened in the garden

"She went after them alone?"

"Tis what they said she must do," said Glenda. "Time was running out and we couldnae think of another plan, nay one that wouldnae add to the danger the bairns were in. Lady Ilsa did just as she was told, but she did say we could send someone along later, that she would keep Geordie and his woman's attention fixed upon her."

It was a blow to realize that he had been so wrong about Geordie, but Diarmot shook that small grief aside. "Good, where did she go?" He did not like the identical looks of chagrin the women wore.

"She didnae leave the wee map with us," said Gay. "We think she did that on purpose so that we couldnae follow her."

"So, Ilsa is alone with Geordie and Margaret."

"Margaret!" Fraser cried out in surprise.

"Aye, Margaret," said Diarmot. "I will explain it all to ye later. Right now I need to find a way to get to my foolish wife."

"I ken where she is, Papa," said Odo, gazing up at Diarmot. "I followed." He cast a wary glance at Fraser.

"We will discuss why ye are a naughty wee lad later," said Fraser.

"Where did your mama go, lad?" Diarmot asked Odo.

"To that wee house where ye got stuck under the bed," Odo replied.

"Did ye follow her all the way there and then come home verra fast?"

"Aye, Papa. I came home verra, verra fast."

Diarmot crouched down in front of the boy, hugged him, then held him by his small shoulders. "Think hard, lad. Were there any men outside, guards like we have here at Clachthrom?"

"Nay, Papa. There was no one about. Mama walked right up to the cottage. There wasnae e'en a mon at the door. Then the lady opened the door and Mama went inside. It was that lady ye were going to marry before Mama came home, Papa. Why does she want to hurt Mama, Alice, and the bairns? Is it because ye chose Mama instead of her?"

"That is some of it, my brave lad. If ye still have questions, ye may ask me later. After I have brought your mama and the others home." He kissed Odo on the cheek, then gently pushed him toward Fraser. "Ye were wrong to run off on your own, lad, and we will have to talk about that, too," he said as he stood up. "But, ye did weel, my wee knight." He looked at Gay. "Are ye verra sure it was Geordie?"

"Aye, m'laird," replied Gay. "He wore a mask, but, aye, twas Geordie. What I felt was certain was confirmed by what Ilsa had just seen. She followed Geordie when he slipped away from Clachthrom. He went to that cottage and met with that woman. Tis certain now they were confirming their plans to take the bairns, but Ilsa was on foot. Thinking it had just been some lover's tryst, she didnae hurry home and was cursing herself for that."

"Jesu, doesnae anyone in this family stay where they are put?" cried Nanty. "I leave for but a few hours and ye are all running about the lands alone and unguarded."

"It makes one wonder if that maid's body was meant to be found now, meant to draw ye away from Clachthrom," said Diarmot.

Nanty shivered. "She had obviously been dead since the day she went missing or soon after. I cannae conceive of anyone wanting to carry that around."

"It worked." Diarmot looked at Sigimor. "We will need fresh horses, I think."

"I will fetch them," Nanty said and, with Tom's help, led away the weary horses Diarmot and the Camerons had ridden in on.

Sigimor watched the women take Odo back into the keep. "If ye e'er want to foster that lad out for a wee while, I would be proud to take him in. Dinnae believe in sending the bairns off to someone else for near all their life, but some of them are served weel for a wee bit of training elsewhere."

Diarmot stared at Sigimor for a moment. "Arenae ye e'en a wee bit worried about Ilsa?"

"More than a wee bit. Tis why I talk about other things." He shrugged. "It helps keep the bloodlust from getting too strong. Mon cannae think clear when that happens."

Somerled nodded. "And when one thinks clear, one recalls that our Ilsa isnae some sweet, shy lady who thinks a knife is only to eat with. She is a Cameron. She willnae let them hurt her or the bairns without shedding some blood herself."

"Margaret may be easily defeated," said Diarmot, "but Geordie is a big mon."

"So are ye, but she knocked ye on your arse," said Tait.

"Ilsa is also clever and has dealt with men bigger and stronger than her for her whole life," said Somerled. "Ye dinnae think she survived all of us by being sweet and smiling prettily, did ye? Aye, the lass is in danger, nay doubt about it, and it isnae certain she can win this fight. But, I promise ye, she went there armed, she plotted every step of the way, and she will be watching close for a weakness. I am fair certain these enemies of yours already have one verra serious weakness."

"And what would that be?" asked Diarmot.

"All they see when they look at our Ilsa is a wee lass who could probably be blown away in a strong wind."

Somerled and his brothers were right, Diarmot thought, and felt his fears ease back just a little, enough for him to pull forth the strength and clear head he would need. Ilsa was slender, delicate, yet strong. He had felt the strength in that lithe body often enough. She was clever and would understand the need of a clear head and a steady hand. Her love for the children and her need to keep them safe would also make her a force to be reckoned with. All Ilsa would need was for Geordie and Margaret to make a few simple mistakes and there was a very good chance she would survive this.

CHAPTER TWENTY

"Weel, ye have already made one serious error, Precious Love," Ilsa said, gently nudging the children back until they were behind her, pressed against the wall.

"Have I?" Margaret glanced at the sword in her hand, then smiled at Ilsa. "What would that be?"

"Ye killed the only real threat to me."

"Ye dinnae see this weapon as a threat?"

"Nay in your hands."

"I have used one before." She looked at Alice. "I will be grieved to hurt Alice. She looks so verra much like Anabelle. Tis as if Anabelle lives on in her child."

"Wheesht, I hope not. Anabelle was vicious. She used people. She used ye, too, Precious Love."

"Ye didnae ken Anabelle," snapped Margaret. "Ye could ne'er understand her. Those men, those swine, thought they had beaten her, but she rose victorious o'er them. She made them crawl, exposed their filthy weakness to all the world. Aye, she used them, but she loved me." Margaret sighed.

"If twas possible, I would spare her child, raise her as my own. It cannae be, however. If I am to have my revenge upon Diarmot, ye all have to die."

"Since ye have killed Geordie and Lucy, just how do ye plan to explain our deaths?"

"Oh, I shall make sure it looks as if Geordie killed ye, then poisoned himself. Guilt drove him to it, of course. Mayhap I shall leave a wee note wherein he confesses all. Lucy's death, too. I must nay forget that."

"Och, nay. I dinnae suppose ye have considered the possibility that I may offer a few objections to your plans. Or, did ye expect me to simply hold my hair out of the way and direct ye to the best place to strike?"

Ilsa could see how angry Margaret was growing and decided her plan was working. It surprised her a little for she had not completely expected it to. She had hoped to make Margaret so angry, so agitated, she would act without thought, would be blindly eager to spill her blood. Then Ilsa could make a run for the door, drawing the woman outside as Margaret chased her. More important, it would draw Margaret and the sword she held away from the children, out to a place where Ilsa would feel it safe to draw and use her own weapons, to fight. It was a plan with only a small chance of success, she had thought, but apparently she had been wrong.

"Do ye nay understand that your wee life is in my hands?" Margaret hissed.

"What I understand is that ye obviously lost your wits years ago. I dinnae fear ye. Ye are naught but a murderous whore, just like your lover Anabelle was."

Margaret's rage came so hot and swift, Ilsa

nearly missed her chance, a mistake that could
have been deadly. She raced for the door even as
Margaret lunged toward her, sword raised. Margaret
quickly followed, screaming curses. Ilsa was prepared
to run a long way, but then she heard Margaret
stumble. She turned, hoping to take advanatge of
it, but Margaret was already getting back on her
feet, the sword still firmly grasped in her hand. Ilsa
slid her hand into the hidden slit in her skirts and
clasped the dagger that was sheathed there. Now
she had the freedom to draw her weapons and
fight. Although she did not want to kill Margaret,
she was ready to do so if needed. The woman's obvious madness had eaten away at Ilsa's bloodlust.

"Margaret is going to kill her," said Diarmot.

He started to move into the clearing surrounding the cottage only to be yanked back by Sigimor,
who said, "If ye go charging in there now, ye will
distract Ilsa and that could certainly get her killed."

Diarmot did not move, his gaze fixed upon Ilsa,
but he wondered aloud, "Where is Geordie? Or
Lucy?"

"Gone from here or dead, I should think. They
would be watching this if they were able. Dinnae
think Ilsa would have gotten Margaret outside wav-
ing that sword about if Geordie was still close at
hand. Or able."

"Nay, I think ye may be right. So, my children
could be all alone in the cottage."

"Ah, aye, and that makes sense. That is why Ilsa
has drawn this madwoman out here. Now Ilsa can
draw her own weapons and fight without fearing
that the children will be hurt." Sigimor looked to

the rear of the cottage and smiled faintly. "Ye do breed some fine children, Diarmot."

Diarmot followed the direction of Sigimor's gaze and nearly gaped. Alice was coming out of the back of the cottage dragging a blanket upon which rested his sons. The little girl was having a difficult time, stumbling as she fought to pull the blanket along. It was a lot of weight for the child to haul, but she appeared very determined.

"Come on," said Sigimor. "I think tis safe enough for us to go round and come up behind the cottage."

After one last look at his wife, Diarmot followed the others. He wanted to rush down and end the threat Ilsa faced, but forced himself to accept the judgment of her kinsmen. They knew her strengths and skills far better than he did. He could, however, help his daughter and sons.

By the time Diarmot reached Alice, she was crying silently and was badly scraped from falling down so often, but she was still struggling to get her brothers away from the cottage. Her eyes widened when she saw him and the others, but she obeyed his signal to be quiet. A moment later, he was holding her in his arms while Sigimor carefully checked the twins for any injuries.

"They wanted to hurt my brothers, Papa," Alice said quietly.

"Ye were a verra brave lass to try to save them," he told her, speaking in a near-whisper.

"Odo says we have to take care of each other."

Liam came out of the cottage, crouched near them, and said, "Only Margaret is left."

"I think Geordie broke something in Lucy," Alice said. "Mama covered my eyes so I couldnae see him do it."

"And Geordie?" Diarmot asked.

" 'Member when ye told us Mama was sick because she dranked bad wine?" Diarmot nodded. "I think Geordie dranked bad ale." She glanced toward the front of the cottage. "Are ye going to help Mama now?"

"Aye, sweet Alice, I am."

"I will stay with the bairns," said Nanty.

"Would m'lady like me to fetch a damp rag, mayhap a wee bit of water, to clean her wounds?" Liam asked Alice.

Free of Diarmot's hold, Alice sat down on the blanket and looked at Liam. "Aye, sir. I gots dirt on me and I dinnae like it."

Diarmot followed the Cameron twins and Tait along the side of the cottage until Margaret and Ilsa were in view. As he watched his wife, Diarmot began to doubt that anything would distract Ilsa from Margaret and that sword. Ilsa had the intense, watchful air of a warrior, one alert for danger or the opportunity to strike. Sigimor drew his dagger and Diarmot was a little surprised to feel himself relax. He had not realized how confident he had become of Ilsa's brothers. There was no doubt in his mind that Sigimor would use that dagger with deadly skill at the first hint of a real threat to Ilsa's life. For now the decision silently made was that they would let Ilsa deal with Margaret.

"Put aside the sword, Margaret," Ilsa said. "I dinnae want to kill ye."

Margaret laughed. "How can ye kill me? By drowning me in your own blood? I have the sword."

Ilsa drew her dagger. "I am nay unarmed. I could

have this buried deep in your heart ere ye completed one swing of that sword." She nodded when Margaret frowned, looking uncertain. "Lay down the sword. Ye willnae hang for this," she promised, hoping Diarmot would agree. "We can send ye to your father, have him protect ye from yourself."

"My father?" Margaret laughed, but it was not a pleasant sound. "My father cannae protect me, willnae protect me. He ne'er has. He didnae protect me from his own brother, did he? Or my cousins. Or his foul drunken friends!"

Her father was obviously the wrong person to speak of, Ilsa thought. Now she knew where Margaret's madness had been bred. Ilsa could weep for the frightened, abused child Margaret had been, could find mercy in her heart for the scarred, troubled woman facing her, but she would kill her if Margaret pressed her to do so. She was not sure Margaret really understood or believed that.

"I must have my revenge," Margaret said. "Diarmot took Anabelle away from me. I will take ye away from him."

"Ye gave the woman the potion that killed her, Margaret."

"That mon had got another bairn on her and wouldnae accept it as his! She would have been shamed!"

"That woman was carrying some other mon's bastard and, if she was shamed, she brought it upon herself by being a whore."

"Nay! Ye didnae ken her! She was a warrior. She showed men their own weakness and foulness. She conquered them in their hundreds. She could make e'en the most pious mon desire her, show him and the world that he was nay any better than the beasts in the field."

"Ye think she was some great battle maiden because she could get a mon's rod stiff? It doesnae take any great skill to do that. Wheesht, a mon can wake up alone in his bed with a stiff rod just because he had a passing thought about breasts. And getting a mon to rut on her was nay a great victory. If a mon is hungry enough he would rut on an ugly woman with boils on her arse. He would just squint a lot. She lied to ye. Mayhap she lied to herself, as weel. I dinnae ken why she did what she did, but it wasnae any great victory. Are ye really prepared to die for those lies?"

"She didnae lie! She was shaming them all and that is why she is dead!"

Margaret lunged at her, but Ilsa was ready for the move. She nimbly moved out of the way and tripped Margaret. The sword fell from the woman's hand and they both dove for it. Ilsa found herself in a hard battle, but Margaret had no skill. She fought like an angry woman. Ilsa fought like a youth facing a bigger and stronger opponent—dirty. In but a moment, she had the woman pinned to the ground.

As she caught her breath, ignoring the squirming, cursing woman beneath her, Ilsa glanced toward the cottage. Out of the corner of her eye she caught sight of an all-too-familiar head of bright hair. She was no longer alone. She did hope that her rescuers had only just arrived or she would suffer from a lot of teasing about her crude remarks.

"Margaret," she said. "I can kill ye. Ye must ken that by now. Ye have a chance to live, though twill probably be in the care of nuns or the like. But e'en that is life. Do ye surrender?"

"Aye," said Margaret. "I yield."

Ilsa carefully stood up, never taking her eyes off the woman. She realized she had dropped her dagger in the fight and quickly drew another from inside her sleeve. Margaret had recently assured Geordie that she would not poison him so Ilsa had a very good idea of how empty the woman's promises could be.

The moment she stepped back and Margaret got to her feet, Ilsa knew it was not going to be that easy. Margaret also had a dagger and lunged at Ilsa. Cursing softly, Ilsa slashed the woman's hand, making her cry out and drop her dagger. Then Ilsa punched her in the jaw. She shook her hand to ease the sting as she watched Margaret collapse into the dirt.

She stared at Margaret for a moment to be sure the woman was unconscious, then turned to go to her children. Her brothers and Diarmot were just stepping into view when Ilsa heard the whisper of movement behind her. She had erred, should have taken Margaret's dagger completely out of her reach. There was no choice for her now. She stood between the men and Margaret so they could not take this burden from her. With a heavy sigh, she turned and threw her dagger.

Margaret stood, her dagger still clutched in her hand, and stared at the knife buried in her chest. Slowly, she collapsed to her knees. Even as Ilsa stepped up to her, the woman fell almost gently onto her back. Ilsa stared into Margaret's eyes and saw the haze of impending death begin to cloud them.

"I told ye I could kill ye," Ilsa said. "Why didnae ye believe me?"

"Oh, but I did," Margaret whispered.

So, she had been chosen as the executioner, Ilsa thought and she leaned down and gently closed Margaret's lifeless eyes. Diarmot reached her and pulled her into his arms. She leaned against him and glanced around at her brothers Sigimor, Somerled, and Tait. A moment later, a small body wrapped itself around her legs, and Ilsa smiled down at Alice. Liam and Nanty walked up, each carrying one of the twins.

"How did ye find me?" she asked as she eased out of Diarmot's hold and picked up Alice.

"Odo followed ye," said Diarmot, standing so that Alice could not see Margaret's body as the Cameron twins took it into the cottage.

Ilsa shook her head and idly rubbed Alice's back. The child was clinging to her, but did not seem overly upset. Ilsa prayed there would be no scars left by this adventure. She then noticed that Alice had a lot of scrapes upon her arms and legs.

"What have ye done to yourself, dearling?" she asked, looking more closely and seeing that someone had already tended to the small wounds.

Diarmot smiled and stroked Alice's hair as he told Ilsa what Alice had been doing. "She was a verra brave, clever lass."

"Och, aye." Ilsa kissed Alice's forehead. "Ye did verra weel, lass. Verra weel indeed."

"May we go home now?" Alice asked.

"Tait, Liam, and I can take them back to Clachthrom," said Nanty. "I dinnae think—" he hesitated and glanced toward the cottage.

There were bodies to deal with, Diarmot realized. Geordie and Lucy could simply be buried in the wood for all he cared, but Margaret had kinsmen who would wonder what had happened to her. He would have to take her back to her cousin and try to explain all that had happened. That was not going to be easy, he thought, then kissed both his daughter and wife on the cheek.

"Aye," he said. "There is some work to be done here."

"Diarmot," Ilsa began. "Margaret—"

"I learned about Margaret at Muirladen. This wasnae a great surprise. Tis why we rode back here after but a day at Dubheidland. I will tell ye all about it later." He kissed her again and went to join the Cameron twins in the cottage.

Ilsa soon found herself seated in front of Liam holding Cearnach in her arms as they rode back to Clachthrom. She felt very tired and she knew it was not solely because of all she had done. There was blood on her hands now and, deserved or not, it would be a while before she could fully accept that burden with ease.

"Ye had nay choice," said Liam. "In truth, I think she made ye do it."

"She did," said Ilsa. "She made that clear just as she died. I will accept it. I almost do e'en now. And I think it may have been a mercy in this case. She was quite mad. There was nay reasoning with her, nay making her see how insane her belief was about Anabelle and all the woman was and had done."

"Aye." Liam was silent for a moment, then murmured, "Actually, I have a question or two about some of your, er, beliefs. An ugly woman with boils on her arse?"

Ilsa saw Nanty and Tait grinning at her and sighed. They had been there to hear her just as she feared. Now the teasing would begin. Although she sighed again rather dramatically, she inwardly smiled. It would undoubtedly grow annoying but, for now, she welcomed the distraction.

Diarmot sighed with a mixture of relief and exhaustion as he left the bathing room off the kitchens and started toward his bedchamber. The day had held more triumph than tragedy, but he was not sure he would even have the strength to make love to his wife. Even the confrontation with Margaret's kinswoman had been easier than he had expected. The woman had assured him that there would be no demands for revenge, that Margaret would be quietly buried and all forgotten.

He frowned as he realized that Margaret's cousin had not really been surprised by the madness that had surely infected her cousin. Diarmot had to wonder if Margaret's father had suspected that his daughter was not quite sane. If he had, the man should never have tried to marry the girl to him. Diarmot decided there was no gain in fretting over it, but he would be very careful in his dealings with the man in the future. It was to be hoped that, after this tragedy, those would be few and far between.

The other thing that left him an odd mixture of exhausted and tense was that he had had a revelation. He loved his wife. He had suspected as much as soon as his memory had fully returned at Muirladen, but now he knew it for certain. That first sight of her facing the sword-wielding Margaret had finished what had begun as he had stood in the copse and recalled their first time together. He had known that he would not find life very sweet if he did not have Ilsa at his side.

Once she had loved him too, but he was no longer certain of that. He had hurt her, could recall the hurt in her eyes all too clearly as time and time again he had abused that love. Although he had done it all unknowingly, he suspected the damage done was the same. Diarmot was not sure how he could mend it. He was very afraid that he may have killed that love he now knew he needed as much as he needed air to breathe.

He was going to have to woo his wife, he decided as he entered their bedchamber and looked toward the bed. It was not something he felt he was very good at, but he would do his best. While matters were so uncertain between them, he did not think he should suddenly begin declaring his love and need for her. He was going to have to go slowly, show her he trusted her and win back her trust.

Quietly shedding his clothes, he eased into bed and pulled her into his arms. This was where she belonged. A part of him had known it from the beginning, although he had fought it. Diarmot wanted Ilsa to know it, too.

"Diarmot?" Ilsa murmured, turning in his arms and sleepily kissing his chin.

"Aye, sorry to wake ye," he said, even as he realized that he was not quite as exhausted as he had thought he was.

She snuggled up against him and stroked his chest. "Was there any trouble when ye took Margaret's body to her cousin?"

"Nay." He caressed her slender back and smiled when she hummed with pleasure and moved against him. "The cousin wasnae verra surprised at all Margaret had done."

"The family kenned she was insane?"

"I fear so, but it doesnae matter."

"At least three people are dead, one of them quite probably an innocent, and many more were almost killed. I think it does matter."

"Actually, there is a strong possibility Lady Ogilvey was murdered by Margaret." As he continued to caress her, he told her all he had learned at Muirladen.

"Jesu," she whispered. "One has to wonder how it all went on for so long and no one put a stop to it."

Ilsa was a little surprised that her passion was stirred by his touch despite the horror of what they were discussing. She decided it was because she had faced death today, and dealt it out. The warmth of his body, the heat of his touch, were helping to ease the chill all of that had set into her bones. Here, in his arms, was life, and the passion they shared was delightful proof of that.

"I wouldnae trust Lesley Campbell much in the future, if I were ye," she said, and gasped softly as he licked her nipple through the thin linen night shift she wore.

"I have nay intention of doing so."

He tugged off her night shift, then settled her lithe body beneath his. "I have been gone for a sennight."

Ilsa kissed his strong throat. "I did notice that ye werenae about much."

"I was aware of a certain absence meself, especially at night."

"What? My brothers didnae keep ye good company?" Ilsa slid her hand down his stomach and stroked his erection, enjoying the soft sounds of pleasure he made.

"They certainly couldnae provide me with the company I was hungering for." He kissed the soft skin between her breasts. "They dinnae smell as sweet, either."

She laughed, but it was quickly choked back when he took her nipple deep in his mouth and suckled. Ilsa tangled her fingers in his hair and gave herself over to the hunger he bred in her. This was what she needed and it was obvious that he did as well. At least here they were still well matched.

Their lovemaking quickly turned fierce and wild. Ilsa could not get enough of the taste or feel of him. Diarmot acted as starved as she felt. When he finally joined their bodies with one hard thrust, she could not hold back, falling into that sweet oblivion he always gifted her with. She clung to him as he swiftly followed her there.

"Now I truly am exhausted," Diarmot murmured as, finally able to move from her arms, he tucked her up against him and nuzzled her hair.

"My brothers couldnae make ye tired, either?" she asked sleepily and grinned when he grunted.

"Your brothers could weary a saint. I was, er, astonished when I first entered Dubheidland," he said as he idly stroked her stomach. "I have ne'er seen so many redheads in my life. Twas near to blinding." He smiled when she giggled. "My welcome wasnae verra warm at first, but Sigimor explained everything."

"Oh, dear."

"Aye, whilst some of your kinsmen accepted me after that, there were a few who watched me as if they expected me to start drooling and babbling at any moment." He laughed along with her, then kissed the side of her neck and closed his eyes. "Tis over now, Ilsa."

"Aye, a sad ending, but still a relief."

"Now we can cease peering into every shadow and just live our lives. Now we can take the time to work on our marriage."

Ilsa waited for him to say more, but then heard him snore softly. The tension that had suddenly gripped her eased away and she sighed. She should have expected something to be said, some change to happen now that he had regained all his memories and their enemy had been defeated. Yet the thought of any change made her extremely uneasy and she did not really understand why.

Their marriage was not perfect, but it was far better than most. They shared a delicious passion and, slowly, had begun to share other things. They had a large family already and many friends. Now they would be able to accept friendship and make new ones amongst the people of Clachthrom since they no longer had to suspect everyone of being a traitor or the enemy. She did not know what more he thought they should have and realized, to her great surprise, that she did not really want to know.

What had happened to her dreams and her hopes, she wondered? Had they also disappeared that day she had entered the church to see him about to marry someone else? Had hurt and anger bred a fear she had not fully recognized until now? There was a lot she had to think about before she could accept any more changes. Unfortunately, she had the strong feeling Diarmot would not give her any time.

That was just like a man, she thought crossly. His mind was now at ease, his enemy was dead, and now he would turn his attention to his wife and his marriage. All was clear and simple in his manly mind.

She took a slow deep breath to calm herself, realizing she was working herself into a temper. It was late, she was exhausted, and it was not the time to think about anything as important as her marriage. Or as complicated as her own feelings, she mused with a tired sigh as she closed her eyes. She would find the time to think about it all on the morrow.

Ilsa placed her hand over his where it rested upon her stomach and felt a brief pang of lingering grief over the child that had been stolen from them. Diarmot had become a very good father and she wanted to give him another child. Glenda had quietly told her ways to halt the seeding of her womb and Ilsa was determined to use them. She had made that decision because she had not been certain of what would happen to them or what Diarmot felt and wanted. Now it seemed she would hold to the decision because she no longer knew what she felt or wanted.

CHAPTER TWENTY-ONE

"I dinnae understand why we are doing this," complained Gay.

Ilsa sighed as, deciding they were well out of sight of the men on the walls, she helped Gay mount her horse. She then mounted her own and settled the sling a cooing Cearnach was in more comfortably in front of her. There probably had not been a need to sneak out of Clachthrom. No one would have stopped her or asked any questions, nor did she need a guard at all times. She was hoping that a little stealth would make it difficult for Diarmot to guess what she had done, a least for a few hours.

"I told ye, the mon is driving me insane," Ilsa said as she nudged her horse forward.

"He is wooing ye," Gay said as she followed. "He has been wooing ye verra nicely for two days now."

"I ken it, but why?"

"Mayhap because he wants ye to be more than a bedwarmer now?"

Ilsa ignored that. "I cannae think with him about."

"Wooing makes it difficult for ye to think clearly? I thought that was what it was supposed to do."

Gay had grown very confident and strong over the last few months, Ilsa mused. She was delighted that the girl had recovered from her ordeals so well. At the moment, however, she rather missed the somewhat shy, meek Gay.

"Tis difficult to explain. I think I had finally accepted what I had, the way my marriage was. Now the fool wants to change everything and it makes me nervous."

"I think ye are afraid."

Ilsa started to vehemently deny that, then grimaced. "Mayhap I am, but I am nay sure of what or why. Every time I find a moment to think about it, to try and understand what is troubling me, there is Diarmot, kissing me, telling me sweet things, or giving me little gifts."

"Ah, how cruel and unthinking of him."

"There is a distinct lack of sympathy in ye for my confusion."

"Quite possibly. I am nay the one afflicted, so mayhap I cannae understand. Howbeit, if ye think ye have to get away from the fool for a while, then get away ye shall. I am just nay sure why we had to be so secretive about it. Why didnae ye just tell him that ye wished to visit with your family for a wee while and leave with your brothers?"

"Because Diarmot would probably want to come with me and then I would have to try to find a reason why he couldnae, or why the children couldnae, or why—"

"I understand. Actually, this may be for the best.

Ye really dinnae have any time to yourself, to think, and to sort out what ye feel and what ye want. First it was someone trying to kill ye and Diarmot, then there are all the children ye were given as a bridal gift, and there were all the troubles caused by his loss of memory and mistrust. Aye, mayhap a few days at the cottage with only your fourteen brothers and two score and then some cousins is just the quiet repose ye are needing."

"Just as I thought ye were understanding, ye slap me offside the head," Ilsa murmured, almost able to laugh at Gay's words. It was hard to ignore the humor of them no matter how she felt. "I may nay explain myself weel, but I do need this. I am certain it will clear my head."

"If Sigimor doesnae knock it off your shoulders when we catch up with him."

"Ah, weel, there is that possibility," she said and tried not to think of the coming confrontation with her brothers.

"But, why did she go away?" asked Odo.

Fraser sighed, understanding some of Ilsa's need to get away from Clachthrom and her husband for a little while, but not sure she could make it understandable to the children. "Tis a woman thing, lad," she finally said and ignored Glenda's snort of amusement.

Ivy frowned. "Tis a woman thing? That makes no sense. I think we need to talk to Papa."

"Aye," agreed Odo. "He will ken what Mama is doing and where she went to do it. She probably told him."

"I doubt it," murmured Fraser as she watched

Alice, Aulay, Ivy, Odo, Gregor, and Ewart leave the nursery.

"Are ye just going to let them go and ask the mon?" asked Glenda. "I think the laird is still asleep."

"Good." She smiled when Glenda laughed.

"I dinnae ken what the lass is thinking," admitted Glenda. "The laird has finally come to his senses and is wooing her and she runs away. Where is the sense in that?"

"I think she is afraid, Glenda. She loved him deeply when they handfasted, then found herself deserted, and when she comes here, what does she find? Anger, mistrust, and some madwoman trying to kill her. Mayhap her fear comes from holding out her heart all those months ago and having it so thoroughly stomped on. She kens it isnae all the laird's fault, but I doubt that lessened the hurt any."

"Nay, I doubt it did. Weel, then mayhap this is for the best. Mayhap those two need to cease tiptoeing about each other and have it out."

"Have it out?"

"Weel, do ye think that the laird is going to be all smiles and sweet words after he has chased her down?"

"Nay," said Fraser and frowned. "Yet, how is that supposed to help?"

"If the laird goes to her breathing fire and outraged male pride, our lady is going to spit right back at him. Somewhere in all that spitting the truth will out. One or the other of them will surely say something that makes it all clear and they can get on with being lovers again."

"I am nay sure if that makes any more sense to me than what Ilsa said."

"It will. Now let us just wait and see how loud the laird bellows."

"Ye find enjoyment in the strangest things, Glenda."

"Papa. Papa."

Diarmot grimaced as a small hand patted his cheek. He stretched out his hand, but Ilsa was not there. Since he could not toss whatever the problem was into her lap, he slowly opened his eyes. Odo looked especially sweet as he smiled and that made Diarmot very uneasy. He looked again and realized all six of his older children were standing around his bed, although Gregor was doing his best to pull himself up onto the bed.

"Is the keep on fire?" he asked as he rubbed a hand over his face.

He was tired. Not only had he been up late talking with Ilsa's brothers and cousin, who had left at dawn, but his wife had kept him awake for a long time after he had come to bed. That had been very enjoyable, he mused, then quickly smothered the memory as his body began to react. He did not want to have to explain that condition to any of the children and he had no doubt at least one of them would notice. Probably Odo, he thought as he pulled himself up into a seated position and collapsed against the pillows.

"Nay, Papa, the keep isnae on fire," said Odo.

Clutching the covers that Gregor nearly pulled off as he finally got his plump little body up on the bed, Diarmot grunted as the little boy threw himself onto his chest. "Then why am I blessed with your company so early?"

"Tisnae early, Papa," said Alice. "Tis nearly noon."

"Aye? Weel, I didnae get to bed until verra late. So, what is it ye have all come here to tell me?"

"Where has Mama gone?" asked Odo.

"I beg your pardon?"

"Where has Mama gone," Odo repeated, speaking very slowly.

"She must be around the keep somewhere."

"I dinnae think she told him, Odo," said Ivy. "She must nay have wanted him to ken about this woman thing."

"What woman thing?" asked Diarmot, wondering if this was some new strange nightmare caused by the rather large quantity of ale he had drunk last night.

"Mama has gone away and Fraser said it was a woman thing," replied Odo. "We thought ye would ken where she has gone and why she would go there. We thought she would have told ye. I think maybe Mama has been a wee bit sneaky, aye?"

"Aye," agreed Diarmot as he lifted Gregor up, kissed him on the cheek, and set him on the floor. "Go back to the nursery. I need to get dressed and find out what has happened."

The moment the children left, Diarmot got out of bed. He puzzled over what they had said as he washed and dressed. He also experienced a growing sense of unease. The children thought Ilsa was gone. From what they had said, so did Fraser, and the woman had tried to explain it, badly. Lacing up his doublet, Diarmot hurried to the nursery.

The way Glenda and Fraser eyed him so warily as he entered the nursery did not put Diarmot at ease. "Where is Ilsa?"

"She has gone back to Dubheidland," replied Glenda.

"I thought we werenae supposed to tell him where," said Fraser, frowning at Glenda.

"Ye promised nay to say where. If ye noticed, I didnae promise, didnae say anything."

Diarmot stood right in front of the two women, knowing he towered over them as they sat in their chairs with their mending in their laps. They did not look very intimidated, however. There were obviously some disadvantages to being surrounded by strong women.

"Ilsa has gone back to Dubheidland?" he asked.

"Aye, m'laird," replied Fraser. "She left here about an hour or so after her brothers and that lovely lad Liam rode out."

"If she is going back to Dubheidland, why didnae she just ride out with the Camerons?"

"Oh, she didnae wish them to ken what she was about until later."

"When they were far enough away from Clachthrom that they would have to listen to her, couldnae simply drag her right back here and continue on their way," said Glenda.

Diarmot was stunned. Ilsa had left him. She had spent hours last night making love to him until his eyes crossed, then gotten up out of bed and ridden away. That made no sense at all.

"I dinnae understand," he muttered and dragged a hand through his hair.

"I am nay sure I do, either, m'laird," said Fraser. "The lass said she needed to think, needed to get away alone and sort matters out."

"Sort matters out? Alone? There are fourteen brothers and two score and more cousins running about Dubheidland! A leper wouldnae be alone there!"

"Now, he has a point," murmured Glenda, and grimaced when both Diarmot and Fraser glared at her. "Mayhap ye ought to go and get some food in your belly, m'laird. Break your fast. Think about it a wee bit. I believe a mon always thinks better on a full stomach."

Fraser's eyes widened slightly when Diarmot growled and strode out of the nursery, six children hurrying after him. "I dinnae think he is going to be understanding about this."

Glenda laughed.

Diarmot had to admit he felt a little better now that he had eaten. He leaned back in his chair and studied the six children seated at the head table with him. Gregor and Ewart wore more food than they had eaten, but all six children had sat quietly, sharing the meal with him. Unfortunately, he also knew they waited for him to tell them what he was going to do. Even though he felt better and his head was clear, he did not have an answer for them. He certainly did not have any explanations for why Ilsa had left.

"Did ye do something naughty, Papa?" asked Alice.

The peace had ended, he decided. "Nay, I am sure I didnae do anything naughty. That isnae why Ilsa left."

"Ye gave her flowers," said Odo. "Mayhap she didnae like them."

"Odo, she spends hours every day in the garden. I think she likes flowers." Diarmot sighed. "This makes no more sense to ye than it does to me. Did Fraser tell ye anything else?"

"She said it wasnae because of us," replied Odo, then frowned. "But, if it isnae us and it isnae ye, what is it?"

"A woman thing," said Alice.

Diarmot thought the look of disgust Aulay and Odo gave their sister was very similar to the sort many men must give women they did not understand. He wished Ilsa was here so that he could give her that look. "Now, I ken ye might nay understand all I am about to say, but listen anyway. There were some problems between Ilsa and me, a few difficulties in our marriage."

"Because your wits were rattled," said Alice.

"Aye, that says it rather weel," murmured Diarmot. "Sometimes a mon and his wife dinnae understand each other verra weel. Misunderstandings can arise. I think that is what has happened here. Ilsa has gone back to Dubheidland to think about everything and try to come to some understanding."

"Are ye going to just leave her there then, Papa?" Odo asked. "If she doesnae understand something, shouldnae ye go and explain it? Men sometimes need to set a lass down and talk sense into them."

"Ye have been talking to your uncle Sigimor, havenae ye?" Diarmot smiled when Odo nodded. "A word of advice, some lasses dinnae take weel to being sat down and talked sense to, especially if tis a mon doing the talking."

"She will come back, willnae she?"

"Of course, because I intend to go and get her."

"Today? Will ye go and get her today?"

"Nay. I will set out after her in two days' time. She wanted time to, er, think about things. Two days should be enough, I am thinking. I cannae leave until then, anyway, as I have things I must get done first. A few meetings and some decisions that can nay longer be put aside. So, in two days, I will go and see if she understands things better."

"And if she doesnae?"

"Then she can come back here and do her thinking. She belongs here and tis time she understands that little matter." For a moment he was afraid he had let too much of his growing anger into his voice, but six little children mimicked the stern look he suspected was on his face and nodded in full agreement. It was nice to have allies.

"I hope ye have a verra good explanation for this, lass," said Sigimor as he helped Ilsa dismount and took Cearnach into his arms.

Ilsa grimaced as Tait helped Gay down then took the horses away. It was dark and she had nearly missed finding her brothers. Fortunately, Liam had realized they were being followed and had found her. She tried not to feel like a naughty little girl as she sat down near Sigimor by the fire and smiled her thanks to Somerled when he served her a bowl of rabbit stew.

"I am nay sure I do," she finally admitted to Sigimor.

"Lass, ye have left your husband and that is a verra serious thing. Now, when he was being an idiot and his wits were rattled, I might have understood. Wheesht, I probably would have helped ye. But, that isnae how it is anymore, is it?"

"Nay," she muttered and quickly filled her mouth with stew so that she could have a little time to think about what to say next.

"Nay. In fact, the mon was wooing ye verra prettily, if I am nay mistaken."

"Aye, I think he was wooing me. Dinnae ken why. Why does a mon need to woo his wife? Does that make sense to ye?"

"Aye and nay. A husband needs to keep his wooing sharp, I think, to keep the wife happy. In your case, the husband needs to do some wooing because he hasnae been that kind to ye since ye arrived at Clachthrom. He remembered everything and now kens that he has been unkind. I think he was trying to mend things or make apologies, or something."

"Aye, he woos me after he remembers everything. He didnae woo me just because he wanted to when his wits were rattled. Nay, he waited until his memory was back and then he thinks, oh, Ilsa isnae so bad, is she? So, then he starts wooing."

Sigimor looked at his brothers and Liam, but only Liam was smiling. Somerled and Tait looked as confused as he felt. Since Liam was smiling, he fixed his gaze on him, and jerked his head toward Ilsa, silently urging his cousin to deal with it.

"Ilsa, what are ye running from?" asked Liam.

"Why would ye think I was running?" she asked, and frowned when, suddenly, it was only her and Liam sitting at the fire. "Cowards," she muttered.

Liam laughed. "Aye, they are. Ye are running, Ilsa, but ye are a clever lass. I think ye ken ye cannae run far enough or fast enough to escape what is troubling ye."

"I loved him, ye ken," she said quietly.

"I ken it. Ye never would have let him seduce ye if ye didnae. Nay, ye would have left him a piece or two short and his ears ringing with curses."

"Wheesht, I dinnae think I was quite that bad." She sighed. "I am just so confused. When I got to Clachthrom and found out he didnae e'en remember me, weel, that hurt. Then I decided to accept that and start all over. All that time that he had no memory of me, I tried to get him to care for me as I ken he used to. It didnae work, nay verra weel."

"Ah." Liam nodded. "Then he gets his memory back and all is weel, except that ye remember several months where naught ye could do would make him care."

Ilsa blinked and stared at her cousin. "I think that might be it. I also think I am a coward."

"Weel, in matters of the heart a great many of us are cowards. Love and all that can leave a deep wound and it cannae be stitched. I think the bleeding can last for many a year."

"Mayhap for the rest of your life," she whispered then shook her head. "I went from being his lover and someone he cared about, to being a liar and mayhap a killer, to just being mayhap a liar, and suddenly back to being his wife and someone he may care about."

"And thus a verra great confusion."

"Exactly. When he left for Dubheidland to find out the truth, he was at the point where he thought I might be lying just a wee bit. Then he returns, our enemy is defeated, and suddenly he is like the Diarmot I kenned a year ago. I just need time to think about it all."

"Aye, ye do. I wouldnae take too long to think and think hard, though."

"Ye think Sigimor will make me go back?"

"Och, nay, for all he may start growling about wives and the rules they ought to follow." Liam exchanged a grin with Ilsa. "Nay, love, I think your husband will be coming after ye."

Ilsa was not so sure about that. Diarmot was a proud man and she had just left him without a word. He would have to explain her absence to everyone. That was not going to make him very happy.

To her relief, nothing more was said. She rode home to Dubheidland with her brothers and Liam and it was just as it always used to be. It was also not the same, she realized. No matter how hard she tried to put him from her mind for the length of the journey home, she kept thinking about Diarmot. By the time she reached her little cottage, she was tired of thinking of the man.

"So, here ye are, lass," said Sigimor as he set her bag down in the cottage. "Just as ye left it. I will send some lads down here with some food and ale."

"Thank ye, Sigimor," she said as she let Gay take Cearnach so that she could slip away and feed the twins.

"I ken Liam said I should just leave it be, but—" he sighed and dragged a hand through his hair.

"Just say it, Sigimor. I think whatever it is ye are thinking has probably been gnawing away at ye for the whole ride here."

"He is a good mon, Ilsa."

"I ken it."

"I think ye could have a verra good marriage and all those bairns love ye."

She winced. It was hard not to think about how her leaving might have hurt the children. Even telling herself that it was best for them if she could rid herself of the mass of tangled emotions within her did not ease her guilt by much.

"Weel, that is it," he said and kissed her on the cheek. "Ye do your thinking then. Just remember that ye have a good mon for a husband and six wee bairns that love ye. I ken ye think I am nay being fair by mentioning them, but I dinnae think ye can make any decision without considering them."

"Nay, ye are right. I cannae."

"Think hard and fast, lass."

"Hard and fast? Why?"

"Because I am expecting your mon to come after ye e'en if ye arenae."

Ilsa cursed as he left. She had come to the cottage for peace and time to think. If Liam and Sigimor were right, she was not going to be given much of either.

"Weel, ye took your time in coming here," said Sigimor as, three days later, Diarmot strode into the great hall of Dubheidland, Nanty and Odo by his side.

"I wasnae planning to make a journey," said Diarmot as he sat down, set Odo down on the seat next to him, and helped himself to a tankard of ale. "There were a few things which needed to be done ere I could leave." He smiled his thanks at a young boy who poured Odo a tankard of goat's milk before sitting down next to the boy. "And ye are?"

"Fergus the last," the boy replied and grinned. "Have ye come to take that stubborn, senseless sister of ours back home to Clachthrom?"

Diarmot looked at Sigimor. "Been ranting about her, have ye?"

"And ye havenae?"

"I think he has," said Odo, "but he mumbles a lot and I cannae understand what he is saying. Glenda said that was probably a good thing as most of it was probably cursing."

"Aye," agreed Sigimor. "And why have ye come, lad?"

"I was chosen by the others to make sure Papa doesnae say anything stupid."

Sigimor and the other Camerons gathered in the great hall roared with laughter and Diarmot sighed. He thought it very traitorous of Nanty to join in with them. Even Odo giggled. He had tried to convince the boy that he did not need the help, but there had been no dissuading him. Diarmot had not had the heart to simply refuse to take him, either. The children had been very accepting of Ilsa's leaving, but he knew that was because they depended upon him to bring her back. Odo, he supposed, was their little guarantee.

"Have ye had a hard time of it, then?" asked Sigimor.

"Weel, nay," replied Diarmot. "The children have been verra patient. I was pressed to explain things a little better than Fraser did. She told them it was a woman's thing." He was able to join in the laughter this time.

"She has set her arse back in that wee cottage. Liam keeps an eye on her," Sigimor added and grinned.

"Does he. How kind of him."

"He thinks so. Now, dinnae misunderstand me, as I am nay blaming ye or her, but Ilsa is troubled. I had to leave it to Liam to talk to her because she started saying things that made my head ache. I am nay verra good at understanding her at times. Liam tried to explain it to me. It seems ye erred by nay wooing her when your wits were still rattled." He frowned. "Something about her being one thing then another then another and she doesnae ken what she is to ye or what she wants to be."

"Weel, that is as clear as mud."

"So thought I. I think ye were supposed to want to woo her when ye didnae ken who she was. Wheesht, that doesnae sound any better, does it."

"Nay. It doesnae matter. I will go and speak to her."

"And it looks as if ye chose a verra good time to do so." Sigimor nodded toward the door of the great hall.

Diarmot looked to see Gay enter carrying Finlay followed by Liam carrying Cearnach. Gay's eyes widened as she saw him, but before she could retreat, Odo was hugging her legs. Diarmot just smiled as Odo dragged her back to the table.

"Greetings, m'laird," said Gay as she let Diarmot take Finlay for a moment. "I just brought the lads here to visit with their kinsmen."

"As they should." He handed Finlay back to Gay and took Cearnach from Liam. "In fact, I think it would be verra good for them if they visited for a good long while. Let us say a whole night."

"Oh. If ye think they should."

"Aye, I think they should."

She sighed and nodded, then frowned slightly at Odo. "Why have ye brought him?"

"I came to make sure Papa didnae say anything stupid," said Odo and he grinned when Gay laughed. "I was chosen."

"Weel, that doesnae surprise me." Gay looked at Diarmot. "I dinnae believe she was intending to stay away verra long."

"Mayhap not now, but after a few days? Or a few days more?" He shrugged. "She has had her time to think. Now tis time to talk."

Diarmot did not find the way Gay grimaced very encouraging, but he stood up and started for the door. He smiled faintly when Odo, Nanty, Tait, Sigimor, and Liam all fell into step behind him. For a long time he had been a very solitary man, morose and lost in his own troubled thoughts. It appeared that was most definitely at an end.

As he made his way to the little cottage where he and Ilsa had spent two blissful weeks after their handfasting, he told himself he must be calm, gentle, and understanding. Ever since she had come back into his life, Ilsa had been confronted with one trouble after another. It should be no surprise that she might be upset or uncertain.

The cottage was coming into view by the time he gave up trying to convince himself that he was not mad, or hurt, or insulted. He was all of those things. He was also afraid that he had lost the chance to have back what he had so briefly enjoyed a little over a year ago. That soured his mood as well.

If Ilsa had just stayed at Clachthrom, they could have quietly sorted this out as the adults they were, he thought. Instead he had had to leave Clachthrom at a very busy time of the year, come to Dubheidland to face her vast army of kinsmen, and fetch her home where she belonged. Everyone at the two keeps knew his wife had run away from him. It was embarrassing. Ilsa obviously had not considered how it would look. His pride had been badly bruised by the whole affair. Few said anything, but it was easy to see that everyone thought he had done something to make her go away. He had had to endure a great deal of unasked-for advice about the management of wives.

By the time he reached the door of the cottage, Diarmot had worked himself up into a fine temper and was feeling sorely abused by his wife. He would give her some time to talk about whatever she thought was important, and then he would take her to bed. After that, he would take her home and there would be no more of this nonsense about needing time to think. That decided, he did not even bother to knock upon the door, just threw it open and glared at the woman who was causing him to act so irrationally. The brief look of horror that crossed her face when she saw him pleased him. Perhaps if she was a little afraid, he would not have to deal with much discussion. They would go to bed, exhaust themselves, and then go home. He crossed his arms over his chest and silently dared her to give him an argument.

CHAPTER TWENTY-TWO

Ilsa screeched softly in surprise when the door to the cottage was abruptly flung open. She turned to scold whichever brother had made such a rude entrance and nearly gaped. Diarmot stood there looking extremely cross, his arms folded over his chest as he glared at her. Odo stood beside him looking exactly like his father despite the darker hair. Behind them she could see Tait, Liam, Nanty, and Sigimor, all of them grinning in a way that made her want to slap them.

She desperately wanted to say something clever, but nothing came to mind. Since she had fled her husband like a frightened child, she doubted she could say anything that he would find particularly amusing. She silently admitted to herself that she was embarrassed by her behavior, but she would rather nail her feet to the floor than admit it to anyone else. Neither would she let everyone know that she recognized her own cowardice.

"Greetings, husband," she said pleasantly as she grabbed a jug of ale and set it on the table. "Ye must wish a drink as I think ye have had a long, rather swift journey." She wondered why he had waited three days to follow her, then told herself not to be so petulant. She had wanted time to think, had she not?

"I see." He watched her set out tankards on the table through narrowed eyes. "Verra weel, we shall play the game your way for a wee while." He moved to the table and sat down, Odo quickly sitting down beside him.

Looking at the four men peering in the door, she asked, "Are ye joining us?"

"We were just deciding if it was safe," said Tait as he led the other three men inside and sat down next to Odo.

"And why wouldnae it be?" Ilsa poured each of the men some ale, then gave Odo a small tankard of goat's milk.

"Mayhap they understand how irritated a mon might be to wake up and discover his wife has deserted him?" Diarmot asked. "Crept away like a thief in the night?"

"Actually, I crept away at dawn. Ye must have slept late."

Ilsa watched the other men's eyes widen even as Diarmot's narrowed again. She noticed that even Odo had stopped drinking his milk to gape at her. What made her goad her husband, she did not know, but she suspected she was not going to stop. Since the other men were drinking their ale rather quickly, she also suspected she and Diarmot would soon be alone together. Ilsa was not sure that was what she wanted.

"I needed my rest after my wife wrung me dry during the night," Diarmot drawled and took some pleasure in her blush, even though she looked strongly tempted to throw the jug of ale at his head. "After such a night, I was, naturally, quite surprised to find she had slipped away home."

Even as Ilsa opened her mouth to respond to that outrageous remark, Sigimor leapt to his feet. "Thank ye for the ale, lass. We will be leaving ye and your husband alone to talk." He grabbed Odo up in his arms and hurried toward the door, the other men close at his heels.

"But I was supposed to stay to make sure he did-nae say anything stupid," protested Odo.

"I think that a great many stupid things are about to be said, lad," said Liam. "Best let them go at it. Ye can return later to mend things if tis needed."

Ilsa stared at the door as it shut behind her cow-ardly relatives, then looked at Diarmot. He smiled. It made her wish she had not allowed Gay to take the twins to visit their uncles at the keep. The way he idly sipped at his ale told her he was far calmer than she felt, despite the signs of anger she had seen. That did not bode well. She poured herself a tankard of ale and sat down opposite him.

"Are ye done thinking?" he asked, and almost smiled again when she scowled at him.

The faintly amused look upon his handsome face annoyed her. She had realized it had been cowardly, even childish, of her to run home be-cause she was upset and confused, but to have him apparently think the same was irritating. Ilsa also realized that she was afraid. She was afraid that he would simply take her back to Clachthrom with nothing settled between them. She was even more afraid that he wanted all she had given him a year ago, but would still not be returning it in kind.

In the time she had been back in her little cottage, Ilsa had done a lot of thinking. She had given Diarmot everything she had had to give when they had first become lovers. In recalling all that had passed between then, she had come to the sad realization that he had never spoken of love, that she had foolishly seen love in sweet words and heated embraces. When he had left her, she had clung to her dreams and her faith in him, certain that he would return for her. With each month that had passed with no word from him, those dreams and that faith had slowly turned to ashes, and it had been a constant grief to her.

Her love had never died. Ilsa was not sure it could. She had buried it, however, buried it very deeply. Despite all of her plans to prove herself and win his heart after reaching Clachthrom, she now knew that she had never really intended to completely free that love again. She had not dared, had always feared a return of the pain she had felt when she had thought herself deserted, then found herself forgotten. In many ways she had liked their marriage as it was, that she had only wanted there to be trust between them. It had been passionate, but safe.

Then he had started to woo her. The sweet words, the tenderness, the hints of affection had beckoned to that love she was trying so hard to keep safely tucked away. That part of her so eager to give him everything—heart, soul, and mind— had begun to stir to life again and it had terrified her. It still terrified her.

"Ilsa," Diarmot said, a little annoyed by the way she seemed to be ignoring him, "why did ye leave?"

"To think," she replied, struggling to subdue the panic she could feel coming to life inside of her. "Aye, to think, just as everyone has obviously told ye. There are many things I need to think about. Since I arrived at Clachthrom it has been one shock after another. Margaret, becoming mother to eight children instead of just two, someone trying to kill ye, then kill me, too, and your loss of memory. Weel, there was nary a moment with some peace to just think, was there?'

"Ilsa, ye are babbling," he murmured and took her hand in his. "I ken it hasnae been easy for ye. Ye have been sorely pressed." He kissed her hand. "And I was most unkind much of the time. Aye, my memory was gone, but I cannae use that to excuse all my faults. Ah, but now, my Ilsa, I can remember it all. How sweet ye were, those passionate trysts in the copse, the plans and promises made. I want that back, Ilsa."

He was startled when she yanked her hand free and jumped to her feet. For a moment he was hurt, feeling the sharp sting of rejection, but then he looked closely at her. Ilsa looked more than just upset or confused, she looked terrified. This trouble between them was a lot more complicated than he had realized.

"Why must ye try to change everything?" she asked, a strong hint of desperation in her voice.

"I was hoping nay to change things so much as return to what we once had together."

"I cannae. Dinnae ye understand?"

"Nay, I dinnae. Ye stay whilst I am being unkind and flee when I try to fix things, things I had made wrong."

"It went wrong o'er a year ago! It went wrong when ye ne'er came back for me, ne'er sent word."

She stamped her foot and placed a hand over her eyes when she realized she was crying. "I tried so hard to believe in ye, in what we had shared. For near three months I kept trying and then I had to face the truth, that ye werenae coming back for me. I accepted that." She placed her other hand over her heart as she felt a stirring of that old pain. "And then, and then I had to hunt ye down. We had two sons. I couldnae just hide here, denying them what was theirs by right. And, oh, I found ye, dinnae I? Kneeling afore the priest exchanging vows with Margaret."

Shock over the sight of Ilsa crying had kept Diarmot stuck to his seat, but now he stood and cautiously approached her. It sounded as if she was saying that her love for him had died from the force of too many blows. Yet, if she had lost all love for him, why was she so upset, so afraid to hear his fumbling words of affection?

"Ye ken why I was marrying Margaret," he said. "I had forgotten—"

"I ken it! I ken all of that, I truly do. In my head, I ken it. The forgetting of me, nay kenning that the twins were your sons, the suspicions, all of it." Try as she did to stop crying and calm down, all Ilsa seemed capable of doing was crying harder. "So I accepted. I decided we would simply begin anew. I would prove myself to ye. Twas necessary. I accepted that, too."

"But now ye think ye cannae accept me? Is that it?" He stood close by her side and lightly stroked her hair.

"Dinnae be such an idiot."

Her small fist connected somewhat forcefully with his side and Diarmot grunted. Then he smiled faintly. He did not know what was troubling Ilsa, but it was not that she did not care for him. How he could be so sure of that simply because she called him an idiot and hit him, he did not know, but he did. Now he just needed to puzzle out what she was talking about. He hated to see her cry, to see her so upset, but he hesitated to try and soothe her. The truth was tumbling out. It might require some untangling, but he knew it needed to come out. He was going to have to tell a few truths himself if there was to be any hope for them.

"I thought once ye trusted me again, all would be weel," she continued. "I thought I kenned what I wanted, but then ye got your memory back, and ye started to give me sweet words and gifts and I realized I didnae ken what I wanted at all. Ye were stirring it all up again and it made me afraid. I cannae bear it. I am nay that strong."

Diarmot could not hold back any longer. Her tears were painful for him, especially since he was the cause. He pulled her into his arms, kissed the top of her head, and gently rubbed her slim back.

"Hush, Ilsa, twill be alright," he said.

"Nay, it willnae." She held herself stiff for a moment, then wrapped her arms around his waist and pressed her cheek against his chest. "I am a coward, a puling weakling." Although her crying had eased a little, she felt drained.

"Ye are one of the strongest women I have e'er met."

"Och, nay. I ran away. I ran away because ye were stirring it all up again and it terrified me."

"What was I stirring all up?"

"All that love and faith I had, all that I had given ye so long ago. I thought it was what I wanted, but I didnae. I cannae bear it," she said, fighting the urge to start wailing all over again. "It hurt so much when ye didnae come back for me."

"Ah, Ilsa, I wish I could change that, but I cannae."

"I ken it. But, dinnae ye see? I put it all away, buried it, locked it up. When I came to Clachthrom I realized I had let it slip free a wee bit and there was all that pain again for ye didnae want me, didnae remember me. And, now, ye are plucking at it again and I cannae seem to keep it all locked away."

"Ilsa, my sweet, what makes ye think I dinnae love ye?" He felt her grow tense in his arms.

Ilsa wondered if all her crying had rattled her wits. "I beg your pardon?"

Diarmot gently cupped her small face in his hands and turned it up to his. "I love ye." For one minute the look upon her face was one of a gratifying wonder and delight, but then she scowled at him.

"Ye couldnae mention that ere now? Ye couldnae have said it ere ye left me o'er a year ago or when ye suddenly remembered it? Mayhap say it as ye gave me flowers or that wee ring or e'en whilst we made love?"

"Ah, weel, I wasnae sure until I saw Margaret trying to run a sword through ye."

Ilsa nearly gaped at him. She stepped back and furiously rubbed the tears from her face with her hands. It was not the fact that he had been so slow to know he loved her that upset her. She knew men could be very slow to grasp such an important fact. It was that he had known for two or three days, but had said nothing.

"If ye had said that but once, I wouldnae have been going near mad with wondering, fretting about what I could or couldnae do, or what I wanted or didnae want."

Diarmot quickly pulled her back into his arms and kissed her. "I wanted to woo ye, to soothe some of the wounds I ken I had inflicted." He kissed the hollow by her ear. "I remembered ye telling me ye loved me and was trying to woo ye into saying it again." He traced the delicate curve of her ear with his tongue, felt her shiver, and relaxed. "Ye can say it now."

"Say what?"

"Ilsa," he growled softly against the side of her neck.

"I think I might just wait as long as ye did ere I tell ye."

"Two or three days?"

"Nay, about fifteen months." She smiled sweetly when he looked at her. "Ye cannae force such words, ye ken."

"Nay?" He picked her up in his arms and headed for her bedchamber. "We shall see. I suspect I can make ye say it."

Obviously, he could, Ilsa thought as she lay sprawled on top of him, struggling to recover from their lovemaking. She had known what he would do once she had thrown him such a challenge, and was glad he had not surprised her this time. There had been a touch of resentment in her heart as she had thought of all she had suffered for the want of three little words. Passion had burned it away. Passion had also made it easy for her to cast off those last shields around her heart.

She murmured a protest when he nudged her onto her side and got out of bed. A minute later, she blushed as he cleaned away the remnants of their lovemaking. When he climbed back into bed and pulled her back into his arms, she went willingly. Ilsa rested her cheek against his chest and began to idly trace his ribs with her fingers.

"When did ye suspect ye might love me?" she asked.

Diarmot absently stroked her back. "When I stood in that copse where we had first made love. I confess I didnae think of love, except that I could almost hear ye say it and I wanted to hear ye say it again as ye just did. Three times." He smiled fleetingly when she lightly pinched him. "What I remembered was the passion, the sweet ferocity, and the peace I felt."

"The peace?" Ilsa had thought she had brought him some peace back then, but had recently begun to have doubts.

"Aye, the peace. It had been a long time since I had felt at peace. I had ceased to reach for it in a woman's arms almost a year before I met ye. Your cousins were wrong about the maid at the alehouse," he hastened to say when she started to speak. "Aye, she was giving me inviting smiles and I did wonder on accepting, but had decided it would be a waste of precious coin. In truth, one reason I had decided to marry Margaret was because I had been celibate for a year. Couldnae understand why. I think a part of me did remember ye. That was the trouble. I was verra reluctant. I also kept feeling it was wrong to marry Margaret and the nearer the wedding day drew, the stronger those feelings grew. Then there were those dreams."

"What dreams?" Ilsa began to kiss his chest.

"I kept having dreams about an angry redheaded

elf surrounded by a horde of fiery demons." He smiled when she collapsed against his chest, giggling.

"So, a part of ye did remember me and my family." She started to kiss her way down his chest.

"Aye. Ye proved a sore trial to me."

"Good." She lightly nipped his taut stomach.

Diarmot laughed. "I had to keep reminding myself that I must nay trust ye, that ye were the only true suspect I had, the only one who would gain from my death."

She could hear the regret in his voice. "I didnae like how ye mistrusted me and, aye, it hurt, but I did understand."

"Ye accepted it."

"Aye, I accepted it."

"As ye accepted my six children, some of who might nay e'en be mine?"

Ilsa looked at him even as she caressed his strong thighs. "They are your bairns. Just because your seed made them doesnae mean they must look just like ye. Many of them do. Odo has your eyes, as does Ewart. Ivy has the look of a MacEnroy, and Alice and Gregor have hair verra much like yours. But, e'en if your seed didnae make them all, they are all your bairns. Ye are Papa. I wasnae just giving them soothing words when I told them a family doesnae have to be one of blood. It can be one of heart, soul, and mind."

"They do feel like my bairns." The last word came out as something perilously close to a squeak as Ilsa curled her fingers around his staff.

"And how does this feel?" she asked as she stroked his staff and kissed his thighs.

"Like more."

A heartbeat later she gave him more. He closed his eyes and savored the feel of her lips and tongue as the heat of them replaced the soft caress of her fingers. When she took him into her mouth, he thought he could have the strength to enjoy that pleasure for longer than he had yet been able to since they had so recently made love. He soon realized he was wrong, that his emotions were still too high, feeding and strengthening his need for her.

Diarmot caught her up under her arms and gently tossed her onto her back. He gave her a grin that made her eyes widen as she recognized the passionate threat he silently made. Then, pulling forth every ounce of willpower he had to rein in his need to join with her, he did his very best to drive his wife wild with need.

Much later, as he roused himself from a thoroughly sated doze in Ilsa's slim arms, Diarmot raised himself up on his elbows and looked at her. He grinned. Ilsa looked beautifully ravished and utterly exhausted. He silently patted himself on the back as he brushed a kiss over her lips. Then he moved off of her, lay down on his side next to her, and tugged her into his arms. Once he got her settled with her back pressed close to his front, he kissed the top of her head, and closed his eyes. At last, his sense of peace, of quiet joy and satisfaction was back, and he reveled in it.

The thumping noise dragged Diarmot from his sleep and, after a moment of confusion, he realized someone was banging on the door of the cottage. Pulling away from a still sleeping Ilsa, he got up and donned his braies. It was undoubtedly one of her massive family, he thought crossly. As he hurried down the steps, he realized it was barely past the dawning hour and he felt a tickle of unease. Throwing open the door, he stared sleepily at Odo, noticing an equally sleepy Liam slumped against the side of the cottage.

"Odo, what are ye doing here?" he asked.

"I came to see if ye made a mistake," Odo replied, then frowned. "Where are your clothes?"

"Somewhere in the bedchamber. Odo, everything is fine."

"Ye didnae say anything stupid?"

"Och, I suspect I did and so did your mother, but everything is fine now."

"So she will be coming back to Clachthrom with us?" he asked, a hint of trepidation in his voice.

"Aye." He lightly tousled the boy's dark curls. "She will be returning with us. On the morrow. So, ye can have a fine visit with all your new uncles and cousins. Your mother and I will come up to the keep later."

"May we go back and get something to eat now?" Liam asked Odo.

"Aye." Odo let Liam take him by the hand, then grinned at Diarmot. "Now ye can start making me some more brothers."

"I shall do my best."

"We need nine."

"Nine?"

"Aye, so I can have more brothers than Fergus."

"Of course."

Diarmot shut the door on a grinning Liam, then grinned himself as he started back to bed. He had tossed aside his braies and was just crawling back into bed, when Ilsa turned to look at him. She looked adorable when she was half asleep, he mused, and gave her a brief kiss.

"Did I hear someone at the door?" she asked as he pulled her into his arms.

"Aye, twas Odo," he replied and nibbled at her ear.

"Odo came here from the keep all alone?"

"Nay, Liam was with him."

"But," she glanced out the window, "tis barely dawn."

"Odo was anxious to make sure I hadnae said anything stupid." He smiled against her throat when she laughed. "And, once assured all was weel, he asked for some more brothers."

There was a strong hint of laughter in his voice which made Ilsa very suspicious. "How many?"

"Nine. He wants more than Fergus has."

"Oh, dear."

EPILOGUE

Nine months later

"There is an army of redheads approaching your walls," announced Nanty as he strode into the great hall.

Diarmot stopped pacing, his four oldest sons doing the same, causing the still-new-to-walking Finlay and Cearnach to walk into them. As Diarmot untangled the boys, he frowned at Nanty. "How the devil did they ken it was today?"

"Mayhap they simply felt it had to be soon."

"Ah, that could be it." He started to pace the room again.

Nanty watched Diarmot and the six little boys for a moment, then laughed and shook his head. "What are ye doing?"

"Pacing," said Diarmot.

"Aye, pacing," said Odo. "Fraser said men pace when women have bairns. She is helping Mama and sent us down here to pace with Papa."

"Ivy and Alice arenae allowed to pace?" asked Nanty.

"Nay, Glenda says ladies sit and sew and tell each other it willnae be long now."

Diarmot gave his brother a disgusted look when Nanty started to laugh so hard he had to sit down. He was about to scold him when the horde of Camerons entered the great hall led by Sigimor. Sigimor quickly decided simply pacing was not manly enough and started drinking. Diarmot was glad of the diversion, even if it was not quite enough to keep all of his thoughts off Ilsa. He wanted the birthing done, wanted to see her safe and well, their child in her arms.

The thought had barely finished crossing his mind when Glenda appeared in the doorway and cried, "Tis a lass!"

Chaos was the only word for what ensued. Diarmot found himself squeezed out of his own bedchamber as it filled up with huge redheaded Camerons and eight excited children. Then Glenda and Fraser, who had been nudged out of the room as well, grinned at him. He watched in amazement as the two women cleared the room with a judicious application of elbows and equally sharp words. He was stunned when he suddenly found himself in his bedchamber, alone with his wife and new daughter.

"Come see the lass, Diarmot," said Ilsa.

Diarmot just reached the side of the bed when Odo appeared on the other side. He sat down on the side of the bed with a sigh. "Odo, why are ye still here?"

Odo peered at his new sister for a moment, then patted Ilsa on the hand. "Tis a fine bairn e'en if tis a lass," he said and started for the door. "I am sure ye will do better next time."

"How can ye laugh?" Diarmot said after Odo was gone and he looked at a giggling Ilsa.

"How can I not?"

"He spends too much time with Sigimor," Diarmot said as he studied the tiny babe she held in the crook of her arm.

Ilsa grasped him by the belt buckle she had finally given him, presenting it on the morning after they had both confessed their love, and tugged him close. "Dinnae fear. I willnae be giving ye one of these each year."

He smiled and kissed her. "I will welcome whate'er comes. Just remember that I want ye more."

"I want to be sure to stay here and let ye want me until we are both too old to see each other even when we are in the same bed."

Diarmot laughed as he sprawled on his side next to her, and reached over to stroke the baby's soft cheek. "Weelcome, little one." He kissed Ilsa's cheek. "I love ye."

"And I love ye."

"She is going to be unbearably spoiled, ye ken."

"With so many uncles and brothers, how could it be elsewise."

"What shall we name her?"

"Peace."

Diarmot looked at the newest addition to his family, thought of the horde down in the great hall, and grinned. "Aye, Peace. Whene'er I look upon her, I shall remember that, no matter what chaos surrounds us, we can find that sweet, comforting peace with each other."

"Aye, my braw knight, always and forever."

"Always and forever."

"How can ye laugh?" Diarmot said after Odo was gone and he looked at a giggling Ilsa.

"How can I not?"

"The spends too much time with Sigimor," Ilsa said as he studied the tiny babe she held in the crook of her arm.

He grasped him by the hair until she had finally given him, preserving it on the morning after their wild bout, confessed their love, and tugged him close. "Diarmot Ian, I will ne be giving ye one of these each year . . ."

He smiled and kissed her. "I will welcome whate'er comes. Just remember that I promise more."

"I want to be sure to make sure, and let ye want me until we are both too old to see each other every when we are in the same bed."

Diarmot laughed as he spreaded on his side next to her, and reached over to stroke the babe's soft cheek. "Welcome, little one." He kissed the soft cheek. "I love ye."

"And I love ye."

"She's going to be unbearably spoiled, ye ken."

"With so many uncles and brothers, how could she be else?"

"What shall we name her?"

"Free."

Diarmot looked at the newest addition to his family, thought of the horde down in the great hall, and grinned. Odo. Peace. Where'er I look upon her, I shall remember that no mean, that peace surrounds us, the peace that that sweet, comforting peace of each other."

"Aye, my brave knight, sharp and honest."

"Always, and forever."

Please turn the page for an exciting sneak peek of
Hannah Howell's newest historical romance
HIGHLAND WARRIOR
now available from Zebra Books!

Scotland—1472

"Satan's big toe!"

Fiona cautiously stood up, steadied herself, and vainly tried to rub away the throbbing pain in her backside as she watched her horse disappear over the hill. Her brothers were going to kill her, slowly. Gillyanne, her sister by marriage, would probably not come to her aid this time. Fiona had the lowering feeling that she had sunk herself deep into trouble this time, had, in fact, been utterly witless. She was miles from home, had no supplies, and the sun was rapidly sinking below the horizon. Even worse, no one at Deilcladach knew where she had gone.

"Weel, you certainly showed Connor who is in control, didnae ye," she muttered as she tried to discern exactly where that cursed horse had dropped her. "If only Connor had asked nicely instead of commanding me in that irritating way he

has. Nay, nay, this isnae his fault. Tis yours and
yours alone, Fiona MacEnroy. Tis ye who is to
blame for this disaster."

She looked around and realized it was not only
the people of Deilcladach who did not know where
she was. She did not know, either. Her annoying
mount had dropped her in a place she had never
been before. The wild ride she had just survived had
left her uncertain of which direction she should
turn in to head home, not that she was very good
at finding her way around under the best of circumstances.

This was undoubtedly the most reckless thing
she had ever done. There was only one good thing
about it that she could think of. The madman who
had precipitated her long confinement at Deilcladach could not possibly know where she was, either.
The man may have succeeded in causing her to do
something completely witless, but at least he would
not benefit from it.

Fiona idly rubbed her finger over the scar marring her left cheek. *He* had given it to her the first
time he had cornered her, along with a matching
one on her right cheek. She could almost feel the
others he had inflicted before her family had
caged her behind the thick walls of Deilcladach
until they could hunt the madman down and kill
him. Just thinking about the man sent chills of fear
throughout her body, yet she had briefly, foolishly,
forgotten that danger. She had succumbed to a rag-
ing need to ride free after too many months of
confinement.

A sound caught her attention and she tensed.
Horses were coming her way, fast. Even as she
looked for a place to hide, the riders crested the

small rise directly in front of her. Fiona drew her sword and dagger, then stood with her feet apart. She knew she had no chance of successfully defending herself against ten or more men, but decided it was better to die fighting than to allow that madman Menzies to keep slicing away at her.

Then she realized Menzies rarely had more than a few men with him. There were at least a dozen riders in front of her. One good look at the huge dark man at the fore of the troop told her this was not Menzies. Fiona held steady in her fighting stance, but had to fight back a wave of fear. Menzies might be insane, but he did not want her dead. She could not be sure these men would have that much restraint.

"Jesu, look there, Ewan!"

Ewan MacFingal just grunted in response to his brother Gregor's cry. He was looking, but he was not sure he was seeing too clearly. Surely there could not be a small female facing them with a sword in one hand and a dagger in the other? Could she not count? There were twelve of them and only one of her, a very small, delicate one.

Signaling his men to halt, Ewan slowly rode toward the woman. She was dressed as a lad in a jerkin, breeches, and boots, but there was no doubt she was a woman. It was not just the long, thick honey-gold braid hanging down to her slim hips which gave her away, either. The lad's clothing could not fully disguise her lithe feminine shape. Her face was definitely that of a woman, as well. A very beautiful woman.

When he was close enough to see her eyes, he

felt his breath catch in his throat. They were big
eyes, the long thick lashes surrounding them several shades darker than her hair, as were her finely
arched brows. They were also the color of violets.
He did not think he had ever seen eyes that color,
or eyes so stunningly beautiful.

The rest of her heart-shaped face was equally
captivating. She had delicate bones, from the soft
curve of her high cheekbones to the line of her
faintly stubborn jaw. Her nose was small and
straight, her skin clear and fine with a hint of gold
to it as if she had been gently gilded by the sun,
and her lips were full and tempting. He idly wondered where she had gotten the scars, one on each
cheek. They were neat, a rather gentle mark beneath each of her lovely cheekbones.

He silently cursed as he dismounted and drew
his sword. If he was thinking that even her scars
were beautiful, she was more dangerous than she
looked. Ewan knew how intimidating he looked so
was rather surprised when she only blinked once,
slowly, looked him over, and then tensed in the
way a warrior does when braced for an attack.

"Ye cannae be thinking to fight with me, lass,"
he said scowling at her.

"And why shouldnae I?" Fiona asked.

"Because I am a mon, bigger than ye in height
and breadth."

"I did notice that."

It was impossible not to notice that, Fiona
mused. He had to be a foot or more taller than her
own meager five feet three inches, if she stood
very straight. She suspected he might even be
taller than her brothers. He was broad of shoulder,
lean of hip, and had long, well-formed legs. His

loosely fitted jerkin and breeches did little to hide the strength in his body. His sword looked rather impressive as well.

Fiona knew she ought to be shaking in her boots, but she was not. It puzzled her for there was no softness to be found in his harsh features. There was a predatory look to the man. His bone structure was good, from the high cheekbones to the strong jaw, but there was a hardness to the face that stole away the elegant handsomeness it should have had. His nose had probably been once long and straight, but a break or two had left a lump at the bridge of it giving it a hawkish look. Despite his dark scowl, she could see that his mouth was well shaped, a hint of fullness to his lips. His eyes were an intriguing bluish gray, like a clear summer sky when the clouds of approaching night started to seep into it. And he was lucky to still have both of them, she mused, as she glanced at the scar that ran from just above his right eyebrow, down his right cheek to his jaw, passing within a hair's breadth of the corner of his eye. There was a hint of softness to be found in those eyes, however, in the long, thick lashes and neat brows that held the touch of an arch. His long, thick, pitch-black hair, hanging several inches past his broad shoulders, was braided on either side of his face and only added to his look of a fierce, dark warrior.

And, he was very dark, indeed, she thought. Even his skin was dark and something told her it was not from the sun. There was the inky shadow of an emerging beard which only made his face even darker. Fiona wondered why she, a woman who had spent her life surrounded by fair, handsome men, should find this dark man so attractive.

"Then ye will nay be fighting with me," Ewan said, subduing the urge to back away from her intent study.

"They do say that the bigger a mon is, the harder he will fall," she murmured.

"Then old Ewan ought to fair shake the ground," said the young man holding the reins of the dark man's horse and the other men chuckled.

"I willnae fight with a wee lass," Ewan said.

"Ah, that is a relief as I had no real urge to get all asweat and weary. So, I accept your surrender."

"I didnae surrender."

That deep, rough voice produced an impressive growl, Fiona decided. "If ye arenae going to fight and ye arenae going to surrender, then what *are* ye planning to do? Stand there all day blocking out the sun?"

If Ewan had not suspected it would be a serious error in judgment to turn his back on this woman, he would have scowled at his snickering men. "Now that ye have had your wee jest, I suggest ye surrender."

Fiona knew she had little choice, which made her feel distinctly contrary. She still felt no real fear, either. The man had made no attempt to attack or disarm her. The amusement of his men did not carry the taint of anger or cruelty. There was also a look upon the dark warrior's face that she found oddly comforting. It was the same look her brothers gave her when they found her to be excessively irritating and were heartily wishing she was not a female so that they could punch her in the nose. Fiona knew instinctively that this man would not strike her any more than her brothers would.

"I wasnae jesting," she said and smiled sweetly. "I am ready to accept your surrender now. Ye can just pile your weapons up neatly by my feet."

"And just what do ye plan to do with a dozen prisoners?"

"Ransom ye."

"I see. And we are all supposed to just sit quiet like good, wee lads, and let ye rob our clan."

"Oh, I dinnae wish to rob your clan. All I want is a horse and a few supplies."

"Ah, lost yours, have ye?"

"Mayhap I ne'er had one."

"Ye are miles from anywhere. Do ye expect me to believe ye just popped up out of the heather, ye daft wench?"

"Wench? Did ye just call me a wench?"

Ewan did not think he had ever seen a woman's humor change so rapidly. He had just begun to understand her game. In an almost playful way, she had been testing him, trying to see if he could be spurred to violence against a woman. She had begun to relax. Now it appeared that, with one ill-chosen word, he had set her back up and set the progress of their odd negotiations back several steps. Before he could say anything to mend matters, his brother Gregor spoke up and made the situation even worse.

"Actually, he called ye a daft wench," said Gregor.

"I hate being called a wench," Fiona said.

She sheathed her dagger, grasped her sword with both hands, and attacked so swiftly and gracefully, Ewan was struck with admiration. So struck that he came very close to getting wounded. As he met her attack, however, he realized it would have been little more than a scratch, that she had not been aiming for anything vital. He also realized that she had been well trained. She might lack the strength and stamina to outlast a man in a long, hard battle, but she definitely had the skill and agility to give herself a fighting chance. A touch of good fortune or an error on the man's part and she could win a fight. The silence of his men told Ewan they also recognized her skill. What he did not understand was why she had attacked him. He was sure it was not because he had called her a name she did not like. Ewan wondered if this was another test of some sort, one to judge his skill or to see just how hard he would try not to hurt her.

Fiona knew within minutes that this man did not want to harm her. He was fighting her defensively and she was certain that was not his way. Even as she wondered how she could now extract herself from this confrontation, it was ended. He blocked the swing of her sword and somehow ended up within inches of her. The next thing Fiona knew her sword was gone from her hand, her feet were pulled out from beneath her, and she landed flat on her back, hard enough to knock the breath out of her. As she struggled to catch her breath, she braced for the blow of his body landing on top of her. It not only surprised her, but impressed her, when he somehow managed to completely pin her to the ground with his body yet rested very little of his weight upon her.

"Now, are we all done with this troublesome nonsense?" Ewan demanded, fighting to ignore the feel of her beneath him and pushing away the tempting images it tried to set in his mind.

"Aye," Fiona replied, panting a little as she regained her ability to breathe. "I will accept your surrender now." The man truly could growl impressively, she mused, and wondered why that rough noise should send small, pleasurable shivers down her back.

"Enough," he snapped. "Ye are now my prisoner. Do ye have any other weapons?" he asked as he took the knife sheathed at her waist and tossed it aside, his brother Gregor quickly appearing to collect it along with her sword.

"Nay," she answered and could tell by the way his eyes narrowed that he knew she lied.

"Surrender your weapons, woman."

"I told ye, I dinnae have any more." Fiona wondered if the fact that the knife sheathed at the back of her waist was digging painfully into her back was the reason her ability to lie was so hampered.

That thought had barely finished forming when she found herself caught up in a fierce wrestling match with the man as he tried to search her for weapons. She got some pleasure out of his curses and grunts which revealed she was at least discomforting him. Unfortunately, it did not deter him. He quickly began to find all of her knives. His curses increased as he took the two strapped to her wrists just inside the sleeves of her jerkin, the two tucked inside her boots, and the one sheathed at her back. He even found the subtle slits in her breeches that allowed her to reach the knife strapped to each of her thighs and took those. All of her struggling halted abruptly when he ran his big, long-fingered hands over her breasts and found the knife sheathed between them. As he tossed that to the man collecting her weapons, he yanked her to her feet, and she wondered why she could still feel the warmth of his touch.

Ewan stared at the collection of weapons a widely grinning Gregor had piled up. He suddenly realized that, at any point during their confrontation, she could have pulled out one of those well-hidden knives and thrown it at him, or slipped it between his ribs. There was no doubt in his mind that she could have done so with speed, stealth, and deadly accuracy. He had obviously not failed any of those tests she had been putting him through. When he looked at her and she smiled sweetly, he immediately grew suspicious.

"Any more?" he asked.

"Of course not." She met his narrow-eyed stare for a full minute before she sighed. "Just one."

"Hand it to me."

His eyes widened as she reached behind her head and pulled a knife from out of the thick coils of her braid. When she slapped it into his outstretched hand, he ignored the hilarity of his men and studied the weapon. It was long with a narrow blade, sheathed in thick, soft leather, and the hilt had been made in such a way it looked like no more than an ornate hair ornament, yet was still perfectly usable.

"Why are ye so heavily armed?"

"Weel, it wouldnae be wise to ride about alone without a few weapons," Fiona replied as she undid her sword belt and tossed it down with the other weapons, then began to remove the sheaths for her knives that she could reach discreetly.

"'Tis nay wise to ride about alone nay matter how weel armed ye are."

She scowled at him and he tried to fix his attention on her ill humor, but it was not easy. His gaze kept falling to where her hand had slipped inside

the clever slits in her breeches to remove the knife
sheathes strapped around each slender thigh. Ewan
could all too clearly recall the feel of that soft skin.
It had taken a lot of willpower to resist the urge to
linger there, to stroke that soft skin, and to recall
that he was disarming her beneath the amused
gazes of his men.

Even worse, his palms still itched with the need
to feel those firm, plump breasts again. He had all
too briefly felt how perfectly they had nestled into
his hands as he had searched her for more weapons.
Despite her clothes and the fact that she had been
bristling with weapons, he could not ignore the fact
that she was a woman, a soft, temptingly shaped
woman. Worse still, he seemed incapable of ignoring the fact that he desired her.

"What is your name?" he asked her as Gregor
put all of her weapons in a sack.

"Fiona," she replied and met his hard stare, one
that demanded more information, with a smile.

"Fiona what? What clan? What place?"

"Do ye expect me to sweetly reply and give ye all
that is needed to rob me and mine?"

Cleverness in a female could be extremely irritating, Ewan decided. "Where were ye headed?"

"Nowhere in particular. I was just riding about
enjoying the rare sunny day."

"Then how did ye end up here?"

"Ah, weel, my mount is a contrary beast. He
bolted. I think I must have hit my head on the saddle pommel or the like for, after a rough ride, I became quite dazed. When I finally came to my
senses, the wretched beast was moving at a calmer
pace, but, as soon as I tried to grab the reins which
had slipped from my hands, the horse bolted

again. After yet another long, rough ride, he tossed me to the ground and left me here."

"Is that the beast over there?"

Fiona looked to where he pointed and softly cursed. The big gray gelding stood only a few yards away idly feasting on soft grass. If she had known he was so close, she would have tried to catch him, might even have escaped the trouble she now found herself in. Then she sighed, accepting her fate. Since she had truly needed a horse, it was certain that aggravating beast would never have allowed himself to be caught.

"Aye, that is him," she replied.

"What is the name it answers to?"

"Several, actually, but, if he is feeling particularly contrary, the best one to use is Wretched."

"Wretched? Ye call your mount Wretched?"

"Tis short for Wretched Pain In The Arse. He is also called Curse To All Mankind, Limb of Satan," she stopped when he held up his hand.

"Mayhap he wouldnae be so contrary if ye gave him a proper name," Ewan said.

"He has one. Tis Stormcloud. He doesnae often answer to it, however. And he has weel earned the others."

"If he is so much trouble, why do ye ride him?"

"He is big, strong, fast, and can go for miles without a rest. Of course, that isnae such a fine thing at the moment," she muttered and glared at her horse, who looked at her, neighed, and tossed his fine head as if he was enjoying a fine laugh at her expense.

"Stay here," Ewan commanded. "Watch her, Gregor." He started toward the horse.

Fiona crossed her arms over her chest and

watched him approach Stormcloud. To her utter surprise and a flash of extreme irritation, the man easily caught Stormcloud. The horse did not even try to elude him, and seemed positively enraptured. She cursed as he led the horse back to her. When the animal looked at her and gave her a horsey snicker, she stuck her tongue out at him. Her captors found that worthy of a hearty laugh. Even the big man holding Stormcloud's reins grinned.

"Mayhap, if ye spoke sweetly to the beast," Ewan suggested, "he would feel more kindly toward ye."

"I *have* spoken sweetly to him, in the beginning, when I thought he was a reasonable beast," Fiona replied. "I spoke so sweetly honey fairly dripped from every word. It ne'er worked. Watch." She stepped closer to the horse and began to flatter him. "Such a fine gentlemon ye are, Stormcloud. Big, strong, fair to look upon." She concentrated on keeping her voice low and coaxing, struggling to think of every compliment she could as she wooed him.

Ewan quickly lost interest in the game she played with her horse. He was caught firm in the magic of her voice. It was low, slightly husky, and dangerously seductive. The flattery she filled the horse's ears with could all too easily flatter a man as well. He glanced at his men and realized they were being as seduced as he was, or nearly so. Ewan hoped their bodies were not growing as taut with need as his was or there could be trouble.

Just as he was about to end the game, to try to break the spell she wove, she reached for the reins. The horse lowered his head and shoved her away forcefully enough to cause her to sprawl on her back on the ground. Stormcloud then produced that sound which all too closely resembled a human snickering. Ewan tried his best not to laugh, but the loud hilarity of his men broke his control.

Fiona cursed softly as she got to her feet and brushed herself off, then glared at the laughing men. "I dinnae suppose ye would have let me ride on him anyway."

"Nay, I wouldnae," Ewan said. "Ye are our hostage."

"Might I learn just who plots to drag me off to his lair and try to use me to pick clean the purses of my kinsmen?"

"We are the MacFingals. I am Sir Ewan, the laird of Scarglas, and the mon weighted down with your vast array of weaponry is my brother Gregor. Ye can learn the names of the rest when we camp for the night."

"Just how far away are ye taking me?" she asked as he searched her saddle and packs, handing Gregor her second sword and three more knives.

"Ye didnae think ten knives and one sword were enough?"

"I might have lost one or two weapons in a battle. What are ye doing?" she asked when he mounted Stormcloud.

Ewan grabbed her by the hand, relieved when she nimbly swung up behind him and offered no argument. "I am riding this horse. He has had more rest than mine own. I am taking ye to Scarglas, a little o'er a day's ride from here. When we get there ye will tell me who ye are and where ye are from. Or, ye can save us all a lot of trouble and do it ere we get there."

Before she could tell him exactly how small his chances were of her granting that wish, he kicked

Stormcloud into a gallop and left her wih no choice but to hang on. He might have a lot of questions for her when they camped for the night, and she might even give him a few answers. She had a few questions of her own, however, such as who in the world were the MacFingals of Scarglas?

ABOUT THE AUTHOR

Hannah Howell is an award-winning author who lives with her family in Massachusetts. She is the author of thirty Zebra historical romances and is currently working on a new historical romance featuring the Murrays. Hannah loves hearing from readers and you may visit her website: www.hannahhowell.com.

More by Bestselling Author
Hannah Howell

Available Wherever Books Are Sold!